MEET ME AT HOME

MEET ME

BOOK ONE

VERONICA WYNNE

For Frank.
I am who I am because of you.
I love you always.

TRIGGER WARNINGS

Dear reader, I am a fan of trigger warnings—mostly because I have some triggers, myself. If you don't need them, you can ignore this page, but I want them to be here for those who do.

Meet Me at Home is a contemporary romance that discusses heavy topics, including the death of a spouse, suicidal ideation, pregnancy loss, divorce, and moderate parental abandonment (if such a thing exists). Please take care of yourselves.

PLAYLIST

marjorie - Taylor Swift

Coming Home - Dirty Money and Sean Combs (with Skylar Grey)

when the party's over - Billie Eilish

Landslide - The Chicks

Unsteady - X Ambassadors

The Lakes - Taylor Swift

Christmas Lights - Coldplay

Winter Song - Sara Bareilles and Ingrid Michaelson

Auld Lang Syne - Ingrid Michaelson

Below My Feet - Mumford & Sons

Owner of a Lonely Heart - Yes

Headspace - Lewis Capaldi

No Sleep 'Till Brooklyn - Beastie Boys

You'll Be Okay (Acoustic) - Michael Schulte

To Die For - Sam Smith

Lifetime Ago - Greg Laswell

Wings - Birdy

Answer - Phantogram

Bridges - Aisha Badru

Breathing - Lifehouse
Fade Into You - The Moth & The Flame
In My Blood - Shawn Mendes
Atlantis - Seafret
Getting Over You - Jake Etheridge
i can't breathe, Bea Miller
Believe - Mumford & Sons
It'll Be Okay - Shawn Mendes
Anti-Hero - Taylor Swift
Wait - M83
Stick Season - Noah Kahan
Running Up That Hill (A Deal with God) - Kate Bush
Hesitate - Steve Moakler
Surrender - Natalie Taylor
New Year's Day - Taylor Swift

You can listen to the playlist on Spotify here.

1

STARTING OVER

Kate

I remember a time when I didn't stare blankly into the abyss. I can still remember what happiness felt like. What it was like to laugh so hard that I couldn't breathe, and my face hurt from smiling too much.

I remember feeling like my life was perfect. I remember his eyes, his smile, and how his fingers felt interlaced with mine. I remember falling in love with him gradually—so slowly that I didn't even realize it at first.

I remember the glorious, heartwarming parts, even if it feels like someone else experienced them at this point.

The point is: I remember it all. And that's what I'm thinking about today in order to avoid the thing I'm *supposed* to be thinking about.

I found a particularly pretty swirl in the hardwood floor a few feet in front of the table a little while ago and that's what I've been staring at. The people around me are talking, but I can't bring myself to care. I should care. I know that. But I can't engage.

Being present and in the moment is not a thing I can do today. If I do, there's no telling what will happen. My track record doesn't inspire confidence as of late.

So instead, I'm staring at the swirl in the hardwood and thinking about the one person I wish was here with me.

I picture his handsome face and the way his eyes used to soften when he looked at me. I see his face light up with that massive smile, his eyes crinkling at the corners and I remember a conversation we had months ago while I was dabbing wrinkle cream onto my face.

"Why do they call them crow's-feet anyway? It sounds rude. Like the lines around my eyes are the dirty feet of a huge blackbird."

He laughed. "Well then, let's call them something else." He paused and watched me for a moment, then wrapped his arms around my waist from behind. "What about eye smiles? *Because they mean you've lived a life so happy that your smile reached all the way to your eyes."*

I rested my head against his chest while I considered it. "Eye smiles… I guess I can agree to that."

He bent his head to kiss my cheek, and then he whispered in my ear. "I have them too, you know. You've made me the happiest man on the planet."

I suck in a deep breath and swear I can smell his cologne. I close my eyes, trying to capture the scent. It's fleeting—just barely there, and I feel like I'm grappling for it in the dark.

Suddenly, the voices in the room go quiet and I open my eyes with alarm. I don't want them to think I'm purposefully not paying attention or that I've fallen asleep like I'm completely bonkers.

That probably won't help my case. Or maybe it will…?

I look to the judge, who is watching me with an expression somewhere between annoyance and concern, and then to Sophie, my lawyer (and also my stepmom), who is looking at me with wide eyes and a very clear *what the actual fuck, Katherine* expression on her face.

"Counselor, is your client all right?" the judge speaks up.

Sophie's eyebrows creep up on her forehead in question.

I nod, rolling my lips between my teeth and finding the swirl in the hardwood again.

"Yes, Your Honor," Sophie's voice cuts through the silent room and I release a breath as the tension dissipates just a little bit.

"Please continue," the judge says. I realize I don't know who she's talking to because I've been focused on green eyes and rain-scented cologne, so I look up to figure out what I've been missing.

The prosecutor is looking at me. He might be trying to figure out just how batshit crazy I am. He doesn't look angry though. Mostly concerned.

He clears his throat before speaking. "Thank you, Your Honor. As I was saying, the people are happy to be lenient. The hospital administrators and the defendant have agreed upon a financial settlement that would cover the costs of the damages caused by Mrs. Rafferty, and in return for dropping the charges, they'd like her to seek counseling. Of course, there's a court-mandated fine listed in the paperwork, as well."

I can feel the shame of this experience weighing down my shoulders. I want to turn around to sneak a peek at my dad— I know he's behind me in a chair. I know he'd be here to support me even if I were on trial for murder. He's just that kind of guy. The very best dad. Which is why I can't bear to see any disappointment in his eyes.

Plus, I don't want the judge to pause for my wandering mind again.

The judge shifts her stern gaze from the prosecutor to Sophie. "I assume that's agreeable for you and your client?"

"It is, Your Honor," Sophie confirms.

The judge nods slowly, moving her eyes over to me—and then leaves them there. Her watchful gaze feels like a boulder and I can't hold it. First off, I don't want her to think I'm challenging her. This is very much a standoff, and I have no intention of winning.

I swallow and look down at my hands. I'm ashamed. I'm so nervous. I can feel my eyes start to burn, so I squeeze them shut.

Don't cry in court.

Don't cry in court.

It will make you look like you're faking it to cement the settlement.

I swallow again, trying to ease the tension in my throat, just as the judge speaks up again.

"Does your client have anything to say for herself, counselor?"

The question is directed at Sophie but shoots alarm through my body. My head snaps up to look at Sophie. She tried to prepare me for this. We wrote a statement that I need to read, and suddenly, I'm worried I won't be able to get through it.

"Your Honor, she prepared a statement she'd like to read if it pleases the court."

"Proceed." The judge motions to me with a nod of her head.

Fuck fuck fuck.

I stand, wiping my sweaty palms on my pants, slapping a hand over my belly when nausea rolls through me.

Sophie hands me a piece of paper from her manila folder and gives me a very small but encouraging smile.

You can do it, Kate, it seems to say.

I have my fucking doubts, but I also don't have a choice.

After a deep breath, I begin reading the statement Sophie helped me write.

"Your Honor, Prosecutor O'Malley, St. Vincent's Hospital Administrators, doctors, and staff,

"I stand here today, incredibly embarrassed and ashamed of my behavior on July fifteenth. I was in shock over the unexpected death of my husband, and I lost control of myself and my emotions.

"I want you to know that I am not typically a violent person. I have never before in my life behaved the way I did that day. I never will again.

"I am deeply sorry for any emotional trauma I may have caused the nurses, doctors, or other staff who witnessed the incident. I cannot imagine such a thing happening at my place of employment, and I'd be terrified if it did. I hope they can find it in their hearts to forgive me.

"Additionally, I want to thank them for providing such a high level of care for my husband and then for me during and following the incident. Men and women who would have been rightfully terrified just moments prior took charge and made sure I was properly cared for while my brain caught up with the circumstances. I owe them a massive debt of gratitude."

I have to stop for a moment because my throat is tightening and I can feel my voice wavering. I close my eyes and bite my lip, trying to ground myself to finish. When I feel like I won't start crying, I continue.

"I am committed to seeking counseling in regard to this matter and am grateful for the administrators' leniency and understanding.

"Thank you for all you do on a daily basis to care for those who are ill and in need of critical medical attention.

"With sincere apologies and gratitude, Katherine Rafferty."

My voice falters at the end, but I get through it. I remember Sophie telling me to make eye contact with the judge after I finished reading, so I steel my resolve and look up to meet those steely eyes.

I remain standing, as Sophie instructed me to do, trying to wait as patiently as possible while she considers the facts in front of her.

I try to imagine what she's seeing. I try to put myself in her shoes so I can find peace with whatever she says when she finally speaks.

I try to imagine my thirty-two-year-old body, wearing clothes that are too big because of all the depression and stress-induced weight loss. I picture my hair, which badly needs to be cut, but a trip to the salon to prepare for court wasn't in the cards this week. Fuck, it's a miracle I'm here.

I think about what paperwork might be in front of her—specifically, my criminal record. Prior to last month, the only thing on it would have been a speeding ticket that came off my license years ago. Prior to last month, I was a law-abiding citizen who'd rarely spoken to a police officer, and when I had, it was at an event. It was most certainly *not* because I was being arrested.

I continue to watch her, even though she broke eye contact first and is now looking at the papers in front of her and throwing the occasional glance to the gallery, where I know my father is sitting, and probably representatives from the hospital.

Finally, *finally*, she speaks.

"All right, Mrs. Rafferty..."

My spine goes ramrod straight and I clasp my hands in front of me, hoping she doesn't go against the settlement.

Not that I deserve it. I deserve at least a little jail time, and I know that.

"In my opinion," the judge continues. "This is a pretty light sentence."

My heart stalls in my chest, and I suddenly can't breathe.

"In other circumstances, I'd reject this settlement, but based on what I've heard here today and the fact that the hospital has agreed to these terms with you and your counsel, I'm inclined to let this stand with one modification."

I force air into my lungs, squeezing my hands together in front of me.

"You will pay the damages, as stated here in the judgment, as well as the fine outlined by the court. You will also enter court-mandated therapy for at least one year. I see here that your counsel has already chosen someone her office works with frequently. I know Dr. Maddox and have seen the kind of work she can do firsthand. I believe she's a good fit for you."

I gotta be honest, I'm not thrilled about therapy, but I'll do it to avoid jail time, so I keep my lips zipped and keep my eyes on the judge.

"I will, however, make one addition, and that is community service. I'd like you to complete one hundred hours of community service in the next year. I think it would do you good to give back to the community you disrupted so violently…"

The word makes me flinch, and I have to look away from the judge. I close my eyes just long enough to see flashes of that day, which makes me open them again quickly, just to make it stop.

But the judge isn't done.

"… but I don't think it's a good idea for you to volunteer at the hospital."

I return my eyes to the judge. I know she's right. If I were in their position, I wouldn't want me anywhere near their hospital.

"I'll allow you to choose a different charity to work with —I find that typically works out better anyway because people are more interested in completing their service, and the benefits are greater for everyone involved. Are there any objections from either party?"

The prosecutor pipes up first. "No, Your Honor."

Sophie looks at me and tips her head toward the judge, indicating that I should answer for myself.

"No, Your Honor."

"Good. By chance, do you have any idea where you'd like to do your community service? If not, I can provide a list of worthy charities in the area."

That's not something I need to think about. I already know.

"The Animal Protective League, if that's all right with you, Your Honor."

"That's fine with me."

She picks up a fancy-looking pen and scribbles on a piece of paper, then gathers up a bunch of paperwork into a neat stack.

"Mrs. Rafferty, you will pay your damages and your fine in the next thirty days or otherwise make mutually agreed upon arrangements, as overseen by your attorneys. You have three hundred sixty-five days from today to complete your community service requirement of one hundred hours. I see here that your first appointment with Dr. Maddox is set for next week, and remember that you're court-mandated to see her as often as she sees fit for the duration of *at least* one year. Failure to meet any of these requirements will be considered a violation of your settlement, and you will face jail time. Do you understand?"

"Yes, Your Honor." I feel my head nodding even though I didn't mean to.

"Good. Court is adjourned."

The judge bangs her gavel, picks up her stack of paperwork, and leaves the courtroom.

I don't even have time to process the events of the past hour before Sophie turns me and wraps her arms around me. I think I hug her back. Probably out of habit more than anything. I might be in shock.

"You did it, Kate."

She's not proud. I know that. But I think she's grateful I made it through this hour without fucking things up for myself.

"Yeah…" I agree, just to keep her happy.

That's when I look up, and I see him.

My husband's best friend, Doug Jarrett.

He works at the hospital, which is a major reason I got such a lenient settlement.

He's looking at me, meeting my eyes for a brief moment before flitting away. A couple of hospital administrators are with him. One of them stands up and bends down to say something to him, slapping his shoulder before walking away. He responds to the administrator and then stands, buttoning his suit jacket in the process.

I let go of Sophie and gather my hair to drape over one shoulder. I know I look like crap. I'm fully aware. I just can't be bothered to care. At least I have makeup on. Sophie turns around to talk to my dad, who I *still* can't make eye contact with, so I return my attention to Doug.

… who is making his way over to me.

I bite down on my bottom lip and shuffle over to him, stepping behind the barrier.

Graciously, he starts.

"Hi, Kate."

I manage a small *hi* in return, but I'm quickly looking back to my feet, the judge's bench, the table where I'd been sitting for the past hour, anything to not look at him.

I steel myself for what I know I need to say to him. I'm fidgeting and suddenly very itchy. I want to get this over with though, so I force myself to look up and make eye contact because that's what he deserves.

"Listen, Doug, I…"

My eyes start burning, so I squeeze them shut for just a second and swallow down the lump in my throat.

"I owe you an apology—a massive apology. I said terrible things to you… that day. They were unfair and uncalled for. I can't take them back. I can't unring the bell, but I wish I could. I was horrible to you. I'm so sorry."

He's looking at me with somber eyes. All I can see is compassion and concern, and it calms me just enough to continue.

"I also wanted to thank you. Sophie told me that you went to bat for me with the hospital. I really appreciate you sticking up for me." I have to look away for a moment. God, this is painful. But I gather my wits and look back up. "I probably don't deserve their leniency or even your support at this point. But I'm grateful."

Doug shakes his head and shrugs a shoulder. "I just did what I thought was right. You were… not yourself."

Fuck fuck fuck.

My eyes close on their own as flashes of that day blink through my mind like a goddamn movie. My breath stalls in my chest as I see that blonde nurse duck behind the nurses' station and feel the security guard grab me.

At this moment—and so many others since July fifteenth —I hate myself.

I manage to snap out of it when someone drops something and the sound echoes.

"Still though…" I continue. "You could have just let them hand out whatever punishment they wanted."

He stands there for a moment, just staring at me with soft eyes. When he speaks, his voice is quiet. Gentle. Everything I don't deserve.

"Nick was my best friend, Kate. I'm going to take care of his wife as best I can. It's the least I can do for him."

Except that I'm not Nick's wife anymore.

The pain that lances through my chest at the thought is debilitating, but I'm still in public. I'm not interested in another public meltdown. I curl my fingers into my palm and dig my nails into the skin to ground myself.

"I have to get to the hospital to check on my patients," he says, voice still as gentle as can be. "Kate, please let us know if you need anything. Anything at all. Michelle and I will do whatever we can."

I force myself to give him a tight smile and nod. "Thanks, Doug. I think you've done quite a lot already."

He lifts his arms toward me hesitantly, silently asking if he can hug me.

I can't deny the man I berated in front of his colleagues a simple hug. So I step toward him and give him a quick hug.

He doesn't say goodbye. He doesn't say he'll see me around. He just turns and walks away.

I watch him push the door open.

I'd spent countless evenings at Doug and Michelle's house, helping to wear out their kids before bedtime, eating dinner, drinking wine.

After dinner, Michelle and Doug would take their kids upstairs to get them ready for bed while I stayed downstairs with Nick, smiling and laughing with him like we had decades ahead of us.

When the kids were tucked into bed, Michelle would whisk me off into the living room with glasses of wine in hand, calling behind her, "The cook doesn't clean!" Doug and Nick would clean up the kitchen while we ladies caught up on our respective weeks.

Michelle and I had become friends. We bonded over the fact that our husbands had been joined at the hip since childhood.

Now, watching the door swing shut behind Doug, I somehow know I'll never see them again.

2

SHE CERTAINLY WAS

Liam

I'm coming home.

I moved away years ago, and while I've been back to visit, I haven't *lived* here in a long time.

Some things look the same. The bridges look older, more worn. The roads have been patched with tar and asphalt in various places. The harsh winters and the snow plows do their fair share of damage.

Other things look different. New buildings. New businesses.

The lake is still beautiful. That's the part I'm looking forward to. And being closer to my family, of course.

I grew up here, and I have great memories of this city. I miss the food. I miss my family. Coming home is exciting.

The reasoning for my return is… less so.

I lost my wife.

As of today, it's been five years, three months, and twenty-seven days.

Losing Jill was a long and arduous process. She was a ballet dancer—a really great one. She managed to get a job in Chicago, so that's where we ended up. As a corporate trainer, I could get a job almost anywhere, but Jill? She had limited options.

The thing is, Jill had ALS.

For someone who depends on the physical well-being of her body, being diagnosed with an incurable degenerative muscular disease was basically the worst thing that could happen to her. It slowly ravaged her body and held her hostage—her mind intact, her body weakened and eventually, something I knew she wouldn't recognize if she would actually look in the mirror.

The doctors assured me she wasn't in any pain. I always figured she'd hide it from me. But when it got worse, I finally asked her specialist.

But that didn't make it hurt less.

She worked as a dancer for as long as she could. When her physical abilities deteriorated, she remained on staff, writing choreography with the other dancers and stepping into an artistic role that allowed her to remain close to the action… still involved in the company.

But that hurt, too.

Back then, I was mostly just happy to still have her in my life. Truly, I felt that way most of the time, even until the end. I was grateful that she was able to talk to me. Interact with me. Even when it got more difficult, we figured out ways to interact.

But then one day—five years, three months, and twenty-seven days ago—I watched the first of the light go out in her eyes. It was the first day she had to just *watch* rehearsal instead of getting up to dance even a little of it. She couldn't even demonstrate anymore.

When she came home that night, I could feel that something had shifted. I just knew.

I picked up carryout from her favorite place. I brought home a bottle of wine. We watched a movie full of blood and gore and action heroes. Later that night, I held her while she cried herself to sleep.

It took a lot longer for her to actually die. Every single day of it was painful.

The day she died was no less painful. My therapist said that some people felt relieved when a sick loved one passed— that they were glad this person they loved was no longer in pain, physically or emotionally.

To some extent, I could see why people felt that way. I was—and still am—grateful that Jill is no longer suffering.

But for me? My suffering has not ended.

My wife—my very best friend and favorite person in the world—is gone.

I don't want to rehash it all. But I was there. I was there all the time.

I worked from home most of the time in her last months. I stayed in her room—the guest room, where her hospice bed was set up—as much as possible. I worked in there. I slept in there. I read to her. I talked to her.

When she was sleeping, I made sure I touched her in some way so she'd know I hadn't left. I'd put my feet up on the bed to rest against hers. I did that a lot when I was working—I could have both hands free, but she knew I was there.

I held her hand. Or rested my hand on her leg.

The day she finally let go, I was reading to her.

One moment, I was reading her favorite passage to her,

and the next, the room was oddly silent. There wasn't a telltale beeping like you'd see in a hospital drama. Even if there would have been monitors to beep, she had a DNR. *Do not resuscitate.*

But it felt different to me. The air shifted somehow.

Her face... Jill's face *looked* different. Peaceful.

And that's when I realized she was gone. Completely this time.

I don't really know what happened after that. I remember my face being wet with tears. I remember the hospice nurse talking to me. I somehow remembered her wedding ring—she'd wanted to keep wearing it but wanted to make sure I took it before they took her. So I slipped it off.

I remember my brother showing up. He handed me a beer and put on some action movie full of explosions and blood.

I drank as much as I could handle.

When I woke up in the morning, I was in bed alone with a raging headache and my brother was asleep on the couch in the living room.

Given the length of her illness, all the funeral arrangements were already made. As much as I loathed talking about it, Jill was determined to make sure it was taken care of early on in her illness. She was right when she said I wouldn't be in a good frame of mind to make decisions. When I woke up that following morning, I was so grateful she'd done all that work already.

She'd donated her brain and spinal cord to science, and she'd already decided where she wanted her ashes spread. Her final gift to me was making her own decisions when she was still able to do so.

We did have a gathering though. Just a little service where people spoke about her—me, her parents, and a couple of friends. There were a ton of people there, including people she'd danced with over the years.

It was cathartic to be around people who cared for Jill. People who will miss her. People who won't forget her. I loved all the stories people told of her when she was full of life, adventure, and determination.

But every time someone referred to her in the past tense, a tiny knife stabbed into my chest.

Jill *was* graceful.

Jill *was* kind and thoughtful.

Jill *was* very beautiful.

They weren't *wrong*. Somehow, knowledge of the facts didn't provide me any comfort. It still hurt like hell.

My brother stayed for a couple of days after the funeral to make sure everything was settled. But before he left, he planted a little seed in my brain, *Would I consider moving back home to be closer to family?*

Jill and I moved to Chicago because that's where she got a job. Professional dancers don't have many high-earning opportunities and she managed to land one, so that's where we went. I've never regretted it once.

I got a stable job with a large company that allowed me room for growth—even in a new city, should Jill get a different job elsewhere. My main goal was to help Jill dance for as long as she could.

I'll admit that I hesitated about my brother's suggestion to move back home. Leaving Chicago felt like leaving *Jill*, even though she wasn't really *there* to leave any longer.

I stayed for a few months, going back and forth about the decision. Eventually, I just couldn't be in that condo anymore.

Being surrounded by memories of Jill, knowing she'd never come home to me, was too much. I couldn't even go into the guest room where her hospice bed was.

The bottom line is simple: nothing was holding me in Chicago anymore.

I started applying for jobs and as soon as I got one, I put the condo up for sale and packed up my shit.

So here I am, driving over the final bridge into the city I called home for my whole childhood. It's farther south than Chicago, so the October air isn't quite as cold. Today has been perfect driving weather. It's sunny and moderate, the air crisp enough to crack your windows open without freezing.

This is my favorite kind of weather.

It's like the city is welcoming me back.

I pull up to my brother's house and cut the engine. I've barely stepped out of the car when a tiny body wraps itself around my legs.

"Uncle Liam!"

"He's really here!"

A second voice yells before another body wraps itself around my legs. My lower body is completely covered by my nephews and I'm on cloud nine.

"Hey boys!" I tousle their dirty-blond hair and tickle their tiny ribs, and the sound of their laughter lifts my heart in my chest.

"Boys, you didn't even give him a chance to close the car door." My brother appears in front of me with a massive smile on his face, even as he's admonishing his children.

He may be younger than me, but Joe has always been louder. More boisterous. We're obviously brothers—if we're standing next to each other, you'd know it without knowing who we were. We have the same green eyes, but his hair is a slightly darker shade of blond than mine, his nose just a little bit longer. I have maybe a half inch of height on him.

We're built similarly—borderline tall, standing at six feet (or five feet, eleven and a half inches, in his case) with broad shoulders and strong muscles built up from years of playing sports that conditioned us to keep exercising even after we were done with teams.

"They're fine, Broseph." I look up to meet Joe's eyes and offer a reassuring smile before I pry the boys off my legs and squat down to pick both of them up—one under each arm.

Two adorable squeals escape them as I jostle to keep them both within my grasp.

"Oh man, you guys have packed on some pounds," I joke with them. They're so much bigger than the last time I saw them. I swing them gently to get that little squeal out of them again.

"I'm forty-five pounds now, Uncle Liam!" The younger one is clearly proud.

"And I'm fifty pounds!" His older brother obviously cannot be outdone.

"I can tell," I exaggerate a groan as I set them back down on the ground.

"Welcome, brother." Joe sticks out his hand and pulls me into a bro hug that lingers for just a second longer than usual. It might not seem like a big deal to anyone watching, but I know what it means. *I'm glad you decided to come back.*

I nod, not really sure what to say.

"Let's grab your bags and get you inside. The beer's cold."

That's a sure way to get me inside quickly. It's been a long drive.

"Which one of you guys wants to help me carry this really heavy bag here?" I ask as I pop the trunk open.

Both of my nephews slingshot around the car, talking over each other in their haste to deem themselves the stronger brother.

"I can do it!"

"No, I can do it!"

"I'll get a heavier one than you!"

"No way, I'm bigger!"

"All right, all right," I cut in, stifling my laugh. They're just like Joe and me growing up. "I'm sure there's something that each of you can carry that will be sufficiently heavy to demonstrate your strength."

I move a suitcase aside and reach for the hidden gift bags. "In fact… Josh, it looks like this one has your name on it." I hold it up to the eldest and watch his eyes light up.

"You brought me a gift, Uncle Liam?" He takes the bag with barely restrained greed, crumpling it a bit.

I pull the second one out, handing it to Jackson. "And this one's for you, my man."

Jackson gasps and grabs the bag from me. "Can we open them, Uncle Liam?"

"You sure can, but let's run inside and do it. Your dad and I are right behind you."

Both boys whoop in celebration and tear off toward the front door.

"What'd you get 'em?" Joe asks me as he hefts a suitcase out of the trunk.

"Oh, nothing too bad. Couple of toys. Couple of books. Massive bags of M&M's. Simple fireworks. You know… the usual."

Joe smirks and shakes his head at me. "Well, as long as they're simple fireworks."

I clap a hand on Joe's back and start walking toward the house. "Come on, Broseph. That beer is callin' my name."

With a suitcase rolling behind me and my brother bringing up the rear, I look up to the house, lit up at dusk.

The house isn't huge, but it's comfortable for Joe, his wife, and their kids. I'll be sleeping on the couch in the den. It's not ideal, but it's certainly not the worst thing.

For now, it's home.

3
WHERE'S THE WINE?

Kate

You know that saying, *Time flies when you're having fun?*

It's true, of course. The lesser-discussed aspect of that saying is that time moves at the rate of a fucking sloth when you're miserable.

That's basically how the past three months have been for me. My court date was in August and now it's November—very close to the holidays, which I am not looking forward to in the slightest.

I went back to work shortly after my court date. Sophie made sure I was set up to start volunteering at the APL and I had an appointment with my new (court-appointed) therapist, Gwen. She encouraged me to return to work if anything for the distraction. She said it would help me find a new sense of normalcy.

To say that my eye roll was so intense it gave me a headache is not an exaggeration.

I don't want to find "a new normal," and I'm pretty fucking bitter about it, to be honest.

But working *is* helpful. It gives my brain something productive to do for a while. I'm a commercial real estate agent. My dad owns our firm. One day—assuming I don't get arrested for throwing shit in hospitals ever again—I'll take over the business.

With no one to come home to except for Nick's cat, Beaker (I suppose… my cat, now), time passes slower than molasses.

Since the holidays are approaching, I've noticed people are reaching out more. My brother, Ben, has been texting daily and calling at least once a week. My dad seems to find no shortage of excuses to stop by the house.

It's all well intentioned, I know. They're all trying to help me.

Frankly, it's annoying.

I mean, I appreciate it, but it's still annoying because I can't even handle my own shit and their constant outreach makes me feel like I need to put on a performance to ensure them I'm not about to off myself. It's *exhausting*.

It's not like I'm pretending to be happy, it's just that I'm not letting them see the worst parts. The dark parts.

And that's how I've ended up in my car, on my way to my best friend Elliot's house for a Friendsgiving dinner. They do this every year on the second Saturday of November. It's just close friends—chosen family—for games, drinks, and far too much food for any reasonable amount of people to eat.

It's the first time in years I've gone alone.

I've been dreading it.

Don't get me wrong—I want to go. I just also… don't want to go.

Seeing Elliot and his husband, Leon, is always a joy. I love those two. They lift my spirits on hard days. But lately, I'm not all that interested in watching a happily married couple move effortlessly around their gorgeous house full of love and hope.

If it weren't for Elliot—and the fact that I live in the same neighborhood as them—I would have canceled and sent an edible arrangement in my stead. But I can't let Elliot down. He's never one time, in the decade and a half that I've known him, let me down.

And honestly, I know Ben will be a dick about it if I skip this party. He might even come home to check on me and that's not a thing I'm willing to risk.

So here I am, wearing decent clothes (that Elliot made me shop for because I've lost so much weight) with a store-bought apple pie and a bottle of red wine in tow. Most people will make whatever they bring, but I'm not trying to fool anyone in this regard. I'm not a cook and I have no desire to become one. Especially now that it's just me.

Beaker eats food from a can, for fuck's sake.

I use the walk from my car up to the front door to mentally prepare myself. I know there will be plenty of well-meaning (albeit nosy) people asking how I'm doing. I'll tell them I'm fine and then redirect them to another question about them.

Listening to them talk about their happy lives is far preferable to talking about my shitty one.

Happy people are obnoxious.

I allow myself one eye roll before I arrive at the front door. Then I take a deep breath and steel myself for the noise. I promise myself—again—that I will try to smile… that I will not bring the party down. For Elliot.

I clench my jaw and ring the doorbell.

Within seconds, I hear footsteps. My heart picks up speed, so I close my eyes in one last effort to gather my strength and fling them back open when I hear the handle turn.

My eyes land on Leon's handsome face, his mouth stretched into a blinding smile.

"Kate! Oh, sweetie, it's so good to see you!" His voice is so warm and kind that I can't help but smile a bit in return. "Come on in, it's cold!" He steps outside and puts an arm around my shoulders to usher me in. I wonder absently if he thought I might flee the scene if he didn't *physically* bring me into the house.

And if I'm being honest, the act brings a genuine smile to my face. I'm not much for physical touch these days—I find it overstimulating—but Leon has known me for years and I know he loves me dearly.

"Hi, Leon," I finally return. "It's good to see you, too."

"I hope you're hungry," he says, shutting the door behind us. "There is *so* much food here. Holy cow."

"Speaking of…" I hold up the pie and the bottle of wine.

"Oh, that looks marvelous, thank you! Here, I'll take that pie."

He takes the plastic container and places it on a dessert table in the next room, then gestures for me to hand him my coat as he's chitchatting about the weather and their Thanksgiving travel plans.

"What can I get you to drink, dear?" he asks as he turns me toward the hall that leads to the kitchen. His arm stays around my shoulders, so I slip mine around his waist. He's a tall, thin man who can seem cold at times—a byproduct of his job as a corporate attorney—but right now, he feels warm and inviting.

"Whatever's convenient."

"Well, Elliot is drinking this beautiful red that my friend Liam brought. Do you remember Liam Anderson? I think you've met him a couple of times."

I try to think back. His name rings a bell.

"I think so? Is he the one married to a dancer?"

Leon winces, his voice dropping to a near whisper. "Um… *was* married to a dancer. Jill passed away in January. She had ALS."

I suck in a breath, unable to get much oxygen. "Oh my god, I had no idea. That's horrible."

"Yeah… it was very sad. Remember that they lived in Chicago? He moved back here recently, so we thought he could use some company. He's been helping us cook today."

I suddenly feel so much comradery toward this person I barely remember. I have a million questions that I desperately want to ask but also *don't* want to talk about myself, which is what will definitely happen because he's probably a nice person and will ask me similar questions.

"Is someone here, Leon?" Elliot's voice is coming down the hall from the kitchen. "I thought I heard the doorbell."

"Kate's here! We're coming!" Leon gently pulls me from the spot where I'd apparently frozen when he dropped the bomb about Liam's wife. "I'm sure he'll have some sort of job for you…" he adds quietly.

"Not if he wants it to be edible," I quip.

Leon chuckles as we round the corner into their giant chef's kitchen. Neither of them is a chef, but Elliot could be if he wanted to. He's very talented. I'll eat anything he makes. Even if it sounds disgusting.

"Kate!" Elliot's voice reaches me, and I feel calmer already. Elliot is one of my favorite people on this planet. He is everything good there is in the world. Loyalty, kindness, curiosity, and the perfect amount of snark. We met in college and were inseparable from day one.

I was a business major and he was a marketing major. He worked in his home state for a bit after college and ended up moving here when I finally convinced him to work for us. He met Leon at a charity event. Between Leon and me, we've roped him in for good.

Elliot wipes his hands on a dish towel and rushes over to me, wrapping his long arms around me and crushing me to his chest. In so many ways, Elliot will always feel like home to me. He's my safe place when I'm drifting. I know he's squeezing me extra tight because of all the shit he witnessed following Nick's death. He's my ride or die.

"I'm so glad you're here," he says quietly into my ear before gently pushing me away to inspect me at arm's length. "You look beautiful, as always. I love this sweater."

"You should. You picked it out."

He smiles broadly. "I know. I have great taste. What can I get you to drink, dear?"

Leon chimes in from beside me. "Pour her some of that red you're drinking—I already told her it was delightful."

"Oh, it is," Elliot confirms, turning to get a wineglass for me and pouring a generous amount.

I love you, I mouth to him.

I know, he mouths back and winks at me.

Just as I'm about to take a fortifying sip of what smells like the best wine I've had in ages, Leon's hand is on my shoulder.

"Kate, you remember Liam," he says, gesturing across the kitchen island to a tall man with blond hair and green eyes cutting up carrots with a professional-looking knife. "He's been helping us out today. You know my husband—if he's cooking, he's cooking for an army…"

Leon is still talking, but I can't pay attention because Liam has put down the knife, is wiping off his hands on a kitchen towel, and is walking toward me.

I blink repeatedly as I stare like an idiot.

Before I know it, he's right in front of me. He's taller than he looked across the room. I'm average height for a woman—

about five-six—but he's taller by inches. His blond hair is short, although long enough that he'd need to style it and it suits him.

"Hi, Kate. It's good to see you again." He sticks out a large, strong hand and I look at it, then back at him, and through some *miracle* of muscle memory—of having shaken thousands of hands during my professional life—my right hand comes up and my mouth forms words.

"Hi, Liam. Of course, it's good to see you, too."

My palm meets his, the grip firm but not overbearing. He uses the perfect amount of pressure and he's making eye contact with me.

I am literally starting to sweat. I can feel my skin flushing. *What the fuck is wrong with me?*

It must be the fact that he touched me. In fact, he's the third person who's touched me since I got here. I'm on touch overload. That must be it. I release his hand and take a step back, holding my breath as Elliot's steady voice infiltrates my thoughts, pulling me back to his kitchen.

"Sweetie, have a seat. I'm going to assign the cheese board to you."

I look at him, eyes wide, trying to cognate what might be involved in creating a cheese board worthy of an L.L.Bean party.

That's what I call them. What I've always called them. They're two peas in a pod with *L*s in their names.

Elliot sees my panic and laughs. "Don't worry, Kate. I'll give you everything you need. Just cut up the cheese and arrange it on the board. Sprinkle in some olives and salty meats."

"Whatever you say," I acquiesce, easing onto a plush stool at the island. "You'll just redo it if it looks bad anyway."

"You're right, I will," he deadpans. "But the cutting is the time-consuming part."

I figure now is as good a time as any to start drinking that wine. That first sip hits my tongue and I immediately look to Liam, who is back at his cutting board, deftly cutting up the carrots.

"Holy crap, this really is good," I say to no one in particular, but probably also Liam.

He looks up, kind eyes meeting mine as he smiles. "I'm glad you like it," he says simply before returning to his work.

I take that as my cue to focus on my own task. I cut up various cheeses and arrange them in a fashion that I hope against hope is good enough for Elliot. He gives me fancy, dark olives and shows me how to arrange them into little flowers between the cheese. I only give him a tiny amount of shit for it.

People arrive and I hold my wineglass like a shield when they talk to me. Elliot keeps filling it up. I worry I'll need to catch an Uber and pick up my car tomorrow. I switch to water before dinner is served to slow myself down.

And the food?

Holy fuck, it is amazing.

Elliot usually goes all out for this, but it seems like he's outdone himself this year. In the dark recesses of my mind, I wonder if he did it for me and Liam.

There are appetizers galore—bacon-wrapped scallops, baked brie with figs, sweet potato crostini with crème fraîche and dried cranberries, spiced mixed nuts (which I couldn't help making a joke about—I'm depressed, not dead for fuck's sake), veggies with a homemade dipping sauce that is somehow better than ranch dressing, and of course, my beautiful cheese board.

Elliot is the person I always consult when I need to bring a dish to something. Typically, he just makes it for me because he knows how inept I am in the kitchen. I prefer the times he comes over and cooks in my kitchen while I drink wine and entertain him. Not that that's happened in the past few months, but still. It was fun when it happened.

Some dickhead voice in the back of my head tries to remind me the holidays are coming up, but I push it way back, cussing at it.

After dinner (which was, again, over the top—perfect steak with crab legs and green beans in a butter sauce), a spirited game of charades begins. There's lots of screaming and yelling and cheering and booing in every round.

My brain is overstimulated. My chest starts to get tight—giant bands squeezing me, making it difficult to breathe. I can feel my breathing get more shallow, less productive, like I'm suffocating.

I find myself making a beeline for the patio door. I know I need air. I need space. And if I have a full-blown panic attack (as I've been prone to do lately), I don't want to do it in the middle of all these people and ruin their fun.

I skirt the edges of people, hoping that I'm not so conspicuous that anyone follows to make sure I'm all right. I just want to be alone.

I open the door as quietly as I can, hoping that the noise of the game will drown out the sound of my escape, and pull it shut behind me. The second it closes, I step out of the light shining through the door, turning quickly to face the backyard and rest my head against the cool siding of the house.

Tangentially, I can feel the cold in the air. I know somewhere in my mind that it's freezing outside. I should have a coat. I just don't care. I close my eyes and breathe in the frigid air, feeling it cut into my lungs a thousand times and taking a tiny bit of pleasure in it.

The pain assures me I'm still alive.

I feel like my new therapist would be rather irritated to hear me say that.

I feel justified in it though, because she also says my feelings are valid. So eat shit, Gwen.

A quiet noise pulls me out of my thoughts—a shift in weight, then a clearing of a throat.

My heart leaps in my chest and I involuntarily gasp. My hand flies to my stomach as my eyes fly open and my head whips in the direction of the sound.

"I'm sorry," a soothing, familiar voice says in the darkness. "I didn't mean to scare you."

It's Liam.

Holy shit, it's just Liam.

He's sitting on a bench on the other side of the patio, his kind eyes on me.

My heart is galloping in my chest, my pulse pounding in my ears as my body tries to calm itself down. I sag against the house in relief.

"Jesus, Liam." I take a deep breath and let it out. It's cold enough that I can see its white cloud linger in front of me. "I didn't know anyone was out here."

"I know. I'm sorry," he apologizes again.

I swallow and take a step toward him. "It's okay. I'm fine." I look around for anyone else as I make my way over to his bench, sliding my hands into my back pockets to keep them from shaking. "What are you doing out here?"

He glances through the glass doors. "I just needed some air."

I nod. "Me too."

He moves over on the bench and gestures toward the empty space, offering it to me silently.

I watch him settle into his new position and decide that it would be super awkward if I *didn't* sit down. So I do. I walk over to his bench and I sit down, leaving a solid foot of space between us. We don't look at each other. We both just stare into the abyss or at our own hands.

It's not as awkward as I would have expected it to be between us, this silence. I feel oddly connected to him as a person who has lost a spouse. I remember him and his wife together in the limited interactions we had. I remember him being so sweet with her, always touching her if he had the chance. Like he couldn't *not*.

I swallow the lump in my throat. "I'm really sorry to hear about Jill."

I feel his attention shift, so I look up and find him looking at me, too. After a brief moment where we just look at each other, he nods.

"Thank you," he finally says. "I'm sorry to hear about Nick."

I can't hold his eyes after he brings up Nick. I avert my gaze and focus on an empty pot, trying to turn off my emotions. Focusing on something typically helps with that. It worked in court a couple of months ago and Gwen encouraged me to keep using that tactic whenever I needed it. She followed that up with some psychiatrist babble about how you have to feel your feelings in order to process them. *Again, eat shit, Gwen.*

"Thanks," I manage to croak out.

Sitting there in silence, the cold starts to seep into my bones. I press my lips together to try to force some feeling back into them. It was stupid to come out here without a coat, but at least Liam made the same mistake. He's wearing a sweater over a button-down shirt, but because men somehow rule the fashion world, his sweater is thicker than mine. It's far more functional than my own.

Figures. It's always that way. Women's clothing never has functional pockets either.

I fold my arms over my midsection to conserve my body heat.

Liam apparently notices.

He straightens his spine. "Do you want to go back inside?"

I shake my head. "Not yet. You can though, if you're ready."

He relaxes back on the bench. "Not yet."

"I hear you're moving back to the area?" I ask. For reasons I cannot fathom, I want him to keep talking.

"Yeah." He nods. "Technically, I already did. I just don't have a place to live yet."

That makes me frown. "Where are you staying?"

"With my brother and his family."

"Oh… well, that's nice that you have someone to crash with."

"Yeah, it is. I get to play with my nephews. Take them out. Fill them up with candy. It's a pretty good deal."

A bittersweet feeling slices my chest, but I'm still able to muster a small smile. "That's great."

He takes a deep breath before agreeing. "It is. It's cramped though. I'm technically sleeping on a futon."

I wince. "At our age? Ouch."

He smiles. "It's all right. It's not permanent."

"You're looking for a place?" My brain goes into realtor mode instantly. I may not do residential real estate, but the principles are the same: finding a space that makes sense for your needs. And I know the area… the market.

"Yeah. Not entirely sure what yet, but maybe just an apartment for now. I don't know." He shrugs. "I've looked at a bunch of places online and I just can't figure out what I want."

My realtor brain is basically taking the wheel at this point.

"Why not?"

His mouth twitches like there's a joke I don't know. "I guess that age-old buying versus renting debate. Do I really want to buy a house to maintain all by myself? Or do I want to rent for a while?"

"I get that." I do. I really do.

Someone telling a story—loudly—inside catches both of our attention and we look through the glass to the culprit. They're waving a wineglass around with one hand while they talk. I can't tell if they're angry or just invested.

I glance back to Liam, who has returned his gaze to his hands, resting in his lap, fingers intertwined. His back curves against the bench. He's not *relaxed,* per se. I might describe it as *resigned* instead.

Suddenly, a thought occurs to me. Something that could be completely brilliant or brilliantly stupid. But I have absolutely nothing to lose, so I go ahead and open my mouth.

"Listen…" I pause to swallow and gather the last vestige of my courage. I nearly lose it when he looks up to meet my eyes, but I know what I'm about to suggest would be good for him—and let's face it, for me, too. So I look back to the empty pot and force myself to continue.

"This might sound like a weird offer, but… I have a huge house. I have three empty bedrooms right now and a giant kitchen I don't even know how to use beyond microwaving something. It seems like a waste for one person. So… if you want a place to rent until you decide what you want to do, you're welcome to one of my spare rooms."

I chance a look at Liam's face. His eyes hold just a hint of surprise with something else I have trouble identifying. Apprehension, perhaps.

Does he think this is a stupid idea? I guess it kind of is. We don't *really* know each other.

Holy shit, now I'm sweating.

What the actual fuck am I doing?

I mentally smack myself in the forehead.

"That's very generous of you," he says, his voice gentle and sincere.

"Well, you don't have to decide right now. Think it over and let me know. No pressure or anything."

I roll my lips between my teeth and bite down on them. I can feel his eyes on me, escalating my embarrassment. I feel like my skin is crawling. What a stupid thing to offer. Maybe he'll do the polite thing and just pretend this never happened.

Jesus Christ, Kate.

There is no way he doesn't think I'm batshit crazy now.

"I will think about it," he says. It seems like he's trying to assure me. Like he can sense my discomfort. "Can I call or text tomorrow to let you know what I decide?"

My eyes snap to his. He's *actually* thinking about it? He's either as desperate as me, or he doesn't think I'm completely insane. Maybe a combination of both.

I blink rapidly, trying to make sense of what he just asked. "Sure."

More blinking.

"Yeah."

He reaches into his pocket and pulls out a phone. His face unlocks it and he quickly navigates to his contacts. He starts to type in my name—which is when I notice he doesn't bother typing in a last name—and when he gets to the phone field, I rattle off my number.

Liam sends me a text so I have his number. I assume my phone dings somewhere in the house.

"Thanks, Kate. I'll sleep on it… let you know tomorrow."

"That's fine." I nod my head. "And again, no pressure. It's just unused space. Seems like a waste."

He watches me carefully before nodding.

I need to get out of here. It's time. I clear my throat and straighten. "Okay… I'm freezing."

His head tilts toward the door. "Go on in. I'll just be another minute."

I offer one more tight nod before standing, taking the few steps to the patio door, and slipping back into the warmth of the house.

I'm immediately accosted by Elliot.

"Honey, where were you? I was just looking for you."

I don't have to force a smile with El. It stretches across my face, pulling my frozen cheeks. "I was just getting some air, is all." I throw a thumb over my shoulder.

For some reason, I don't mention Liam's presence outside. I feel like I should protect his right to have a few more moments alone. I suppose that's what I'd want if the roles were reversed.

"Oh, okay." His smile grows. "I wanted to ask for your help with dessert."

I feel my sense of humor come back with a vengeance.

"Oh, you need someone to ruin it? I'm your lady."

Elliot's head falls back as he laughs and pulls me toward the dessert table. "Darling, you underestimate yourself. And besides, I'm only asking you to cut the pies and unwrap cookies."

I can't help but laugh. It's not full-bellied, but it's something.

"How do I cut a pie again? Like wedding cake?"

I'm teasing him. He knows it.

He laughs again and wraps his arm around my shoulders.

"I'm so glad you're here, Kate."

As much as I hate to admit it, I am, too.

4

PITTANCE FOR A PALACE

Liam

Kate's neighborhood is insane. I'm not even sure it can be called a neighborhood. The houses are not "close" together and they're all massive. I don't know if these houses existed when I lived here last, but I was definitely never in this area.

Obscenities fly out of my mouth with each house I pass as my GPS assures me I'm getting close to her place.

I'm fully aware that this might be a crazy idea—considering moving into someone's house right now. Someone I barely know. I get that it's impulsive and might cause people to question my judgment. There's just this voice in the back of my head telling me this will be good for me. Maybe the voice is Jill. I have no idea. Regardless of where it's coming from, it's been loud and insistent since Kate went back into the house last night.

I sat on the bench for a bit, considering her offer. On one

hand, there's the very obvious benefit of sleeping in a real bed, as opposed to a futon with a bar down the middle, that makes restful sleep essentially impossible. Also, it would be nice to not sleep in a shared space of someone else's home. I feel as though I'm a great imposition on my brother's family, even though I'm certain he would vehemently disagree.

Last night, I wasn't sure I'd have much more privacy living in a relative stranger's house, but now that I'm seeing these houses, I'm legitimately wondering if we'd each have our own wings. Maybe I'd never see Kate.

A large part of me wants my own space. I want… something that I can just have to myself. I've lived my entire adult life with a woman I was—am—madly in love with. I asked her to move in with me so quickly. I wanted to spend as much time with her as possible. Every place we ever moved into was decided upon with the desire to make Jill comfortable. It needed to be accessible for her. We needed an elevator—no walk-ups for us.

Don't get me wrong, I would have gladly made every accommodation for her for the rest of my life. That's what I signed up for. But now that she's comfortable wherever she is, I don't have to worry about her anymore. I think she'd want me to just think about myself. I think she'd be happy to see me moving on and building a new life for myself.

The more I thought about it last night, the more excited I was to move out of my brother's house. Whether that meant moving into Kate's house or into an apartment on my own, I wasn't sure I cared. It's time to pick up and keep going. Jill would want me to.

Grieving is a strange process. It ebbs and flows. It's waves, not lines. It doesn't happen all at once or in a straightforward manner. While time does help lessen the pain, it doesn't mean that after a certain period of time, it won't hurt anymore. But it does mean that—with time—the pain is more manageable, sometimes more predictable, and not nearly as sharp. Don't get me wrong, I know there will be times when the pain is still so acute it feels as though it just happened. But you have to remember that my wife's life ended years before she died. I've already been through many seasons of grieving. And this is simply a new one.

Talking to Kate, though… was completely different.

It was a breath of fresh air.

Kate's eyes weren't full of pity, like most people's eyes when they look at me these days. No, Kate's eyes were filled with her own pain. Pain she was clearly trying *very* hard to mask—probably for Elliot's sake. I know they've been friends for a very long time.

Perhaps because she knows grief, she didn't behave at all the way other people do when they hear my wife passed. She didn't spend her time with me asking about the gory details of Jill's death, how we spent her last days, or if I felt relieved that she wasn't suffering anymore. She didn't ask me any questions about Jill. She simply acknowledged it happened and then dropped it.

She didn't even try to cheer me up. She asked relevant questions and then made me an incredibly generous offer.

I figured—at the very least—it was worth checking out the house. I tried to talk myself out of it many times, but as I said, there was this persistent voice in the back of my head telling me to give it a chance.

So I called Kate this morning.

And that's why I'm currently doing what the GPS tells me to do and turning left into a driveway with stately-looking stone pillars on either side of the drive and a wrought iron fence extending around the property.

Oh, and the driveway? It's not short. It's rather lengthy, in fact. If I squint, I can see the giant house at the end of it, peeking out through the trees that line the drive.

Expletives that would absolutely make my mother furious leave my tongue before I even realize it. This looks like an estate. Like someone very important lives here because they can fly under the radar instead of living in some penthouse downtown.

I reach the end of the tree line and the driveway opens up on both sides. There's an area to the left with some space for parking and the area to the right seems to go toward a garage. There's shrubbery in front of me, so I have to pick a side. I go to the left and park my car. Holy shit, I feel like I'm out of my element.

I check Kate's text one more time before I get out of the car, making sure I'm at the right place. Her text matches the house numbers I see etched into the stone by the front entrance. That's surrounded by pillars.

Jesus.

I'm staring up at the house in awe when I hear the front door open. Kate appears between the pillars, arms crossed over her chest, hands holding her biceps as if she's hugging herself to save some warmth.

I manage to shut my slack jaw and meet her eyes as I walk toward her.

"Kate… this is your house?"

She looks up above her at the portico, the large light fixture hanging above her, then back toward the front door before nodding. "Yeah."

"It's incredible."

"Thank you." Her voice is soft. She seems a little uncomfortable, though I'm not sure how to solve that problem.

"Do you want to come in?"

"Of course. Lead the way." I motion for her to go ahead of me. She pivots toward the door, her arms falling to her sides as she walks purposefully into the house.

I follow, shutting the door behind me. The door feels expensive. No builder's grade bullshit in this place.

"I can take your coat," she offers from behind me.

I take it off and hand it to her, tucking my scarf in one of the armholes.

She watches me do so with curiosity in her eyes. "I've never seen anyone do that before."

I nod. "I hadn't until I saw Jill do it. It's pretty smart."

"It is," she agrees, putting my coat on a hanger and tucking it into a hall closet. Just then, a screeching noise comes from another room.

"Oh, I was just making tea. Do you want some?"

"Sure."

She walks around a corner, out of the foyer, so I slowly follow her, taking in the space as I go. There's a dining room off to the immediate right and straight in front of me, there's a huge living room with floor-to-ceiling windows overlooking a backyard surrounded by the same wrought iron fencing I saw at the entrance.

Looking around for Kate, I see her in the kitchen, off to the right. It's modern. Clean white cabinetry, marble countertops, and stainless steel appliances. Huge island in the center, where Kate is standing, pouring hot water from a kettle into two mugs.

There are cushioned stools on the side of the island facing me, so I pull one out and sit down. "Thank you for the tea."

"No problem." She selects a tea bag from a box and then slides it across the island to me.

The box has multiple rows of tea bags. There's more variety here than I'd ever know what to do with. I look through them long enough to find English Breakfast—because that sounds safe—and rip open the package to plop it into the hot water.

"So how long have you been here?" I ask.

"Um…" She seems to be lost in thought for a moment, her brow furrowed, one hand slowly moving the tea bag around in her mug. "About five years, I guess."

"Well… I know I'm already here and everything, but I wanted to let you know it's okay if you change your mind. This is an incredibly generous offer and I appreciate it. But if you don't want me to stay here, I completely understand. We'll have tea and I can leave. No hard feelings."

She looks up at me, her eyes assessing, her expression difficult to read. "I'm not going to change my mind." She shakes her head and looks back to her tea. "But thank you."

I watch her for a moment, wondering what the hell is going through her mind. I wonder if that's just what it's like to know Kate… to wonder what's going on in her brain.

I decide to break the silence with a concern of my own.

"I haven't had a roommate who I'm not married to in a long time."

Her eyes snap to mine and her head tilts to the side. "Me either."

"Think we can hack it?"

Her lips tug at one corner, like she kind of wants to smile but is stopping herself. "I figure it will be awkward at first. But we'll either work it out or… you'll leave."

I can't help the smile that splits my face. I don't think she was trying to make a joke, but the delivery was deadpan and, for some reason, strikes me as very funny. I somehow manage to stop myself from laughing. "Fair point."

"Do you want to see the place?" she asks me.

"I'd love to."

She picks up her mug of tea and drops the tea bag into a trash can. I follow suit and then trail behind her as she begins the tour.

"Kitchen, obviously. Garage is through that door." She

points to a door off to the left. "You can park in there. There's plenty of room. Formal dining room over there." She points to a room at the front of the house. "That room also opens up to the foyer. You may have seen it when you came in."

Barely. I was too busy gawking at the chandelier and the high ceilings.

She moves past me into the living room, and I scurry after her.

"The main living room. There's patio furniture outside in the summer that you're welcome to use." She pauses to look out the back windows, at which point my jaw hits the fucking floor.

I'd noticed the fenced-in backyard, but I'd failed to notice the lake just beyond. I knew she was close to the water, but I didn't realize she was *on* the water. I must have said that part out loud because she responds.

"It's pretty close."

In the silence that descends between us, I can almost hear the seagulls and the sounds of children's laughter. "It's very peaceful."

She nods but doesn't look at me. She's staring at the water with unfocused eyes.

"Do you ever get down to the beach?"

She sucks in a breath like a spell has broken. "Umm... I run on the boardwalk a lot. Sometimes, I sit on the beach and read."

"Are you ever worried about security being so close to the beach?"

"We—" she stops abruptly, clamping her mouth shut and swallowing. "There's an alarm system. The fence should probably be higher, but I don't want to block the view. It would still be a bitch to climb over."

She slides her free hand into the back pocket of her jeans,

and I avert my eyes to keep my own eyes from following the movement. I tell myself it would be fifty shades of creepy to look at her ass. Fortunately, she continues talking.

"Technically, this part of the beach is private for residents. The public beach is a couple of miles down. Residents haven't had many issues over the years. I don't think about it very much." She looks over to me. "Shall we?"

"After you." I nod.

"There's another living room over there." She points off to our right to a doorway before we ascend the stairs. There are photos lining the wall as we go up. Kate and Nick on their wedding day. The two of them standing in front of the house, surrounded by vibrant fall colors. A landscape of New York City. The Eiffel Tower. Old family photos. Kate doesn't even look at them, whereas I'm devouring them.

At the top of the stairs, she points toward an open landing that looks to the front door on one side and the living room on the other. On the other side is an open door.

"That's my room. There are three bedrooms on this side, though only one of them has its own bathroom."

She walks into the one closest to the stairs and flips on the light. "It's this one. Bed, dresser, and nightstand are already here. But if you want to move your own in, you can. I can get this stuff out of here. Bathroom is over there." She juts her chin to a doorway by the window.

I take a peek inside the closet and bathroom, then look out the window. It overlooks the entrance and the driveway. "This is really nice. I'd have my own little suite to myself."

She nods. "And really, there are two other empty rooms, so if you wanted to put a desk in one, you could have an office. I don't have any extras lying around. The rooms are over here."

I follow her into the hallway again, shutting off the lights as I go.

In one room, there's extra furniture—a dresser, a bookshelf, and a bunch of boxes. In the other is nothing at all.

"You can have whichever room you want. Or two of them. All of them. Doesn't matter." She shrugs.

"Have you thought about rent?"

"Yeah…" Her hand comes up to her brow for a second before dropping back down to her side and sliding up to her lower back. Whatever she's about to say, she seems nervous. She throws out a number that is absolutely insane.

"That's a joke, right?" I shake my head, smirking.

"No…" She blinks a couple of times. "Is that too high for you?"

"No, no…" I huff a laugh, trying to defuse the tension for her. "Kate, it's not enough. That can't possibly be half the mortgage."

"Well, it's not." She averts her gaze, suddenly finding her tea *very* interesting. And then she tells me what the mortgage, property taxes, and insurance cost per month. Quick math tells me she's basically trying to charge me half of what she should.

"Okay, so let me pay half. I'd be paying that if I rented an apartment or even bought a place."

"But you don't own it," she argues. "It's my responsibility."

"Kate, I have to pay you more than a pittance to live in a palace."

She looks around the landing, the living room sprawled out below us and throws out another number that still isn't enough.

I shake my head. "I'll tell you what: I'm going to pay you half of that total amount every month for letting me live in your gorgeous house while I figure out what the hell I'm going to do." I pause, studying her. "That cool with you?"

She looks startled. "That's more than double my initial offer."

"Your initial offer was woefully undervalued, and you know it."

She has to know it. She's a real estate agent, for fuck's sake. Commercial or residential, she still *has* to know better. I have no idea why she's low-balling me… if it's pride, or maybe Nick left her a ton of money and she doesn't need anything from me. Whatever the reason, I have pride, too. I have to pay at least half of her mortgage.

With a sigh, her shoulders sag. "Okay, fine. If you're sure."

I don't hesitate in my response. "I'm very sure."

"There's no need for a lease unless you feel strongly about it. You're free to go at any time if you find a place of your own. Until then, you're welcome to stay here."

I offer my hand to seal the deal. Her lips press into a firm line when she takes my hand and squeezes once before letting go.

"Listen, Kate, this is incredibly generous of you. I really appreciate it."

"It's nothing. It should work out for both of us, really."

I nod and look back down in the living room. I've never dreamed of living in a house this nice, and definitely not with anyone other than Jill. I could see her down there though… twirling around on the hardwood, carefree and relaxed, running through choreography. She would have absolutely loved this place.

A cat meowing interrupts my thoughts.

"Hey, bud." Kate's face transforms into something soft and *relieved*. She sets her tea on the newel post and bends to pick up the cat—who is pointedly ignoring me—and snuggles it against her chest.

She glances up to me, nerves present in her eyes again. "You're not allergic to cats, are you?"

"No." I offer her a smile when I shake my head. "What's this little one's name?"

She smiles when she looks back to the cat, who is happily purring in her arms. "Beaker. You know… like the Muppet?"

"Oh, right."

"Because he's kind of a mess. He'll warm up to you eventually. We've been pretty much attached at the hip for the past few months, though."

Something strange tugs in my chest watching her with that cat. I don't know what it is… but it feels warm and lovely in a way that makes me feel uncomfortable. I don't know her well enough to have any kind of feeling about her.

I press my fingers to my sternum, frowning.

Her attention snaps to me and when she opens her mouth, her voice is full of fear. "Are you okay?"

I pull my hand away, remembering with a start that Nick died from a massive heart attack. "Yes. I'm fine."

She studies my face and then looks back to my chest, where my fingers had been just seconds ago. "Are you sure?" Her voice is still off, but it's quieter.

"Yes." I nod, trying to reassure her. "I promise."

Her eyes travel back up to mine and move back and forth between them, watching me. She's hugging the cat tighter and I feel horrible. I make a mental note to never touch my chest in front of her.

I step to the side and pick up her mug of tea. "Come on. You bring Beaker. I'll bring the tea. We'll finish these downstairs and I'll talk about getting roommates as adults in their thirties."

I throw a smirk in her direction and see that she's still eyeing me warily but is at least starting to follow me toward the stairs.

Whatever that feeling is in my chest is not something I want to examine at this moment. Maybe later. Or never. But definitely not soon.

5

I NEED SOMETHING STRONGER

Kate

It's Thanksgiving.

Cue my obligatory comment about how I don't have much to be thankful for this year, including the fact that my entire family has plans that do not involve me.

My mom is with her boyfriend's family in Portland. My dad and Sophie are on vacation with Sophie's sister and brother-in-law. Even Elliot and Leon are in Minnesota visiting Leon's family.

My dad did feel terrible when he realized the trip was over Thanksgiving. He said he'd talk to Sophie about canceling, but honestly, what's the point? He'd cancel a trip full of sunshine and happiness to hang out with his Debbie Downer of a daughter? No thanks.

Therefore, I was fully prepared to spend this wretched fucking day alone.

But then Nick's sister called. Marie, the eldest.

Nick had a huge family. He had six siblings: Marie, Matthew, Molly, then came Nick, then the twins Martha and Mark, and Maggie.

So yes, Marie called. Specifically, she called to tell me I was welcome at the Rafferty Thanksgiving Feast.

"You don't have to bring anything! We'd just love to see you!" she'd claimed through the phone.

Do I want to see Nick's family? A little bit, yes. I want to see Maggie, in particular. Maggie and I had been close. But since Nick died, I haven't been able to do much of anything, let alone hang out with someone who constantly reminds me of him.

What I *want* to do is stay at home in my pajamas with at least one bottle of wine and a healthy Netflix binge session. *The Great British Bake Off* released their holiday episodes recently and while I might not enjoy cooking or baking or literally anything that happens in a kitchen other than eating, I love seeing what they come up with. It's like magic.

But I know that's not what I *should* do. So I compromised a little bit. I agreed to go to Thanksgiving at the Raffertys', but I would skip out earlier than usual to come home and do my own wine and Netflix session. I could be alone to weep silently if that's what I wanted to do.

And since I'm about to have a roommate, weeping on the couch will probably be in poor taste soon, so this might be the last night it will happen for a while.

Decision made, I'd told her that I'd bring something, but promised I wouldn't cook it.

Marie laughed and I could almost hear the relief in it. Whether it was because I wasn't cooking or because she'd be glad to see me, I wasn't sure.

So yesterday, Elliot brought over a green bean casserole, which I will cart over to my in-laws' house.

This morning, I'd given up on my restless sleep around

seven a.m. When it was finally light enough to run safely, I went for a run. Three miles down, three miles back. And then I realized I was so close to a 10k, I figured I'd stick out the final stretch, so I ran past the house. I walked back to cool down and then stood in the shower for a while, cursing the passage of time.

Dinner was set for three p.m. I was told to arrive any time after two p.m., so I aimed for two thirty, hoping I could get in, hand off the casserole, grab a drink, ask if I could do anything to help (yeah, right), and sit down to eat, suffering through as little conversation as possible in the meantime.

And that's how I ended up standing on my mother-in-law's front steps, staring at the door.

I stare at the burgundy door and breathe in the cool air, enjoying the way it stings my lungs. Elliot's words from yesterday echo through my head: *One step at a time and get a drink as soon as you can. Text me when you get a chance.*

I take another deep breath and tell myself it's just a couple of hours—okay, a few hours—and it won't be that bad. I place my finger on the doorbell and force myself to press it.

The chime sounds on the other side of the door and the dull murmur of voices accompanies it. Footsteps grow louder and before I even register the door opening, Nick's dad is standing in front of me.

Suddenly, the air is frozen in my lungs. I haven't seen him since the funeral. Seeing him now is like a mirage—an older version of Nick I'll never get to see. I'd certainly noticed the resemblance between the two of them, but I never spent much time thinking about it.

Now, with him standing here in front of me, I'm gutted. I'm staring at a future I was robbed of. I'll never get to see how he would age, how his face would change, the silver starting at his temples and spreading over time. Forever, Nick would remain thirty-seven years old.

I feel an intense urge to hand Mr. Rafferty the casserole and run back to my car. But I know if I do that, Gwen will be pissed. I know exactly what she'll say... *You chose to go back to your empty house instead of socializing with your in-laws who love and care about you?*

So instead, I'm frozen. Standing on the front porch of a house I used to visit at least monthly, staring at a handsome, lined face with a broad smile stretched across it.

His mouth moves, but I don't hear anything come out over the blood rushing in my ears.

My lungs start to burn, and I realize I haven't taken a breath this entire time.

"Kate? Are you all right?"

His voice finally cuts through the fog, and I breathe in, just in time for the sound of joyful children playing games to punch me right in the stomach.

I blink a few times, trying to clear my head. "Hi..."

My voice sounds like I haven't used it in days.

"It's so good to see you!" His smile gets wider and my chest cracks at the fondness in his eyes. "Come on in! Here, let me take that from you."

He reaches out and takes the casserole dish from my hands, then beckons me inside the house.

The familiar scent fills my nose. It's a mix of cleaners, old hardwood, and home cooking. The decorations are exactly the same as they were last year—fall colors, signs painted with sayings about being thankful, and a basket filled with gourds on the hall table. It looks like nothing at all has changed, even though every single one of us knows that *everything* has changed.

A memory of the first time Nick brought me here seeps into my brain like warm honey. I'd been so nervous to meet all of them. They hosted a big family dinner on the first Sunday of every month and everyone came—siblings, spouses, children. So it wasn't like I was meeting his parents… I was meeting all of them. At once.

Even now, all these years later, I can remember being introduced to each of them. It was complete chaos, which I later learned was just par for the course for the Raffertys. Matthew had been carrying one of his boys under his arm on his way to a diaper change. Marie had been half in the oven, pulling out a huge chunk of meat. Molly was chopping vegetables while complaining about something or other under her breath. Martha and Mark were playing with the kids (loudly). But Maggie was just observing me, waiting for her turn.

She took my hand, dragged me out of the room, got me a glass of wine, and attached herself to my hip. Maggie was my favorite Rafferty (that wasn't Nick, of course) for so many reasons, but we were a strange pairing and that made her interesting to me.

We had plenty in common (being the same age, for one), but we also were polar opposites in so many ways. Where I was happy to marry Nick, settle down, and build a life with him, Maggie had a bit of a rebellious streak. I loved her immediately.

I still do love her. I'm just… a mess now.

I know she's here and my nerves are suddenly flipping my stomach uncontrollably. I don't want her to be mad at me. I feel guilty that I've fallen off the face of the planet.

"Let's get this to the kitchen," Nick's dad breaks into my spiraling thoughts and snaps me back to the present.

I follow him down the hall to the kitchen. I can already see the dining room table I have spent countless hours at, talking and laughing with Nick's family. I always loved hearing their stories, but today the thought of childhood Nick stories makes me want to puke.

We round the corner, and it takes less than one second before someone announces my presence.

"Kate! You came!"

My eyes cut to the source of the voice—it belongs to the person I've been most nervous to see, aside from Nick's mom, which I'm dreading with every fiber of my being.

I swear to you, a record scratches somewhere. Utensils are set down clumsily. Drinks are almost spilled. An audible gasp fills the room. Every single person in the room has stopped what they were doing and is staring at me.

This house has never been this quiet. Not for a single minute.

I scan their faces and watch as their eyes quickly shift from surprise to sadness, filling with tears.

I look away because I just can't. I can't watch them cry. And now I'm uncomfortable. And I wish I hadn't come.

I clear my throat, trying to defuse the situation by distracting them. I gesture to the casserole dish Nick's dad is holding. I can't bring myself to look at him as I do it.

"Green beans… they'll need to be heated up."

Marie—thank their Catholic god—took charge like I hoped she would. She wipes her hands on her apron, blinking away her tears quickly and crossing the kitchen to take the dish from her father. "Of course!"

We make very brief eye contact before I avert my gaze. It physically hurts to look at her eyes. They're the same dark green as Nick's.

"Thank you for bringing them, Kate. It was very kind of you."

I don't have a chance to say anything because Molly can't —or won't—hold back. Before I know what's happening, she throws her arms around my neck and sobs loudly in my ear.

Holy shit.

Oh shit, oh shit.

I can't breathe.

I don't want to be touched.

She's not letting go.

My brain is overloaded before I can feel it start to shut down, turning off every single emotion and sense trying to invade it. I find myself staring at the counter behind her, my arms bent at a ninety-degree angle as if I were going to return her hug, but my hands aren't actually touching her.

I probably look crazy. I can't be bothered to care.

"Molls…" Maggie's voice cuts into my reverie. Her body steps in my line of blurry vision and she touches Molly's shoulder. "Come on. Let her breathe."

Molly lets go of me (finally) and pauses in front of me long enough to stammer, "I'm glad you're here," before running to the bathroom to blow her nose.

Fuck, this is awkward.

Everyone is shifting awkwardly, trying not to make eye contact. Nick's dad lays a hand on my shoulder for only a second, squeezes once, and turns to leave the room.

"Well, Kate, let's get you a drink, huh? Hang up your coat, maybe?"

Maggie to the rescue.

I realize in that moment how much I miss her. How much I rely on her presence in my life. My guilt triples.

I remove my coat as people return to their previous tasks, no doubt assigned by Marie. The eldest of seven, she had four children of her own and had everything in her life down to a goddamned science. I often appreciated her efficiency. In the Before Times, of course.

"Come on," beckons Maggie, jerking her head toward the other room, which I fully remember is where the liquor cabinet is.

She takes my coat, throws it on the coat rack, and then steps over to the place I know we both want to be. She takes out the good scotch and pours two fingers into a tumbler for me.

"Thanks." I offer a weak smile before taking a fortifying sip.

Maggie nods. "How you holdin' up?"

I can't do anything but shrug. "Some days are better than others."

She nods again, this time slowly. Thoughtful. Her eyes snag on the chain around my neck and her eyebrows draw together. Her hand reaches out to touch it, pulling it from beneath my shirt.

I try not to bristle at the contact. If I get overstimulated, I might cry. Or drink too much and then cry. I have to keep everything shut off in order to function on a daily basis under normal circumstances, let alone the first time I'm seeing Nick's entire family since the week he died. And truthfully, I don't really remember seeing them then.

Maggie gently holds the ring on the chain, letting it slip onto her index finger, twirling it with her thumb around the digit. Her eyes soften, but she doesn't cry. "Yeah… yeah, I think it's like that for all of us."

I can't.

I close my eyes and struggle to suck in a breath.

Get your shit together, Kate. Don't cry until you get home.

"I'm glad you came, Kate."

I take one more breath and open my eyes. Maggie is looking directly at me, studying me. She sets the ring back down, where it rests against my sternum.

"I've really missed you."

Oh, the guilt.

I tuck Nick's ring back into my shirt and am sure I imagine it when it sears my skin.

My throat burns. My eyes sting.

"I've really missed you, too," I manage to tell her.

When I meet her eyes again, I see she has tears in them. She quickly clears her throat.

"It seems you're still an evil shrew."

I can't help it. I laugh. Maggie has always been hysterical. A tear escapes my eyes against my will. I wipe it away as I respond, "Glad to see you're still a spiteful hag."

Maggie laughs, wiping at her own escaped tears.

And then we laugh together. It becomes infectious. We're laughing at the absurdity of our lives. At the fact that we missed each other and she managed to bring back an old inside joke to remind me subtly that she loves me despite the fact that we're not technically "in-laws" anymore. We're laughing to keep from crying. We're laughing about the fact that we're both laughing.

Besides, if we're laughing, then the tears are because of laughter and not sadness.

I can't breathe, but right now, it's because Maggie is funny and my side stitch has nothing to do with grief or pain or anything else. It's honestly refreshing.

"Maggie?" Marie's voice startles us both and we look at her, standing in the doorway.

We try to stifle our laughter, but both of us are still sputtering uselessly.

Marie frowns. She looks confused. "Maggie, I could use your help in the kitchen."

Maggie clears her throat and wipes more tears from her face. "Yeah, sure. I'll be right there."

Marie nods once, still frowning, and walks away.

I look back to Maggie. "Thank you… I desperately needed that."

"Glad I could help." She wipes the rest of her tears away, blotting at her face with her sleeve.

"Where's your mom?" I ask the question before I can think better of it.

She glances through the doorway where Marie was just standing. "Last I saw, she was in the living room." Her voice was somber once more.

I can tell by her expression that the formidable Helen Rafferty is not doing well.

I wouldn't have expected anything else, frankly.

I haven't been dreading seeing Nick's mom because I don't *like* her. Quite the contrary. I *love* Nick's mom. Nick's mom is everything anyone could ever want in a mom. Everything I never had in a mom. She's nurturing and kind and patient. Warm and loving. Generous. Lovely.

I take another sip of scotch for courage. "All right. I'm going to go find her."

"I'll see you in a bit."

I nod and turn, heading across the house, trying not to remember countless things about my time here with Nick as I go. I dodge a few kids who are running around. I weave around the debris they left in their wake.

When the living room comes into view, I see Helen sitting on the couch, staring blankly at the TV. She's holding a tumbler of scotch, just like me. Some football game is on the screen, but she isn't watching it. Not really. Her eyes might be fastened to it, but she isn't paying attention.

I glance around the room and find a photo of Nick and me on our wedding day on the mantel above the fireplace, with lit candles on either side of it. I want to look away from it... I just *can't*. I remember how happy I was that day. How Nick laughed when I ripped my heels off my feet at the first opportunity. How he tenderly slipped a pair of sparkly flats on my feet in the limo. The look in his eyes and the swell in my heart when he introduced me as his wife for the first time to colleagues.

Fuck fuck fuck.

I clench my jaw and wrench my eyes away from the

photo. But ultimately, my gaze lands back on my mother-in-law and I know it's time.

So I blink away the memories and the tears that accompanied them, then silently walk over to the couch and sit down next to Helen.

She doesn't acknowledge me at first. She just keeps staring at the TV.

So that's what I do, too.

Every few minutes, I glance back up to my wedding photo, unable to help myself, craving the sight of his joyous face, defined by his disarming smile. The way he's holding my hand to his chest is a fucking sucker punch that I can't seem to get enough of.

"You came," Helen's voice cuts the silence, shocking the hell out of me.

"I did." I nod. "You seem surprised."

"I am, a little."

I huff a humorless laugh. "So am I, to be honest."

Helen turns her head now and looks at me. I don't meet her gaze, but I can feel the weight of it. "What made you decide to come?"

I sigh, trying to figure out how to even answer that question. Truthfully, I'm not sure what compelled me to come here today. I just wanted to lounge around in sweats all day, alone in my giant house with unlimited Netflix and a cat on my lap.

Instead, I'm experiencing the complete opposite. I'm sitting next to my mother-in-law. I'm wearing skinny jeans with knee-high boots and a sweater. I'm still wearing my scarf as if it provides extra body armor. I even put on makeup and blow-dried my hair after my shower.

But really, what it comes down to is that... when I married Nick, this crazy bunch of weirdos became my family. I'm a Rafferty like all the rest of them. They made me feel welcome from that very first visit. Even when I felt like an outsider, all twelve hundred times they told inside jokes I didn't understand because I didn't grow up with them. They loved me—*love me*—like a real family member… not just someone who married into the family.

They're my family, the same way Elliot is my family. They aren't my blood, but I've chosen them all the same. And with that crushing thought, I realize that I haven't been choosing them since July and I feel absolutely wretched about it.

So I take an unsteady breath and turn my head to meet Helen's eyes. "You guys are my family."

Her brows knit together, a line forming between them. "Of course we are, dear." She reaches for my free hand with hers, squeezing tightly. "We'll always be your family. No matter what. You're ours."

My eyes immediately sting, followed by my nose and my throat and I feel my chin wobble. I squeeze my eyes shut and whisper, "Thank you."

Helen squeezes my hand again. "I'm so glad to see you, Katherine."

And then I can't hold back my tears anymore. They slip out past my closed eyelids and I can't stop them. Helen lets go of my hand and wraps her arm around my shoulders, pulling me into her side. I acquiesce, leaning my head on her shoulder.

I can hear her sniffing, too, so I know she's crying along with me.

I'm fully aware that I'm a mess.

I have no tissues. Neither does Helen. And because each of us is holding scotch—that we're absolutely not willing to give up—neither of us can reach any form of tissues. So we just sit there together, crying as quietly as we can manage, a blurry television in front of us.

* * *

DINNER—WHAT I'm able to stomach—is delicious. I eat small bites. I switch from scotch to water so I can drive home responsibly. I don't contribute much of anything to the ongoing conversation and no one asks me how I'm doing.

After dinner, Helen and I start cleaning up the kitchen. Marie tries to stop us, telling us to sit back down and rest, but Helen (mercifully) shoos her away.

When she tries to object, Helen snaps at her in a mom voice I was never familiar with but would have obeyed immediately if she'd used it on me.

"Marie, I'm not going to tell you again. Kate and I are perfectly capable of doing dishes. Now leave us alone."

We're left to our repetitive, productive tasks of hand-washing and drying Marie's wedding china. I actively try *not* to think about the fact that Marie has been married for nearly twenty years. I try so hard *not* to think about how she's used this china every holiday season since. I try *not* to think about the fact that we didn't register for wedding china because it seemed stupid.

I try and I fail.

I want to smash the fragile plates against the tile.

But I manage not to. Somehow.

Helen and I work in silence. I mostly appreciate the opportunity to avoid after-dinner conversation. I'd been keeping to myself in hopes that I could pass up the Catholic Inquisition (people *do* expect it). I don't want to answer his siblings' questions about his stuff. Or his house. Or the missing meat on my bones.

When the kitchen is clean and Helen has refreshed her drink, Marie comes back into the kitchen. She starts putting away the china, neatly and carefully, in its proper cabinet, even going so far as to place thin foam pieces between each dish.

"How's Beaker, Kate?"

See? I told you to expect it.

She's trying to lighten the mood. I know that. I swallow before I can say something sarcastic, but I don't miss Helen's eye roll and annoyed glance at her eldest daughter. It makes me smirk and does a better job at breaking the tension than Marie's question.

"He's hanging in there. He's figuring things out," I offer.

"Nick just loved that cat. He's such a funny creature."

I can't help but smile just a little. Beaker is indeed a funny creature. "Yeah, he's a good egg."

I could practically see Marie's brain searching for another topic to bring up. I suppose now is as good a time as any to throw the grenade and run out the front door.

"Listen…" I force out the words before Marie can ask another question. "I wanted to talk to you guys about something and I'd rather not do it with everyone around."

I set down the last piece of china I am drying and begin to fiddle with the hand towel, needlessly inspecting the pattern.

"The house is a lot for me. I'm going to be getting a housemate tomorrow."

Marie freezes, a small line forming between her eyes. "Oh…"

"He's a friend of Elliot's—"

"*He?*" Marie's eyes look like saucers—exactly the way Nick's did when Beaker broke the Tiffany vase we received as a wedding gift.

I steal a quick glance at Helen, who is silent but looks surprised.

Don't get defensive. Don't get defensive.

"Yes… *he* lost his wife at the beginning of the year. He's originally from the area, but he lived in Chicago with Jill. She was a dancer with Joffrey. He moved back here recently and has been sleeping on a futon at his brother's house with his wife and two kids ever since."

I stop to take a breath, having rushed all that information out.

"I have a four-bedroom house I share with a ridiculous cat. He has three other bedrooms to choose from. And frankly, I would appreciate some noise in the house."

Helen and Marie seem to deflate a little.

"I didn't want you to think I had some random man living with me. And I certainly didn't want you to hear it from anyone else. It's not..." I can't even continue the thought. I can't say it aloud. As if there could ever be anyone else. "I promise..."

There's a moment of silence before Marie clears her throat. "Well... if that's what you need."

I watch her for a moment. I can tell she feels uncomfortable with the information, but it's not her choice. She has no say in the matter. It's none of her business.

I shift my gaze to my mother-in-law, who looks paler than she did the moment before. But she doesn't look angry.

"Kate, you're a grown woman." Her voice is quiet and tight. "You do what you have to."

Marie offers a quick, slight nod.

My chest feels lighter, but fatigue suddenly overwhelms me. I choke out a quick, "Thank you."

I take a deep breath and hang up the towel on the oven door. "Thank you for inviting me today. I really appreciate you reaching out." I meet both of their eyes so they can see I mean it, even though I'm about to flee like my ass is on fire. I can't stay here. Being with Nick's family is like watching him walk around in pieces. His mother's nose. His father's build. His siblings all have the same kind eyes. Maggie has his little twitches. It's so fucking painful.

"I should get home to Beaker."

They both nod and look away in a strikingly similar manner, their eyes shining.

I make hasty goodbyes to the others, who are now playing Trivial Pursuit in the basement and having a heated debate about the accuracy of a particular card. Google is being consulted. Maggie offers to walk me to my car. I hit the remote start button as we walk out the front door.

"What are you doing this weekend?" she asks me.

Court-mandated community service.

Not that I'll admit that to Maggie. I literally haven't told anyone who wasn't in that courtroom.

I shrug. "Nothing, really."

She tilts her head, hesitating briefly before asking, "Have you started decorating for Christmas?"

I huff a laugh. "No. Not feeling particularly festive this year."

I'm literally a shell of my former self. Who gives a fuck about Christmas this year?

"Well, you have to do something to that gorgeous house," she argues.

"I suppose," I admit, sliding my hands into my coat pockets.

"I'll tell you what… I'll come help you," she offers. "This weekend or next—whatever works. I'll come put up the tree, deck your halls, drink your wine."

I can't help but smile. Of course she's offering to spread holiday cheer. I also know that she wouldn't offer to do this for just anyone. She'd only do this kind of favor—while she's grieving, just like I am—for someone she really loves.

"It'll be good," she insists.

I force my eyes to hers so I can accept her offer genuinely. "I would really like that if you're game."

"Of course I am."

"All right, then."

"I'll text you," she promises.

"Thanks, Mags."

I look down at my feet, trying to gather the courage to tell her the thing I know I need to tell her. I want to keep my mouth shut. I don't want to say it again. But I know Maggie will be pissed if Marie is the one who tells her about my roommate situation.

"I um..." I swallow hard and look anywhere but at her. "Someone is moving in with me tomorrow. A friend of Elliot's. His wife died earlier this year and he just moved back here. He could use a place to stay." I glance at her. She's watching me with a look of mild surprise, but she's silent. "I could use some noise in the house," I tack on needlessly. I'm uncomfortable. I just want her to say something.

The silence stretches for another tense moment before Maggie clears her throat.

"Jesus, if you're that lonely, you just need a vibrator. You don't need to get a whole-ass housemate. I could give you some recommendations."

A startled laugh flies out of my face.

I'm not embarrassed. I have no problem with sex toys. It's just that... who fucking says that during a serious discussion like this? Maggie, that's who.

Fuck, I love her.

"You know what? You caught me," I manage to speak through my laughter. "We can revisit this discussion this weekend. Give me all your pointers."

"I'm full of useful information, Katherine, you best not forget it."

I laugh again.

"I would never do you such an injustice," I assure her.

"I should hope not." Her expression is defiant with a

touch of arrogance, but I can see her eyes twinkling with mirth under the streetlight.

She reaches her foot out and taps my leg, her face growing serious. "I love you, you know that. I'll support you no matter what."

I reach my foot out and tap her leg in return. "I know. I love you, too."

She pulls me in for a quick hug, squeezing tight before pulling back. I swear her eyes are a little glassy when she separates from me. "I'll text you later."

I nod. "Elliot's out of town. I'm in desperate need of interior design assistance."

"Then I would not miss it for the world."

6

HOME FOR NOW

Liam

I'm staring out the back windows again.

I have a feeling this is where I'll end up a significant portion of the time I live in Kate's house. It's just unreal.

I've lived on a Great Lake most of my life.

I lived in Chicago for years. I grew up a few miles away from this very lake that I can't tear my eyes away from. But I've never seen anything like this from my place of residence.

The view from Kate's backyard overlooking the water is *magnificent*. I don't know if it's nostalgia or grief or my new beginning, but I swear it's calling out to me. Some essential part of my being knows that I've made the right decision moving in here.

Today is the day after Thanksgiving. I moved in this morning.

I'd already put a bunch of my stuff in storage because there wouldn't be much room for any of it at Joe's house. I'd sold everything I could or left it behind for the new condo owners. I just didn't see the point in spending the money to relocate it and then store it all for an undetermined period of time.

The point is, I didn't have much to *move in*.

I'm not even sure you can call it *moving in* if you only roll two suitcases over the threshold. This might just be a booking at an extended-stay hotel or an Airbnb.

Kate gave me the garage code when I was here last. It's six digits and something tells me it's something related to Nick. Maybe their anniversary.

There was a set of house keys on the kitchen counter with a note telling me to make myself at home and a Wi-Fi password scrawled at the bottom.

Getting settled took all of an hour. All I had to do was unpack my suitcases, hang my suits and dress shirts, then get the rest of my clothes organized into the dresser. I stashed the suitcases in the closet and put my favorite picture of Jill on a little shelf next to a candle that was already sitting there.

By the time I was done, it wasn't even end of business. I'd taken the day off, but Kate hadn't. I didn't expect her to. That meant I was alone in the house, so I took the opportunity to wander around. I didn't go in her bedroom, and there was a set of double doors that were closed by the front door that a little voice in my head told me to leave alone. But otherwise, I took my time wandering around and taking note of the little design elements. I looked at the photos of Kate and Nick, happy and vibrant. I gathered that whoever decorated had a modern eye.

I think I stopped in front of the window so I could space out and process the events of the past two weeks.

The house feels… strange. I can't put my finger on why. I wonder if the house feels to Kate the way my condo in

Chicago felt to me. I just couldn't be there anymore—not without Jill taking up as much space as possible.

Then again, it's not my house. It might feel strange because it's still new to me. I'm sure that's part of it, no matter what else might be at play.

I decide I want some tea. Kate had told me to make myself at home. I put the kettle on and search the cabinets until I find the box I remember from last week. I look for something without caffeine since it's getting so close to dinnertime and wander over to the breakfast nook by the back window while I wait for the kettle.

There's a beautiful patio made from big stones. There's a table with six chairs just outside the window I'm standing by and over to the left—by the back door in the living room— there's a row of four white Adirondack chairs. It reminds me of a beach house. I suppose, in many ways, it could be considered a beach house, given its proximity.

Behind me, the kettle screeches, so I pour the water into a mug and drop my tea into the mug. While the tea steeps, I put the box away and peek through the cabinets I haven't touched. For a woman who claims to not know what to do with a kitchen, Kate sure has a lot of kitchen gadgets. I assume these are all wedding gifts.

After throwing the tea bag in the trash, I head outside to claim an Adirondack chair so I can watch the sunset. It's chilly outside. I should have put on a coat at least, but I don't really care. I grew up around here, so I'm used to the cold. And besides, Chicago is colder. My blood is plenty thick at this point in my life.

Looking out into the backyard, I wonder again how Kate can feel safe in this house... all alone with a beach so close and a fence anyone taller than my nephews could scale. I certainly wouldn't have wanted Jill to be in this position.

At the very notion, the dull ache in my chest begins. I

close my eyes and try to ground myself using the hot mug in my hand. The air smells crisp, but I can also smell the tea. I can hear seagulls. I can feel the cold wood under me. I open my eyes and I can see the glorious pink-and-orange sky over the blue water.

I know in the back of my mind that a fresh wave of grief will be coming soon. Jill passed in January, which means the anniversary of her death is only two months away. In some ways, it feels like she's been gone forever and in others, it feels like it was just yesterday.

The woman I fell in love with—the woman I married, even—was nothing like the woman I cared for in her final days. The woman who danced with abandon became a person who couldn't bear to see photos of herself performing, hair tightly drawn into a bun, sparkly, dramatic makeup on her face, tights stretched over her long legs, finished off with pink pointe shoes. She asked me to put away the photos, so she didn't have to see them.

It was one of those photos I put up in my new bedroom. That's how I choose to remember her.

The sharp, stabbing pains of grief aren't as frequent anymore, but January is coming up, and I'm anticipating a rough time.

I close my eyes in resignation and suck in a deep breath of cool, wintery air, letting my head fall back against the chair. If I concentrate hard enough, I can almost catch the subtle scent of her perfume.

The sound of the sliding door cracking open snaps me from my thoughts. I turn my head to find Kate poking her head out the doorway.

"Hey," she greets me with a mild look of worry on her face.

"Hey," I return, trying to shake off the heavy thoughts I was just having.

Her eyes dart around the backyard. The sunset is almost over, still shooting orange and pink into the horizon. She blinks at it for just one second before returning her eyes to mine. "You all right?"

"Yeah. Just resting."

She nods, seemingly satisfied with my response.

"Do you have plans tonight?"

She shakes her head. "Just gonna hang here, I guess. I don't really like running in the dark. I didn't get home soon enough to beat the sunset." Her head tips in the direction of the water.

"Do you want to have dinner with me?" I hope my voice sounds normal when I ask the question. Part of me wonders if my loneliness will shine through.

A look of surprise flashes across her face and she blinks a few times. After a moment of silence, she blurts out a response with a shake of her head. "I don't cook."

"That's okay." I smile. "I wasn't asking you to. I could cook. Or we could order carryout."

"Oh…" she seems a little relieved that I—her tenant—am not asking her to cook for me and feed me. "Okay, sure."

"Great."

I swing my legs over to stand up from the chair and she hesitates briefly but opens the sliding door farther for me as I walk toward her.

"Carryout is really fine. You don't have to cook for me," she says.

"All right. You pick the place. Dinner's on me."

Her brows knit together. "That's not necessary."

"I know it's not necessary. It's a thank-you for offering me a place to live."

Her face is almost made of stone while she considers that offer. If I studied her face for a full hour, I'm not sure I'd be able to decipher what was going on in her head. She just looks at me for a few breaths before nodding. "All right. Thank you. That's very kind."

"It's not a big deal," I assure her. "What are you in the mood for?"

"Whatever. I'm not picky."

I remember a new Indian restaurant that opened recently, so after some perusal of the menu, we agree on it and I place the order online. Thirty minutes later, a delivery man appears at the front door with piping-hot food in Styrofoam containers. I unpack the food while Kate opens a bottle of wine, and we sit down to eat in the breakfast nook.

"Thank you for dinner," she says.

"You're welcome."

"It's pretty good. I haven't found a lot of great Indian food around here."

She's pushing her food around her plate with a fork. I can tell from the photos around the house that she's lost weight and those times when eating seemed like a chore spring to my mind. I make a mental note to see if she'll eat with me regularly so she at least eats something before bed.

"Yeah," I agree. "This will definitely do. Jill and I used to get takeout from this place down the street from our apartment in Chicago all the time. I've missed it since I got back."

Something flashes through her eyes when they snap to mine, but it's gone so quickly I can't even begin to figure out what it is. She takes a deep breath and looks back to her plate, pushing a piece of tofu around.

"Do you have any plans this weekend?" I ask, trying to change the subject.

She stops toying with her food and is completely still for a moment. She doesn't even blink. She's just staring at her fork, and I can't peel my eyes off her. I wonder if she's okay. I wonder what my question triggered.

But then she takes a sudden breath and seems to snap out

of whatever trance she'd been in. "My sis…" her voice is weak, so she clears her throat and looks up at me. "Nick's sister is coming over to help decorate the house for Christmas."

"That's nice of her." I nod. Truly, it sounds incredibly kind. Even I don't want to think about decorating this season, and I'm months—if not years—ahead of her in my grief.

"It is," she agrees. "She said it would essentially be a travesty to not decorate this house and I'm… not exactly in the mood." Her eyes widen meaningfully, so I offer her a smile that I hope conveys my grasp of the situation. "She'll be here tomorrow," she finishes.

"I'll be out of your way," I assure her.

She frowns. "Oh, you don't have to do that. She knows that someone is… moving in with me." Her voice cuts off as a blush appears on her cheeks that I find both endearing and inexplicable. What's causing it? Embarrassment? I decide to ignore it for both of our sakes.

"Well, I have plans with my family," I offer. "My parents were out of town visiting extended family on Thursday, so we're all doing Thanksgiving together tomorrow."

A soft smile lit up her face, but I could still see the melancholy in her eyes. "How many of you?"

"Me, my parents, my brother and his wife and their two kids."

Her mouth opens like she wants to ask another question, but she changes her mind and takes a sip of wine instead.

I'm tempted to fill the silence, but I don't. I know it's awkward. Sometimes, the silence is better than small talk.

Instead, I stand to clean up the leftovers. She quickly follows, scraping the food from her plate back into the Styrofoam container that it came in. Together, we clean up the kitchen, putting our dishes in the dishwasher and stashing the food in the refrigerator.

It seems like it should be awkward, but somehow, it's not. I don't necessarily know where everything (or anything) is, but Kate directs me and before I know it, we're done.

"Thank you again for dinner," she says. She's standing a few feet away from me, her hands clasped in front of her, fidgeting.

"My pleasure."

"Um… please make yourself at home. I can't really claim to be a gracious host at this point," she huffs a quiet laugh with a quirk of her eyebrow. "I have almost nothing in the fridge, but you're welcome to whatever you can find."

She's charming. That's my first thought, and I personally find it alarming. I frantically search for anything to say to break my own thought process.

"I'll probably head to the grocery store Sunday."

She chuckles as she looks toward the refrigerator and screws up her face into a self-deprecating expression. "Yeah, that's probably a smart move on your part."

"I'm a grown man." I laugh. "I can take care of myself."

She nods, her tongue peeking out to lick her lips. "All right, well I'm going to get to bed. You have a key and the garage code, yes?"

"I do."

"Good. I'll see you tomorrow, then."

"Sounds good."

Kate turns and heads toward the stairs, her heels clicking on the hardwood as she walks, her footfalls diminishing as she hits the carpeted steps.

I look around the kitchen one more time.

This is home, for now.

7

AN EVIL SHREW

Kate

Maggie should be here any minute.

Letting her help me decorate for Christmas seemed like a decent idea at the time, but now I'm really regretting it. I want to be alone. I don't want to have to put on a brave face for anyone. Then again, if I'm going to allow anyone into my house when I feel like this, Maggie is the person who would be the most understanding. So I'm going to suck it up and let her help me.

I'm cleaning while I wait for her… just to keep my hands busy. The house is clean. I don't really need to do it, but that's my thing these days. I clean obsessively because it feels productive and it makes me *appear* to have my shit more together than I do. So when people stop by unexpectedly (as they're wont to do lately), I don't look like I'm two steps away from lying on the floor and wishing for death.

Even if that's exactly how I feel.

I made it through Thanksgiving (barely) and now I'm staring Christmas in its stupid, sparkly, joyous face. I'm sure I'm not hiding the extra weight of my grief these days. The weight hadn't really lifted much at all and now it's the fucking holiday season and honestly… I'm angry. And bitter. And yes, deeply depressed.

Gwen—my court-appointed therapist—assures me that the way I'm feeling is normal right now. The holidays are difficult for anyone who is grieving, especially when that grief is so fresh. This is my first Christmas without Nick, so it's bound to be challenging.

Every time a commercial on TV talked about spending time with loved ones this holiday season or making time for family this year, my eyes rolled so hard I was afraid they'd get stuck in that position.

My favorite loved one is gone. I will never again get to spend a holiday season with him. My loved one will not be attending parties with me this year. Or any year from here on out, for that matter. We were—quite literally—out of time.

Letting Maggie come over to decorate the house accomplishes two goals: trying to show people I'm not going to off myself and it gets me quality time with Maggie, which is something I should never turn down. She's my second favorite Rafferty.

A little voice in my head reminds me that with Nick gone, Maggie is bumped up to first place by default and I kick that voice until it shuts the fuck up.

Dick.

Along the lines of keeping up appearances, I took extra care today to make myself look less pale than usual. I put extra blush on my cheeks, along with some eyeshadow and plenty of mascara.

My face still looks… odd. Drawn. Pale. But it's not as bad as it looked this morning.

Liam isn't due back until later tonight, so I'm alone while I wait for her. I finish unnecessarily scrubbing at the windows and then take a moment to stare at the view. In the gloomy afternoon haze, the first time I was ever at this house pops into my mind.

Nick had told me he wanted to drop off a housewarming present at a client's house—a tradition he'd picked up from me and my dad.

He drove us through the neighborhood while I marveled at the giant houses set away from the street. I knew we were close to Elliot and Leon's house and I wanted to stop by to see them, but El wasn't answering my texts. I remember being annoyed about that.

When we pulled up to the house, Nick offered to show me around the house, which freaked me out because his client wasn't home. Nick assured me it was fine—that his client had given him the garage code and it would not be a surprise to his client that we were already there.

So we walked around the house together. He let me wander as I liked, pausing to gape at the view, remark at the size of the tub in the master bathroom, and make comments about paint color under my breath… you know, just in case his client walked in while I was disparaging something he actually liked and did on purpose.

When I was done snooping, I wound up right here… in front of these windows, staring at the sloping lawn framed by the wrought iron fence with the lake visible beyond.

My knees nearly gave out when he told me the house didn't belong to his client.

He'd bought the house.

Nick bought the house.

For *us*.

And while I was still reeling from that information, he asked me to move in with him.

My immediate reaction wasn't elation or excitement. I was furious.

We'd discussed moving in together. His lease was coming up on his condo, so he was considering buying something. My lease was up a couple of months after his, which of course brought up the idea of us cohabitating. But at *no point* did we discuss him buying a *giant house* on the *water*.

I felt like he was skipping a few steps. He'd passed over the starter home entirely, was assuming we'd be able to handle living together and was moving straight to "forever home" territory.

So yeah… I was pretty pissed.

I remember yelling at him. Right here, in front of these gorgeous windows. The volume of my voice stemmed more from disbelief than actual anger.

Up to that point in our relationship—two happy years into it—we'd barely argued, minor issues only. Neither of us had ever yelled at the other.

Nick liked surprises and I'd been getting used to them. They were sort of his love language. He usually put a lot of thought and effort into surprises. In his own way, he was telling me how much he cared about me, how much he prioritized me in his life.

But a house? On the water? It was too much.

Therefore, the yelling was one-sided. He let me process my feelings (loudly) while he stood quietly a few feet away with his hands in his pockets, waiting out the storm.

When I was finished yelling, he told me he understood why I was upset—and then asked me if I liked the house.

I did. Of course. I still do.

When I told him I loved it, his face split into that gorgeous, arresting smile and my anger disintegrated.

Surely, you can guess that I moved in with him. Who wouldn't move into this ridiculously beautiful house with someone they're completely in love with? Although, I did swear the argument wasn't over because I simply couldn't encourage such behavior. He promised to never again make a major purchase without consulting me.

And honestly, it worked out. Nick was right. We were so happy here.

Looking around the living room now, I struggle to find the same peace I felt just months ago when Nick and I would sit around eating popcorn and watching Netflix. These days, that kind of happiness feels like trying to catch a firefly—you see it and then it disappears and you're wandering around in the dark, trying to catch it.

The house feels foreign to me now. It feels haunted. Ghosts of my former self and my dead husband living happily within these walls stalk me as I wander around, obsessively cleaning and trying not to look at the photos on the walls.

I have a love-hate relationship with the photos of Nick in that I love seeing his face, his smile, the vibrant spirit evident in his eyes. But I hate that those photos are a constant reminder that he's not actually *here*.

Of course, the photos are all I have left of him. So I keep them up.

I find myself staring at them when the doorbell rings. I don't know how long I've been there, but my eyes sting and my throat is burning. I clear it and squeeze my eyes shut, telling the tears to fuck off into the sunset. I did my makeup, for fuck's sake. With one final deep breath, I walk to the front door and catch a glimpse of Maggie through the window.

I don't have to fake a smile when I open the door. Her mass of curly hair is barely tamed and her expression leaves me believing that she knows something I don't. It's just like old times.

"Haven't seen you in months and now twice in one week? I feel so special," she quips as she hugs me and then makes her way to the kitchen with take-out bags.

I know she means it as a joke, but I still feel the dig. "I know... I've been pretty reclusive."

I set my hands on the island across from where she's standing, taking containers out of the bags.

She looks up at me and frowns. "I'm sorry, Kate. I didn't mean it like that..."

"Yeah..." I wave her off. "Yeah, I know."

I didn't know, but the look on her face is genuine.

"Seriously, it's fine. Don't worry about it." I peek inside the take-out bag to change the subject. "This smells delicious."

With one more hesitant look at me, Maggie starts digging the food out of the bag.

"It's Chinese food. Nothing particularly fancy. But I did get extra egg rolls."

"I would expect nothing less," I tease as I head over to the wine rack to grab a bottle.

For Maggie's benefit, I make sure to eat two entire egg rolls and some of the broccoli and rice. After we finish, I take her upstairs to the large closet in one of the spare bedrooms, where all of the Christmas decorations are stored.

"Well, the tree is a given. We have to do that," Maggie announces, looking around at the tote bins, boxes, and bags of decor. "I also think we should do your mantel... and the stairwell."

She slides the tree box out of the closet and picks up tote bin (after tote bin after tote bin) and sets them on the floor by the bedroom door. Then, she returns to stare at the remaining supplies.

"Oh, good! You still have that huge wreath. That needs to go on the front door."

I do whatever she tells me to do. I don't have it in me to enjoy the celebratory fanfare of the season, but I can follow directions and enjoy the sound of Maggie's voice for a little while.

As we move through the house, putting up lights, garland, wreaths, and knickknacks, Maggie catches me up on all the siblings and their children—what's going on with them, how various sports are going for the kids, and how work is going for herself. As usual, Maggie is a chatterbox and I'm perfectly content with it.

"How are things with Ethan?" I ask.

She heaves a sigh for the first time during the evening. "Good, I suppose."

I lift an eyebrow and look at her meaningfully.

She sees my expression and rolls her eyes at me.

"He's fine. He's wonderful. He's Ethan."

I stop wrapping garland around the staircase and frown at my beloved sister-in-law (but also… not my sister-in-law). "What does that mean?"

She rubs her forehead, stalling or trying to stave off a headache, I'm not sure which.

"He's just… concerned, I guess."

I avert my eyes, knowing her well enough to realize she probably wants some space to process what she wants to tell me. I return to my task, winding the garland through the balusters at even intervals. Truthfully, I'm grateful for the distraction—Maggie is frustrated about something and that is something I can focus on. It's something I can use to alleviate the tension in my own mind.

"He's in my space and asking me what I need and sometimes, it just feels suffocating," she blurts out all at once, shaking her head at the silver bell she's holding in her hands.

I let her words hang in the air for a moment because I want her to realize how ridiculous she sounds. "It's nice that he's concerned," I start softly. "If he weren't, I'd think less of him."

Maggie huffs out a laugh. "I guess so, yeah." She stops and studies the silver bell. "I feel like it's a lot sometimes, though. Like, I'm not going to kill myself or anything. I'm just..."

Silence permeates the air. I watch her as she appears to struggle with her next words.

"Depressed?" I ask quietly.

Maggie's eyes snap up to mine before dropping away with a flush in her cheeks. Her jaw tics just before she nods.

I finish wrapping the garland while I try to think of comforting words. *Any* comforting words. I cross the room to where she's standing and I take the silver bell from her hands.

"I think it's sweet that he's hovering."

She shoots impressive side-eye my way.

"I know, I know." I hold a palm up between us to indicate surrender. "I get it. I'm just saying that Ethan understands how painful... how traumatizing this is for you. He's known you for years. He wants to take care of you." I pause and wait for Maggie's eyes to meet mine. "He's trying to take care of you. He loves you, Mags."

Maggie sighs and closes her eyes. "Well, when you say it like that, I sound like an asshole."

"Nah..." I tsk. "You're not an asshole. A spiteful hag, yes. But not an asshole." I wink at her for good measure, just to make sure she knows I'm messing with her.

She laughs quietly and lifts her eyes to the ceiling. "God, you really are an evil shrew."

"We all have our strengths," I deadpan. "More wine?"

"Is the Pope Catholic?"

8

FROM UNDER THE CHRISTMAS TREE

Liam

Christmas is less than two weeks away. I'm out shopping with Joe—we're getting gifts for the kids and he's still trying to figure out what to get for Tracy. He thinks he still has time, but I roll my eyes at him. He's basically at the point where he needs to find something he doesn't need to order online or order something pretty quickly in case shipping is delayed.

Making sure your wife has presents under the Christmas tree that she did not have to plan, purchase or wrap is the second most important thing that all husbands need to know. I tell my brother this, shocked he doesn't already know better and wondering how much it irritates Tracy.

"Come on, Liam. It'll be fine. I'll find something and she'll have presents and she'll be happy."

I shake my head. "I'm tellin' you, man. Don't wait until the last second. It's a simple thing you can do for her… showing her you care about her and you're thinking about things that will make her happy."

We sidestep a family standing in the middle of the aisle—obviously arguing about something—and then come back together on the other side of them.

"If you're frantically trying to come up with an idea *just* so she has a gift, she's going to notice," I point out.

"It's not that deep, man. Christmas is really more about kids once they're around."

I frown. "You sound awfully dismissive of the woman who grew both of your sons for forty weeks and pushed their giant heads out of her body."

"What?" He looks confused. "It's not like that. I'm not trying to be *dismissive*. I'm just saying… Tracy gets it. I'm sure she feels the same way about buying gifts for me."

We've hit a traffic jam, so I can look over at him for longer than a second at a time. I study him and realize he actually believes that.

I heave a sigh and look over the heads of people in front of us to see how long this traffic jam will take to unclog.

"What?" Joe asks. "What's that big, dramatic sigh for?"

Memories of Jill on Christmas flood me. I try not to think about the last Christmas we spent together. I try to dig for the early Christmases. The ones in college when everything felt new and exciting. The ones when we were newlyweds, and we already knew we had a time limit.

I spent a lot of time thinking about Christmas gifts for her. She didn't really want *stuff* and in many ways, that made it more difficult. So instead, I bought her experiences. Or I did travel research for her. I had to adapt as her illness progressed. But she always looked so pleased… so happy that I'd put so much thought into her gifts.

"Liam?" Joe's voice cuts into my thoughts and I automatically look at him.

He frowns. "What's up?"

The traffic jam lets up before I can answer, so we keep walking through the aisle, looking for items on our list for the kids.

He flicks my shoulder with the back of his hand and lifts his chin when I meet his eyes, silently beckoning me to speak my mind.

I rub the back of my neck nervously. I don't have a problem talking about my feelings—I've been in therapy for years, so I could learn how to cope with the impending death of my wife and best support her as she declined.

But talking about my feelings in public where anyone can hear me? That I'm not all too comfortable with. Not to mention, I'm going to say something that might upset—and possibly guilt-trip—my brother and that's not really my goal here.

"Listen…" I clear my throat and lower my voice. "I have a different perspective than you at this point, okay?"

His eyes soften with understanding.

"I'm not telling you this to put a damper on the day. I'm just saying…" I glance around us to stall for time because I can feel my holiday-amplified emotions threatening. "You just never know, man. You should put in the effort."

His head rears back. "Dude… I put in effort. I love my wife. You know that. *She* knows that."

"I know…" I say because I *do* know.

"Then what are you tryin' to say, Liam?" He looks offended. Maybe blindsided.

I know I'm being kind of intense for Christmas shopping. I can't help it though. Jill is getting to me. This is fucking hard. I miss her. I would do anything to have her back, but I don't want her to suffer. I want able-bodied Jill back and I know that's not what I would have if she were still alive. She'd be bedbound and angry.

I take a deep breath before I say the thing that I think I've been trying to say, but it hasn't been coming out right.

"The first rule of being a man who is married to a woman is to always remember that you loved her first." I meet his eyes. "Before anything. Before you got married, before you had a house or kids. You loved her first."

His eyes drift down and to the side like he's trying to run through his memory for something. I clap a hand on his shoulder and squeeze once before continuing my search for gifts.

Those boys have uncles on Tracy's side, too and I'm determined to be their favorite. Whether I like it or not, toys are one of the ways to their hearts, so I'm looking for some of those, but I'm also looking for things we can do *together*.

I know better than most that it's the quality time you share with the people you love that matters more than anything.

* * *

I'M EXHAUSTED at the end of the day. Joe and I ate dinner and had a couple of beers at a restaurant downtown before he headed home to help with bedtime, and I drove to my own (albeit temporary) home.

Grabbing a few bags of gifts from the trunk, I decide to leave the rest for later. I'm glad to be done shopping. Stores get more intense as Christmas nears and I don't like fighting against the last-minute shoppers.

I make my way through the garage door into the kitchen and set the bags down so I can strip off my winter gear. The house is quiet except for Christmas music playing over the sound system.

The lights are dim in the kitchen and completely off in the living room. I can only see the light from the Christmas tree that Maggie helped Kate set up right after I moved in. But the fireplace that separates the kitchen and the living room is on, providing a soft glow throughout the first floor.

Leaving the bags on the floor against the wall and my boots by the door, I head toward the living room. Maybe Kate is reading or something.

When I pass the fireplace wall, I scan the room only to come up empty. Maybe she's upstairs?

Upon a second scan, something catches my eye around the corner of the couch, and I do a double take. It looks like… legs sticking out from underneath the tree?

A certain degree of alarm floods my veins instantly and I find myself walking toward the tree without explicitly thinking that I should. I lean down enough to confirm that yes, it is Kate and yes, she is breathing. I can see her chest rise and fall. And thankfully, I don't see any blood. So she must not be hurt.

I quietly approach her, but not so quietly that I'd startle her and then lower myself to the floor next to her, lying down a couple of feet away from her.

I glance at her out of the corner of my eye and notice the lights reflecting off wetness on her face, but I don't point it out. This is her first holiday season without Nick and her wounds are fresher than mine.

So I join her on the floor, looking up at the lights of the tree. The lights don't blink. They're steady, bright and colorful. A perfect metaphor for what we both need right now, even if we aren't asking for it.

Jill is still heavy on my mind, as I've expected her to be. Not only is this my first Christmas without her, but this is my first Christmas without her in over a decade. The day has already been hard enough, and I don't have the energy to dwell on the depressing parts—it won't bring her back, anyway.

Instead, I try to think about the happy times. I picture her on our wedding day. Her long, flowing white dress with lace accents and a simple flower in her auburn hair. I think about our first vacation together—a long weekend at a cabin on Fox Lake about an hour outside Chicago. We'd hiked and fished during the day and spent our evenings huddled in front of the fire, drinking spiked tea and playing cards.

I think back to our first date. We didn't do anything particularly special that night… just met up at a dive bar for cheap beer and ate greasy pizza afterward. But looking back on it, that night changed the course of my life in ways I never could have imagined at the time. I can't say I fell in love with her that night, but I remember the feeling of being with her. She was exhilarating, her energy unstoppable.

I picture our first apartment with its hodgepodge of hand-me-down belongings—no order anywhere in the chaos. I see the crinkle between her brows that she always got when she was reading in bed at night. I can almost smell her perfume. I can definitely smell the gallons of hairspray from performance nights.

That familiar bittersweet tang settles in my chest. I know I'm allowed to be sad. I know I'm allowed to miss her. But I also feel like crying in front of my new roommate is crossing a boundary, so I realize I need to get my shit together—and fast.

I take a slow, purposeful deep breath in, drawing the air deep into my belly and then let it out. I keep going until the sting of tears threatening me finally dissipates, my jaw relaxing.

I risk a glance at Kate and when I realize her eyes are closed, I let mine linger on her prone form. Her eyes are closed, but a tear has escaped the corner and tracks down her face to her wavy hair. Her breathing is a bit ragged, as if she's trying to stop herself from crying.

I feel a strong urge to comfort her, to reach out and hold her hand, but I don't want to intrude upon her. I might already be stepping on her boundaries just by being here. Especially *here* under the tree.

I force my eyes back to the lights above me and let my eyes lose focus as my thoughts return to Jill. To stolen moments in the kitchen while we cooked dinner. To her eyes lit up with happiness and a bright smile plastered on her face. To the sound of her laughter bouncing off the walls of our apartment. To the way it filled my chest with something light and heavy at the same time.

But as I'm trying to recall every single detail about Jill, the woman next to me is growing increasingly agitated. Her breathing is shallow and quick, often irregular.

Sliding my eyes back to her, I can see her chest heaving, her hands balled into tight fists and pressed into her stomach. I turn my head to look at her fully and realize she's on the verge of—if not already headfirst in—a panic attack.

Before I even realize what I'm doing, I'm reaching out for her hand. When my hand makes contact with hers, she gasps and looks over at me for a split second, during which I spot the embarrassment easily.

She doesn't rip her hand away, but she does cover her eyes with her other hand.

I gently coax her fingers out of their tight shape and lace them with mine, squeezing her hand firmly.

"Can you take a breath with me?" I ask quietly.

She turns her head toward mine, eyes scared and sad and embarrassed all at the same time. She shakes her head ever so slightly.

"Can you try?" I take an exaggerated breath myself, breathing in through my nose and out through my mouth. Her gaze holds mine as she struggles to follow my lead.

I keep breathing regularly. In, out. In, out. In, out.

"You're doing great," I encourage her, keeping my face as relaxed as possible. I don't want to sound condescending. I've been where she is. There's no shame in it. I'm just trying to help her through it.

We breathe together until she's calm. I can see the signs of relief on her face, and that helps me relax, too. I want to say something, but everything in my head sounds wrong. So instead, I squeeze her hand again. After a moment, she squeezes mine in return and nods as if she can tell what I'm thinking.

Her eyes return to the lights above us, but she doesn't let go of my hand. We lie there together until she whispers a soft "thank you" and sits up carefully. I sit up next to her, resting my elbows on my bent knees.

"I've been there," I say, looking forward to a random plank in the flooring. I don't want to make her feel self-conscious.

I can feel her gaze on me after a moment, so I turn to look at her.

Her eyes are glassy and her face splotchy. If she was wearing makeup earlier today, it's long gone now. And she's still striking. She always is.

She nods her head and averts her eyes. "I'm going to try to get some sleep."

"Sounds like a good plan." I stand and hold a hand out to her. She accepts it, allowing me to help her off the floor. She purses her lips into something that might resemble a tight smile and then walks up the stairs toward her bedroom.

My eyes follow her against my will. I feel creepy to an extent… she's been crying and I'm thinking about how beautiful she is.

If I could punch myself in my own face, I would.

Instead, I make sure all the doors and windows are

locked, then grab the presents and make my way upstairs to my own bedroom.

When I'm lying in bed later that night, my mind is warring with itself. I should be thinking of Jill and how I'm going to spend this holiday season without her—and I am, of course. But I'm also thinking about the brunette across the landing, wondering how she's doing. Wondering what I could do to support her through her grief.

I have no intention of preying upon this woman amid her grief, but I also can't help the attraction I feel to her or the common experiences we're sharing.

It takes far too long to drift off to sleep, and when I finally do, it's filled with guilt-laden dreams about Jill.

9

HAPPY FUCKING NEW YEAR

Kate

Christmas was… a day.

I spent the day with my dad, Sophie, and Benji, who was in from New York for a few days. He'd offered to stay at my house, but I told him it wasn't necessary… that he should stay with friends he'd been missing. I insisted I was doing all right.

It's a lie, but he doesn't need to know that.

Liam spent the day with his family. We saw each other in the morning before we both left the house, but not for very long. We were both in our own worlds, probably processing our bullshit on our own.

All in all, it didn't look or feel like Christmas morning for me. There were no presents under the tree. No stockings hung by the chimney with care.

That's the line I'd drawn when Maggie was helping decorate. I just didn't see the point.

Who would fill the (one, singular) stocking?

Me? By myself?

Fuck that.

So Liam and I kept to ourselves. I drank coffee in my bedroom by myself, watching reruns of *Law & Order*.

Otherwise, the house was silent. There were no gleeful screams of children or the sounds of happy laughter. The sound of paper being ripped off boxes was notably absent.

Being with my family was nice but truly exhausting. By the time I got home, I couldn't fathom talking to anyone else. I grabbed a bottle of wine and went straight upstairs to my bedroom. I turned on *Law & Order* and tried to escape my reality.

I vaguely heard Liam return to the house, but I wasn't sure what time it was and I didn't really care. I didn't bother to look at the clock. Eventually, I fell asleep.

But now it's New Year's Eve and we're both expected to be at Elliot and Leon's house for a party. I can't speak to Liam's mindset, but I only agreed to go because I didn't want to disappoint Elliot.

There's something about a new calendar year that is gutting me. It's a year in which Nick will never live. He'll never see what the new year will bring. He won't kiss me at midnight. Come to think of it, I'll have no one to kiss at all.

What a lovely thought.

Liam drives us over to Elliot and Leon's. He stays sober, only imbibing two beers the entire night.

I try to keep it in check, mostly because I don't want to become the sad, sloppy, crying drunk at the party. That's never a good look. I stop myself after two glasses of wine.

Midnight is approaching and I'm nervous. I'm not sure what anyone around me will do or how they'll react to me being here, alone. All I can think about is all the couples pairing off to kiss each other in a few minutes and I'll just be standing here among them.

I can feel my chest starting to get tight, so I meander toward the back of the room. I can still see the TV, but I'm not surrounded by so many people. I zone out, trying not to notice the sights and sounds of happy people. I think a part of me hates them in this moment. All of them… just going about their lives while mine is falling apart.

I roll my eyes at my own dramatics and let my head fall back against the wall behind me.

"Hiding?" a low voice asks to my left.

I look over to find Liam mirroring my position against the wall. He's not looking at me. He's looking at everyone else.

I follow suit. "A little."

"I get that."

That's all he says before falling silent, just standing next to me, keeping me company.

A million thoughts swirl through my head—ones that are threatening my careful composure. I'm trying desperately to keep my feelings stuffed down for the evening and I'm afraid that if I try to talk to Liam, I'll start crying. Or have another panic attack like the one below the Christmas tree.

Whether I like it or not, that moment cracked something open. It shifted our… arrangement. It brought us closer together. While we haven't spent much time together over the past week, I don't think he's upset about it. He's been mourning the first holidays without his wife in the same way I have been. It's a very personal experience and I think he just understands that I need to deal with it in my own way.

But if I'm being totally honest—and I might deny I said this later—I kind of missed Liam over the past week. Which doesn't make any sense. We don't really know each other.

The parts of him I've experienced though? I like them. I like them a lot.

The thing about Liam is that he's *steady*. He's just standing next to me, silent. Like if I need him, he'll be there, but if I don't, it's okay with him. I'm grateful. This might be just what I need. This stoic, steady presence who won't smother me.

When the clock strikes midnight, I try my hardest to take a deep breath, but it's just not working. My lungs won't accept the air.

Everyone around us is kissing, smiling, singing. And the two of us are just standing next to each other, letting the wall hold us up, facing a new year without our beloved spouses.

"Happy New Year, Kate."

His voice reaches through my impending panic attack, stopping it in its tracks. Suddenly, I can take a deep breath and the oxygen gives me a sense of relief.

I turn my head to face him, studying his face for a long moment before returning the sentiment.

And then Liam leans toward me, placing a soft, chaste kiss on my cheekbone. When he leans back, our eyes meet and hold.

He has this small, sad smile on his face and I'm sure my eyes are wider than usual. My skin tingles where his lips touched me.

Before I can spend any length of time analyzing his actions and my reaction to them, Elliot and Leon appear in front of us with gleeful shouts, snapping the moment happening between us.

"Happy New Year, my darling!" Elliot wraps me up in his strong arms and kisses the cheek Liam did not. Out of the corner of my eye, I see the same thing happening between Leon and Liam. The two men switch then, Leon kissing my cheek and pulling me into a gentle hug before turning to face the room and joining in the chorus of singers attempting to belt out "Auld Lang Syne."

I can't find the holiday cheer to sing along, but I certainly don't complain when Elliot tucks me into his side, his arm slung around my shoulders as he sings. I slip my arm around his waist and after a moment, I feel a warm hand take my free one.

I glance down to find my hand engulfed by Liam's. Leon is on the other side of him, his arm around Liam's shoulder the same way Elliot is standing with me, essentially forming a protective barrier around us, their grieving friends.

The love and support flowing between them is a tangible thing. It threatens to overwhelm me, but just for a moment, I let myself feel it… *really* feel it. I let it lift me up just enough that I feel just a little less weighed down by the past six months. I imagine it flowing through me like magic in a fairy tale, sinking into my bones and fortifying me.

When I feel the prick of tears behind my eyes, I shut it all off. I stare straight ahead and tune out the music.

Except that a moment later, Liam squeezes my hand.

I blink and remember how he squeezed my hand under the Christmas tree and I know that he's trying to remind me to breathe.

So I do.

I take a slow, deep breath in through my nose and let it out through my mouth. And then another. And one more for good measure.

After the third breath, I feel a tiny bit better, so I squeeze Liam's hand in return.

* * *

THE NEW YEAR DID NOT, in fact, bring anything new.

Unless you count a more comfortable living arrangement between me and Liam.

Against my will, his simple, caring gestures on New Year's Eve—standing with me as I avoided the happy crowd around us, that sweet peck on the cheek, his gentle reminder to breathe—managed to break down my armored walls just the *slightest* bit.

Okay, maybe more than a *slight* bit.

I've actually started *wanting* him to be around. I like seeing him in the evening. Watching whatever Netflix thing we want to disassociate with for a while. We have dinner together often. A couple of times when my run ended after dark, I found all the back lights on and him waiting for me out in the dark with a cup of tea.

It's kind.

Liam is kind.

I've continued my community service at the animal shelter every Sunday morning, and of course, I've been attending my court-mandated therapy with Gwen.

That's where I am now—my first appointment of the new year.

"Do you think Nick knew how you felt about him?"

And apparently she's not pulling any punches.

The fuck?

I can't do anything but blink at her. I shake my head because I honestly can't cognate that question.

She's only been this direct with me one other time and it was when I first started. She wanted me to talk about the day Nick died and I didn't fucking want to, but she told me we needed to because it was really important. So I did and then I spent the rest of the hour curled into a ball on the couch, sobbing. And then, in true therapist fashion, she gently told me the hour was up and scooted me out the door—makeup smeared down my face and looking like a literal clown.

I'm not kidding. A kid in the waiting room stared at me, gasped, and clung to his mother.

Since then, Gwen has been gentler. The rational side of me knows that she needed to hear about the day Nick died. She needed that information—and not just what was in my criminal record—in order to... whatever she's supposed to be doing... helping me? Leading me through the grieving process? Keeping me out of jail? Whatever.

But this question? Jesus fucking Christ. I can't wrap my mind around why in the actual fuck she would ask me something like that. Is she implying I was this way—this shell of a person, closed off and bitter—when I was married to Nick?

So I literally ask her, "What kind of question is that?"

"It's just a question," her calm voice comes out, her kind face smiling, and I wish I could bottle it up like Ursula, except that I wouldn't use it for myself. I'd lock it up forever, so I don't have to fucking listen to it anymore. It feels patronizing.

I roll my eyes and throw my hands in the air. "We were married. We lived together. Of course he knew how I felt about him."

Gwen is quiet for a long second and then nods. "That's good."

"Why are you asking me that?" I'm offended. And angry with a side of belligerence.

Look at me naming my feelings, Gwen!

"Some people worry after the death of a loved one that they never adequately expressed their love or appreciation to the person. It's good that you believe Nick knows how you felt."

I frown at Gwen in silence before I start to second-guess myself. I look out the window without really seeing anything, scanning my brain for any kind of memory of a time when Nick might have seemed needy or unsatisfied or upset with me and I come up with nothing. Absolutely nothing.

"I… I mean, I…" I swallow the lump in my throat. "I think he knew." My vision blurs with tears. "I hope he knew."

"I'm sure he did." Gwen's gentle voice doesn't grate on my nerves this time. It's actually soothing. I want to believe her.

"Can you tell me about your favorite day with Nick?"

I look back over to her, surprised by the topic shift. "My favorite day?"

"Yeah. It could be anything—something ordinary or something exciting. Whatever day sticks out in your mind."

Since I'm already scanning through my Rolodex of Nick memories, I keep going. The highlights pop up easily. "The first night we really talked—at my dad's company holiday party. Our first date. Our wedding day. The night he proposed. The day he bought me a house—that was actually an emotional roller coaster, but it ended well for the most part." I shrug a shoulder and shake my head. "It's hard to pick a favorite."

"Is there a particular moment you've been thinking about lately? Anything that keeps coming back to you?"

I take a deep breath, close my eyes (don't worry, I roll them after they're closed), and resign myself to provide a real answer. "I keep thinking about this night during grad school…" I find a familiar spot on the carpet a few feet in front of me and try to disconnect from the memory, but it won't let me. It's tugging me back, begging me to talk about it. To bring Nick to life with a spoken memory for just a minute.

Fucking therapy.

I rub my forehead and force the words out of my mouth. "It wasn't extraordinary in any way. It was just this night when I was slammed with schoolwork and real work, and I'd come home from class at like… ten o'clock at night to find

Nick waiting outside the door of my building. I wasn't expecting him, but he'd shown up to surprise me because I mentioned earlier when we'd spoken that I hadn't eaten a real dinner… just a small bag of chips or something."

I feel a little tug on the corner of my mouth—an attempt at a smile without my permission.

"So he just showed up at my place with dinner. He'd already eaten, but he brought me a burger and fries from this place down the street from my apartment. It was just a bar with decent food—it's closed now. But sometimes I went there for takeout when I was really busy."

For once, I feel that beautiful wistfulness that some people claim happens when you remember a happy time prior to a tragedy. I feel calmer than I did when I started talking. My chest aches, but it's not as sharp.

"Actually," I continue (for reasons I could not explain if doing so would save my life). "I think it was that night when I realized I was in love with him. Because… like, who does that? Who shows up at their girlfriend's apartment at ten o'clock at night with dinner? And you don't even bring enough for yourself?" I picture him standing outside my apartment building, smiling at me as I approached. I remember the way my heart swelled when I saw him. And the sharp pain is back.

"Nick did that kind of stuff though… he was quietly romantic a lot. Doing thoughtful things. And over-the-top ridiculous things, too, like buying us a house. But mostly, it was the little things that made me realize how much he cared about me." I stop and stare at my hands, realizing the point. "I'm not sure I did the same for him."

The rest of the evening plays in my mind. Laughing on the couch, him rubbing my feet, kissing him, him staying the night, waking up wrapped in his arms in the morning. I'd give anything—absolutely anything to have another night like that. It's not the big stuff you miss. It's the tiny moments that build your life with someone. *That's* the good stuff.

"I'm sure he knew how you felt, Kate." Gwen's voice breaks my thoughts.

I meet her eyes, unsure. "Are you just saying that so I don't have a breakdown about it?"

Gwen smiles. "No. I think people who don't feel their affection is reciprocated don't keep doing such things. If he didn't feel loved that night he brought you dinner—and most subsequent nights, for that matter—why would he have bought you a house? If he didn't feel you appreciated the grand gesture of the surprise house, why would he have proposed? If he didn't feel you loved him deeply, why would he have married you?"

As much as I hate to admit it, Gwen is making some sense. It makes me want to steal her voice again. Instead, I sigh and tell her the truth. "I suppose you could be right. I hope you're right."

Gwen sighs quietly and leans forward over her notebook. "Kate, I didn't ask you if Nick knew how you felt to make you question your actions while you were together. I asked because some people find comfort in knowing they did the best they could."

10

FUCK, OUR LIVES ARE DEPRESSING

Liam

Today marks one year since Jill died.

It's a weird feeling because I know in my rational mind that she died on this day, three hundred and sixty-five days ago. But Jill wasn't Jill when she finally died. The Jill I fell in love with was barely there anymore. I could see that spark still in her eyes when we spent time together, but I also saw storm clouds glaze them over.

Jill didn't believe she was Jill without dancing.

Today, the sharp pangs of grief are back. It doesn't feel as fresh as it did last year, of course. But it's not a dull ache the way it usually is. Today, it hurts a hell of a lot more than that.

I'm sitting in an Adirondack chair on the back patio. It's cold. I'm wearing a hoodie over a waffle shirt with jeans and thick socks. I made tea that had the word "calm" in the name and I'm staring into the inky black sky, listening to the sounds of the lake.

My therapist back in Chicago would be proud of me, I think. I've dealt with my grief in the best ways I know how—with his help, of course—and have begun to rebuild my life. He encouraged me to move back home and surround myself with family.

I've made progress. I know that.

But moving on... fuck, it's hard.

I never *wanted* to move on from Jill. I wasn't given much choice in the matter.

I suck cold air into my lungs and hold it for a few seconds before releasing it and watching my hot breath become a pale-white cloud for a moment.

The back patio door opens with a crack and Kate is suddenly filling the open space. "Hey." She tips her chin up to me. "You all right?"

"Hey." I sit up straighter and adjust so I can see her better. I want to say I'm all right, but it doesn't feel accurate. Instead I shrug and admit it was a hard day.

Her brows pull together and she chews on her bottom lip while she eyes my mug of tea. "What are you drinking?"

"Just tea."

"Well, I think a hard day calls for bourbon and it's cold as fuck, so I'm going to grab that and a glass. You want some in your tea?"

I can't help but smile at her. She's trying to cheer me up even though she has no idea what's wrong. Maybe she guessed.

"Sure."

"Good. I'll be right back." And then she shuts the door, turns back toward the kitchen and disappears.

I wasn't sure how I'd feel about seeing Kate today—or anyone, for that matter. But now that she's home, I'm actually glad to see her. I'm looking forward to sitting with her out here.

But maybe I'm getting ahead of myself. Maybe she's just going to pour some booze in my tea and go back inside.

You are a lost puppy.

I roll my eyes at myself.

Kate's back a moment later, wearing a hoodie of her own (or maybe Nick's), sweatpants, and slippers with socks. She's carrying a bottle of Blanton's and a tumbler. She sets both down on the patio and then starts hefting another Adirondack chair closer to mine.

I immediately start to sit up. "I can help…"

"Sit," she silences me. "I don't need help."

And truly, she doesn't. She's done already. She moves the bourbon and the tumbler closer to her chair and then goes back inside. When she comes back, she's carrying a giant blanket.

To my surprise, Kate settles herself down in the chair next to mine and throws the blanket over both of us. Then, she picks up the bottle and pours us both some bourbon— mine in my tea and hers in her tumbler. She has a heavy hand and it makes me smile.

"Thank you."

"You're welcome." She nods and sets the bottle back down on the ground. This time, it's just behind our chairs, so we can both reach for it if we need a refill.

"I'm kinda surprised you're out here," she starts.

I scratch my five-o'clock shadow just to stall for time. "Just needed the air."

"I get that."

I look over at her to find her staring intently into her bourbon. Something tells me she truly does understand why I need to sit outside in the cold.

"You wanna talk about it?" she asks just before looking up to meet my eyes.

Hers hold the same guarded sadness they always do, but

her face is open. It seems like she's actually asking and is interested in hearing the answer.

I draw in a deep breath before I say the thing I don't want to say aloud. "Today is the day Jill died."

I can hear her small intake of air before she clamps her mouth shut. Her gaze is still focused on me, but I'm looking out into the inky blackness of the sky.

"I'm glad I brought out the good bourbon, then." Her voice gets muffled as she brings the tumbler to her mouth for a sip.

I laugh. I can't help it. No one else would have dared to make a joke today, but here's Kate making a quip about good booze on a bad day.

A glance in her direction lets me know that she's watching me laugh, a tiny, barely there smile on her face.

"I appreciate the thought," I manage to get out as I try to reel myself back in. "And the laugh."

Kate pulls her knees up to her chest, nesting her tumbler between her chest and her legs like she's trying to keep all her body heat close. Then she pulls her hood up over her head. It's obvious she's cold, but she doesn't complain.

When she's all settled, she asks, "Do you want to talk about her?"

I think about it for a moment and decide that… "Yeah… yeah, I do."

She beams a wistful smile at me and rests her head against the back of the chair, tilted so she can look at me. "How did you meet?"

The memory fills my mind and I'm sure the same kind of wistful smile stretches across my mouth. "Uhh… we met in college—at a house party. She was there with some of her friends. The host was a friend of mine."

My vision loses focus as I think about the details. The air, the people, the house.

"I was in the backyard with some guys. We were playing cornhole. I don't even know what made me look up, but… she was coming out the back door."

I can see her clear as day, like she's standing across the yard now.

"I couldn't take my eyes off her. She was stunning. I think she felt someone looking at her, or maybe she was searching for someone—she kept looking around." And then I realize how that sounds, so I look at Kate and clarify. "I wasn't staring at her in a gross way. I was just… drawn to her. Stealing glances, seeing who she was talking to, trying to figure out if she was there with a date."

Kate smiles softly and it puts me at ease.

"Anyway, eventually we caught each other's eyes. She glanced over a few times. I tried to play it cool, but I was doing a horrible job. Before I knew it, she was just walking right over to me." I chuckle at the memory of her making her way across the yard to me. "I couldn't believe it, honestly. It took guts to leave the safety of her friends and waltz up to me with all of mine. But there she was. Her hair was down, but she had this clip in it to hold it out of her face. It was fall, so there was a chill in the air. She had jeans on with a green sweater. Gold necklace. She was even more beautiful up close. We talked for the rest of the night. I got her number when her friends came to get her before they left. I called her the next morning. I couldn't wait." I shake my head. "We went out on an actual date the following weekend. My life was never the same."

"How old were you?"

"Hmm… I guess I was already twenty-one, but she was a few months from her birthday."

"Did you know?"

I frown and look over at Kate. "What do you mean?"

"That she was the one. Did you know right away?"

I think about it for a long moment, and Kate stays quiet. She doesn't try to interrupt me or ask me a different question. "I knew she was someone special. I didn't know she was the one for a while. But it didn't matter—we were inseparable after that."

"That's very sweet," she says quietly. "What about after college?"

"We stayed in Chicago because that's where she got a job. I can work anywhere, really. Dancers don't have that luxury."

She nods before she asks, as gently as possible, "When was she diagnosed?"

The familiar dull pain in my chest rears up and pushes against my ribs. I nearly press my fingertips to my sternum, but then I remember Kate's reaction the last time I did that, so I adjust my seated position instead and clear my throat.

"A couple of years after college. She was having some trouble moving around in rehearsal. She'd fall for no apparent reason. Obviously, that's kind of a problem for a dancer. She was twenty-four."

"Ugh… that's awful." Kate frowns into her bourbon. "That must have been heartbreaking for her."

"It was," I admit. "She was *really* angry for a *really* long time. She tried to break up with me at least once a week for a couple of months. Told me she didn't want to tie me down. She didn't know at the time that I'd already been saving up for a ring. I knew I wanted to marry her. It was only a matter of time. And when we found how little she had…" I trail off. There's no good way to end that sentence. I finally settle on, "I just didn't want to waste it."

Silence descends between us, nothing but the sound of the waves crashing in the darkness. It feels… comfortable. Like I don't need to fill the silence. Like she and I could sit here in silence for a while and it would never become tense.

Part of my mind wants to explore that conundrum, but the part that's swimming in grief shoves it away.

"Fuck, our lives are depressing," Kate suddenly says, reaching behind us for the Blanton's.

Her comment makes me laugh again and I gladly accept a refill. Once she refreshes her own glass, she puts the bottle back down behind us.

I take a sip and enjoy the burn in my throat as I think about the next part of our story.

"I proposed to her three times over the course of three months." I laugh quietly. "She turned me down the first two times."

"No… are you serious?" Kate's eyes are wide with surprise.

"Yeah," I confirm. "She kept telling me she didn't want to wrap me up in all that mess. Didn't want to drag my life down with hers. All the same reasons she tried to break up with me, but there wasn't a thing she could have done to make me leave her. She didn't see it the way I did—not that I blame her. But what kind of person would I be if I abandoned the woman I loved when she was sick? In sickness and in health, right?"

Kate sighs and lays the side of her head on her knees. "Of course you wouldn't leave her. That's not who you are."

I meet her eye. She's right. That's not who I am. I'm just surprised she knows that already. I nod to confirm what she said.

"If you…" She hesitates.

"If I what?"

"If you knew—that night at the party—if you knew how it would turn out… would you still go through with it? Would you still call her the next morning? See her the following week? Marry her?"

I don't have to think about the answer. "Yes."

She's frowning at me, her eyebrows drawn together.

"She changed my life for the better in ways I never imagined. We weren't destined to celebrate our fiftieth wedding anniversary, but we made it to our tenth. We were together for thirteen years. I wouldn't wish away any part of the time we spent together. I'm going to love her for the rest of my life. Do I wish she were still alive? Yes, of course." I push my fingers through my hair and tug a little bit, trying to ground myself back in this moment. Jill is not here. She never will be. "But she meant everything to me. I don't have any regrets. She was an incredible person and I'm just lucky to have gotten to share some of her life with her."

Out of the corner of my eye, I see Kate wiping at her eyes and I'm reminded how much fresher her wounds are than mine.

"Would you…" I start but stop when she looks up at me, eyes shining.

"Is it your turn to start questions without finishing them?"

I huff a small laugh and rest my head against the back of the chair, closing my eyes. But then I feel something hit my leg—the back of her hand, I think.

"Come on. Would I what?"

I roll my head to the side to look at her. She's mirroring my position, leaning back against the chair, the side of her head resting against it, eyes on me.

"Would you still marry Nick? If you knew what would happen?"

Her eyes leave mine and lose their focus somewhere beyond me. She's quiet for a long moment. So long, I wonder if she's going to answer it at all, but then she breathes in sharply and turns her head toward the dark yard and the lake beyond the fence.

"To be totally honest…" She pauses again before continuing in the smallest voice I've ever heard. "I don't know."

I watch her for a moment, letting her words sit in the air around us. I remember my therapist in Chicago talking to me about the way people grieve and how no two people process it the same way.

"Does that make me a bad person?"

Her whisper is so quiet I nearly miss it while I'm thinking back on those early days of therapy.

"No," I say gently. "It doesn't make you a bad person."

She casts me a disbelieving look, her eyes brimming with tears again. "I wouldn't be so sure about that."

I smile. "It doesn't, Kate. I promise."

"Then how are you so sure you'd still do it? And what does that say about me that I'd consider throwing away really good years of my life because it ended so terribly?"

"Everyone processes grief differently…"

She scoffs and rolls her eyes. "Now you sound like my therapist."

I can't even fight the huge smile on my face. "Where do you think I heard it?"

Kate's head snaps in my direction, shock and horror on her face. "From my therapist?!"

I crack up, hand on my stomach, eyes squeezed shut, ending on a wheeze.

"What are you laughing at?" The back of her hand hits my leg again, but it's playful.

I manage to open my eyes long enough to glance at her, finding her incredulous. "I'm sorry…" I wipe my eyes of the tears that are miraculously happening because of humor instead of grief. "I'm sorry, but the look on your face… it was priceless. Kate, *my* therapist in Chicago told me that everyone grieves in different ways."

Her shoulders sag and she hides her face with one hand.

Without thinking, I reach up to grab her wrist so she can't hide. "Kate, grief is… very personal. It's unique to each person and the circumstances and a million other factors. The way you feel is completely valid."

She looks at me with drawn eyes, like she's sad but also leery of me. It's only when she squeezes my hand that I even realize I never let go of hers.

"If you say so," she whispers.

"Kate, the circumstances surrounding Jill's death were very different from the circumstances surrounding Nick's death."

She visibly shudders in her chair, so I squeeze her hand.

Her lips purse as she returns her gaze to mine.

"I've been through a *lot* of therapy. I wasn't thinking this way a year ago. Or even two years ago. Or five years ago, for that matter. I was angry about Jill's diagnosis, too. It took me a long time to get to where I am."

Kate sighs. "Or maybe you're just less broken than me."

"That's not it at all. I've spent a very long time trying to reframe my thinking. And you're not broken, Kate." I make sure to meet her eyes when I say it because it's fucking true and I hate that she thinks that about herself.

She rolls her eyes.

"What's that stupid cliché? *Don't cry because it's over, smile because it happened.*" I scoff and roll my own eyes. "I know it's annoying, but it's not wrong. I can't do anything about what happened to Jill. I did my best to give her whatever I could and make her feel loved while I had the chance. I may not be able to change it, but I can choose to accept my time with her for what it was. Special. Meaningful. Loving."

Kate takes a gulp of her bourbon and rests the glass against her forehead.

"People look at me with pity, and I get why. But I don't usually feel sorry for myself. I'm a lucky man for having the opportunity to know her, and for her to agree to spend the rest of her life with me. But I did *not* feel that way all the time, and sometimes I still don't." I shake my head and pause to regather my thoughts. "It's a process."

The look Kate is giving me clearly states her skepticism. Her eyes are sad and her mouth is shaped into a frown. I want to cheer her up.

I blow out an exaggerated breath and let go of her hand to reach behind us for the bourbon. "Fuck, we really are depressing."

A laugh bursts out of her and I'm grateful for it. The smile on her face lifts me, too.

I don't feel so alone tonight.

11

BONDING OVER BLOOD-THIRSTY DINOSAURS

Kate

It's Valentine's Day and I'm working late because... why not?

I have no one to celebrate with.

I'm going home to a roommate and a cat.

Under the guise of finishing *just one more thing*, it's going on six thirty and I know I should stop working, but... why?

I have no plans. My friends are all out with their significant others. And the idea of being around happy people is making me borderline violent.

I should go home. I know that. There's just no one there waiting for me.

Except Liam.

Fuck.

I honestly don't know what Liam is doing tonight and I suddenly feel guilty about that. I pick up my phone and text him.

Me: What are you up to tonight?

Just as I set my phone down, my dad appears in my doorway.

"Katie, what are you still doing here?"

I blink at him.

He stares at me.

I blink slower.

He sighs as his shoulders sag.

"I think the better question is: what are *you* still doing here?" I volley. "Don't you have plans with Sophie?"

"I'm meeting her at the restaurant." He glances at his watch—a real one, not a smart smartwatch. It's a Tag Heuer that I helped Sophie pick out for him for his sixtieth birthday. It's simple, no nonsense. Just like him. "I need to get going."

"Well you'd better not keep her waiting." I make sure there's enough sass in my voice to make him believe I'm doing just fine.

He puts his hands in his pockets and studies me. I tilt my head to the side and wait for the commentary.

"What are you doing tonight?"

I shrug. "I don't have any plans."

His mouth hardens and I can almost see his brain whirling. I know what he's about to say, so I cut him off.

"No, I do not want to go to dinner with you and Sophie."

"But—"

"But nothing. I do not want to go to dinner with you and Sophie," I repeat before adding, "Or anyone else. I do not want to be in a restaurant surrounded by happy couples."

Saying it bluntly is the only way I can get him to leave, and I know it.

"I'll be fine. I'm going home. I'll eat takeout. Or cereal. I'll watch a movie," I assure him.

He pinches the bridge of his nose. "Katie, I'm—"

"I know," I cut him off again. "I know you're worried."

He meets my eyes and I nod my head to acknowledge his feelings.

"Dad, I…" I let my head fall back on my chair and I stare up to the ceiling while I gather my thoughts. I can't think of anything better than, "I'm doing my best."

He frowns and takes a step closer to my desk. "Honey, I know you are."

"Okay, then please… go to dinner with Sophie. I'm going to be fine."

My dad—the loving, kind, wonderful human that he is—purses his lips and looks down at his feet. He wants to say something else. I can tell.

I've known him for over three decades. First, as the dedicated father who taught me how to ride a bike and properly hang things on walls, and then later as the fierce protector of his family. He and I have been through happy times and sad. We've navigated choppy waters together.

I stepped up to help with Benji after Mom left. When dad was building his company—the very one I'm currently working for—I was making sure that Benji did his homework and ate dinner. When Benji was sad about Mom being gone, I was the one who talked to him. I was the one who put a walkie-talkie on my nightstand so I could talk to him whenever he woke up in the night and needed someone to talk to but felt like he was too old to go running to a parent or sibling's room. I was there for Benji, and dad was there for me. We figured it out together.

In this moment, I'm painfully aware of the fact that my father is trying his absolute damnedest to be there for me… he just doesn't know what else to do, nor do I know what to tell him to do.

Oh, how the tables have turned.

Just as I'm opening my mouth to make up some kind of lie that might make him flee the office to meet Sophie, I'm saved by the literal bell.

My phone chimes on the desk with an incoming text.

> Liam: I have a very hot date with Indian food.

> Liam: Want to join me?

"Ah, look at that," I say to my father, still searching for words. "Liam is bringing home Indian food. We'll eat dinner, probably watch a movie, and make fun of happy people."

He looks up, and even though there's a look of sadness in his beautiful hazel eyes, I can tell he feels relief that I won't be spending the evening alone.

"See? All set." I nod my head for emphasis.

He still looks skeptical.

"Go. Meet Sophie."

He watches me, so I make sure to keep my gaze neutral. I only break it to text Liam back.

"There's wine at the house. And bourbon, obviously. I don't have any beer though," I say aloud, like I'm maybe texting Liam that he should pick up beer if he wants it.

> Me: 1) Did you just make a pun about spicy food? 2) That sounds perfect.

> Me: I'm about to leave the office. Want me to pick it up?

I look back up to my father, setting my phone on the desk again.

"Where are your reservations?"

He sighs and that's all it takes for me to know where he's going.

I smile. "Make sure you get the Manhattan."

His head falls. "I know you love their version of that drink," he says quietly.

"I do. I make it at home now. I just buy ginger beer at the store. They always do it better, but mine isn't half-bad."

"Katie…"

"Dad, please stop."

I *need* him to stop. I can't. I just can't. I don't want to spend the rest of this day being sad about my dead husband. There's nothing I can do about it. And frankly, today is no different than yesterday, or the day before that, or the month before that. Nick is still dead. I still miss him. I'm still broken. The date doesn't change anything.

My phone chimes again.

> Liam: I might have made a spicy food pun, but I swear it was an accident.

> Liam: It would be awesome if you could pick up the food. I just got home and was about to order.

His use of the word *home* isn't lost on me. My home is currently his home and I'm honestly… honored. He's mending his broken heart under the safety of my roof and not judging me for how I'm mending my own. He didn't have to choose my house, but he did and I'm grateful to have someone else to go through my weary days with.

> Me: Sure, sure. Try to take back the spicy food pun.

I include an eye-roll emoji because it feels necessary.

> Me: Order my usual, please. Anything else while I'm out?

"I'm picking up the food, so I need to leave soon."

My father watches as I lean back in my chair and interlace my fingers over my stomach, my elbows on the armrests.

He nods. "Okay, Katie. If you're sure."

"I am."

He studies me for another moment, like he's waiting for me to crack. Eventually, he takes a deep breath.

"Fine. You win. Please call me if you need anything."

"I will," I assure him. But I know I won't call him, even if I do need something. "Tell Sophie I said hello."

"Okay."

With one final look at his feet, he turns and heads toward my office door. When he reaches the threshold, he stops, hesitating for a prolonged second.

"I love you, Katie."

He doesn't look at me when he says it. He's still facing the hallway, his head tilted to one side, his voice soft.

I swallow a lump in my throat before answering.

"I love you, too, Dad."

Mercifully, he leaves the way he came, headed back down the hall toward his own office.

I let my head fall back against the headrest and I close my eyes.

I try really hard not to lie to my father. For a lot of reasons. First and foremost, because he's always been there for me. Even when he was stressed. Even when he was busy. Even when it felt like his own world was crashing down upon him. Jack Holloway has never, not one time, let me down and I feel like I've let him down far too many times in the past few months.

Second, because I'm the heir to the throne. Even if he were able to see past our personal, familial connection—which he definitely is not able to ignore—I'm the person who is supposed to take over this business one day. And that person cannot be mentally unstable or make headlines for causing scenes in the ICU.

Shame settles over me at the memory and I sink further into my chair.

Fuck fuck fuck.

I don't want to spiral, but I can feel my brain trying to throw me headfirst into a sobbing panic attack. I can feel my body trying to betray me, my heart rate picking up, the backs of my eyes stinging, my nose burning, my breathing coming faster.

The hospital seeps into my memories and suddenly, I feel like I'm right back there, face down on the floor with a security guard's knee in my back, Doug's face in my line of vision.

My phone dings on the desk, mercifully distracting my spiraling thoughts. Doug's face disappears like a balloon pop and I blink my way into my office, behind my desk. I take a few deep breaths to calm myself down and then pick up my phone.

> Liam: Not unless you want anything else. I looked in the freezer. We don't have any dessert.

I chuckle to myself. Liam is worried about having dessert in the house in case either of us needs (or wants) to eat our feelings. It's sweet. It's kind. It's thoughtful.

It's distinctly Liam.

> Me: Well, that simply will not do. I'll pick something up. Any requests?

I hit send and then shut my laptop and gather my things. I do love this city, but I don't enjoy all the winter accessories required. Heavy coat, gloves, boots, a scarf, maybe a hat, but at least ear warmers. It's all annoying. And then you're inside and sweating. It's only when you walk outside do you feel *normal* and then you're angry because the cold is biting at the exposed skin on your face.

Why do I live here?

I'm about to button my coat when my phone dings again. I pull it out of my purse to check the text.

Liam: Anything with peanut butter.

Me: Hell yes. Leaving in a minute.

He sends me back a thumbs-up emoji and I head out the door. It's only when I've already picked out ice cream (one with peanut butter and one without), picked up the food, and am driving toward the house that Liam's text really sinks in.

We don't have any dessert.

We.

Not I.

We.

* * *

IF YOU HAD TOLD me when I was a child that one day, I'd find Jeff Goldblum attractive, I'd have laughed in your face. It would have seemed preposterous.

And yet, somehow, I'm sitting on my couch with my roommate, watching the original *Jurassic Park* and I can't help but realize that I do, indeed, find Jeff Goldblum attractive. I can't say I love the *Jurassic Park* haircut, but I can overlook that part right now.

Nick and I never had the kind of relationship where jealousy ran rampant. Your ability to recognize an attractive person doesn't end when you commit yourself to someone, so we didn't have stupid disagreements about stuff like that.

That being said, Nick *never* looked at other women in front of me. He never made comments about them. But if I said something about how an actor was cute, he didn't react harshly. He'd smirk at me, then kiss some part of my body—my hand, my head, whatever he could reach. It was a subtle way of reminding me that he was here, no matter what happened, no matter who caught my eye or his. We were in it together. In it to win it.

And here I am, looking at 1993-era Jeff Goldblum and getting sappy over the fact that my husband isn't pulling me into his side and kissing my hair.

Ugh.

As the T.rex eats the dude on the toilet, I hear Liam make a noise from his section of the couch.

I look over at him to see what's going on. He's grimacing.

He sees me looking at him. "It's the bone crunching for me." He shivers dramatically and it makes me laugh.

I throw a piece of popcorn at him. He picks it up from where it lands in his lap and pops it in his mouth with a smile.

In the back of my mind, I remember that this is not Liam's first Valentine's Day without Jill. He's already had one and it was very soon after her passing. I suddenly wonder if he's hanging out with me for *my* benefit rather than his own.

I'm sipping red wine and watching a movie full of blood and bloodthirsty dinosaurs that are supposed to be extinct on what is supposed to be one of the most romantic holidays of the year. Nick always did a big thing for this ridiculous holiday. Neither of us particularly *loved* the holiday itself, but we did enjoy the excuse to do something special together. Sometimes, he'd cook dinner and we'd stay in. Other times, we'd go out to a fancy dinner or we'd see a show. He usually bought me something sparkly—earrings or a necklace—and I'd arrange for something to be done for him. The man had everything, so it wasn't like he *needed* anything. I'd have his car detailed or ask Benji to send me a photo he'd taken that I knew Nick loved and I'd have it framed for our gallery wall on the stairs.

He was always happy with whatever it was. He was happy with *me*.

And that thought is bringing me down hard and fast, so I'm grateful for the distraction of the Ford Explorer going over the ledge into the T.rex enclosure. It lands in the tree and the roar of the T.rex shakes the living room.

"This is scary in a different way for me as an adult than it was when I was a kid." Liam's voice cuts through the air after the rumbles stop.

"In what way?"

"Well…" His head tilts as he watches Tim's rescue and the terrified looks on both kids' faces. "I think it's because I have nephews. Like, how much older are these kids than my nephews?"

My brain comes to a screeching halt and I feel my chest tighten. I deflect. And quickly.

"I can see that. I definitely had nightmares after seeing this as a kid." There. Acknowledge his feelings and then change the topic. "But what I keep wondering is how the hell they made this movie in the early nineties."

He makes a thoughtful sort of *hum* and studies the brachiosaurus taking a branch from Dr. Grant's hand.

"I suppose we'll have to watch one of the new iterations soon to compare."

My brain tries to latch back on to his use of *we*, but I quickly push the thought away.

"I don't think I've seen any of them."

"No?" He looks over at me and I shake my head. "I'm sure we can rent them somewhere online."

"Didn't they make up new dinosaurs for the new movies?"

Liam pulls out his phone. "I think so…" He taps away with the thumb of his free hand while the kids are getting some food in the café. I find that I'm just as disgusted by the wobbly gelatinous thing they're eating as I was as a kid.

"Indominus rex... a T.rex-velociraptor hybrid. And there's some water dinosaur called a Mosasaurus..." he trails off and I glance over to find him frowning at the screen. "Apparently, that's based on a real thing though, which is terrifying."

"The water dino?"

"Yeah, but it was a giant lizard. The indominus rex was—thankfully—not a real thing."

"So basically, that thing is just a finely tuned killing machine... all the most terrifying parts of a T.rex and a raptor combined into one giant body."

"Sounds like it." He tosses his phone onto the couch cushion next to him.

I sit with that for a moment, wondering if the whole *don't move and the T.rex can't see you* thing is real and then think about how that doesn't apply to raptors and I've never been more grateful that I live in *this* time period and not *that* one.

"Why would you even do that?" Liam asks.

"Do what?"

"Create a mutant dinosaur that is more lethal than the *other* lethal dinosaurs?"

"Well, I figure that's kind of the point of the movie." I raise an eyebrow at him. This is an easy answer.

He meets my eye and gives me a self-deprecating smile. "Yes, okay, fine. Fair."

My own smile widens, but I try to hide it by taking a sip of wine.

We fall silent while we watch the kitchen scene with the kids hiding from the velociraptors.

"It's the raptors opening the doors for me," I say.

He blows out a breath and shakes his head. "You've got a point."

I know the kids will get out, but I also know that in the moment, they're terrified and part of me just wants to break the tension with dialogue. Any kind of dialogue. So I start talking.

"If the point of the first movie is *'just because you can doesn't mean you should'* then perhaps the point of the newer movies is a continuation of that."

I see his head turn toward me out of the corner of my eye, so I meet his gaze, a question in his eyes.

"Like you said… *'why would you even do that?'* It's a completely valid question, but I think one that is at the center of *this* movie." I gesture toward the screen, where the kids are reunited with Doctors Sattler and Grant. "But the newer movies…"

I pause and shake my head, trying to formulate a cohesive sentence.

"I think the question there is, *'Did you learn nothing from history?'*" I take a generous sip of wine, suddenly feeling like the liquid courage is spurring me on. "I mean, they already tried this, right? And it didn't work out. People died. But they're trying *anyway* and they're being *even dumber* about it, creating *new* mutant dinosaurs."

Am I rambling?

I'm a little tipsy and even I can recognize that what I'm saying has a deeper meaning that I have absolutely no desire to examine it.

Silence descends upon us for a long moment.

People run from dinosaurs, some successfully, others not so much.

And then Liam's calm, gentle voice breaks through the space between us.

"Maybe they thought it was worth the risk."

12

I'M A SAD, LOST PUPPY

Liam

I think I'm in trouble. I might be—okay, probably am—in over my head.

Valentine's Day was a lot less awful than I expected.

Kate and I had carryout and drank wine and watched a movie on a Friday night.

It was actually *fun*.

I wondered initially if it was the wine warming me up to her. If maybe I was getting tipsy and that's why I was feeling the way I was. I'm obviously attracted to her. She's gorgeous. I'd have to be blind not to realize it. But that night was the first time I had trouble dealing with it.

The thing is, the more time I spend with Kate, the more I *enjoy* spending time with her. The more time I *want* to spend with her. And that thought fucks me up.

When I moved back here from Chicago, my therapist referred me to someone he knew in the area. I've talked to

123

him about this a couple of times and he's assured me that what I'm feeling—guilt about developing feelings for someone new—is completely normal. He said that even if this happened a year from now, I might still feel this way.

But it's happening *now*.

And for my *roommate*.

My gorgeous, grieving roommate.

No matter how many times I tell myself this is a stupid, pointless endeavor, I can't help the way I feel about her. I can't help that I'm attuned to her when she's near me. I can't help that I want to talk to her about anything and everything. I can't help that I want to know everything about her. I can't help that I want to slide my fingers through her wavy hair. Feel her lips against mine.

And *fuck,* that's a dangerous thought spiral.

I've been finding excuses to be out of the house to try and avoid her, but I also don't *want* to avoid her. So then I cave and stay in to spend time with her and then I just end up wanting *her* and then the cycle begins again.

I'm not really sure how this happened.

I'm also not sure how to stop it—or if I *want* to stop it.

So now it's St. Patrick's Day and I'm taking an alternate route back to the house so I can skip the hordes of people going out to drink green beer. It's a Monday and I'm too old for this shit. I bought Guinness cans yesterday and put corned beef and cabbage in the slow cooker this morning before I left for work.

I'm not sure what Kate is up to today. I didn't see her this morning. I heard her come back from her run while I was getting dressed for work and then I was gone before she came out of her bedroom.

I'm trying not to think about it. About her.

It's obviously going well.

I'm a little bit surprised when I open the garage door and

Kate's car is already there. I typically get home before her. Even taking the long way home, I still expected to be here before her.

I open the door leading to the house from the garage and immediately smell the corned beef. My mouth waters. Every year, I slow cook corned beef in Guinness. There's no better way to make it.

I peek through the glass top of the slow cooker and my stomach growls. I can hear the TV on quietly in the living room, so I hang my coat up on a hook and make my way in. The fireplace is lit. Kate is huddled under a blanket on the couch. I can see just her head—the rest of her is covered. Her hair is up on the top of her head, a glass of something amber-colored is on the coffee table, and she's asleep.

Beaker pops his head up from behind her knees, where he's made a little bed for himself. He gives a little chirp and stands up to stretch, then stares at me.

He and I have a tentative relationship. He's a pretty skittish cat, but he's a good boy. I've been slowly trying to show him he can trust me.

I take a slow step forward with an easy smile on my face. "Hey there, boy," I say quietly, trying not to wake Kate up.

He eyes me warily, but without the panic I usually see, his muscles typically taut and ready to run. Instead, he's sitting, watching.

I take another step. "Did you get a good nap?"

His head moves with each step I take and when I reach the end of the couch, I put my hand out for him to sniff. He leans forward and slowly, slowly, slowly moves toward me on careful feet, stepping around Kate's legs.

I stay as still as I possibly can. I don't want to scare him off. This is a lot of progress for us.

His pink nose edges closer to my knuckles and when it makes contact, a static-electric shock jolts him back. "Oh, no," I murmur. "Sorry, Beaker. It's just the cold. No moisture in the air."

This seems to satisfy him and he tries again, this time without the shock. But to *my* shock, he pushes his gumline across the back of my hand.

I remember someone telling me once that cats are forever trying to rub their scent all over things and that this is one of the ways they do so… rubbing their spit on things.

"Such a good boy," I say with a wider smile. "See? I'm all right."

Apparently, he agrees because he sits down and pushes his head into my hand, so I cautiously flip my hand over and scratch behind his ear the way I've seen Kate do. He pushes harder into my hand and I hear the *faintest* of purrs, like he's reluctant to show me he's actually enjoying himself.

I chuckle, and unfortunately, it rouses Kate. She breathes in sharply and lifts her head, eyes squinting like she's confused.

Beaker abandons me for Kate—not that I blame him. He steps lightly around her body and headbutts her face.

"Hey, bud," she says through quiet laughter. "I guess I fell asleep, huh?"

I'm not sure she knows I'm here, so I shift my weight and put my hands in my pockets, clearing my throat softly.

Her head snaps in my direction, eyes wide.

"Hi."

"Hey…" She pushes up to a seated position, the blanket falling off her shoulder and pooling next to her. Beaker moves into her lap. "I didn't hear you come in."

I shake my head. "I just got home a minute ago."

She nods in acknowledgment and pets Beaker in the same way I did a moment ago. His purrs are louder.

"No St. Paddy's Day plans tonight?" I ask.

The smile melts off her face. She leans forward to get her

drink, smooshing Beaker a little bit, but his protest is short-lived when she continues to scratch his ears.

"No," she says after a sip of what I assume is whiskey. Maybe bourbon. "No plans tonight."

I nod, wondering what the change in her demeanor is about, but not wanting to push. "Well, I've got corned beef and cabbage in the slow cooker if you want some."

She glances up at me with a stiff smile. "Sure. That sounds nice."

"I'm gonna go get changed, but I'll be right back to prep it."

The smile she gives me this time is a little less stilted. A bit more gratitude—not that I need it. "Thanks."

I turn toward the stairs and make my way up to my bedroom, trying to ignore the fact that I can feel her eyes on me as I move. When I close the door, I lean my forehead against it for a moment.

I have no right to want to be her confidant. All in all, I'm a new person to her.

But the bread crumbs she's given me—our talk in January on the anniversary of Jill's death and the tiny details I've seen from living with her... all of that has just made me want to know more.

I change out of my work clothes and into sweatpants and an old baseball shirt.

I may not be able to solve Kate's problems or take her worries away, but tonight, I can put good food in her belly and keep her company. If she wants that, anyway.

With one last deep breath, I head back downstairs. She's in the kitchen emptying the dishwasher.

She told me that since she doesn't cook, she's always on top of dishes. She believes it to be a fair trade—equity in meals. I briefly think about what a good team we make... how we've fallen into such an easy routine together. But then

I push it to the very back of my mind because we're not a thing. I'm just a moron who developed a crush on my roommate.

My gorgeous, grieving roommate.

I get out a big cutting board and set it next to the slow cooker. Carefully, I take out the hunk of meat, set it on the cutting board, and start cutting slices. I lay the cabbage at the bottom of a serving dish and lay the corned beef on top of it.

When I look up, Kate is staring at the platter with a strange look in her eyes.

"Kate?" I ask.

Her eyes snap to mine.

"Hmm?" She's doing her best to school her expression, but I can tell something's bothering her.

"You don't have to eat it…" I start.

She frowns. "What? No, it looks delicious."

"Then… why are you making that face?"

"Am I making a face?" Her eyes show genuine confusion.

"A little bit, yeah," I concede gently.

"Oh…" She glances out the window above the sink. "I just…"

I don't dare move. I stay as still as possible, hoping for another bread crumb.

Sad, lost puppy.

She swallows hard and I can see her eyes glistening. She sucks a breath in, like she's fortifying herself. "Nick's family is super Irish. His dad is literally one-hundred-percent Irish. It's a big part of their family culture." She meets my eyes for a prolonged second before looking back to the dish and gesturing toward it. "This is just… something they'd do. That's all," she ends with a shrug of her shoulder.

I nod my head slowly. "I see."

I don't know if it will help or hurt her to talk about it, so I opt for turning this meal into a silent tribute to Nick.

"Well, I'm sure the real Irish do it differently, but this is cooked in Guinness and we can have Irish coffee later."

Kate looks back up to me, something soft in her eyes. She gives me that same grateful smile she did earlier on the couch and then nods.

"Grab some plates. Let's eat it while it's hot."

And we do. We sit down at the little breakfast nook that overlooks the backyard—not that we can see it right now, thanks to the short days of winter—and we eat. I give a silent toast to Nick when I take my first sip of the Jameson Kate set on the table.

She doesn't eat a ton, but she eats and that's something. She tells me it tastes delicious. She thanks me for making it and for sharing it with her. It's nothing, of course. I'm happy to make food and share it with her. But I also know what it feels like to be at this stage of grief when small acts of kindness feel big.

When we're finished, I package up the leftovers and put them in the fridge while she starts the cleanup process. We've agreed to watch *Jurassic World,* so I pull up the app that will let us rent it. Once I have it ready, I look up recipes for Irish coffee. I do a quick mental inventory of the ingredients in the kitchen and am grateful we have some heavy whipping cream leftover from something I made last week.

Perfect.

I head back into the kitchen to prepare a little bit of decaf coffee just as she's wiping the slow cooker dry with a towel.

"Whatcha doin'?" she asks.

"Prepping some decaf for Irish coffee later." I finish placing the grounds in the filter and slide the coffee maker back against the backsplash.

When I look back up at her, she's watching me with a wholly new expression on her face. It's kind of like a mixture of surprise and sadness that I can't even begin to untangle, but I watch her anyway, waiting for her to resolve whatever thoughts are going through her mind.

It should feel weird, us looking at each other like this. And maybe, to some extent, it does, but I find that I cannot look away. Her eyes are a beautiful hazel with yellow surrounding the irises in a way that reminds me of sunflowers before fading into a striking green ring on the outside. They look like they hold a story. A million stories. Ones of love and heartbreak and immeasurable joy.

I want to hear all of them.

And they're none of my business. Not really.

"Are you okay?" I manage to make my vocal cords work, but they sound like they're moving around gravel.

She blinks a few times and averts her eyes. Whatever spell we were under is broken.

"Yeah..." Her voice is gravelly as well, so she clears her throat. "Yeah, I'm all right."

When her eyes meet mine again, it feels like it holds weight. It hits me in the sternum, and I feel an actual pressure there, just like that time on the stairs when I came to look at the house.

What the fuck is going on?

I feel my hand touch my chest before I even realize I'm doing it and I see her eyes widen as she tracks the movement.

She sucks in a breath, but I can see the color drain from her face anyway.

"Hey..." I'm suddenly right in front of her, pulling her into my arms.

How did that happen?

I can't answer my own question, but her arms are around my waist. I cradle the back of her head with my hand, and I feel her press her forehead into my shoulder. Hear her take a breath in and feel the hot air of her exhale through my shirt. Register the scrape of her nails as she fists my shirt against my back. Catch some kind of floral scent from her hair and I can't help but dip my head lower so I can smell it better.

Her head turns so her ear is pressed against my chest. When she takes another breath in and holds it, ear still tightly against me, I realize she's listening to my heart, and I swear mine skips a few beats.

I take a calming breath of my own and squeeze her a bit tighter.

"I'm okay," I whisper. "You're okay."

She doesn't respond verbally but holds me tighter.

So we stand there, holding each other in the kitchen. Quietly supporting one another. At some point, I gently run a hand up and down her spine. This seems to relax her, so I keep doing it.

I don't know how long we stand there. Honestly, however long it was, I would have been happy to stand there longer.

Finally, she lets out a deep breath and loosens her hold. She steps back just a smidge, but her hands are still on my waist, so I let mine stay on her arms. I force my eyes to stay locked on hers instead of dropping to her mouth because what I really want to do is kiss her. But that would be extra-ordinarily inappropriate at best and taking advantage of her vulnerability at worst.

I force words past my lips. "Do you still want to watch a movie? I have *Jurassic World* queued up."

This makes her eyes dance with amusement and a smile stretches across her beautiful face. "Blood and gore? Count me in."

We settle onto the couch with Irish coffees and watch the movie. There's a respectable distance between us and Beaker chooses to take it, hugging up against Kate's leg. I've never been envious of a cat before, but in this moment, I am. I find that I want to be the one pressed up against Kate. I want an arm around her shoulders and her head on my chest. I want the quiet nights at home with her.

As the search for the indominus rex gets underway (when, of course, it's just hiding because it's a fucking genetically modified superdinosaur), I realize just how much trouble I'm in.

13

WHAT THE FUCK IS THIS?

Kate

"This wasn't a fair match-up! You run miles every single day."

I roll my eyes and try to hold back my smile. "Sounds like you should take up the habit."

When my baby brother crests the final staircase and meets my eyes, I wink at him. He flips me off.

I'm in New York visiting Benji for my birthday. He lives in a four-floor walkup in Brooklyn with a friend of his from NYU. They have half of one floor. I haven't seen it yet because they just moved in last year and I've been... well, I haven't been in a good place for traveling, or visiting, or company. But it's my birthday and I'm trying.

Or rather, my dad insisted. I'm pretty sure they teamed up to make sure this trip happened. Benji has been begging me to come out to the city and when we got closer to my birthday, dad told me to take a long weekend. When I protested—because what the actual fuck would I do with myself at home alone on a weekday—he told me he'd already booked me a Thursday evening flight and a return flight on Monday morning.

Of course, when I told Gwen, the therapist, she was quite excited.

So here I am, standing on the third-floor landing, waiting for Benji to haul his sorry ass up the last few steps.

I shouldn't be too hard on him. He *is* lugging my suitcase behind him.

He lets us into his apartment—a beautiful space with old hardwood floors, crown molding, a fire escape down the back, a balcony on the front, and enough character to have its own drama on a major network.

Since I flew out after work, it's already getting late. I don't want to go out (people… gross), so we stay in and he shows me some of his most recent photo shoots. I'm doing my absolute best to not get teary-eyed because I don't want to ruin his good mood, but he gets better and better with every job he takes and I'm just *proud*. So fucking proud.

We drink wine (which he bought specifically because I was coming) and he talks about his work and what's going on for the weekend and I just listen. This is the most content I've felt in a full year, and I don't want to go to bed, but eventually, I can barely keep my eyes open. Benji insists that he'll sleep on the couch and says I should take his bed. It's not worth the argument, so I acquiesce and let the sounds of the city lull me to sleep.

Friday is my actual birthday and Benji has a photo shoot scheduled, so I tag along as his unofficial assistant. I keep track of his equipment, hold reflectors, adjust lights, and just *watch* him. He's so talented. Seeing him in his element is one of my favorite things and it reminds me that I *do* have favorite things.

That I *do* have reasons to keep pushing through this life.

That I *do* have things—people—to live for.

And *that* thought reminds me of Liam, which sobers me up and kicks me back into the moment where Benji is asking me to adjust the reflector I'm holding.

Snap out of it, Katherine.

Don't think about St. Patrick's Day. About that moment in the kitchen. About how he made you dinner and Irish coffee and distracted you with bloodthirsty, genetically modified dinosaurs.

I distract myself by really focusing on what Benji is doing. On the people he's photographing. On the way subtle lighting adjustments make a difference.

We end up having dinner with Benji's roommate and some of their other friends at their favorite pizza place. Then, we go bowling and drink pitchers of beer and finally stumble back to the walk-up at one in the morning. I'm buzzed. And the closest thing to happy I've been since last spring.

I barely even notice that no one has asked me about the fact that I'm a widow who is still wearing her wedding ring.

Before I pass out, I realize I have a text from Liam wishing me a happy birthday. For some reason, this only serves to buoy my bubbly mood. I text back a thank-you, along with some photos from the bowling alley.

Saturday, we go to a farmers' market, where we eat crepes and drink coffee and people-watch on a bench before meandering through the booths and pick out ingredients for dinner.

And by that, of course, I mean that *Benji* did those things because he didn't want to risk me burning down his apartment—or worse, the entire apartment building.

By the time we reach the apartment, his roommate confiscates the groceries, claiming that Benji isn't much better than I am at cooking. So Benji and I follow explicit instructions in prepping ingredients while a beautiful meal is cooked for us. Two other friends who hadn't been able to go bowling join us for dinner and we hang out until the wee hours of the morning chatting.

One of the women—Cassandra—asks me a bunch of questions about commercial real estate and we trade stories about real estate in New York City versus smaller towns in the Midwest. I notice my brother sneaking glances at her and I make a mental note to interrogate him about this later.

For her part, Cassandra is much more subtle in her glances toward Benji.

Sunday, we did tourist stuff—the Metropolitan Museum of Art, Ground Zero to see the memorial and pay our respects, then to the Statue of Liberty on the ferry before heading back to Brooklyn.

When I checked my phone in the afternoon, I found another text from Liam. This time, there was a photo of Beaker sound asleep on his favorite rug by a roaring fire.

Me: 😜 😜 😜

Me: Thank you for the update. I was worried he'd freak out with me being gone.

Liam: He's been okay. I told him you're coming back tomorrow.

That makes me laugh. My poor cat.

Liam: Did you have a good birthday?

I take a moment to think about that question and have to admit to myself that I did… I really did have a good birthday. Probably thanks in large part to my dad and Benji. I'm feeling more like myself than I have in so long. I can hardly remember ever feeling this way.

It's been my experience that grief changes your concept of time. I have absolutely no idea how much time has passed, even with the calendar telling me that it's late April and my husband died on July 15. It feels like more than the nine months it's actually been.

Each day is a different version of the same bullshit: wake up, pretend to care about being alive, feed the cat, play with the cat, try to mask my depression around everyone.

Everyone except Liam.

I certainly haven't told him much, but I've told him more than most people.

I skip all of this in my reply.

Me: I did, actually.

For some reason, I can see Liam's smile in my mind. It's quiet and lazy. Gentle. Happy.

Liam: I'm glad to hear that, Kate.

And now I'm smiling, which I only realize because my face fucking hurts after this wonderful weekend with my favorite brother. (Yes, I know he's my only brother.) But I also feel guilt, and I know that if anyone on this planet understands that feeling, it would be Liam.

Me: I feel kind of guilty about that, though.

I press send and hold my breath, suddenly nervous that I've revealed this *thing* about me that feels shameful. I feel like I *shouldn't* be having a good time. But I am. And I'm *glad* I'm having a good time. It feels really good after so much darkness for so long.

Liam: About having a good time, you mean?

Me: Yeah.

I chew on my bottom lip while I watch the three dots dance back at me and release a breath when his reply comes through.

Liam: I understand that. I felt similarly the first time I had fun after Jill. It felt… wrong. Like I should still be miserable.

Relief. That's what I feel. Instantly.

Me: Yes, that's it.

The dots appear again, so I sit down on the bed to wait for his response. I take off my shoes and stretch my back and legs. I haven't been running since I've been here, but I've walked a lot.

My phone dings.

Liam: I know Jill would have been angry with me if she knew I was trying to not have fun. She would be furious if she knew I was intentionally being miserable just because she was gone. I know people say that "they wouldn't want this for you," but I can say with certainty that it was true in Jill's case. So I let myself have fun. Little by little. It's still a work in progress.

I know he's right. Not specifically about Jill, but the sentiment rings true in Nick's case. He wouldn't want me to *try* to be miserable. He would want me to find joy where I could and try to live a good life.

In the dark recesses of my mind, I know that the question

remaining is: *do I actually want to keep living so I can try to have a good life?* Because that feels like a choice. One I'm not ready to make. So I push it back into the dark spaces of my brain and tell it to shut up.

Me: Thank you, Liam.

His reply is immediate.

Liam: You're welcome.

I breathe a sigh of relief and stand up to head back to Benji in the living room. But my phone dings again.

Liam: I'm here. I hope you know that. If you need anything.

I stare at that text and I have no idea what to say. It stirs something in me that I cannot identify. Something that makes me uncomfortable but also *not* uncomfortable. I can't explain it. I don't know what to do with it.

But I do appreciate what he's saying.

So I touch the message and add a heart reaction to it.

* * *

"Do you remember the walkie-talkies?" Benji asks me.

We had dinner at his place again, just the two of us. It was chilly outside but not unbearable. So we bundled up and took a bottle of red wine onto the balcony so we could chat for a bit.

"Of course I do. Those were on our nightstands for like…" I pause, doing some mental math. "God, it had to have been twelve years or more."

A wistful smile spreads across his face.

"You kept that thing on every single night," he says, his voice soft with nostalgia and low with something else—perhaps something sheepish. "Whenever I turned it on and spoke into it… you answered every damn time."

The bright lights of the big city allow me to watch him through the dark. He's staring blankly at his wineglass.

"It wasn't even on a regular basis," he continues. "It was sporadic. And it didn't matter. You were always there."

He swallows hard and fidgets before speaking again tentatively. "I'm sure I… I'm sure I never told you how much that meant to me." He spares me a cursory, nervous glance before finishing. "For keeping the walkie on."

I can't help the flinch that takes over, my head snapping back, eyes wide. "Benji, you don't need to thank me for that. Jesus. You're my brother. I love you. I wanted you to have someone—" A lump in my throat cuts off my speech. I avert my eyes to my own wineglass and clear my throat to buy myself some time to get my own emotions under control. "You needed someone who was there for you. Just you. It was a hard time… you were having a hard time."

"Yeah… but not that whole time."

I can feel him looking at me. He stays silent, waiting for me to meet his gaze again. Eventually, I give in and turn my head.

"It was hard at first… that's true." His eyes are intense, clear. "But you kept that thing on until you left for college. *Years* after it stopped being hard for either of us. And when you left for college, you left it on your nightstand."

I try to shrug it off, but if I'm being totally honest—which I'm only doing because I'm on my second glass of wine—I was sad I couldn't take it with me. I wished we could have kept it going. "Well, it wouldn't have reached me all the way on campus."

He rolls his eyes, an amused smirk brightening his face. "I

realize that, but the distance isn't the reason I brought it up. I looked at it like…" He pauses, staring out into the city lights. "Like you were telling me you'd always be there if I needed you."

I can't take my eyes off him. I'm holding my breath. I want to know if I *have* been there for him. If I've royally fucked that up in the past nine months. But I don't want to know, either, because I'm not sure if I could handle that disappointment. Both his and our father's.

"And you were… you have been. You've always been there, Katie."

I release the breath I was holding as relief floods my chest, followed by guilt. I know I haven't been there for him recently. I know I've been rude, mean, condescending in my refusal of his help. And he's not holding that against me.

My eyes are starting to burn. I take a fortifying sip of wine as a million thoughts roll through my head and threaten to fly out of my mouth, but I don't trust myself to speak just yet.

The truth is, I raised Benji just as much as my dad did. Hearing him talk about something so small and seemingly insignificant that had had such a large impact on him is… a lot. It's emotional and surprising and I don't know how to handle it. So I make a joke.

"Well, you've always been my favorite sibling."

He scoffs, surely understanding what I'm doing and why. "I'm your only sibling."

"It doesn't matter." I can feel that the mood is already lighter and I'm running with it. "Even if we had more—if Dad and Sophie would have had more—you'd always be my favorite. You were just a cool kid. And you're a cooler adult. There's just no arguing with facts, Benjamin."

He laughs. "You're full-naming me?"

"Yes. You're lucky I'm not middle-naming you."

He laughs harder.

"Why? Why would I be in trouble for telling you something important?"

I smirk, then laugh, squeezing my eyes shut and doing my very best Ron Burgundy impression. "I'M IN A GLASS CAGE OF EMOTION," I shout into the night.

Benji laughs so hard he wheezes.

I can't stop the laughter bubbling up in my chest. I laugh so hard I cry.

After a few minutes of our inability to control ourselves, someone with a heavy Brooklyn accent yells at us.

"Would you shut up? It's late, for cryin' out loud!"

It only makes us laugh harder.

Eventually, we fall asleep—me in Benji's room and him on the couch (stubborn man)—both of us a little drunk and very exhausted but grateful for the time we were able to spend together.

The following morning, we have breakfast at a local Jewish deli that Benji loves before bidding farewell. I Uber back to the airport and spend the flight home reliving my time with my brother.

This weekend with Benji was the first time in a full year that I felt anything like myself. I think back on my text conversation with Liam about how I feel *guilty* that I had fun. I had a great time. I enjoyed each day. I looked forward to the next day.

That might sound absolutely absurd. Like that's how normal people live every day. But... that's not how I've been living.

I think about the upcoming week and realize that I have an appointment with Gwen on Wednesday and I roll my eyes at the thought of telling her I had a great time. And then I frown because I realize that I actually *want* to tell Gwen about my weekend. *You have to make an effort in order to stay within the terms of your court mandate.*

I'm proud of myself for enjoying myself. I am. But I'm also painfully aware that one weekend will not cure my depression or undo all the trauma I've experienced in the past year.

I allow myself for just a few minutes to remember my last birthday with Nick. Of course, I didn't *know* it would be my last birthday with him, so I don't remember as much as I wish I could.

I remember that he (reluctantly) agreed to go on a run with me. I remember that he took me out to a lovely dinner. I remember that we sat on the patio at night drinking bourbon, huddled under a blanket on a lounge chair together.

While the roaring of the airplane surrounds me, I close my eyes and try to remember what his arms felt like around me. The sharp scent of his cologne mixed with his skin. The way his stubble would scratch the top of my head. The look in his eyes. His hands on my face.

I curse my brain for not being more photogenic, for not remembering every tiny detail of Nick, both inside and out.

I feel my throat tighten and my eyes begin to burn, so I clench my jaw against the sensation and take deep breaths. I'm not about to start crying on an airplane full of strangers. Absolutely not.

Once I get myself under control, I open my eyes and stare out the window. Farmland passes below me, followed by patches of cities in a pattern that repeats for hundreds of miles before we finally begin our descent into the city.

Collecting my baggage and getting my car happens in a haze of nostalgia and grief. I miss Benji already. My brain and body are on autopilot as I maneuver through the familiar streets, finally ending up in my driveway.

I pull the mail out of the mailbox and toss it on the

passenger seat as I make my way to the garage. I park the car, lug my suitcase inside, drop the mail on the counter, and then promptly abandon both because Beaker is bounding toward me.

"Hello, handsome man!"

I pick him up and nuzzle him for a few minutes, talking to him and hugging him close until he decides he's had enough and wriggles to let me know he wants down.

I refill his water bowl and put fresh food in his dish, then start sorting through the mail.

There are some envelopes for Liam. Some for me. But … one is addressed to Nick.

My mood plummets through the floor. There's a logo in the upper left-hand corner, signifying the company that sent the envelope, but I assume it's junk.

Regardless of who sends each piece of mail to Nick, I resent each and every one of them. Doesn't anyone ever update their fucking mailing lists? The fact that I'm *still* opening mail addressed to my husband nine months after his death is infuriating to me.

Infuriating and *triggering*.

Every time I see an envelope with his name on it, I have a panic attack. I've gotten better about managing and mitigating them, but right now, my heart is racing just the same.

It's just an advertisement. Just open it and throw it in the shredder.

I take a fortifying breath and rip open the envelope.

It's a letter addressed to Nick and signed—actually signed, not printed or stamped—by someone named Marcy.

I blink hard. Take deep breaths. Shake my head. Read the letter over and over.

While I know very little with certainty in this life, I know one thing for sure: this letter is some kind of mistake.

And I'm mad at whoever the fuck Marcy is because she

has destroyed the ending to my wonderful weekend. Because the panic and despair I try so hard to keep at bay are clawing their way up my throat.

I dig my phone out of my purse to call the number listed at the bottom of the letter and ask where the actual fuck this came from.

Marcy answers the phone.

I do my best to stammer out questions and assumptions that the letter is just part of a scam. I tell her that I have no idea what's going on, but I tell her that this letter is wrong. It just has to be.

Marcy assures me that the letter is accurate. That she has a copy of the documents in her records and they hold my husband's signature, signed May 11 of the previous year.

I feel my head shaking back and forth.

This isn't possible.

Marcy tells me what the next steps are. What to do. Offers her condolences—she had no idea Nick died. Tells me she'll check back in with me after a week if I haven't called her yet.

I hang up and drop my phone on the counter. I read the letter *again* as if it would say something different the fifth time I read it.

None of this makes any sense. Gripping the letter in one hand, I run to Nick's office and shove the double doors open. I haven't been in here in months, but I try not to think about that fact because I'm on a fucking mission. I'm in here for a reason.

A very important reason.

I rip open the bottom drawer on the right of his desk, which I know is a little filing cabinet. I sift through the meticulously labeled tabs until I find what I'm looking for.

And that's when I freeze.

I spend a few moments staring at the name on the folder,

wondering what the fuck I'm supposed to do with this information. Eventually, I force myself to take the file out and open it up.

I shuffle through the contents, hands shaking, tears obscuring my vision.

But when I find the handwritten note, my chest tears in two. A sob rips from my throat, echoing off the foyer walls.

I end up on the floor, though I'm not totally sure how I got there, and I'm crying. For Nick, who isn't here to comfort me. For myself, who is still grieving so deeply and desperately needs something. Anything. Maybe some*one*.

But I'm alone.

All alone.

14

THE DEAD KEEP SECRETS

Liam

I t's the first really beautiful day of the year.

The sun is out and it actually feels *warm*. It's not like the colder days of winter when the sun comes out, but it's so cold you still don't want to be outside.

No, today it's sunny and cool and perfect. It's that perfect day we get, maybe a handful of times each year, that reminds me spring is coming and with it comes a renewed sense of hope and a lightness most people haven't felt in months.

Me included.

It's only about fifty-five degrees, but no one around here cares. We'd put on shorts and a tank top just to get the vitamin *D*.

The thing is, the first nice day of the year makes everyone who works in an office miserable because they want to be outside. Of course, this year, matters are exacerbated by the fact that today is the worst day of the entire week: Monday.

Recognizing that I didn't want to be inside either, I let everybody on my team go home at three p.m. After their initial shock wore off, they grabbed their belongings and sprinted toward the door, like I might change my mind.

Not a chance.

First of all, it really is a gorgeous day and I really do want to be anywhere but in my office.

But I'd be lying if I said it didn't also have something to do with the fact that Kate should be getting home any minute. She was away for her birthday and I want to do something special for her. This was her first birthday without Nick and I want her to feel loved and cherished and safe.

And no, I don't really want to examine that any further.

So I hopped in my car, rolled the windows down, and took the long way home just to enjoy the sunshine.

When I open the garage door with the remote on my visor, I see Kate's car and I get far too excited about it. My stomach is suddenly full of butterflies and my heart is pounding faster.

Cut it out, dude.

I take a couple of cleansing breaths before I let myself get out of the car. She's not in the same place that I am. She isn't ready. I know this.

But I still can't help that I jog up the steps into the house, eyes immediately searching for Kate when I open the door. I don't see her, but I do see a suitcase against the wall and a half-opened pile of mail on the kitchen island.

She may have gone for a run.

I set down my bag on the bench by the door and start looking through the mail. There are already two piles: one for me and one for Kate. I finish sorting it and that's when I see the open envelope addressed to Nick.

I feel my face contort into a grimace. Getting junk mail

addressed to your dead spouse isn't any less painful than the actual mail you have to deal with. Getting off mailing lists is extraordinarily difficult and often not even worth the fight. I hadn't had to deal with it for too long—I'd moved back home after our lease was up a few months after Jill died. If she was still getting mail, the new owner was throwing it all in the trash.

Now I'm honestly *hoping* she went for a run. It might help clear her head. I look around for a note, but I don't see one. I check my phone, but the last message I have from her is that her flight landed safely.

"Kate?" I call out, but I don't get a response.

I walk into the living room and peer out the back windows. She's not on the patio. Not in the yard. Perhaps she went upstairs to her room, upset and wanting to be alone.

But if that mail really did upset her, she may need someone.

In the very back of my mind, I wonder if I'm projecting that feeling onto her, but I push it away.

Instead, I move toward the staircase and just as I'm about to climb the first step, I hear something near the front door. I follow the muffled sound to a set of double doors in the front entrance that I've never once seen open in all the months I've lived here.

They're carelessly open. Like they'd been thrown open and the force ricocheted them back, but not with enough force to actually close them.

I hear ragged breathing inside, interspersed with whimpers and sobs, and it propels me forward. I push one of the doors to find a massive walnut desk with a chair behind it, pushed aside and facing the window. There are shelves of books, knickknacks, and picture frames behind the desk.

I can hear her, but I cannot see her. So I follow the sound farther, walking around the desk.

When I see her, that familiar stabbing pain blasts through my chest. The pain of grief. Of loss. Of utter despair.

Kate is on the floor, back against the bookshelves, surrounded by papers, sobbing hysterically.

I'm moving toward her before I even realize it.

"Kate…"

She hears my voice, head snapping up to meet my eyes for just a split second before hugging her knees into her chest and letting her head sink down to her arms, hiding her face.

"Hey…" I try to soothe her with a soft voice as I sink down to the floor next to her. My arm wraps around her shoulders on its own volition and pulls her into me. "What's going on?"

It surprises me when her body crumples, falling helplessly against my side as sobs still shake her chest.

I remember this. I remember how horrible this feels. But I also don't know what's set her off today, specifically. So I stay quiet, holding her head against my shoulder and stroking her hair while she cries. Even after a few minutes, she's still not calming down. Her breathing is so uneven I'm worried she'll pass out.

"Kate, try to take a deep breath," I say gently.

Fortunately, she hears me and responds, albeit nonverbally.

She hauls herself upright and I pull my arm out of the way so she can sit up straight. Her head falls back against the books as she tries to take deliberate breaths in and out. With her eyes closed and head tilted toward the ceiling, the tears stream down her face and into her hair. I take her hand so she knows I'm there, and she grips mine tightly, her knuckles turning white. Like my hand is a life raft in the middle of a raging sea threatening to drown her at any moment.

When her breathing normalizes and her tears slow, I ask

again, as gently and quietly as I can manage. "What happened?"

She clenches her jaw and takes another breath before opening her eyes, but they stay fastened to the ceiling. Her voice is unsteady when she speaks.

"Mail came for Nick. I opened it… I figured it was junk mail or something. But it was a renewal notice for a life insurance policy that I didn't know anything about." She pauses and closes her eyes again.

I squeeze her hand.

Her eyes flutter back open and meet mine before she looks back at the paperwork spread out on the floor. "I called because I figured it was… a mistake or something. I don't know." She shakes her head. "I thought it was bogus. And this woman named Marcy told me that Nick bought a life insurance policy in May. He just never told me about it."

I'm not really sure how to respond to that, so I go for generically surprised.

"Wow…"

I immediately regret my response.

Brilliant, Liam.

I study her face, trying to determine what's going on in her mind. She's very difficult to read. Not just now… she's always difficult to read.

"Was this his only policy then?" I continue.

She swallows, her throat clearly trying to get rid of a massive lump.

"No… he had one through his employer that was equivalent to his salary. It was helpful, of course. It covered the funeral and the burial, and then…" She pauses suddenly, eyes losing focus before snapping back to the present. "… his medical bills and stuff. But the house… the property taxes, the mortgage, the insurance… it didn't last long."

Kate glances up at me shyly and understanding washes over me.

She was absolutely generous when she offered me a place to live. I truly believe she did it out of the kindness of her heart.

But she *did* need the money.

Which reminds me that she tried to charge me a fraction of what I'm actually paying to live in this house.

I nod, so she knows I get what she's saying.

"Anyway…" She shrugs as she continues. "I figured having you here would buy me some time. You'd have a place to live and I could decide what I wanted to do with the house, but I just haven't been able to bring myself to leave it. I assumed I'd have to list it at some point. With you here though… it's fine. I can handle it."

I tilt my head and pin her with a meaningful look. It says *You tried to lowball me when you needed help.*

She rolls her eyes, one corner of her mouth tugging up in what looks like a resigned gesture.

I just sigh and shake my head. I've never been more grateful I pushed back on her offer.

"Well, what about this policy? Is it valid?"

"Marcy says it is. She just needs the death certificate to complete the payout."

"And will it help?"

She frees her hand from mine—honestly, I'd forgotten we were holding hands—and picks up a packet of papers. With another hard swallow, she hands the stack to me.

I leaf through them, skimming the terms. I know my eyes are wide when I mutter, "Holy shit…"

I glance up at her. She's looking at the remaining papers on the floor.

"Kate… this is…" I search for any appropriate word,

knowing nothing will be sufficient. I finally land on, "...
Incredible."

She huffs a breath out. "Is it? Is it incredible?" Her voice is dry as a bone.

I take her hand again. "I didn't mean it like that..." I stay quiet until her eyes meet mine. "I just mean that... you can keep the house now. You can probably just pay it off. Or invest it. I don't know, I'm not a financial expert. But this is really an amazing thing he did for you."

Her eyes close again and her head falls back against the books.

I keep looking through the papers when it suddenly hits me.

"Why didn't he tell you?"

Kate goes completely still. She stops breathing. Not a single muscle twitches.

When I look up at her, her eyes are open, but her gaze is guarded.

"Kate? What is it?"

She clears her throat, reaching forward to grab a folder. "We were a bit... preoccupied."

"With?" I ask, watching her closely.

She hands me the folder without looking at me. She just stares at the bottom of the walnut desk.

The name of the insurance company that sent the letter is written in pen on the tab. I open it to find a piece of generic stationery with the same handwriting featured on the folder's tab.

> *Kate -*
> *Please forgive me for hiding this from you. I know I*
> *promised to not hide large expenditures from you... and I*
> *promise (again) that I never will again, but this is very impor-*

tant. I need to know that you're going to be cared for if anything happens to me—both of you. I know you don't like to talk about it, but it's in my nature to plan. I promised when I married you that I would always take care of you, so if there comes a day that I can't be there physically, this policy should help you.

I can't wait to start this new adventure with you.

I love you with all my heart.

Nick

I shake my head, confused. "I don't understand." I look up to Kate, but she's still staring at the same spot at the bottom of the desk. I search for answers in the folder and find Nick's signed copy of the policy and a small photograph. I pick it up to examine it more closely.

Black and white. Unclear. But a kidney-shaped blob in the middle.

I've never held one in my hands, but I know what it is. I frantically search for more information on the curled edges of the photo.

I find what I'm looking for in the upper right-hand corner. *Eight weeks, two days.*

All the air leaves my lungs like I've been punched.

"Oh, Kate..." I turn my head to look at her. Tears are slowly running down her cheeks as she stares at the photo in my hand.

I force myself to say the words.

"Kate... you were pregnant?"

15

MY OWN PERSONAL TINY
TORTURE CHAMBER

Kate

"Kate?"

I can vaguely hear Liam saying my name. It feels very far away. Like he's speaking to me through thick panes of glass.

My vision is blurry with tears and I'm staring at the sonogram printout in his hands.

Memories from the day that image was created flit through my mind. The general discomfort and low-key humiliation of a transvaginal ultrasound. My nerves. Nick's jaw slacked open beside me. His hand wrapped around mine and him kissing my palm. The tears in his eyes when he looked up at me.

It's like a tiny torture chamber created just for me.

Liam says my name again and it graciously pulls me from my mental prison.

I look up at him and nod.

He sucks in a breath and holds it. He seems to be at a loss for words. I can almost see the questions flitting through his mind.

It's not a difficult decision to put him out of his misery. There's no point in staying silent about it at this point.

So I take a deep breath and I tell Liam my biggest secret.

"I don't know when he had time to do this. There were only three weeks between that ultrasound and the miscarriage. I assume that's why he didn't tell me... it was kind of a moot point. We would have tried again. He probably assumed he'd tell me after I got pregnant again. Of course, none of that really matters because he died a few weeks later."

Liam takes my hand again, his voice heavy with sadness when he speaks. "Kate, I am so sorry."

I can't talk just yet. I just nod and squeeze his hand in return.

I'm both terrified and relieved that someone else knows this information. For nearly a full year, I hadn't told a soul that I'd found out I was pregnant shortly before my last birthday. And therefore, when I miscarried a few weeks later, I had no one to notify. I was with Nick at the time, so I didn't even have to tell him that I'd lost his child.

And when he died, all hopes of starting a family with Nick disintegrated with him. The finality of it is what nearly killed me. I *did* know we'd try again. It was that hope that kept me from curling up into a ball.

So when Nick died, I had no one to talk to about this massive thing that happened that made the entire thing even more devastating than it already was.

It's this thought process that finally makes what I've just said sink in. My pulse skyrockets and I clasp his hand in both of mine, pleading with him. "Oh my god, please don't tell anyone. *No one* knows. Until just now, I was the only living person who knew."

Liam frowns. "No one?"

I shake my head frantically.

"Not even Elliot?"

I shake my head again, slower this time. "Nick and I wanted to keep it under wraps until the first trimester was over... just in case. Obviously, that was kind of applicable in our case. But also..." I take a moment to figure out how to say this. Men don't get it. But something tells me Liam will at least *try*. "People treat you differently when they find out you're pregnant. Coworkers, clients, everyone. I didn't want anyone catching wind of it and getting weird... thinking I couldn't handle my job anymore. I didn't even tell my dad."

I didn't even tell my lawyer, who was arguing severe emotional distress.

I leave that detail out for Liam. He doesn't need to know the extent of my failings just yet. Or ever.

"Okay, okay... I won't tell anyone." He puts his free hand on top of the pile of mine and his and squeezes. "It's okay."

I sigh with relief, my body sagging back against the bookshelves. I pull my hands free in the process and run them through my hair. Some of it is wet with tears.

Fuck, I'm a mess.

"Thank you."

"Of course."

He's so fucking nice.

"I-I just can't believe this."

Liam stays silent next to me. I can't blame him. What's he supposed to say?

"I wish he would have just told me. It would have saved me a *lot* of stress. I miscarried, my husband died suddenly, and then I thought I was going to lose my goddamn house."

Liam tilts his head and his expression is nothing but

sympathetic. "He probably didn't want to upset you. Planning for your death isn't exactly an uplifting topic."

He would know.

"Well, it was a shitty thing to hide." I know my voice sounds angry, but I don't care. I'm so angry with Nick right now. And I can't even yell at him.

"Even so…" Liam says. "He promised he'd always take care of you. And he did. He kept his word."

My throat tightens and a tear immediately spills from my eye. If I were in a different state of mind, I might be surprised that he reaches up and wipes that tear away with a curled index finger. It seems natural in this moment. Like he hadn't even thought that he shouldn't do it.

"What do you need?" His voice is impossibly soft and it makes me want to curl up in it and go to sleep.

"A drink."

"Let's get you a drink, then."

He helps me to my feet, and when I wobble, he wraps his arm around my shoulders and pulls me against his strong body. He leads me out of the office, closing the doors behind him. Neither of us bother to pick up the paperwork scattered on the floor.

After he ushers me over to the couch and puts a blanket over my legs, he fetches a bottle of bourbon and two tumblers. Plopping down next to me, he pours us each a drink.

"Thank you."

I take my glass and immediately take a big gulp. It's too much and it burns going down, but I don't care. I'll always welcome a feeling that cannot be labeled *debilitating grief* even if it's just for a moment. With a deep breath, I lean back into the soft cushions of the couch.

"What else can I do?" he asks, his voice still so soft, like cashmere.

I take another sip of bourbon and think for a moment, but eventually, I shake my head. "There's nothing. There's just nothing." Another tear slips from my eye and this time, Liam doesn't bother to catch it. Instead, he grabs the tissue box from the coffee table and sets it between us.

"Do you mind if I just sit here with you?"

I look over at him, surprised at his offer, but I immediately realize I shouldn't be surprised at all. This is just who Liam is. He's kind and supportive and obviously has a loving heart. He took care of his dying wife for years. He married her even though they knew she would die young. He's a good person to the core.

Years of societal training that has taught me to be leery of men rears its head.

Go out in groups. Stick together. Don't set down your drink. Don't let other people bring an open drink to you. Don't leave with a stranger.

Maybe don't invite strangers to live in your home.

How have I not thought of this until now?

But he's not a stranger, is he? He's known Leon for years. He's known *Elliot* for years. And looking at Liam right now, I know he'd never hurt me. Something about him makes me trust him. And at this point in my life, that's saying a lot.

After all, he knows the secret I've been hiding for the past year.

In fact, he's done this before. Before Christmas, when I was lying under the Christmas tree, he stayed with me and helped me breathe through a panic attack until I was able to calm down.

He's been sleeping across the landing from me for months now.

Leon is one of his very good friends. He's known Liam for over a decade. You're safe with him.

I blink a few times and finally nod. "Yeah, that's fine."

* * *

I'VE NEVER REALIZED how much my therapist's office looks like Nick's office.

I'm sitting on the couch, staring at the bookshelves that line the wall behind her desk. They look custom made.

Gwen's desk is stained gray. It's modern, as opposed to Nick's traditional old walnut desk he found at an estate sale.

Gwen's bookshelves are off-white, with the inside painted a calming green. Nick's are stained dark to go with the desk.

I think that's why I overlooked the similar layout.

Well, that and I haven't been in Nick's office in months. Not since he died.

Not that I ever spent much time in there anyway. It was his space. I went in there sometimes on a weekend morning when he was checking on things or studying world markets after the closing bell.

I've never really enjoyed being in Gwen's office, but I always assumed it was because of the whole *court-mandated* thing.

You know... that thing keeping me out of jail.

But now that I've recognized its similarities to Nick's office, I'm wondering if that plays a part.

Now, I'm wondering if this room has always reminded me of Nick.

When Gwen enters the room with that familiar manila folder, I force a smile, but it doesn't fool her. She frowns immediately. She settles herself into the chair in front of me and cocks her head to the side.

"Kate, you seem a bit... fidgety today," she begins. "Did something happen in New York when you were visiting your brother?"

"No."

She looks to my foot pointedly, a meticulously groomed brow arching. It's twitching maniacally.

I press my foot into the carpet and my palms on my knees to keep my legs still.

I clear my throat. "No, it was after I got home."

"What happened when you got home?" She asks the question so gently that it nearly pisses me off. At the very beginning, I would have seen this as patronizing. But now, I realize she's trying not to scare me off. Trying to let me go at my own pace.

Goddammit, Gwen.

I look out the window as I gather my thoughts… Monday afternoon replaying through my mind. I'm trying to figure out what the important parts are so we don't waste our precious fifty-five minutes when I'm suddenly alarmed by the thought that I don't want to waste time in therapy.

When the actual fuck did that happen?

"I got a letter… from an insurance company," I start.

I tell the whole story—an abbreviated version of my visit with Benji, making sure to let her know that I actually enjoyed myself and then launching into the life insurance portion. Her eyes are as wide as I've ever seen them, which would probably be unnoticeable to the average person. But I've spent many hours staring at her face at this point.

When I finish the saga, Gwen blinks. Hard.

"Wow…"

"Yeah."

"That's… a lot."

"Yeah."

"And you didn't know anything about it?"

I shake my head. "He must have done it after we found out I was preg—" I swallow the rest of the word, gulping it down and flushing red immediately, hoping Gwen hadn't heard it.

No such luck.

I can feel Gwen's eyes boring into my skull even though I'm intently looking at my hands in my lap.

"Kate. What were you saying?"

"Nothing," I say quickly. Too quickly. I'm not helping my case.

There's a moment of silence, during which I'm *certain* that Gwen is giving me a chance to come clean.

I try to play it off like nothing happened. Like I didn't accidentally spill my deepest, darkest secret that I'd only ever told one living soul. Like I didn't accidentally admit to hiding a major, life-altering event from my *therapist,* who is trying to help keep me out of jail.

I'm both annoyed with myself for being so careless and mad that I hid this from Gwen for so long because I think she's going to be mad at me.

What is wrong with me that I'm suddenly spilling my secrets to people?

"Kate," Gwen begins quietly. "It sounded to me like you were about to say you were pregnant… which is perhaps why Nick bought the life insurance policy." She pauses until I finally relent and meet her gaze, relentless and strong. "Is that true?"

I lick my suddenly very dry lips and look at my hands again. "I don't want to talk about it."

Gwen sucks in a quick breath, like she's genuinely shocked but also fitting some puzzle pieces together. "Kate, this is very important. Were you pregnant when Nick died?"

I swallow the massive lump in my throat and shake my head.

"What happened?"

"I don't want to talk about it," I repeat. My nose, eyes, throat… they're all burning. I can feel the panic rising in my chest. I would do anything to get out of this conversation.

"I understand that… I'm sure it's very painful. I'm only going to ask you one more question, and I want you to answer it. Then we can drop this subject until a later date." She pauses, waiting. Always patiently waiting on me. "Okay?"

I nod, still staring at my hands.

"Did you miscarry prior to Nick's passing?"

I nod again, just once. I want this conversation to be over.

"Okay," Gwen states with finality. "Okay, I'm done asking about it for today."

I nod again, reaching over to the side table for the box of tissues. I don't bother grabbing one. I just take the whole fucking box and set it in my lap, sinking down the couch and staring at the ceiling.

I hear Gwen clear her throat and take a deep breath. In some ways, I feel bad for her. The rational side of my brain knows that this *is* a big deal. I *have* hidden a pretty big secret from her for months.

"Are you sure the policy is authentic?" Gwen asks and I'm so grateful that she's dropping it.

"Yes," I answer. "I called immediately, and then I asked Sophie to look into it just to double-check. It's legit."

"Wow…" she repeats herself. "Kate, that's… kind of amazing."

Jesus fucking Christ.

I roll my eyes and lift my head. It's my turn to stare daggers into Gwen.

Gwen sees the ragey look in my eyes and softens. Her head tilts in the empathetic way I'm accustomed to by now. "I understand that no amount of money is a sufficient substitute for your husband."

"No, it's really not. I'd trade it for him in a heartbeat," I snap.

"I know you would." Gwen is nodding. "But consider the fact that Nick loved you *so* much… he cared for you *so very* much that he wanted to make sure you were properly cared for. It's just…" she trails off.

"It's what?" I demand.

With a resigned sigh and an apologetic look on her face, she admits something it doesn't seem she wants to. "It's a bit romantic, isn't it? Your husband is taking care of you… even though he's no longer with you."

My vision blurs immediately. Familiar pain lances my chest. I fold my torso over my legs and hug my knees, crying into my thighs, unable to hold it in any longer.

And even though it's not exactly proper, Gwen crosses the gap between our seats and sits next to me. She puts a gentle hand on my back and moves it back and forth across my shoulder blades while I sob.

16

THE MOUTH ON HER

Liam

Baseball season is starting.

This is my favorite time of year. The weather is improving, the sun is shining brighter, and the sound of baseball echoes across the city.

I love baseball. Some people love football, choosing to sit in front of the television for three hours every Sunday for seventeen weeks when the weather is awful. Or worse, going to games and freezing their balls off.

Hard pass for me.

I'd much rather be at home watching a baseball game. If I can't be in the stands, that is. I haven't been on the field in years.

I don't want to subject Kate to baseball if she doesn't like it, so I usually watch the game in my room. There's a TV mounted on the wall and I can sit in bed, falling asleep to the sounds of the crowd, baseballs landing in leather mitts, and the crack of a wooden bat against a ball.

Today is Friday. It's been a week since I found Kate crying in Nick's office and I can't stop thinking about it.

For the first few days, she was more timid around me, avoiding eye contact and trying to stay busy with something—anything—every time I was in the room. She's been a little more relaxed in the past couple of days, but it's still not back to normal.

I imagine she's skittish from having told me such a well-kept secret. She might feel awkward that she cried. I'm not judging her for anything that she did or said last week. I just want to make her feel comfortable around me again. But I don't want to push her.

I came up to my room to watch the game even though she wasn't home yet. It's the third inning when I hear the garage door open.

The sound of Beaker's claws digging into the carpet as he rounds the landing to fly down the stairs and meet Kate makes me smile. He and I have been getting along a little better since St. Patrick's Day, but I'm no match against Kate.

To be honest, I don't blame him.

I try to focus on the game even as I hear her voice drifting through the house as she talks to Beaker. It's distracting though. It's getting harder and harder to ignore the way I'm attracted to her. The way my ears try harder to listen when I hear her voice. The way her body moves. It's inappropriate for me to notice. She's my roommate. I need to figure out how to turn it all off.

I'm already failing miserably though, because when she appears in my bedroom doorway, holding Beaker, my eyes are immediately drawn to her gorgeous hazel eyes. I take a deep breath and focus, which makes me realize that she's nervous.

I try to keep my voice gentle, but not so gentle that I'm trying when I greet her with a simple, "Hey."

She gives me a tight smile, but I can see the relief in her eyes. "Hi."

"How was your day?"

"Long," she says, scratching behind Beaker's ears. "I went to my dad's for dinner afterward, though."

"That's nice. What did you eat?"

Beaker is wiggling in her arms, so she bends to set him down in front of her. He pauses to look at me and sniff the air, then turns and runs into the hallway.

She watches him go before turning back to me. "Um, they ordered in. I had a salad."

I nod.

"It had steak on it though, don't worry." She smirks.

I open my mouth to crack a joke when I hear the crack of a bat on the TV. Both of us look just in time to see the ball fly over the right-field wall. Ramirez rounds the bases and high-fives the two runners he brought in.

Damn, that kid's good. Far better than I was at his age.

"Has it been a good game?"

Kate's voice interrupts my thoughts and when I look over, I realize she's closer to me than she was before. She's actually entered the room and is standing near the bed, watching the TV. Her arms are folded over her chest, but she's here nonetheless.

"Yeah… it's been good. They're playing well. Kluber's pitching a good game."

She nods like she's unsure of how to respond.

"Are you a baseball fan?"

She shrugs one shoulder. "My dad is. I used to watch the games with him when he had time to watch them. I was usually doing homework or something. I haven't kept up on it though."

Kate's eyes go back to the TV as the next batter comes up and misses the first pitch.

"You're welcome to stay and watch with me," I offer.

Her head snaps back to me, then skirts around the room.

I want her to stay, I realize. But I also see that she feels uncertain.

"Here…" I sit up fully, then start stacking the pillows up against the headboard. I'm fully dressed, wearing a T-shirt and a pair of sweatpants and I'm on top of the covers. My brain is frantically searching for any possible way this might look like I'm trying to coerce her and realize that there is no possible way for it *not* to look like that.

But she must feel okay about this situation because she's rounding the bed. I quickly retreat to my own side, leaving plenty of space for her. She sits down and crosses her legs in what my nephews call "crisscross applesauce," eyes intent on the TV screen.

It's silent, save for the sounds of the announcers and the game for a few minutes. The umpire is calling pitches. The catcher is throwing the ball back to the pitcher. The steady rhythm of the game seeps into my bones and soothes me in that old familiar way it always has.

That is until Kluber hits the batter in the shoulder with a pitch.

Kate sucks in a breath. I wince.

"Ouch…" she mutters.

"That definitely stung," I agree. I reach up and touch the outside of my shoulder where the ball hit the batter, remembering the times I'd been nailed in that exact same spot.

"You've been watching the games… you must be a pretty big fan," Kate says.

The smile on my face is completely natural. "Yeah, I love baseball. I played for a long time."

"Oh yeah? Little league?"

I glance over at her. Her eyes are soft and a gentle smile stretches her mouth.

"Yeah, but also in high school and college."

Out of the corner of my eye, I see her head rear back. "Really?"

"Yep." I look at her fully this time. She's surprised, but not in a disbelieving way. And I absolutely catch the way her eyes flit down my torso like she's searching for evidence that I might look athletic under these clothes. I resist the urge to puff out my chest and then chastise myself for the urge in the first place.

"What position did you play?" she asks.

"First base."

"And you stopped after college? No pros for you?"

"Nah…" This isn't an uplifting story, but I'll tell it anyway. "To be completely honest, I probably wouldn't have made it to the majors, and I knew that. I'd have been stuck in the minors for years, and that might have been okay—that happens to a lot of guys. Some of my friends even and they still enjoyed their careers for as long as they were able to play. But… it wasn't meant to be for me, and that was fine because once Jill was diagnosed, all I wanted to do was spend time with her. A minor league schedule wasn't something I would have been willing to put up with—riding buses in the middle of the night to get to the next game. The uncertainty of it all. If I had made it to the majors, the schedule would have been even more rigorous. I just didn't want it anymore."

I can feel Kate watching me. She's still as a statue.

"I don't regret it though. I got a job with great benefits and a lot of vacation time, so we could travel and I knew she'd be taken care of. She got to live the rest of her life in a job she loved. And I got to love her."

When I look back over to Kate, there are tears in her eyes

that she quickly tries to hide, clearing her throat and snapping her head in a different direction.

I reach out and squeeze her knee.

She sniffs and dabs at her cheeks with her sleeve. "I'm so sorry, Liam."

"Don't be," I assure her. "I'm not. Not really."

Kate turns back to me with a confused look on her face. My hand is still on her knee, but she makes no move to shift away.

"Obviously, I didn't want my wife to die. But I also wouldn't have changed any decisions that I made as a result of her diagnosis. I'm grateful I stayed close to home for her. I got as much of her as I possibly could have. I knew my years with her would be short, but we got more time together than we thought we would. I'm grateful."

She lays her hand down on top of mine and squeezes. "You're so level-headed and… well-adjusted," she says, dabbing at the corner of her eye a final time. "It kind of pisses me off, to be honest."

That shocks a laugh out of me, my free hand on my chest as it shakes. I hear her chuckle quickly next to me and she squeezes my hand again. It's like she's trying to tell me that she's not *actually* mad at me. I chance a look at her to find her watching me with a soft smile on her face and mischief in her eyes.

"What was it that got you here? Therapy? You probably tried harder than me." Her tone is teasing, but I can tell there's a note of seriousness behind the question.

I laugh her off. She needs to go at her own pace. I'm not going to tell her how to grieve for her husband or how to heal those wounds.

She settles against the stack of pillows behind her. I let go of her knee as she moves, but I don't get the impression she moves just so I will move my hand because she scoots just a tiny bit closer to me.

At the end of the inning, I ask if she played any sports. We've already talked about my baseball days.

"Just track."

Just track like running is a less worthy sport than baseball.

"What were your races?"

"Middle distance, mostly. Eight hundred and fifteen hundred meters."

"Fifteen hundred meters is nearly a mile. You run farther than that now on leisurely runs," I point out.

There's that soft chuckle again. I love that sound.

"Yeah, I suppose so. It calms me down," she admits, stealing a self-conscious glance my way. I smile to reassure her.

"You never went up to long distances?"

She scrunches her nose and shakes her head. "It takes too long. How boring to run around a track over and over again. You might as well run cross-country. At least there would be something to look at."

She makes a fair point. "You basically run cross-country now though."

A brilliant smile spreads across her face and it reaches her eyes. "I suppose I do. Fewer hills. And the view is pretty great."

"Can't beat it."

Kate starts to nod off during the eighth inning, so she says good night and makes a left for her bedroom as she leaves mine.

I brush my teeth and change my clothes, then crawl into bed to finish watching the game. When it's over (they won, in case you were wondering), I turn off the TV, stare at the ceiling, and think about the gorgeous brunette across the landing.

* * *

WHEN KATE WATCHED the ball game with me the other night, I didn't expect it would become a regular thing, but here we are. I was already in my bedroom watching the game when she got home from work. I had an exhausting day and I'm basically ready for bed. I have flannel pajama pants and a T-shirt on. I hear her chirping away at Beaker and then she appears in my doorway. She's wearing dark-gray pants and a white button-down shirt. Her black heels dangle from one hand. Her face brightens with a smile when she sees the game on TV.

She's stunning.

"What's the score?"

I inhale sharply when I realize I've just been staring at her. I look back at the TV. "We're down five to three."

She squints at the screen when the score graphic comes up at the bottom of the screen. "Yikes. It's only the fourth and Bauer's already been pulled?"

A smile tugs at my lips. She doesn't pay that much attention to baseball, but she clearly looked up the starting pitcher ahead of time. Or maybe she talked to her dad about it.

"Yeah…"

"Just having a bad night, you think?"

"Probably." I take a sip of beer and tilt my head to the open space next to me. "Do you want to watch the game? You're welcome to join me."

Her hazel eyes look over to the empty space on the bed and her bare feet shift as she thinks about it. "Sure… I'm going to get changed real quick."

When she reappears in my bedroom, she's wearing leggings and a long shirt and she's holding a glass of wine. She stays until the end of the eighth inning and then goes back to her room.

It happens again and again. Sometimes, I stay in the living room, but most of the time, I watch the game in my bedroom. She joins me often, but not always. The only reason it's not always is that she's not necessarily home or I'm out with friends or family.

We talk about our days, baseball, how her runs have been going, my nephews… anything and everything and nothing.

The more I learn, the more I talk to her, the more I hear her talk, the more I want. More of her, more of this, more of us. More *from* us.

But I won't make the first move. I don't think she's ready. I'll wait for her.

* * *

"Hey!"

Kate's voice cuts into the game noise. She's leaning against the doorframe. Today she's wearing black pants with a green top that shows just the tiniest amount of cleavage, the chain she always wears dipping below the neckline. Her black heels are dangling from her fingers again. Her hair is wavy and framing her face.

Gorgeous.

"Happy Friday," she says as I try not to stare.

"And to you, as well." I tip my glass of bourbon toward her.

"What's the score?"

"Five to one. We're up."

She watches the screen for a moment before I ask if she wants to join me. I always ask. I always wonder if she's waiting for the invitation. Like she needs an excuse to watch with me. Or she doesn't want to invade my space.

"Sure."

"Want a drink?"

"Always."

That makes me smile, not that I need much of an excuse to smile around her. "Go get changed. I'll grab you something. What would you like?"

I climb out of bed, bringing my bourbon tumbler with me. As I get closer to her, she stands up straight and I definitely don't miss how her eyes dip to my chest and *almost* go lower before she jerks her gaze back to my face.

She clears her throat and scratches at her temple while she averts her eyes. "Bourbon sounds good."

I stop two feet in front of her. Close enough but not touching. "Okay. I'll get it."

She nods, staring at the floor between us.

I shuffle back a half step. Nervous is one thing. Uncomfortable is another.

I keep my voice gentle when I ask, "Are you okay?"

Finally, she gives me her eyes again.

I can see the change as it happens. When the anxiety ebbs and she relaxes. She blinks slower, less frequently. Her breathing grows steadier. Her eyes soften. Her shoulders drop farther from her ears.

I clutch my tumbler in one hand and slide the other in my pocket to keep from reaching for her because I'm not sure what she wants.

Me? I know I want to kiss her. I know I want to thread my fingers in her hair so I can see if it's really as soft as it looks.

But Kate? She's probably not in the same place.

So I stay still and keep my hands to myself.

"Yeah…" she answers. "Yeah, I'm okay."

"Okay." I don't mean for my voice to come out as a whisper, but it does.

"All right, I'm…" She scratches her temple again and turns toward her room. "I'm gonna go change."

"Okay."

I head down the stairs as she dashes across the landing and closes her door. I get her a drink, refresh my own and I'm back in my spot on the bed before she returns, her tumbler on the other nightstand.

Kate turns the corner into my room, wearing a loose V-neck shirt and leggings. I keep my eyes glued to the TV as she settles onto what I'm trying really hard to *not* call "her" side of the bed and lifts the tumbler of bourbon to her lips.

"Mmm… perfect," she murmurs as she sinks down a bit, getting more comfortable.

I look at her just in time to see her lick her lips, which is both a blessing and a curse.

"Any fun plans this weekend?" I try to deflect my own train of thought.

"Not really. You?"

"I'll see my brother and his family tomorrow afternoon."

"Oh, that will be nice."

"It will."

The crack of a bat draws our attention, which thankfully means we don't miss a spectacular save from Lindor.

Our respective exclamations threaten to drown each other out and it feels like the most natural thing in the world when we high-five.

"They're off to a good start," she says.

"They are," I agree. And I've enjoyed these last couple of weeks watching with her. "I need to get over there for a game. I haven't been yet this season."

"Really? God, I don't remember the last time I went to a game."

"Who did you go with?"

A wistful smile brightens her face. "My dad."

"Everyone always talks about dads introducing their boys to sports, but I love it when dads and daughters go to games together. Especially baseball, since women don't have their own league."

"And ain't that some bullshit?" she mutters.

I laugh. "It is. They did during the war."

She scoffs and rolls her eyes. "Until they were told to get back in the fucking kitchen when the *menfolk* came home."

The way she says it—like she's personally offended by this, even though she has no desire to play baseball and she did not live during that time period—only makes me laugh harder. Kate's funny when she lets herself relax. When I pry my eyes open, I can see her trying to hide a smile behind her bourbon tumbler.

Tomlin strikes out the last batter to end the inning and we're both cheering again like the team would be able to hear us downtown. The sound of frantic paws on hardwood makes us dissolve into another fit of laughter, Kate calling out apologies for Beaker.

That's how the rest of the night goes. We watch the game, we laugh, we cheer. Eventually, Kate falls asleep on the bed next to me. She looks so peaceful, I don't want to wake her. So I slip into my bathroom and get ready for bed, then take a blanket from the end of the bed and cover her with it. I turn off the lights and lie down beside her—a safe distance away— on top of the duvet.

I turn the volume on the TV down and turn on the closed captions before flipping the channel so I can watch *Sports- Center*. I can hear Kate breathing steadily next to me. One arm is under the pillow, the other resting on the bed between us. The entire scene gives me a sense of calm. And that's the last thing I remember until I feel an arm around me.

Instinctively, I wrap my own arm around the soft one stretching across my stomach.

The sound of a sharp intake of breath makes me open my eyes. I look down to find my hand resting on Kate's. I can feel the tension in her arm and I imagine her entire body is taut at the moment. Slowly, cautiously, I turn my head to look at her face.

Her eyes dart up from where our hands are touching to meet my gaze. There's a little bit of fear there, like she doesn't know what to do. Like she's afraid I'll react poorly. But what Kate might not realize is that I've been dying to touch her. I won't do anything she doesn't want me to. I won't push her. But if she wants to touch me, I won't stop her.

To reassure her that I'm okay with this, I gently interlace my fingers with hers.

Her chest expands with a deep breath and her eyelashes flutter. I wonder if she can feel the tingles shooting up her arm the way I feel them in mine. If her body is warming the way mine is.

But still, I wait.

And then she squeezes my hand.

I want to meet her where she's at. So I slowly roll onto my side to face her, making sure to keep hold of her hand. When she doesn't go flying from my bed, I reach out with my free hand to trace her cheekbone with my thumb.

Her head tilts just the tiniest bit, leaning into my touch. So I brush a lock of hair off her forehead.

She closes her eyes with a sigh.

I have never been more aware of someone's body language. I'm holding myself back in every single way, waiting for her to either lead us forward or bring us to a screeching halt.

But then she scoots just a tiny bit closer to me, bringing our still-interwoven hands to her chest.

It's like we're taking turns. Testing each other. And it's my move.

I trail my fingers over her shoulder, down her side, and to

her hip. I keep my hand in a safe zone—firmly on her side, not touching her butt or her low belly. And then I gently close a small portion of the gap between us.

Her eyes are on my face the whole time and I watch the way her breathing gets more shallow.

To be totally honest, I expect things to end here. I assume we'll snuggle. God knows both of us are touch deprived at this point. I'd be fine with that scenario. Truly.

But then she brushes her lips against my knuckles and my body lights up in a way that it should not light up. This woman's lips have barely touched my body—and a pretty innocuous part of my body, at that—and I'm having a physiological response that I cannot begin to grasp.

My heart is pounding. My breath is coming faster. My skin is on fire. I'm already getting hard and nothing has even happened here.

I'm not even cognizant of my face inching closer to hers until I'm only a few inches away.

Suddenly, she lets go of my hand and I wonder if this is it… the moment she freaks out and jumps out of bed. Instead, she reaches toward me and brushes her thumb over my lips. I feel another rush of heat blast through me and I'm still a bit distracted by the sensation when she closes the rest of the gap between our mouths and presses her lips against mine.

I'm too afraid to move. I kiss her back, of course, but I don't push it. She's in charge here. A moment later, her lips part, so I follow suit. Her kisses are slow, languid, tentative at first and then become more demanding as she gains confidence. It's all incredible. I'll take any of it and truly, I will stop here if that's what she wants.

But it's when her tongue touches mine that I start to unravel.

Fuck.

A groan slips out of my throat and I give in to the urge to plunge my fingers into her hair. As my hand travels up between our bodies, I accidentally brush her breast—I swear I didn't mean to and I freeze when she gasps. My eyes fly open and I study her face, trying to gauge her feelings.

But she doesn't look upset. She looks surprised, which seems entirely fair.

Both of us are breathing harder than we were a few moments ago. My hand is suspended between us by her collarbone.

It's the way she pulls me back to her with a renewed sense of urgency that shows me she's okay. Her arm snaking down to pull my hips closer to hers is also a great sign. So I let my fingers dive into her hair, holding her head steady as we feel each other, taste each other. All the while, I look for signs that she wants to stop. That she's uncomfortable. But she's only had one drink and she's sucking on my bottom lip and pulling my body flush against hers and wrapping her leg around mine and it all feels so *fucking good*.

I press my hips into hers, partially to test her, to see if she actually wants to keep going when she feels evidence of my arousal. She moans, which only makes me harder. She doesn't protest when I slip my hand under her shirt. No, she actually moves her arm to make it easier for me to reach her breast, throwing the last bit of blanket off her body and arching into my hand.

Everything feels amazing and we're still fully clothed. And goddamn, I want her clothes off. I want to feel every inch of her skin. The fire that started earlier is going to consume me and I'm going to let it—so long as she lets this continue. It's all up to her. I'll follow her lead.

But there's still a tiny voice in the back of my mind.

I tear my lips away from hers. "Kate…"

She fuses her mouth back to mine, effectively shutting me up before she actually speaks words. "No talking."

She reaches down and cups me, causing me to gasp and press into her hand. "Fuck…"

"Yes… exactly."

Kate kisses me again and starts working her hands under my shirt, inching it up my torso.

"Kate—"

"I said no talking." She wrenches my shirt up enough to kiss my stomach and chest, her tongue driving me absolutely wild with anticipation.

"I just want to make sure—"

She pulls her mouth from my skin and looks up at me. "Liam. I'm not drunk. I'm *very* turned on. So stop *talking* and start fucking."

Motherfucker, the mouth on her.

I pull her mouth back to mine and guide her backward so she's lying flat. I sit up long enough to rip the shirt up over my head and then help her out of hers. *Fuck*, she's gorgeous. Perfect breasts and a slender waist ending at hourglass hips. I can't get enough of my mouth on her skin. It feels like silk and tastes like honey. I slide a hand under her back to snap her bra clasp open and then drag it from her body. I can't help that my breath catches when I see her bare chest.

"Jesus…"

The look she gives me is nothing short of wanton.

If she's all in, I'm all in. I slide my way down her body, pulling her leggings with me and dropping them to the floor.

I kiss my way back up her legs before looking back to her face. Her eyes are full of lust, with a generous amount of impatience, which only fuels my wicked side. So I stop at the apex of her legs, a slow smirk forming on my face, and when her lips part in anticipation, I finally follow her instructions.

17

WHAT THE FUCK HAVE I DONE?

Kate

I wake up to unfamiliar surroundings. Vaguely familiar but not *mine*.

This is not my bed.

That is not my window.

What the fuck is happening?

I look around and my half-awake brain finally realizes I'm in Liam's room.

Baseball.

I must have fallen asleep—

And that's when my brain fully catches up.

Panic seizes my chest, but I still force myself to look to my left. Of course, that's where I find Liam, sleeping peacefully next to me, his bare chest still exposed, and *no,* I will not be dwelling on how hot he is right now with his mussed hair and golden skin.

Oh my god, oh my god, oh my god. What are you doing, Kate?!

I ease out of the bed as quietly and gently as possible, gather my clothes, and tiptoe out of his room.

I can't remember the last time I snuck out of a man's bedroom, hoping to remain unseen. It had only happened once or twice. Of course, I'd never snuck out, closed the door, and found myself in my own fucking house with nowhere to go.

The thought spurs me forward toward my own bedroom. I shut the door behind me and then press my back against it. The door is cold, which reminds me that I'm naked.

"Fuck."

What the fuck have I done?

I cannot even begin to unravel this predicament right now. I need to move. I need to get out.

I throw on some running clothes, shove a house key in my sports bra, grab my earbuds, and bolt out the patio door.

I keep my warm-up short. My blood is pumping plenty hard right now, all on its own. I don't need to ease into this. Adrenaline is a powerful drug and I'm currently pumped full of it.

The boardwalk passes by more quickly than usual, or maybe I'm just not paying a lot of attention. I pass the turnoff to Elliot and Leon's street and decide to keep going. I barely feel my feet hitting the pavement.

Around the three-mile mark, I pause to stretch. Or at least, that's what I tell myself. I know that at least part of the reason I stop is because I don't want to return too quickly. I'm not ready. I need more time alone. So I sit on a bench and stare out at the lake. It's still too early for people to be at the beach, and it's a bit early in the season for that anyway. No one would be lying out—they'd be walking, running, or fishing.

I watch seagulls forage for food, fly to a new spot, try

again. I watch the waves come in and crash on the beach. I let the rising sun warm my skin.

When the adrenaline starts to crash, I finally face reality.

Last night, I slept with someone.

Unequivocally, it was a terrible idea. I'm a widow. He's a widower. I'm a fucking *mess*. He's much more put together than I am. I'm trying to muster up the courage to get through every day. He's rebuilding his life.

Oh, and there's the small matter that he sleeps across the fucking landing from me. I *can't* get away from him.

I don't even have an excuse. I can't even tell myself that I'd had too much to drink and that impaired my decision-making skills. And truthfully, with the way he was trying to pause long enough to think about what we were doing, he probably wouldn't have let things get very far if I'd had more than that one drink, anyway.

Goddammit, he's such a good person.

Honorable and kind. Gentle.

And also hot.

I feel my body heat up and I fan my face. I'd like to tell myself that I'm just hot from the run, but I know it's a lie. The flashbacks in my head are hot enough to boil my blood.

I'm fully aware that I was the one who pushed us forward. I literally told him to *stop talking and start fucking.*

I drop my head into my hands as a fresh wave of embarrassment washes over me. I'm barely keeping the guilt at bay. I'm trying to remind myself that my husband is dead, that I didn't do anything *wrong*, but then I'm just reminding myself that *my husband is dead* and that makes me feel absolutely wretched.

And that makes me want to do dirty things with Liam to make me forget. Because last night? I wasn't thinking about any of my problems. I was thinking about how hot it was.

How hot *he* is. And how *good* he felt. How good he was at all of the things.

My self-loathing groan is audible and it makes someone walking on the boardwalk turn their head. I force a tiny smile and a half-hearted wave.

I've already been gone for an hour. I need to head back to the house.

Maybe if I'm lucky, I can avoid him. For how long, I'm not sure. But as far as I'm concerned, the longer the better.

* * *

I DON'T TAKE out my earbuds when I get home. I go straight to the kitchen and fill a glass with water. I drink half of it while staring out the window above the sink, music still playing, my mind desperately searching for a reason to leave the house today. I finally decide to shower and head to work.

I refill my water glass and turn to leave the kitchen, only to find Liam standing just a few feet away, scaring the ever-loving shit out of me. A ridiculous, over-the-top gasp escapes me. I jump backward and jerk my arms, promptly spilling most of the water in my glass.

"Shit!"

Smooth, Kate. Real smooth.

"Sorry…" I hear Liam faintly through my earbuds.

I set the glass down on the counter and shake my hands off in the sink. I feel him sliding past me to get paper towels and it sends a shiver up my spine. When I turn, I see him kneeling down to wipe up the water and I finally take out my earbuds.

"Sorry," he repeats. "I didn't mean to scare you."

"No, it's not your fault." I grab some paper towels to help him wipe up my mess.

When we stand, our eyes meet and I'm so *acutely* aware that he's seen me naked. That I've seen *him* naked.

That he is hot both naked and clothed.

Fuck!

"I can take those." I reach out for the paper towels he's holding and then throw them in the trash. "Thanks."

"No problem," he says. He's watching me with curious, cautious eyes. I want to run away from him and I also want to kiss his gorgeous face and those stupid soft lips.

Why were his lips so soft? Men's lips are never that soft!

"Looks like you went for a run," he says. He's trying to break the ice and I appreciate it because I feel incapable of doing so in this moment.

"Yeah," I confirm.

"How far did you go?"

"Um…" I bite my lip while I try to figure it out. I see his eyes dip to my mouth and my conflicting emotions double. *How far did you run, Kate? For fuck's sake, spit out a number!*

"About six miles, I guess."

His eyes meet mine again and he smiles. "Wow… really kick-starting your day, aren't you?"

A tiny giggle—a fucking *giggle*—escapes my lips. *Who even are you, Katherine?!*

"Yeah, I suppose," is all I can muster.

"You've got to be starving. How about I make some brunch?"

I blink at him. *Is he seriously offering to make me brunch right now?*

The silence stretches between us, but he breaks it before it gets too awkward.

"If you have plans, that's fine. I just… I mean, I'm hungry. I imagine you need to eat after running six miles."

"Um…" I don't want to be rude. And I did have sex with this man last night…

If my brain could scream, it would. I mentally face-palm myself. Outwardly, I just scratch at my temple.

"I don't have concrete plans. I was thinking of showering and heading into work for a bit."

He nods. "All right. Well, I'm going to make some food while you're in the shower. If you want to eat before you head out, you're welcome to it."

That sounds reasonable enough. Right?

"Okay… yeah, that sounds… that sounds great." My hand absentmindedly heads toward my hair, which serves as a stark reminder of how disgusting I currently am. "Thanks."

"Excellent."

I force a nod. "Okay, I'm going to get cleaned up." I avoid his eyes as I grab my phone and my earbuds before trying *not* to sprint toward the stairs.

When I get to my room, I shut the door tightly behind me and head to the bathroom to start the water, muttering to myself the whole way.

"Seriously, what is wrong with you, Katherine? You sleep with your roommate—your roommate with the dead wife. And did you forget about your dead husband? That's not making this situation any better."

I rip the sweaty clothes off my body and throw them in the hamper with more force than necessary.

"Having brunch with him won't be awkward or anything like that," I continue. "Fuck, you are so *stupid*, Kate."

In the shower, I try to think of literally any topic to discuss over brunch. The weather—it's supposed to be a beautiful day. I could ask him about work. Or about his plans with his family this afternoon. He mentioned last night that he's supposed to see them today.

Last night.

Unbidden, flashbacks slam into my mind. His wicked

smirk as his head descended between my legs, his broad shoulders above me, his hand in my hair.

Heat that has nothing to do with the temperature of the water spreads through my low belly.

I have absolutely no idea what to do with all of these conflicting feelings. I feel like I could combust. Again, I feel an intense urge to get *out*.

I should have gotten up the moment I started to feel sleepy last night. I should have gone back to my own room. The moment Liam's hand enveloped mine, I realized how badly I'd missed physical contact—the touch of a warm hand, the weight of a man on top of me, soft lips pressed into mine. *And his lips are so fucking soft.*

I know I'm lonely. But I could have chosen *literally anyone else* to fill a lonely void and my dumbass chooses the man who lives in my house who is also grieving. This is very possibly the worst decision I've ever made.

We'd developed such an easy, natural friendship and I fucking ruined it. The *one* person who maybe understood me better than anyone else on this planet right now and I destroyed it with one bad decision. I wish I could go back and undo it.

Even as the thought crosses my mind, I know it's not true.

I don't want to erase it. But I do wish it weren't so goddamned complicated.

I decide I will eat whatever he makes for brunch. He's right—I do need to eat. But I also need to get the fuck out of this house. So I finish my shower, put on tinted moisturizer and mascara, throw on some clothes, and head downstairs.

When I walk into the kitchen, Liam is standing at the sink, washing dishes. The unmistakable scent of bacon is in the air and my whole mouth fills with saliva. I do my best to convince myself the overactive salivary glands are a result of the bacon and not the tall man at the sink with the talented tongue.

Goddammit, Kate! Be cool!

Putting one foot in front of the other (because, *yes, Katherine, that is how you walk*), I make my way to the coffeepot and grab a mug from the cupboard.

"Hey!" Liam looks up at me with the most sincere smile, disarming me immediately. I have no idea what it is about him that calms me down. He can make me relax so easily. "How was your shower?"

"Good…" I hear myself respond. "It was good." I pour myself some coffee and then get out another mug for Liam, since I don't see another out on the counter. "Here you go," I say as I slide the mug closer to the sink.

"Thanks." He shuts off the water and is drying his hands when the oven timer goes off. "Ahh…" Sliding an oven mitt onto one hand, he opens the oven and transports a tray of bacon onto the stove. Then, he pulls a tray full of waffles out of the warming drawer underneath.

"Here are the waffles. You can help yourself. There's syrup, fruit, and powdered sugar on the table over there," he says, gesturing over to the breakfast nook. "Help yourself and have a seat. I'll get the bacon ready."

"Oh… wow." I hadn't even noticed the spread on the table. "This is amazing… I wasn't…" I scratch at my temple again. "I wasn't expecting all of this." Setting my coffee down on the table, I study his hard work.

Never once had a man made me brunch after we slept together for the first time. Not even Nick. I can't remember what we did the morning after our first time together, but it definitely didn't involve either of us cooking. Chances are, we went out to brunch, or we rushed off to our respective workplaces. We were both so busy all of the time… going to work early for this client or that client, rushing to get reports out, putting extra hours in to catch up on something we'd neglected.

The contrast here is not lost on me.

While we never realized how little time we might have, Liam was acutely aware.

Liam appears next to me and sets the plate of bacon down on the table. "You all right?"

Snapping out of my thoughts, I look up to his beautiful eyes and feel that sense of calm he always seems to provide for me. "Yeah… yeah. Sorry."

I turn toward the cabinets and get out two plates, then grab a waffle and sit down at the table. I scoop berries on top, followed by a (heavy) dusting of powdered sugar. Before I dig in, I steal a glance at Liam. He's pouring syrup on his waffle.

"This is really nice, Liam. Thank you."

He looks up at me and smiles. "It's my pleasure."

I manage a small smile and then we both tuck into our meals. We sit in companionable silence, each thumbing through separate sections of the newspaper. I feel like he's intentionally giving me space, even though we're sitting in the same room with only a table between us. I appreciate it.

"Here's the crossword." I hand over the page to him when I find it.

"Oh, thanks." He takes it with brief eye contact and a smile, then goes back to the article he was reading.

When we've finished eating and the paper had been properly riffled through, Liam clears his throat.

"So um…" he says hesitantly. "Do you think we should talk about last night?"

My brain is screaming again. I try to feign calmness by folding up the section of the newspaper I'd been reading and set it on the table.

I swallow the lump in my throat. "Um… I-I don't know. I guess?"

We stare at each other for a moment, the silence stretching before we both chuckle at the awkward moment.

"Are you all right?" he asks gently.

I let myself think about it for a moment and then shrug a shoulder. "I guess, yeah. Maybe. I don't know." I'm not fine. Obviously, I know it. He knows it. I need time to process. "What about you?" I ask.

He also takes a moment to think about it, and then nods. "Yeah. I'm okay." He glances away before continuing, his voice shyer than it was before. "I, um… haven't been with anyone since Jill died, so… I don't know where you are, but I wanted to let you know what's going on with me."

I let the gravity of his words sink in before I respond. "Me too. Same." I feel relieved after I say it.

He nods. "Anyway, I just wanted to make sure you were doing okay. You were gone this morning when I woke up and I was worried about you."

I can see in his eyes that he's telling the truth. He really was worried about me.

"That's kind of you. I'm sorry I—I quite literally ran away."

Liam chuckles. "A few miles away."

I roll my eyes at myself. "I needed to clear my head."

"I understand," he says. And I know he does.

With one more nod, I stand and gather the dishes. "Let me clean this up. Then I'm going into the office for a little bit."

While I clean up, he puts leftovers in the fridge. There are waffles we can eat later, but the bacon is long gone, obviously.

"You're… going to work on a Saturday?" he asks.

I look up from the plate I'm rinsing. "Yeah."

He hesitates before continuing. "Are you going to work because you really have something to do or because you want to get away from me?"

My stupid eyes burn. *How is he this emotionally intelligent?*

Again, I swallow a lump in my throat. "I'm going to take over the business one day. I always have something to do at work."

Liam stares at me for a long moment before responding. "But you *also* need some space." It's not a question. It's a statement. One we both know is true.

"Yes," I acknowledge.

"Okay. Whatever you need." He turns to leave but stops before adding, "Like I said, I'm seeing my brother and his family this afternoon, but I'll be back tonight… if you want to talk or anything."

I nod and attempt to thank him, but it comes out as more of a whisper. I don't really want to talk about this. With anyone. At all.

"All right. Enjoy your afternoon, Kate."

And with that, he turns around and walks up the stairs and even though I'm trying *so hard* to convince myself to finish my task, I can't stop staring at him. When he disappears from my view, I find myself staring into space, lost in a tornado of confusing thoughts and feelings.

It's Wednesday and as per court mandate, I'm sitting in Gwen's office, waiting for her to stroll in.

Something therapists conveniently forget to tell you is that your appointments aren't *actually* an hour. It's more like fifty minutes. Maybe fifty-five. Those extra few minutes are so you can pay your bill and reschedule.

Usually, during this time frame, I'm trying to remind

myself that I'm here to stay out of jail. That I have to at least *try* to put in some effort, so Gwen's reports to the court are in order. Literally, one negative note from her could mean jail time for me.

But today, I'm a ball of anxious energy. I need to talk to someone about what happened with Liam, but I don't know who to talk to. I just can't keep it buried down deep anymore.

I'm staring out the window, stuck in a downward spiral of bullshit (that Gwen would probably call negative self-talk), when she walks in and shuts the door behind her.

"Kate! It's good to see you."

"Hi," is the only thing I can manage.

As usual, Gwen begins our session with a recap and a warm smile. "So… the last time we spoke, we were talking about how—"

"I slept with Liam," I blurt. I don't need a fucking recap. I need her to tell me what to do. How to feel. What to think. How to react.

Gwen looks up at me with surprise in her eyes, but obviously trying to keep a neutral face. After a moment of silence, she says, "Oh."

That's it. Just… *oh*.

I sit there, staring at her while she watches me carefully. It feels like a solid five minutes, but it's probably only a few seconds.

"Okay," she tries again. "And how did that… come about?"

"I don't even know. I… still kind of can't believe it happened." My hands start fidgeting of their own volition, wringing together, flexing into fists and unclenching. Anything to get out the nervous tension shooting through my body. "We've been spending more time together recently. At night, I've been watching baseball games with him. He used to play, which I didn't realize. Anyway, we've been watching the games together—sometimes in his room, which has been *totally* innocuous, but Friday night, I fell asleep in his bed, apparently. When I woke up, Liam was lying down, too and my arm was around him and his hand was holding mine..." I swallow as I get to the bottom line. "And then..."

I didn't really know how to finish that sentence. I couldn't very well say it *just happened* because I was a very willing and very active participant, even if I did tell him to keep his mouth shut. I *wanted* it. It was a decision I made consciously. I could have stopped at many different points, and he definitely tried to stop me. But I didn't *want* to stop. I wanted it. I wanted him.

You also wanted to forget.

I shove the tiny voice in my head to the side and look back at Gwen.

"And then what?" she prompts.

I groan and let my head fall into my hands. "And then I *wanted* to have sex with him," I admit.

"And how do you feel about that?"

"I have no fucking clue," I say, pressing my fingers into my temples. "I'm kinda freaked out, to be totally honest."

"Because you slept with someone or because you *wanted* to sleep with someone?" Gwen asks.

I pause to think about that, watching a couple of ducks land in the pond outside the window. She's asking a legitimately important question and I don't want to answer it.

I see her tilt her head out of the corner of my eye, still patiently waiting. Silently observing.

"Both, I suppose."

"Is Liam the first person you've been with since Nick died?" She speaks in an incredibly gentle voice, like she is worried she'll startle me.

I nod.

"Do you feel like you did something wrong?" Gwen continues. "Like you cheated on Nick?"

"Kind of…"

"Well, it's perfectly normal to feel that way, but… you do know that's *not* the case. Right?"

With a big sigh, I admit that I do know. "But I still feel weird about it," I add.

"How did you react afterward?"

Oh god.

My head lands in my hands again. "Ugh… I snuck out of his bedroom and then went for a run. I literally ran away from him. And when I got back, he offered to make me brunch. Fucking *brunch*, Gwen."

Gwen's eyebrows shot up, amusement dancing in her eyes.

"What's wrong with brunch?"

"Nothing is wrong with brunch. It's very possibly the best kind of meal, but *he* fed me the morning after."

She does that head tilt thing again. "Are you confused by his actions?"

"Yes!" I wince when I realize I basically shouted that word.

"Why?"

"Because why would he do that? Does he think this is going somewhere?"

Gwen shrugs. "I'm sure he was trying to be nice. Helpful, even. But if you want to know the answer to that question, you're going to have to ask him."

I scowl at her.

"I can see you're very excited by that prospect," she jokes. My therapist has *jokes* now.

"Gwen…" I whine.

"What's going on in your mind? Jumbled or organized, whatever. What's going through your brain?"

"I'm—" I huff and rub at my temples. "I'm mad at myself, I guess."

I expect Gwen to say something—anything. But she stays silent, so I continue.

"Everything was going well. And now it's different. I'm so uncomfortable around him. All I can think about is that we've seen each other naked."

"Did you feel that way after sleeping with Nick for the first time?"

I try to think back to the early days with Nick, but I just don't remember that kind of detail. Why would I have committed the morning after we slept together to memory unless it was something remarkable?

"I'm sure it was awkward." I shrug. "I don't really remember feeling mortified or that it had been a mistake. Just the normal awkwardness that comes after you've slept with someone for the first time. You know... being self-conscious and stuff."

"You said 'mortified.' Do you feel mortified now?"

"Yeah, a little," I admit.

"Why?"

"Because he's my roommate and I'm an *idiot*."

Gwen is shaking her head before I even finish the last word. "You're not an idiot."

"Well, it wasn't a *smart* idea."

She fucking chuckles and I mock glare at her. She pulls her lips between her teeth to dampen her smile, but it's still in her eyes.

"It is what it is. It happened. Now you have to figure out how to move forward."

"Yeah, I guess," I concede.

"Have you guys talked about it at all?"

"Very briefly. When we were eating brunch, he asked me if I was all right. He said I was his first since Jill."

"Hmm…" Gwen scribbles something in her notepad. "And you haven't discussed it again?"

"No."

"Have you slept with him again?"

"No."

Gwen hesitates before asking her next question. "Do you want to?"

I honestly don't know how to answer that question. My mouth opens and closes as I try to start, but I quit before I can get a word out.

"Okay, let me put it a different way. He asked if you were all right… are you?"

My head dropping into my hands seems to be my new favorite seated position. "Have no idea," I say through my hands. After taking a moment to gather my thoughts, I look up at Gwen. "I suppose I'm probably not okay. I'm still in love with Nick, but the other night, I slept with someone else. It feels wrong on some level."

I avert my eyes and stare out the window, trying to decide just how much I want to reveal here. But then I remember that Gwen isn't allowed to talk to anyone about what I discuss within these four walls and suddenly I feel emboldened. Like anything I say in here is a wash—a tree falling in the forest. Did I really say it if no one can corroborate it?

Fuck it.

"At the time though… it didn't. Feel wrong, I mean. It felt *good.*" That same sense of calm when I'm around Liam washes through me. "It felt good to be touched. To have someone kiss me like that again. To feel a good—genuinely good—man hold me. It's been almost a *year.* It's not even about sex necessarily… I'm lonely. I miss Nick. I always will. But he's not coming back. He's not going to walk through the door and sweep me off my feet or whatever romantic bullshit would happen in a fairy tale." I take a deep breath and let it out slowly. "My husband is dead. But I still can't believe I did this."

Gwen and I just look at each other for a moment. It looks like she's waiting to see if I'm finished talking and frankly, I'm waiting for her to tell me what to do. So finally, I just ask her exactly that.

"Well, if you're not sure how you feel about this, I wouldn't necessarily think it's a good idea to do it again. You may not want to talk to Liam about the way you feel, but I highly recommend you do. Maybe tell him that you're not ready to be involved in this kind of relationship right now and that you hope you can remain friends."

"You're right. I don't want to have that conversation."

Gwen smiles. "It's not an easy one. But it *is* the most effective if you don't want it to happen again. Or, in this case, if you're not *sure* how you feel about it happening again. You can set some boundaries with him."

I squint at her, trying to think of a better solution. "Or… I could just avoid him."

"That's not exactly a permanent solution. In fact, it's not a solution at all."

Fucking therapists.

"And if I decide I want to keep doing it?" I ask quietly, unable to look at her.

"Well… if that's something both of you want, then there's nothing to stop you. But I still think you should talk to him about how you feel. You've both been through a lot in the past year. You're going to need to discuss it so you can try to prevent further trauma."

I watch her facial expression carefully as she finishes her thought. "But you think it's a bad idea," I say.

Gwen smiles again. "It's not about what I think. It's about what *you* want and what *you* decide is best for you. *My* job is to help you figure that part out."

1 8

CONSEQUENCES BE DAMNED

Kate

When I get home from work on Friday, Liam's car is in the garage. We haven't seen each other much over the past week. I'm not going to lie, I've been avoiding him and I'm sure he knows it. I'm also very sure he's trying to give me the space I need.

It's time though. I've avoided him long enough. It's not fair to him.

I can hear the TV in the living room when I close the kitchen door. I set my purse down and peer around the fireplace to find Liam sitting on the couch, eyes on the ball game. But when he sees me, he bolts upright.

"Hey."

"Hey." I glance up at the TV. "How's the game going?"

"Not bad. They're up. They got an error in the third though."

I nod before turning my gaze back to him. He's nervous. He's watching me like I might bolt.

His instincts aren't entirely wrong.

"You're welcome to sit down and watch with me… if you want." His voice is hesitant, but I know he's being genuine. He's not just offering to be nice. Liam is genuine to his core.

I don't really have to think about it very hard.

"Sure."

"Yeah?"

"Yeah. I'm going to grab a drink first," I say, jutting my thumb over my shoulder toward the kitchen.

"Okay."

I turn back to the kitchen and pour myself a glass of red wine from the bottle on the counter. As I walk past one of the glass-front cabinets on my way back to the living room, I catch a glimpse of myself. Frowning, I tousle my hair and try to tame some of the waves in a flattering manner. It's been a long day.

And why am I trying to look pretty for him?

I ignore the voice in my head and go back to the living room. I choose a distance away from him on the couch that looks… safe. But not an awkward distance.

We sit in silence for a bit, just watching the game. Liam is sipping his beer occasionally, which makes me think about his mouth, and then I have to try to intentionally divert my thoughts.

Aside from the sounds of the baseball game, interspersed with commercials, neither of us speaks for a long time. The silence between us goes on for so long that it starts to feel… tense.

And my first thought for how to break the tension?

Climb in his lap.

Not smart, Katherine! Jesus, what is the matter with you?!

"It's awkward…" Liam finally says, looking over at me.

"Yeah, it is," I admit, meeting his gaze. I could feel the heat in my cheeks just as much as I could feel his eyes shift to my flushed skin.

"I don't want it to be," he continues softly.

"Me either."

"So how do we not let it be awkward?"

"I have no idea."

A broad smile breaks out across his face. "At least we're on the same page."

I nod before choking out the question that's been kicking around in my head the whole week. "Do you um…" I scratch at my temple. "Do you feel guilty at all?"

Liam is quiet for a moment, watching my face carefully, probably trying to figure out what to say that won't make me run out the back door. "A bit, yeah," he finally admits before falling silent again for a moment. "But I shouldn't. She'd want me to live my life. Move on. Be happy."

I keep my eyes on him as his gaze moves to his beer glass. "Do you?" he asks.

I can't get any words out, but when he looks at me, I nod my head woodenly.

"Kate, I don't want to make you feel uncomfortable. It happened. It never has to happen again if you don't want it to."

I nod because I have absolutely no idea what to say. Fuck, he's so sweet. So kind. So thoughtful.

He pats the space between us once and then stands. "All right, I'm going to go upstairs and finish this last inning. I'll see you tomorrow."

"Okay." There's nothing more to say, really.

His smile is tight as he heads toward the stairs. I remain glued to the couch for a few minutes, Gwen's words running through my mind. After I finish my wine, I get a glass of water, check that all the doors are locked, and head upstairs.

Through the crack in the door, I can see the light from the TV dancing on the wall of Liam's room. I pause in front of his door for a moment.

Gwen didn't tell me *not* to sleep with him again. She told me it was my responsibility to figure out what's best for me. And honestly, I don't know the answer to that question. But what I *do* know is that I love the way I *feel* when I'm with Liam. I want more of that feeling. More of what I felt last week when we were in bed together.

With that thought, I raise my hand to knock on his door, but in that moment, the door swings open.

I jump back with a gasp.

"Oh!" Based on Liam's expression, he's just as startled. "I didn't hear you come up. I was just going to grab some water. I'm sorry... I hope I didn't scare you too badly." He smiles, his eyes searching mine, and suddenly, I want nothing more than to sink into his arms and slide my tongue against his.

That feeling is addicting and it's very clear to me that I already have a problem.

"It's... it's okay," I stammer out. "I was kind of in my own world."

"Okay." He nods. But a tiny frown mars his forehead. "Are you all right?"

I nod quickly. Too quickly. "Yeah... yeah, I... yeah. I'm fine."

Smooth, Kate.

He looks skeptical but doesn't push it. "Okay. I'm going to get some water."

"Sure, yeah." I step aside so he can get past me unhindered.

Liam disappears into the darkness while I silently berate myself on the landing.

Seriously, what the hell was the plan there, dumbass?

Beaker gracefully bounces up the stairs and winds his body through my ankles.

"Hey, buddy." I crouch down and rub his tiny head. He purrs happily and pushes his head into my hand. That's how Liam finds us when he comes back up the stairs.

"Hey, Beaker!"

To my surprise, Beaker leaves me and goes over to Liam. I watch in stunned silence as he rubs his side against Liam's leg and looks up expectantly, waiting for Liam's hand to touch him. Being the softy that he is, Liam obliges, kneeling down to pet him.

"Wow… I see how it is, Beaker," I quip.

Liam lets out a low chuckle and my belly flips over. "We're good buddies these days, aren't we?" Beaker lies down on the floor and twists his body around playfully, waiting for one of us to find the audacity to touch his belly. "He's so sweet once you get to know him."

That makes me smile. "Yeah, he is. He takes a while to warm up, but he's a great cat."

"He is," Liam agrees. He rubs the bridge of Beaker's nose just the way he likes it and the purring intensifies.

I try not to take offense, but I can't help but joke about it. "Jeez, Beaker… you don't need me at all, do you?"

"Nah, don't say that. He and I have just been bonding lately."

"Really?"

Where the fuck have I been?

Hiding from Liam, the voice in my head reminds me. I mentally swat at it with the back of my hand.

"Yeah. We hang out when I get home from work."

My chest warms just a tiny bit. Before I even know it, I'm sinking down to the floor to sit with them on the landing, watching this big strong man pet my erratic cat with a gentle, loving hand.

"I'm glad you guys are getting along."

Liam looks at me with a blinding smile and that warm feeling in my chest gets hotter, spreading up to my shoulders and down into my belly. I can't look away from his gorgeous green eyes. It's like they've hypnotized me.

Somewhere in the back of my mind, I know we're just sitting on the floor outside our respective bedrooms, staring at each other. The air between us is getting more charged by the second. Goose bumps break out over my skin.

Flashbacks from last week go through my mind one after the other. His hands. His mouth. The perfect mix of tender and rough.

An obnoxious meow snaps me out of my flashback. I swallow a copious amount of saliva in my mouth (*when did that happen?*) and look down to Beaker, who is aggressively pushing his head into my arm and kneading my leg.

I hear Liam clear his throat as I stare at my cockblocking cat. "It's getting late." He's suddenly standing up and pulling his T-shirt down over his groin.

Based on how hot my face feels right now, I'm sure I'm red as a tomato. I stand up, bringing Beaker with me. *Little fucker.*

"Yeah, you're right."

"Good night, Kate." He takes a step toward his door, making room for me to pass.

"Good night, Liam."

When I walk across the landing, I can feel his eyes on me. But as I turn to close my door, he's gone, replaced by the light from the TV dancing on the wall through the crack in his bedroom door.

I don't see him much the next day. We're both doing our own thing. I have dinner out and am surprised that he's not home when I get there. Out of habit at this point, I check the baseball schedule and see that the game started at 4:05 p.m.

and is long over by now. (They lost, in case you were wondering.)

I'm not tired enough to go to bed yet, so I sit on the couch watching HGTV with a glass of wine and try not to think about Liam. I don't know where he is and it's absolutely none of my business. But for reasons I cannot and do not want to understand, I wish he were here. With me. Sitting on the couch. Watching TV.

I watch one twin get a good deal on a house while the other renovates it into the house of the couple's dreams. It's fun to see an eyesore become something incredible. I love seeing the transformations. And it's not as if I live in anything *close* to an eyesore, but it does make me want to make some changes in the house.

Sometime during the second episode, I hear the kitchen door open and close. When Liam comes into view, I straighten up on the couch. He smiles that beautiful, disarming smile and I feel my chest heat again.

I should really see a doctor about that. Heart disease is the number one killer of women and my husband literally died of a heart attack.

"Hey," he says. "I thought you'd still be out."

I can't help but return his smile. "Nah. We had dinner. Elliot has a bunch of stuff going on tomorrow, so we didn't stay out too late. I came home and started watching HGTV. Been here ever since."

Liam glances at the TV and smirks. "Sounds like fun."

I try to gather all my courage, taking a deep breath and swallowing my nerves. "Join me?" I ask.

He only waits a half second before answering with a simple, "sure." He sits down a couple of feet away from me and starts asking about the logistics of the show.

I explain it to him, including the part where they trick the couple into thinking they can afford a McMansion before bringing them to the crushing reality that they could never afford anything like that.

"Oh, there's two of them." Liam suddenly frowns.

I find that incredibly endearing. "Yeah, they're twins. The clean-cut one is the realtor and the scruffy one is a contractor."

We watch the episode together, him asking me questions about the show and me answering them. Both of us make comments on the design choices and the final product. My wine is long gone, but I don't refill it. I stick to water instead. Liam never gets a drink.

When that episode ends, we watch another. The tension from last night has eased a bit and I'm chagrined to realize that Gwen was right. I hadn't wanted to talk about my feelings with Liam, but I did… at least a little bit. We didn't go as deep as she told me I should, but it's my life, goddammit.

I still don't know where he went tonight, and I find myself far more curious than I have any right to be. So I ask.

"I just went over to my brother's. Riled his kids up. Made bedtime a disaster for him and my sister-in-law."

That draws a laugh from me. "I'm sure they appreciated that."

"I did my best," he says proudly.

Somehow, I know that's true, and not just in the context of this conversation. Liam strikes me as the kind of person who just does their best all the time.

"How was dinner? Where did you guys go?"

"We went to that newish place on Columbus. It's called Fire."

"Oh yeah, I read about that place recently. Was it any good?"

"It was, yeah. I had salmon. Elliot got chicken. Leon got a steak that was practically still mooing."

"Sounds about right." He smirks.

"It does, doesn't it?" I laugh.

He's quiet for just a *tiny* bit too long before asking, "Just the three of you?"

It's been a hot minute since I've dated, but even to me, this sounds like he's fishing. Like he wants to know if I was on a date. Knowing that he might be a little bit jealous does things to my low belly that I'm not particularly proud of.

"Another friend of theirs who's in town for the weekend."

"Oh… the one from Chicago?"

"Yeah, Will," I confirm.

"Will… I'm pretty sure I've met him before."

"He's in town every now and then. He's nice." I shrug.

"I'm glad you guys had a good time."

He seems unsatisfied with my answers, but he doesn't seem angry. He just looks like he's… unsettled.

"It was fine."

When the episode ends, I glance at my watch. "I should get to bed."

With a confirmation glance to his own wrist, he agrees. "Yeah, it's getting late."

I turn off the TV, switch off the lamp on the end table, and double-check that the sliding door is locked. I turn around to find Liam standing still on the other side of the room, hands in his pockets. He smiles—just a small twitch of his mouth.

I move closer to him, stopping when I reach the couch and return his tiny smile.

"What are you up to tomorrow?" he asks.

"Nothing, really." I slide my hands in the back pockets of my jeans and watch his eyes dip to my hips.

"Just a chill day?"

I nod.

"Maybe we could chill together?"

"Yeah."

We're staring at each other again. There are feet between us and yet my heart is pounding, my lungs can't get enough air, and I'm itching to touch him.

The moment stretches and I can't stand it any longer. I want to feel him on me again.

Is that what he wants?

"You're not going upstairs," I say quietly.

He shakes his head slowly.

"Why not?"

A muscle in his jaw tics. "I don't know," he says. But the way his eyes dip to my mouth betrays the actual reason.

His words from the previous night float through my brain. *It never has to happen again if you don't want it to.* Not *we*. *You*. He's giving me the choice. The power.

I nod and then slowly close the distance between us, stopping just inches in front of him. Gently, smoothly, I pull one of his hands out of his pocket and intertwine my fingers with his.

When I look up into his eyes, they're perfectly calm. He doesn't seem nervous or tentative or conflicted. No, there's nothing but patience in his expression and heat in his eyes.

My brain tries to remind me that Liam and I haven't talked about the long-term impact of our actions. That we haven't talked about what I want and don't want. That I don't have a clue what he wants or doesn't want. That we're both kind of a mess… trying to recover from extreme trauma relatively early in our adult lives.

But honestly? I can't be bothered with any of that right now.

What I know deep in my soul is that I feel *good* when I'm with Liam. Even when nothing physical is happening between us. Liam makes me feel like I'm not completely broken. Like I'm more than a shell of my former self. Or at least… that the shell remaining is still worthwhile.

And that? Well, I'm not going to ignore it.

Another glance to my mouth encourages me just enough to take the final step forward so our bodies are almost touching. I slide my free hand up his chest to his neck, guiding his face toward mine and gently press my lips to his.

His free hand finds my waist, pulling me flush against him.

I tease his bottom lip with my tongue, encouraging him to open up for me. He does it willingly but slowly. Enough to tease me. To remind me what's waiting for me if I keep going.

And there's that fucking heat again, shooting straight through my body. There's the gentle warmth in my chest, but also a searing shot down my spine, right to my core.

I thread my fingers into his hair and hold him closer. In response, his grip on my waist tightens, pressing his hard torso into mine.

Fuck, he's a good kisser.

His tongue dances with mine—licking, touching, teasing. His teeth gently bite down on my bottom lip.

Sliding his hand to my tailbone, he presses into me. I can feel him hard against my low belly and all thoughts fly from my head. I don't care about a single thing other than the man I'm touching.

He's still a bit tentative. Like he's moving slowly out of fear that he'll spook me. It's as if he's showing me he's interested if I choose to move forward, but he's letting me lead.

I pull back slightly so our lips part, but I reach back up on my toes to take that perfect bottom lip back into my mouth and suck on it gently. I hear his breath hitch and feel his arm tighten around my body.

I force myself to keep pulling back, but slowly, so I don't give him the impression that I'm trying to stop.

Instead, I step to the side, still holding his hand, and lead him up the stairs to his bedroom.

The second time is even better than the first. There's less awkwardness. More confidence on both sides. He makes me come on his tongue and his fingers before sinking into me and I ride the high because this is the best I've felt in *so long*.

I don't know what I'm doing and honestly, I don't care.

Liam is the calm in my storm. My life vest when I'm drowning.

Right now, he's everything I need.

And I'm not going to think about the consequences.

19

FEELS LIKE HOME

Liam

"Uncle Liam, can I get popcorn?"

We've finally reached the point in the year where the weather is getting more consistently beautiful. It's not quite summer, but the trees and the grass are getting greener and flowers are blooming. Baseball is well underway and the home team is doing pretty well.

This time of year is in a league of its own. There's all this great weather up ahead—it's only the beginning. And that feels apropos right now. I'm facing new beginnings, just like the world around me.

Spring is full of so much hope.

Against many odds, my *life* feels hopeful right now.

I peek down at Jackson as we walk through the crowded stadium. It's an afternoon game on a Sunday—always a family day. There are plenty of activities for kids and they get to run the bases afterward. I haven't been able to do this very often in the past, living in Chicago. And they're finally old enough to walk around on their own and generally follow instructions. Sorta.

"That's not really my call, little man." I burst his bubble.

I hear my brother's laugh drift back to us. He and Josh are walking in front of Jackson and me. He turns his head to talk over his shoulder to his younger son.

"Maybe later, Jack. You need an actual meal first. Popcorn is a snack."

"*Fine.*" Jackson's acquiescence is full of annoyance. I pull my lips between my teeth to keep from laughing. I shouldn't encourage him.

My dad's mirthful laugh reverberates behind me.

I look over my shoulder to see what he's laughing at. I know immediately he's laughing at my brother's expense. My mom has told me how funny it is to watch your children raise their own children, and since you're viewing it from such a different perspective, things seem more *funny* than *obnoxious* at that point.

He catches my eye for a brief moment and it confirms my thought process. There's straight-up glee in his eyes, like he's enjoying every moment of his son getting his karma.

I roll my eyes and shake my head, returning my attention to the throng of people in front of us.

Joe and I are very close in age—we're only eighteen months apart—but we closely align with the stereotypes of birth order. I, being the oldest, have always been the most responsible, while Joe, being the second-born and the youngest, has always had a more rebellious streak.

Unfortunately for Joe, his kids inherited the same roles. Josh is the older of the two and very cool, calm, and collected, especially for his age. Jackson is the wild child, and as a result, he and Joe often butt heads. When I'm around, I try to handle Jackson just to give my brother a break.

Joe's wife finds all of this hilarious.

My dad and Joe have baseball games with the boys down to a science. Seats are located first. Dad stays in the seats with the boys while Joe (now with me) goes to get hot dogs.

And beer, obviously. We're at a baseball game surrounded by tens of thousands of people with two young boys who take after me and my brother. If you're not having a beer, you're a hell of a lot stronger than we are.

But just one. We need our wits about us due to the aforementioned young boys.

"How you doin'?" Joe asks me while we wait for the hot dogs.

The question is pointed. His voice low. He's not even trying to act like he's not asking about grieving, moving back home, and then moving in with a near stranger.

Not that she's much of a stranger anymore.

"I'm doin' fine, bro. You don't have to worry about me."

I'm looking at the menu up ahead of us hanging from giant boards, but I can feel his eyes on me.

"What are you going to get?" I try to distract him. "They have bratwurst. You can get sautéed peppers on it. That sounds really good."

When he doesn't respond, I finally look over to him, trying to pretend like I *don't* know his eyes are boring into my head.

"Are you all right?" I ask, trying to get on the offensive.

His eyes narrow. "Are *you*?"

"Yes," I say. "I'm doing fine. Really, you don't have to worry about me." I return my gaze to the menu and begin to contemplate the outrageously priced beer selection.

"How's your living situation working out?" he asks. "It's been a few months now."

He's fishing. He knows I know it.

I do my best to keep my face neutral. It's none of Joe's business what Kate and I are doing. *Not that I even know what we're doing.* Even if I knew, I wouldn't tell him. At least not yet.

"It's great, actually. I have a room with an en suite. The cat has finally warmed up to me. The land is beautiful." I throw him a glance and a smirk. "I live on the fucking lake, man. Doesn't get much better."

He makes a noncommittal noise. "Well, you're always welcome at our place. I know it's tight, but we don't mind at all."

I try to hide my smile as we move forward with the line.

"I know… I'm not trying to reject your generosity, Joe. I just wanted some space of my own."

"Yeah, but you moved in with someone else."

"Her house is huge. She works a lot. We've literally gone days with only saying a handful of words to each other."

His eyes narrow in a suspicious manner. I decide to deflect again.

"Are you *sure* you're okay?"

"Bro, I haven't even seen your new digs," he blurts.

I frown. "Is that what this is about? You haven't seen where I'm living yet?"

He averts his eyes and shoves his hands in his pockets. "You always visited me at school," he says quietly. "You wanted to see where I was living and make sure I was doing okay. That I had what I needed."

I clench my jaw against the sudden emotion clogging my throat and burning my eyes. I'm not about to cry at a baseball game.

"Well…" I clear my throat. "You're welcome anytime. I'd love to have you."

He nods curtly. "Yeah, I mean, whatever."

I roll my eyes and gently punch him in the shoulder.

"Fine. I'd really like for you to swing by my new place so I can show you the view."

In the back of my mind, a tiny voice reminds me that I'm not living there permanently. That it's not *my* place. That I'm just a visitor in that house.

I try to ignore the pang in my chest at the thought of moving out one day.

"Yeah, that sounds fine. Do you need anything? Cleaning supplies? Plants? New sheets?"

I smile because he's listing off things I brought him when he was in college.

Cleaning supplies? *Don't live like a slob. Your future partners won't appreciate cleaning up after you.*

Plants? *You need some fresh air and something to make it look less like a frat house.*

New sheets? *Those are probably self-explanatory.*

"I think I'm all right," I say with a laugh. We're the next ones in line, so I push us back to the task at hand. "Do you know what you're getting?"

"That bratwurst with the peppers sounded pretty good."

"It does, doesn't it?" I nod.

"With that IPA," he adds.

My little brother is one of my favorite people. I know he's got my back, no matter what. I know he's trying to make sure I'm adjusting to my new normal. I appreciate it more than I'll ever be able to express to him.

We place our order and juggle the food and drinks back to our seats, where dad is trying to make sure the boys know how to properly catch a fly ball so they don't break their faces.

The boys eagerly eat their hot dogs and sip their sodas, sandwiched between me and dad. We let Joe take the aisle seat so he can get a very brief reprieve from his kids—and frankly, so they can get a brief reprieve from him.

As the game gets underway, I take a moment to appreciate the experience… the sights, the sounds, the smells, the *feeling* of being in a baseball stadium again.

The sun shining in the outfield.

The warmth on my face.

The shouts and cheers from the crowd.

The smell of spilled beer and grilled hot dogs.

It smells like baseball.

It feels like home.

* * *

AFTER THE GAME, we drop the boys off at home and let our dad get back to our mom. I invite Joe over for a beer on the patio and he quickly accepts. I send a quick text to Kate to warn her so she can either make herself scarce or choose to meet my brother. I don't mind either way. I know Kate likes privacy and I don't want to surprise her with company.

She responds quickly enough to let me know it's fine, that she might be out running errands but shouldn't be gone too long.

Joe follows me in his car over to Kate's house and parks in the same spot I parked in all those months ago when I came over to take a tour of the place.

Much like mine was the first time I saw the house, his jaw is hanging slack, eyes wide open as I show him around. He's glad to see I have a little suite to myself, but he's hustling out the door and back down to the wall of windows pretty quickly. It was hard to tear him away from it in the first place.

"Bro, no wonder you don't want to stay with us. You think Kate would rent a room to me and Tracy just when one of us needs a night away?"

I laugh. "You could always ask."

"This view is incredible. How do you not just stand here all day?"

"I'm not gonna lie and say I haven't done that many times." I clap him on the shoulder. "Want a beer? We can sit outside."

"Sure, yeah," he says, but he doesn't even spare me a glance.

I grab two beers from the fridge and we settle into the Adirondack chairs on the patio. We talk and Joe tells funny stories about the kids and I am constantly reminded that *this* is why I moved back. The quiet moments where nothing momentous is happening may not be the ones that stick out in our minds, but they shape us nonetheless. It's the times when we're living the mundane banalities of life when we see how people truly care about us.

Sure, people may show up in a crisis to help out, but when things are boring? That's when you see how those people actually feel about you. When they want to see where you're living because that's how you cared for them when they were younger.

When they want popcorn but don't want to get up to make it, so their loved ones do it for them.

There are so many small ways to show someone you love them, and in so many cases, it's the everyday moments when they shine.

I got these moments with Jill and I'm forever grateful for them. Now that I'm home, I can enjoy them with my brother, my parents, and—

"Hey," Kate's voice interrupts my thoughts and I find my head snapping in her direction.

"Kate." I smile as I take her in. She's wearing leggings and a flowing long-sleeve shirt. Her hair is down and wavy. Her sunglasses are perched on top of her head as she assesses the situation in front of her, eyes half-guarded like she's nervous but trying not to be.

She looks from me to my brother, and I'm reminded they've never met.

"Kate, this is my brother, Joe. Joe, this is Kate."

"Hi, Joe. It's nice to meet you." She extends her hand and he scrambles to his feet to shake it. I get to my feet as well, but not as quickly. I repeat to myself that I need to act cool.

"It's nice to meet you, too. Your home is beautiful."

"Thank you," she says, averting her eyes. Over the past few months, I've gotten the impression that she's uncomfortable with compliments about the house, but I'm not sure why. "I'm glad I get to finally meet you," she continues.

"Same," Joe replies. "It was really kind of you to offer my brother a place to stay."

Her eyes move to me, and her eyes transform. It's like they're smiling, though her smile has barely changed at all.

"It's no problem at all." She shakes her head and returns her gaze to Joe. "He's good company."

"Do you want to sit?" I finally find my voice. "We were just having a postgame drink."

Her smile widens. "Sure."

"Can I grab you a beer?" I ask.

"Okay."

I tip my chin to Joe's empty bottle in question. He hands it to me and nods. As I head inside, I can hear them chatting.

"I heard on the radio they won. Did you guys have fun?"

Joe answers her, but his words are lost to the distance between us as I grab fresh beers from the fridge.

Kate doesn't drink beer often, but I doubt she'll scoff at it. Besides, she didn't specifically say she wanted something else.

As I make my way back to the sliding door, I see that Kate has taken a seat in the chair I'd been in and Joe has settled in his. They're facing the water and Kate is pointing to something off in the distance, her sunglasses back down to cover her eyes and Joe is shielding his eyes from the glare.

It strikes me that Joe is talking to a woman I am interested in. Romantically. How many years has it been since that happened?

So many.

I don't know what's going on with Kate. I don't know what we're doing.

What I *do* know is that I am surprisingly happy living with her. I know that I want to *keep* spending time with her.

I also know that I feel something for Kate that goes deeper than our physical connection (which… if I'm not being too crass here, is *incredible*).

And I know that I help alleviate her pain, even if it's only a little. That part makes me nervous. That, and I don't know how deep her feelings go. She might only want to use sex to mask her pain—not that I blame her.

I take a deep breath and head back out, taking a seat in the chair next to Kate so she's positioned between Joe and me. They're still talking, but each of them thanks me quickly when I hand them beer bottles. I sit quietly, listening to them chatter, talking about the beach, the house, the baseball game, my nephews.

I watch Kate closely during the discussions about Jackson and Josh. She gives nothing away.

That's something I've noticed about Kate—that she tries so hard to keep her face emotionless when something is hitting close to home. When we've broached a topic she doesn't want to discuss or that triggers something in her, her face seems to… shut down. Her eyes go distant and her face goes slack.

Right now, I can see that her face is more drawn than

usual, but she's plastered on a small, polite smile while Joe brags about his kids and his wife.

We all chat for a bit until Beaker starts pawing at the door, so Kate excuses herself to go feed him.

"Shit, I should get going," Joe says with a glance at his watch.

We both get up and he and Kate call their goodbyes across the house. I walk Joe out the front door and over to his car.

"What time are you getting to Mom and Dad's next weekend?" he asks.

It's our mom's birthday. We're all going over there for lunch on Saturday.

"Probably about eleven thirty."

"Sounds good."

He gives me a backslapping hug and turns to get in his car, then pauses, one hand on the top of the car, the other on the doorframe.

With a sigh, he turns around and looks at me with an odd expression on his face.

I frown. "What's goin' on?"

He glances back to the house. "Kate seems really nice."

I nod slowly. "She is."

"When did her husband die?"

I have a feeling I know where this is going and it's making me antsy. "Last summer," I say, running a hand through my hair.

He nods, eyeing me carefully. "You already know what I'm going to say."

I huff a laugh. "Do I?"

"You have feelings for her."

He says it so matter-of-factly. I resist the urge to look back at the house. If Kate's watching us, I don't want to give her the impression that we're talking about her behind her back.

I know, I know... we're talking about her, but we're not saying mean things about her.

"I do," I admit quietly.

He's silent and I'm staring down at the pavement between us. I don't know what I'm going to find when I look at him. Judgment? Concern? Confusion?

When I finally meet his eyes, they're soft and a tiny smile is turning the corners of his lips up. "Good for you, brother," he says, just as quietly as I confessed.

I feel my body deflate a little bit, tension I didn't realize I was holding leaving my body.

"I-I don't…" I swallow hard and avert my eyes toward the yard, the trees, anywhere other than the genuine eyes of my only sibling. "I doubt she's in the same place."

I hear him take a breath and let it out. "I'm not so sure about that."

My stupid, hopeful heart skips in my chest. I look at him, searching his expression for any information I don't have already.

Did they talk about me?

He starts without me having to ask.

"I think she cares for you."

At that point, I can't help but look back toward the house. I don't see her in any of the windows.

"But…"

I sigh and look at the cement between us.

"… she's not in the same stage of grief as you."

I clench my jaw against the surge of disappointment. It's not as if this information is a surprise, but hearing it doesn't make it hurt less.

I nod. I can't do much else.

"You know how to find me," he says, stepping forward and giving me a bro hug, complete with a slap on the back.

"Yep."

"See you next weekend."

And with that, he climbs in his car and drives back down the long driveway toward the road, leaving me in a jumble of complicated feelings.

I want Kate. And I don't even totally know what I mean by that right now. I just need her right now. I need to lay eyes on her and touch her skin.

So I walk back into the house, locking the front door behind me. When I round the corner and the kitchen comes into view, I find Kate crouching by Beaker's food bowl, petting his back while he inspects his fancy chicken feast.

She sees me and stands. "He headed home?"

I don't answer her. Not verbally. Instead, I take her hips in my hands and pull her into me. If she's surprised, she doesn't let on. She just lets me do it, and I'm grateful when her arms come up to wrap around my neck. So I pull her in closer and kiss her. She opens for me quickly and before I know it, my body is on fire, and I've got her pressed up against the counter.

I don't know if Kate feels the connection that I do. I mean... I know she's attracted to me. All evidence (panting, moaning, screaming, clenching, shaking, wanting to do it again and again) points to her enjoying our... *relationship*, or whatever it is. But I don't typically pounce on her in the kitchen.

This feels new though.

It feels deeper than it did last month.

Now isn't a good time to bring that up, so I don't. I keep my mouth busy on her. Her mouth, her neck, any skin I can reach.

When I lift her onto the island, she wraps her legs around

my waist and pulls me in tight, fingers threading through my hair and holding me in place while she starts to grind against me.

Goddamn.

I use one thumb on her core through her leggings and she gasps my name.

"I hope you don't have any plans for the rest of the evening," I warn her.

A shiver shakes her body just before I pick her back up and start carrying her toward the stairs. I'm careful as I'm walking us up, so I don't trip, but she doesn't seem worried. She's kissing and licking my neck, hanging on to me like a koala bear.

When we get into my bedroom, I drop us both onto the bed. I'm too afraid to get too far away from her—afraid she'll see something in me that scares her, that she'll go running because of it.

She yanks my shirt up my torso, forcing our mouths to tear apart as my shirt reaches my head. I can feel the desperation in her movements and *fuck*, I feel it, too. But I want to worship her beautiful body and her courageous soul. I want to learn the parts of her I haven't yet.

Stretching her arms above her head, I mold her hands over the side of the bed and whisper in her ear. "You're gonna need something to hold on to."

She blinks at me. I think I've surprised her. I'm happy to show her that there's more where that came from. But thus far, she's been pretty adamant about not talking very much.

My dick is already aching, but I want her to come at least once before I do. Preferably twice. Anything more is a bonus. Frankly, I'm not sure I'll be able to wait that long.

I slide her shirt up and lave attention on her breasts as I tease her through her leggings. She's writhing and gasping before too long, starting to beg just a little, so I kiss a trail down her belly to the waistband of her leggings and peel them off her legs. She takes the opportunity to take off her shirt and bra, throwing them somewhere irrelevant.

Sliding my hands back up her legs is not a task I want to rush, but she's saying my name, which is spurring me on. Her hips are rolling and she's breathing heavily.

As I settle between her legs, I look up and meet her eyes. She's propped up on her elbows to get a better view.

There's no way she could know I'm going to enjoy this as much as she will.

The first lick causes her to stop breathing, her shoulders to collapse back onto the bed. I see the column of her throat bob as she swallows.

"Hang on, baby."

Her head lifts back up and her eyes widen, but she follows my instructions, hands returning to the edge of the bed. So I keep going. And I make sure to fulfill my promise to myself. She comes twice before I start to chase my own release. With her body still pulsing around my fingers, I use my free hand to unbutton and unzip my jeans. Shimmying out of my pants with one hand isn't an easy task, but I don't want to move my other hand.

When her grip on my fingers eases, I slip on a condom and sink into her.

Stars burst behind my eyelids. After a moment, I force myself to open them and look at her. There's a glimmer of something in her eyes that looks like hesitancy, maybe fear, and then it's gone with a single blink, replaced by lust.

I try to savor the feeling of her soft skin against mine. The sound of her moans and gasps. The sight of her below me. The scent of her perfume on her skin. The faint taste of beer on her tongue.

I'm going to explode, so I pull her legs up. I found that spot inside her and I've learned how to best reach it without neglecting her clit. I wait for the telltale signs of her orgasm building—her back arching, the way her brow furrows just a little bit, her thighs squeezing me, the helpless whimpers she makes and how the pitch increases as she gets closer.

It's not until her hands clutch the bed so hard the duvet bunches up into her tight fists that I finally let go.

As we're both trying to catch our breath, I rest my forehead against hers and tangle one hand into her hair. Her arms wrap around me and hold me close.

It feels good.

It feels better than good.

Kate is starting to feel like *home*.

And that should probably scare me more than it does.

20

SO CUTE, IT'S DISGUSTING

Kate

"I'm not sure I've ever seen balloons that big."

Liam has a point. I'm not sure I have either. "I thought these were only available to social media influencers."

Elliot's backyard is dressed to the nines. Their shrubs have been immaculately trimmed and a new lattice has been placed behind them, which is where two massive gold mylar balloons are hanging: a three and a five.

"Hey Leon, how old are you again?" Liam calls to his friend across the lawn.

"Funny," Leon calls back. "You're next, asshole."

Liam responds with an easy smile and it's so fucking endearing I have to clutch my drink to keep from wrapping my arm around his waist and pressing my head against his chest.

I have no idea what's happening with Liam. I'm so acutely

aware of him at all times. I want to touch him. I want him to touch me.

But no one knows about us. No one knows that we're… roommates with benefits?

Jesus, Kate, are you in college?

It's an overgeneralization. It feels like something deeper than that and I am unprepared. Especially here, now, at Leon's birthday party.

"Oh my god, how did I miss your arrival?"

The familiar voice makes me thaw immediately and Elliot's long arms wrapping around my shoulders don't hurt either.

"Hello, my love."

"Hello, to you, too." He kisses the top of my head and then takes a step back to assess me. "You look stunning." He nods once with approval.

"Why, thank you kindly." I do the best curtsy possible while balancing a drink in my hand and he cackles.

If Elliot were my brother, I'd have a hard time picking favorites between him and Benji.

"Liam, it's so good to see you." Elliot steps forward to pull Liam into a hug and then launches into the speech about where food can be found, noting that we've obviously already found the bar. (Duh.)

Then, he dashes off to play host, leaving me and Liam alone again. I take the opportunity to look around the yard to see who else has arrived. Attorneys from Leon's firm are here with their spouses. Mutual acquaintances mill about, sharing information about the latest gossip. Elliot and Leon's parents are all sitting together at a table under a huge umbrella with iced tea (although—because I know them well—I have a strong suspicion that there's some kind of alcohol in there).

Everyone here is happy. They're celebrating Leon,

enjoying cocktails in the sunshine, and spending some quality time together. Their mood is infectious and I'm no exception. The smile on my face comes easily as I listen to people update me on their lives. In the deep recesses of my brain, I wonder what they think of me—if they're glad I'm not bringing Nick up. I assume they're trying to keep the conversation light. I try not to think about it too hard.

The afternoon is gorgeous. Everyone is effervescent.

As the light fades into twilight, Elliot is getting the cake ready and asks me to go grab a box from his office. I slip through the crowds and walk past the photo displays of Leon —high school, undergraduate, and law school graduations, vacation photos, newspaper clippings from high-profile cases. I make my way up the stairs and turn down the hall-way, but I hear footsteps behind me. I turn just in time to see Liam coming before he wraps his arms around me, his lips landing on the side of my neck.

The smile that splits my face should surprise me, but it doesn't. Liam always makes me smile.

"Hey," he whispers into my skin.

"Hey."

He takes my hand and spins me to face him. Both of us are looking around for people who may be nearby. There's no one in sight.

"Do you need any help?" he asks quietly.

"I think I got it."

"All right," he says, just before planting a soft kiss on my lips.

"Kate, can you grab the Harrods bag, too?" Elliot calls up the stairs. I suck in a breath and take a step back from Liam, but Elliot can't see us. We're around the corner.

"Sure thing! I'll be right down," I call to him.

When I look back at Liam, he's stifling a laugh, which

makes me laugh. "Stop it." I smack his arm playfully. "Come on."

He follows me into Elliot and Leon's shared office space. It's a pretty big space with two matching desks facing each other with a big window overlooking the front yard. There's a wedding photo of the two of them on one wall.

They're the cutest.

It's disgusting.

"Which one is it?"

"It's this one." I point to a box on the floor behind Elliot's desk with a Harrod's bag sitting on top of it. It's not big. I don't have concerns about my ability to carry it down a flight of stairs. But Liam is already crouching down to pick it up. I pluck the bag off the top and shoot him a smirk.

"Oh, thank you. The bag was the worst of the weight," he jokes.

"Glad to be of service." I wink.

He can clearly handle the box. The man carried me up the stairs not too long ago.

A shiver runs down my back at the memory. He sees my shoulders move and his eyes narrow with suspicion.

Deflect, deflect, deflect.

I scratch my temple and turn toward the door.

We go back downstairs to the kitchen, where Elliot is grateful to discover that I "found" another set of hands. I'm not a great liar, so I avert my eyes to keep him from seeing something I don't want him to. Elliot knows me too well. He'd know something was up. I'm honestly a little surprised he hasn't grilled me about it yet.

Maybe we're hiding it well.

"Liam, will you put candles on the cake?" Elliot hands gold candles to Liam's outstretched hand.

"That sounds rather dangerous. He's incredibly old."

Elliot laughs. "Oh dear, he's going to be insufferable when

your birthday rolls around. You'll never be prepared for the payback."

"He'll always be older than me," Liam quips in return.

"Just put candles on the damn cake, William." Elliot's voice sounds stern, but I see the playful nature of his eyes.

But wait...

I do a double take with a frown on my face. "William?"

"There's no need to resort to full names, Elliot." Liam glances at me but continues his response to Elliot. "I'll always be older than *you*, after all."

Liam turns toward the cake to begin his task while Elliot runs off to take care of something else.

I open the boxes and count out thirty-five candles. That thing is going to look like a bonfire.

Liam begins placing them on the top of the three-tier masterpiece that will be demolished in a few minutes.

"So, William..."

Liam scoffs and shakes his head, but he has a smile on his face.

"Yes, my full name is William. As is my father's. And his father's. And his father's."

"Jeez," I say, as I do that mental math. "So that makes you William Anderson the Fourth?"

"William Arthur Anderson the Fourth, yes."

Jesus. The legacy.

In the deep recesses of my mind, something is pinging me. It's reminding me of conversations with Nick about baby things and carrying on family names. I kick it away. I don't want to think about this. I don't want to ruin my day. I want to move past it and find that happiness I felt again when Liam wrapped his arms around me upstairs.

"Wow..." I finally squeak out.

"How do you think we should place these candles? All around or just on one side?"

He's moved on. I blink away the thought that won't stop pinging me.

"Go all the way around. Make him work for it."

"Sinister."

"I'm not sorry."

He chuckles as he places the next candle. Leon is going to hate this. I'm not sure exactly what Elliot will think. Regardless, under any annoyance will be genuine affection.

They'll get him back on his birthday. Which reminds me…

"Leon said you're next. When's your birthday?"

"September."

I blow out a breath. "That gives them a good amount of time to plan."

He smirks. "We tease because we love."

Something in my brain pings me again and I cuss at it. I don't care about anything outside of this lovely party and I kind of resent my brain for trying to make me.

For the record, I'm not wrong about Leon hating the candle placement. He knows immediately who did it. Elliot laughs and takes a million pictures.

The rest of the evening is easy. I'm a little buzzed but not drunk. Relaxed. Surrounded by close friends and the warmth of people who love me.

This is the happiest I've been in over a year. If you didn't know me and met me at this party, you might think I'm a normal person. You might think I haven't had a horribly traumatizing year.

The thought of all that trauma tries to dampen my mood, but I push it out of the way. It's not welcome here tonight, at this beautiful party on a gorgeous evening with my very best friend and a handsome man who's looking at me like I'm the most stunning woman here. A man who is quickly becoming very important to me.

Our eyes meet and hold across the firepit. People around us are talking, but the sound is garbled. It's like we're alone. Do moments like this happen in real life? Where it feels like everything else has melted away?

Someone yells Liam's name. He blinks and the moment is over, but I can tell he's upset about it. He's listening to the person who has taken the chair next to him, but he's also sneaking glances at me.

A while later, Liam drives us home. He holds my hand the entire time.

When we enter the kitchen, I set my clutch down on the island and bend down to pet Beaker. I notice Liam moving around out of the corner of my eye, but I'm focused on Beaker. When Beaker runs away from me, I realize that Liam has put more food and water in his bowls.

He's so kind. So caring.

My heart speeds up, galloping off on its own, regardless of the absolute dumpster fire that the last year of my life has been. It's headed straight for Liam and that *terrifies* me.

But then I meet his eyes and I can breathe again.

How does he do that?

He closes the distance between us and runs his thumb along my cheekbone.

A warm feeling spreads throughout my chest. I fight the urge to close my eyes. His green eyes have a choke hold on me in the best kind of way.

His hands slide along my jaw and thread into my hair, his forehead tilting down to gently rest on mine.

The air between us feels charged, like there's something we're not saying. Like we need some magic spell to undo whatever it is that's happening between us.

But do I want to undo it?

I don't think I do.

This is the only time I feel human anymore.

So I close my eyes and breathe him in. He smells crisp, like the chill in the air after a warm day, with a subtle hint of bonfire smoke and burned marshmallows.

His thumbs move under my jaw and tilt my head up. When I open my eyes, a soft, lazy, contented smile stretches across his mouth. My returning smile is automatic. I don't think about it. It just happens, like it always seems to around Liam.

Today, in this moment, I'm content to focus on this wonderful man in front of me. To not think about the potentially catastrophic consequences of what we're continuing to do against all logic or reason.

After all, grief is neither logical nor reasonable.

Today, I feel beautiful in my floral wraparound dress and favorite wedge sandals.

Today, I feel loved and appreciated and *alive*.

Today, Liam had wrapped his arms around me outside Liam's office—so bold and brazen because anyone could have seen us. But he seemed so compelled to touch me that he couldn't *not* do it. And the way he's kissing me now makes me feel like... I don't know. Like maybe I could be a whole person again. Someday.

Maybe in this moment, I'm half of a person and with more days like this one, I could get there eventually.

His hands trail the length of my arms, gently tugging my hands away from his jaw as he pulls his mouth from mine. He lays tender kisses on my knuckles before taking my hand and walking us toward the stairs. I stay close to this side, my free hand reaching across my body to hold on to his bicep.

I try not to think about how natural it feels to have him here, living in my space, spending time with me.

At the top of the stairs, he gently leads me into his bedroom, never letting go of my hand. After closing the door behind us, he pulls me toward him and covers my mouth with his. My arms wrap around his neck on their own and I melt into him, opening wider so I can feel his tongue.

His hands are on my hips, holding me tightly against him, but when our tongues meet, he groans and wraps his arms around my torso, enveloping me completely. So when I take a step backward toward the bed, his body moves with mine like we're one being.

He eases me gently onto the bed, breaking away from me only long enough to slide off my sandals and toe off his own shoes, but then his long body is hovering over me, his hips nestled between my legs.

I feel my way down his sides and slide my hands under his shirt, inching it up toward his shoulders. I need to feel his skin. When I get it up high enough, he pulls his mouth away from mine and, with one hand, grabs the shirt, pulls it over his head, and then strips it from his arms one by one before fusing his mouth to mine again.

It's like our mouths can't bear to separate. Every time we break away, we're back within a couple of seconds. But it's not enough. It's never enough.

I can feel his bare chest—can see all that golden skin—but I need more.

Dress off. Now.

I reach a hand down to tug at the knot tied at my side. As I go for the snap by my breasts, he lifts his torso to give me more room. I yank the dress open. I don't even remember what undergarments I'm wearing, but Liam's breath catches when he pulls back to look at me and I feel like whatever I put on earlier was a good choice.

Oh, right. Light pink with lace.

Liam has seen me like this plenty of times by now. This isn't new for him. My brain tries to get me to think about something else—something related to what my feelings currently mean, but I tell it to shut the fuck up and just enjoy what's happening. Letting my own brain cockblock me is not something I'm going to allow right now.

Emotion is thickening the air between us, like a humid day before a heavy rain and still, I can't bring myself to think too hard about it. I allow myself to acknowledge it but not to analyze it.

He holds his body above me, bracing himself on one forearm by my head, sliding his free hand into my hair. He brushes a soft kiss against each of my cheekbones before dipping lower to my breasts. His hand follows, trailing down my neck as it goes.

My back arches on its own and he takes the opportunity to flick open the clasp on my bra. The sleeves of my dress are still on my arms, so he helps me shrug out of them and pulls my bra off, tossing it to the floor. Then he tugs at my dress, lying pointlessly beneath me, silently encouraging me to lift my body so he can remove it. He trails soft kisses down my torso as he pulls. When he reaches my hips, he pauses and traces the lace at the top of my underwear with a single fingertip, brushing his lips against the soft skin just above the fabric.

Shivers go up my spine, and I have to close my eyes for a moment.

Liam tugs once more on my dress, so I lift my hips. He drags my underwear down my legs as he pulls the dress free, and I hear the fabric hit the floor.

I open my eyes to the sound of his belt being unbuckled. He's standing at the foot of the bed with his hands still on his belt. Our eyes meet and he hesitates for just a moment, as if he's waiting for a sign from me that I want to keep going.

Somehow, I know down to the depths of my soul that if I said the word, he'd stop dead in his tracks and let me walk out the door with no hard feelings.

Well... some hard feelings.

But he wouldn't have any ill will toward me.

But that's not what I want right now. That's not what I want at all.

I want *him*.

So I sit up and kneel in front of him on the bed. I nudge his hands away from his pants, slide the button through its hole, slowly unzip them, and push them down his legs, along with his boxer briefs. He steps out of each leg and then kneels on the bed in front of me, one hand on my hip to guide me backward.

I reach up to touch his face. He's so handsome. Looking at him is no hardship.

He sighs quietly and leans his head into my palm, his eyes fluttering shut. I brush my thumb over his lips, but before I can finish, he reaches up to hold it in place and kisses it.

"Kate…"

His voice is so quiet it's basically only breath.

My stomach flips over and it sort of scares me.

Why is that happening?

I can't understand why my body is reacting like this. It's more than just Liam being hot and good at *all the things*. He says my name like I should be treasured.

I don't want to think about these feelings too much, so I press my body against his, wrapping my arms around his neck and fusing my lips to his. His skin feels like it's searing mine. Like when you stand too close to a bonfire on a cold evening. Shivers make goose bumps pop up all over my body.

He must feel them because he pulls away.

"Are you cold?" he asks, his voice full of concern, his eyebrows knit together.

I can't talk. I can't speak words. My heart is full, and my head is a mess.

So I look into his eyes and slowly shake my head.

Liam breathes out heavily and then crushes his mouth to

mine. Reaching down to my thighs, he lifts me and tilts me backward so I fall onto the bed. I laugh a little when I hit the pillows and eagerly wrap my arms around him when he crawls back on top of me and trails kisses along my chest and collarbones.

His hand slides down my body, ending between my legs. Lust shoots through me and I gasp. Goose bumps break out across my chest as another shiver racks my body.

The smile on his face can't be described as anything other than smug. But it's short-lived because he closes that talented mouth over one nipple, pausing to suck and gently bite before he moves lower.

When I say that Liam is good at *all the things*, I really mean it. It took him almost no time to learn what makes me come and he's currently putting that knowledge to good use.

With his tongue moving over me in earnest, coherent thought evaporates into the air, my brain checking out from reality. The only thing I can register is the heat building in my body and the man causing it.

A natural disaster could occur outside and I'd be completely oblivious. My hands search for purchase in his hair, on his shoulders, and on the hand that is still kneading my breast. Anything I can reach, I hold on to for dear life as my breath escapes my lungs in heavy pants.

The pressure finally explodes, shaking my body and forcing my eyes shut. My senses abandon me completely for a brief moment while my breath stalls out.

When air mercifully enters my lungs again, I hear a condom wrapper being ripped open. I feel Liam's warm skin pressing against my belly. I catch the clean scent of his cologne on his neck. I force my eyes to open and I see him gazing at me with a smile in his eyes. He's braced on his forearms, caging me in, but his thumbs are gently stroking my cheeks. He leans in slowly to kiss me. I can taste him mixed with *me*.

I still can't speak. I may have forgotten the English language entirely.

So I draw my legs up along his and wrap them around his hips, tilting up toward him. He takes it as the invitation it is, shifting his hips and easing into me.

He rests his forehead against mine as he lets me adjust. When I'm ready, I lift my hips and revel in the soft moan that vibrates in his throat. I feel the muscle in his jaw twitch against my fingers and I'm sure he's grinding his molars together.

Our bodies fall into a rhythm easily. I find myself trying to pull him closer, closer, closer. He's literally inside of me and it's not enough for me. He can't be close enough. Can't hold me tight enough.

The way he looks at me takes my breath away. It's amazing and terrifying.

Thankfully, that terrified feeling doesn't last long because Liam closes his eyes as he dives back in for a brutal kiss before pulling my knee up higher on his back and suddenly the only thing that matters is his tongue and the over-whelming heat building in my body again.

Another shiver works its way down my spine, and I feel him tense up, clenching every muscle in his body. He breaks our kiss on a gasp. When our eyes meet again, I try to offer an apologetic (and embarrassed) smile.

"I'm sorry," I whisper. My throat is so dry all of a sudden, but I silently applaud myself for remembering English. I lick my lips and swallow. "I c-can't control it."

"I'm not sorry," he whispers back. "And I don't want you to try to control it."

He drops another kiss on my lips, lingering to suck on the

lower one for a moment before rearing up and pulling my hips up onto his thighs.

Oh fuck, oh fuck, oh fuck.

Any semblance of control I thought I had over my body disintegrates. My back wants to arch, but it can't because of the position my hips are in. My head throws itself back. My eyes squeeze shut. My hands grasp the duvet. I'm vaguely aware of gasping, moaning, screaming as my body gives itself over to the warmth spreading through my limbs. Stars explode behind my eyes. If the sensation wasn't so overpowering, I might be convinced I blacked out for a moment.

But as it stands, I'm still fully cognizant, lying beneath Liam's strong body, and if I still believed in a god, I'd throw up a prayer of thanks for this incredible man above me, worshiping me as if I'm water and he's been dying of thirst.

As our tremors subside, Liam gently slides his thighs out from under my hips and lowers himself to me, softly kissing my neck, my temple, my cheek.

More goose bumps.

He smiles.

So do I.

He seems reluctant as he peels himself away from me to dispose of the condom. When he returns, I slip into the bathroom to clean up. By the time I'm finished, he's settled under the covers, but I can feel his eyes on me as I move toward his bed through the darkness. I nestle into the bedding, shivering again, but this time from the cold sheets underneath and above me.

Liam wraps his arms around me and pulls me into his body, our legs intertwining. I press my ear against his chest and listen to his steady heartbeat.

Sleep takes me quickly, but before it does, I take a deep breath, filling my lungs with his calming scent before letting it out with a contented sigh and a lightness I haven't felt in—

Well… that I haven't felt in what feels like forever.

CALM BEFORE THE STORM

Liam

"It's socially acceptable to drink at a one o'clock baseball game, right?"

I smirk as I lock the car and reach for her hand. She only hesitates for a half second before taking it. It's progress.

"First of all, yes. Of course, it's socially acceptable to drink at an afternoon baseball game."

"Even on a Sunday?"

That gets a laugh out of me. "Especially on a Sunday."

I might be imagining that she squeezes my hand, but I'm also focused on making sure neither of us gets hit by cars as we cross the busy street parallel to the ballpark.

"And second, it's June, which means it's officially summer and the rules are always more lax during the summer."

She shoots a skeptical look my way. "I don't think summer officially starts until the twenty-second."

"I'm not really sure why you're arguing with my ironclad logic for why it's okay for us to have a couple of beers at a baseball game on a beautiful, sunny day."

"You do make an excellent point," she concedes.

As we near the gates, I pull out my phone and get the mobile tickets ready that I bought this morning.

"Where are we sitting?"

"Right field. It's my favorite."

"Why's that?"

We shuffle forward with the line as it moves. I never let go of her hand. She's wearing a tank top, black shorts, and Converse. Her wavy brown hair is in a ponytail, and she has big sunglasses covering her eyes.

Stunning.

"Because I was on first, so I like being able to see down the line."

That answer seems to satisfy her. She nods thoughtfully and moves her thumb along mine as we wait for the line to move again.

After yesterday, I was desperate to get Kate to a ball game. At Leon's house, she was much more relaxed. I'd seen her laugh with and fawn over her best friends. I saw her throw her head back and laugh from deep in her throat. Until yesterday, I'd never seen her laugh so hard she couldn't breathe.

I'm sure her mood had to do with being surrounded by people who love her, but I swear the sunshine helped, too.

Regardless, I wanted to find ways to bring out that joyous, uninhibited laugh of hers that made a peaceful warmth settle in my chest.

I wanted to give her another day like that. She deserves it. She needs it. In the back of my mind, I know we're nearing the one-year anniversary of Nick's death and I remember how hard that day was for me. I want her to see there's still life left to live.

At the same time, knowing where she is in her grieving process makes me feel horribly guilty given the… nature of our relationship.

She's a perfectly willing and active participant. It's not like I'm forcing her or she feels obligated by anything what-soever. But this is uncharted territory for both of us. I never thought about dating after Jill and I'm certain Kate never thought about dating after Nick.

Not that what we're doing could be considered "dating," but you know what I mean.

What I've realized at this point is that I don't want to be the thing Kate uses to numb her pain. It may have started out that way, but I have a sneaking suspicion that her feel-ings run deeper than that now—even if she doesn't want to admit it to herself or can't. It's just a feeling I get. I could be wrong.

What I know beyond the shadow of a doubt is that I want more. Sleeping with Kate was never a way to numb my pain, although I'd be lying if I said it didn't also have that effect. Kate has intrigued me from the very first night at Leon's house when she offered me a place to stay.

Her heart is so fundamentally *good*.

I know she's scared and heartbroken. I know she's trying to find her way.

But so am I.

Scared. Heartbroken. Trying to find my way.

It seems to me that my path has led me to Kate, and I don't really want to take a detour.

Last night was nearly my undoing. Things felt different between us—more intense, tender, open. Her eyes weren't as guarded. She was more communicative, mostly in a nonverbal way. I could feel something different in her touches, her kisses, her eagerness. It all landed differently with me last night.

I didn't dare speak, though *fuck*, I wanted to. I wanted to tell her how good she felt, how gorgeous she was, how I'm falling in love with her.

But I know damn well that she's not ready for any of that. I knew telling her any of those things would destroy that perfect moment with her and everything else about our situation.

So instead, I kept my mouth occupied in other ways, taking my time, tasting her everywhere. I wasn't able to *say* it, but I could do my best to show it.

And I wanted to show it.

I'm sorry... I can't control it, she'd whispered as a shudder ran through her body that nearly made me lose control. It was too good. *She* was too good. It was all too much, but I couldn't be bothered to care.

I didn't trust myself to speak, but I couldn't remain silent after that comment, so I risked two very measured sentences.

I'm not sorry. And I don't want you to try to control it.

And then I kissed her again. I didn't want the words to tumble out on their own.

She'd fallen asleep quickly after we cleaned up, but I stayed awake for a few minutes, basking in the softness of her skin, the scent of her shampoo, and the feeling of her legs intertwined with mine.

I planted one last kiss on her head and let myself think it one time—just once—before drifting off to sleep.

I love you, Kate.

It was on this wave of tenderness that I asked her first thing in the morning if she'd like to go to the ball game with me today.

"Hey," she says, poking me in the side.

I look at her and I'm glad I'm wearing sunglasses because

I think there would be hearts popping out of my eyes right now. *Fuck*, she's beautiful.

"You kinda zoned out there," she continues. "You okay?"

The smile on my face is automatic. "Of course."

What I want to do is pull her into my side and kiss her temple, but I don't think she's ready for that. So instead, I squeeze her hand.

She squeezes it back.

The line has been moving slowly but moving nonetheless. We're not too far away from the front when I hear someone call my name.

I turn in the direction of the voice to find a guy I played college baseball with.

"Holy shit," I murmur.

Daniel Fitzpatrick is heading right toward me, a massive smile on his face, arms already coming up to hug me.

I glance back at Kate, who is watching us with confusion. "I used to play ball with him. It's okay." I squeeze her hand once more before letting go so I can return the crushing hug Fitz is about to give me.

"Holy shit, dude, I can't believe it's you!" Fitz practically yells into my ear when he delivers that crushing hug. He low-key knocks the wind out of me for a second. "William Arthur Anderson the *Fourth*." He laughs as he pulls back. "It has been far too long."

"No shit, man. What are you doing out this way?"

Fitz doesn't live here, last I heard.

"We're back visiting family for a few days."

"We? Is Jen with you?"

Fitz and Jen met during college and got married when Fitz was playing in the minors. He played a few games in the majors, but he never made it big. It's not in the cards for all of us.

"Yeah, but she's with my mom and aunts doing a spa day. Dad and I brought all the boys out for a game."

"That's awesome, Fitz. It's great to see you. This is Kate," I say, turning around to take Kate's hand again, but both of her hands are shoved into her back pockets.

Something in her eyes isn't quite right. It looks maybe like fear or sadness, but it's gone before I can identify it. I try to catch her eye to no avail. She's already offering an easy smile to my former teammate and extending one hand for a shake.

"Hi, it's nice to meet you."

"Nice to meet you, too," he says, nodding at Kate. Fitz undoubtedly knows about Jill's passing. He certainly knew Jill when we were in college. But thankfully, he doesn't say anything.

"Hey, you still got my number?" he asks me. "We should catch up while I'm in town."

"Maybe?" I take out my phone and check that I have the correct number and agree to text tomorrow. Then Fitz runs back to his family, and I finally take Kate's hand again.

The expression on her face is still a little bit weird, but she wipes whatever it is away before she meets my eyes.

"Are you okay?"

"Of course," she echoes my earlier assurance.

This time, I can't help but lean forward and press my lips to her temple. Her hand tightens around mine just a little bit, and I feel like whatever she is feeling will be okay. Maybe she felt awkward about being seen in public with me when we're not really an official thing.

When we get through the gates, we make a loop around the ballpark. Kate says she hasn't been here in years and things have changed quite a bit. We watch people play games for prizes with the merchandise crew that wanders around the stadium. We meander through the largest gift shop, and I buy her a ball cap, which she promptly puts on her head, pulling her ponytail through the hole in the back.

When we make it to our section, we find the nearest vendor with beer and take them to our seats.

And the seats? I love them. Since I'm back here now, I should look into getting a season ticket pack or something, splitting them with Joe and Dad. I'd love to spend weekends here.

I'm never sad that I'm not playing these days. I can still throw the ball around with Joe and my nephews. And realistically, I couldn't still play at my age, anyway. Some young buck would have taken my spot years ago and I'd be warming the bench or gone entirely.

I don't regret any decisions I made—especially where Jill was concerned—but I do miss it sometimes.

You know what, though? I'll happily take sitting in right field with Kate next to me. I'd love to have more warm afternoons at the ballpark, sitting in the sunshine, drinking a cold beer, watching my favorite game with this beautiful woman I've fallen in love with.

She doesn't object when I put my arm around the back of her seat. She even leans into me a bit. I'll take that and run with it.

We share nachos slathered in processed cheese and, later, cotton candy.

When the home team wins, she claps and cheers. I have to resist every single urge to pull her into me. We're not "public." We don't even know what "we" are. I have to keep reminding myself.

We listen to the postgame show on the drive home. I like listening to the coaches' interviews and mercifully, Kate doesn't seem to mind. She watches the world go by through her open window with a content look on her face, still holding the bag of leftover cotton candy.

"I'm beat," she announces as she walks into the kitchen. "Being in the sun wears me out."

I chuckle and get us both a glass of water. "You need to hydrate."

She takes a healthy gulp of water and then plops herself down on the couch. If I'm being totally honest, I'd be down for cuddling on the couch with Kate and maybe taking a nap. She's right about the sun—it wears you out.

Or maybe it's just living in a northern state. We're not used to the sun.

I sit down next to her and rest a hand on her bare thigh. She doesn't flinch or readjust her body. She just stays there, letting me sweep my thumb back and forth over her smooth skin.

It feels natural.

Like we should be doing this all the time, forever.

With a loud meow, Beaker jumps into Kate's lap and proceeds to headbutt her jaw.

"Hey, bud!" she croons. "Did you miss us?"

Us.

I try not to let myself get too excited by her word choice.

I glance at my watch. "I'm sure he did, but I'm also sure he's hungry."

Kate looks at her watch, too. "Oh shit, Beaker, I'm sorry."

She moves to get up, but I press on her thigh to keep her there. "Stay put. I got it."

Kissing her on the cheek feels like an entirely normal thing to do, so I do it, then pick up Beaker and hug him to my chest, rubbing his head as I take him into the kitchen. I serve up some fancy seafood feast for him and put the little treats on top like Kate always does. After I set it on the floor next to his water, I run my hand down his back a couple of times. He's such a sweet cat once you get to know him.

"Speaking of dinner, what should we eat?" Kate calls from her spot on the couch. "We could just order something."

I stand up and move around the fireplace so I can see her. She's stretched her legs out and her feet are resting on the coffee table.

Her legs are toned and tan, and she looks so goddamn gorgeous. She's oblivious to my staring as she takes her cap off and tugs on the tie holding her hair up, shaking it out and letting her waves tumble around her shoulders. She reaches her arms above her head and stretches, her back arching in a way that I'm very familiar with at this point, but during an entirely different activity.

And now I'm picturing her bare chest.

"Liam?"

"Hmm?" Words are hard.

She has a suspicious look on her face, which I only know because I manage to tear my gaze from her body long enough to make eye contact.

"What's going on?"

I hum in response. Again, words are hard.

She watches me as I slowly make my way over to her, sitting on the coffee table next to her feet. I place my hand on her ankle and gently smooth it up her leg, moving to the soft skin of her inner thigh as I get higher. Her eyes track the movement, and she uncrosses her ankles to make room for my hand between her thighs.

When my fingertips graze her core, her eyes flutter shut and her mouth drops open.

Gently picking up her legs, I bend them and slide between before putting them back down so the bottoms of her feet are on the edge of the coffee table.

And then I lean forward and leave open-mouthed kisses on her neck before whispering in her ear.

"I want dessert first."

She makes no objections, and we don't even make it upstairs before she's ripping my clothes off and straddling me on the couch.

If you'd have told me this time last year that this would be my life today, I'd have laughed in your face. But I couldn't be more grateful. I'll savor every moment I have with her.

Because when I head into work the following morning, my boss drops a fucking bomb on me.

22

A KICK RIGHT IN THE CHEST

Liam

I've been staring out my office window at the lake for a solid thirty minutes.

For the first time in a while, my brain is an absolute fucking mess.

The thing about having a spouse with a long-term illness is that you mourn them before they die and then again after, which can fuck with your head. You're essentially living in limbo while they're sick and then one day... they're gone. I feel like I mourned Jill for *years*, so by the time she died, it was more fast-tracked for me. It was horrible and painful, and I hated it. I would have traded places with her in a heart-beat if it were possible.

But I also felt grateful that she wasn't suffering anymore. I was glad she wasn't being held prisoner in her own body anymore. I imagined—still imagine—her dancing wherever she is.

I started seeing a therapist before Jill died because that shit is hard to wrap your head around. *Knowing* your spouse is going to die—not just on some unknown far-off date, but within the next few years—is a total mindfuck.

Dedication to supporting her is the only thing that kept me together, so when she passed, there was nothing to hold me together but glue. And not the strong kind. I'm talking purple glue sticks like my nephews use at school.

It was during that time that I felt like I was wading through water all day long—limbs heavy and sluggish, brain groggy, heart angry and broken.

Right now, my body feels like that, but my brain is moving a million miles a minute and I have no idea how to slow it down.

Every technique my therapist taught me is failing me and I think it's because the main factor in the decision I have to make is…

Honestly, I don't know how to finish that sentence.

About an hour and a half ago, my boss called me into his office and told me about a job opportunity. As corporate trainers, we're sometimes asked to go to new locations and get new offices up and running. It was something I shied away from when I lived in Chicago, taking lower positions that didn't require travel so I could be home with Jill.

But when I started applying for jobs around here in preparation for moving back, I told potential employers I was okay with traveling because… well, there was nothing to stop me. I figured it would be fun to have a change in my routine and that it would let me see new places. It felt like a way to honor Jill, so long as I took the time to see the city.

I've been here for less than a year and I had no reason to believe I was going to be asked to travel to a new location anytime soon.

Until today.

In fact, someone else was slated to be assigned this location, but they'd had a family emergency and needed to pull out.

When my boss said the word *Austin*, I think my whole body froze. I just stared at him, shocked.

I tried so hard to appear grateful—surprised but grateful for the opportunity.

I told him I'd think about it and let him know. He gave me a time line, which is shorter than I'd prefer. I need to tell them within the week. If I pass it up, they'll choose someone else.

My first instinct was to say no. To say that I was finally getting settled and I wasn't feeling up to traveling right now, because really, the reason I don't want to do it is Kate.

It's not a few weeks. It's six months. *Minimum.*

I honestly don't know what the fuck I'm going to do. I don't want to leave Kate, but I'm certain—beyond the shadow of a doubt—that she'll tell me to take the assignment.

I almost don't want to tell her. But that feels like lying. If she ever found out, she'd be so furious. And really… as much as I wish it weren't the case, she and I are *not* in a relationship. We're roommates. We might be more than roommates, but she's not my girlfriend or my partner or anything that could even be described as being part of a couple.

Do I love her?

Yes. My chest physically aches sometimes when I look at her.

Do I want her to be mine?

Fuck yes. I want everything.

I want her mornings, afternoons, and midnights.

I want her tears of joy and sadness.

I want to be the one lying under the Christmas tree with her when she's struggling, and I want to be the one putting her to bed when she's had too much to drink.

Kate is everything I wasn't expecting—not at this stage in my life or ever again.

But I can't deny the way I feel about her.

She's everything.

I'm just… I'm not sure she feels the same way. And the fact that I'm uncertain about it makes my stomach feel like it's made of lead.

I take a step back and lean against my desk, my chest suddenly tight. I'm rubbing at my sternum when I hear a knock at my door, followed by the handle turning.

"Liam, holy shit," I hear from behind me.

I turn to face my closest work friend, Marcus.

"What's up, man?"

He comes in and closes the door behind him, scoffing. "You know exactly what's up. You're getting the Austin location."

I force a smile as he walks toward me and sits in the chair in front of my desk. I spin my chair into place and settle into it. "So I hear."

Marcus frowns, his deep umber skin pinching between his eyebrows. "Why don't you sound excited as all hell? This is an amazing opportunity for you."

Marcus had the last office opening. He was in Washington state for almost a year. He came back around Christmas this year. He's a few years younger than me, not married, and only recently landed a steady girlfriend after being single for a while.

"I know it is," I acknowledge.

His head jerks back. "Then what's the problem?"

I fiddle with a pen on my desk needlessly as I look for the right words. "I guess I'm just surprised. I just moved back home, you know?"

He blinks at me.

I avert my eyes, rubbing my forehead.

"Liam, what's really going on?" he asks.

I take a long, slow, deep breath in and let it back out. "I just… it's not great timing, is all."

He stares at me for a moment, that frown still fixed on his face. "What the fuck are you talking about?"

I don't know how to explain this to Marcus. This thing with Kate is basically a secret. I don't want to betray her trust, so I don't want to talk about her specifically, but I do want to talk to someone about this.

I scrub my hands down my face and tell the truth. Part of it at least.

"I met someone."

The frown melts away and his eyes widen. "Oh."

"Yeah… oh."

"Well… it's only six months or so. She'll still be here when you get back."

Logically, I know Marcus is correct. But it feels wrong to leave Kate. Quite frankly, I don't *want* to. I want to be here with her.

And I also understand a little bit about what she might go through over the next few months, and I don't want her to be alone.

"I know that," I concede.

"So…" It's a question he's asking, though someone who doesn't know him might not think so.

I fiddle with my pen again, spinning it around on the desk. "It's just a bad time, man."

"Look, I know I'm not an expert on relationships, but I feel like Leena would tell me to talk to her. To tell her what's goin' on. I can't imagine she'd want me to give up a really great professional opportunity. Especially knowing that I'd be back at the end of it."

I look up at him and know that he's right. I *do* need to talk to Kate about this. And I love how hopeful he is about Leena. I hope it works out for them. He's a good guy.

"And hey, she can always visit you in Austin. It's a great town." His head falls back and his hand claps over his stomach. "*Ooooh*, and the barbecue. I'm tellin' you, Liam..."

I offer a weak smile. It's all I can muster before I let my head fall back against the chair and I fix my gaze on the ceiling.

"Come on, man," he chides gently. "It's a great opportunity. You should be excited. Are you thinking she won't be supportive?"

The cold hard truth of the matter is that I'm not worried Kate won't be supportive. That thought never even crossed my mind.

"If she's not going to support you, is it even worth it?" Marcus continues.

I huff a laugh completely devoid of humor and shake my head. "Nah. That's not what I'm worried about."

"Thennnnn...?" He draws the word out as if the answer here is completely clear and there are no complications anywhere.

I take a deep breath before I admit the thing that I'm very sure will happen. Because I know Kate. I know who she is and what she believes in. I know what scares her and excites her and makes her fall apart.

My eyes are unfocused, staring at the drop ceiling above me when I finally answer him.

"I'm worried she'll tell me to go."

* * *

KATE IS in the kitchen when I get home. She's crouched on the floor, petting Beaker while he eats.

She turns to look at me and a brilliant smile splits her face.

For a split second, I consider not telling her. Just turning down the job and not telling her. But I know I have to.

More than anything, I want her to be my partner. And partners make decisions together.

I hang up my keys, drop my messenger bag on the bench underneath, and walk straight over to her. She stands up and I wrap my arms all the way around her. She stiffens at first, like she's surprised, but then she relaxes and melts right into me. Her arms wind around my neck. I bury my face in her hair and try to be discreet about inhaling. I'm probably not successful.

When she loosens her grip, I force myself to do the same.

"How was your day?" she asks.

I swear my heart skips a couple of beats. She sees the immediate change in my face.

"What's wrong? Did something happen?"

I don't want to say it yet. Holding her jaw in my hands, I kiss her. I don't want to pop the bubble, but I have such a terrible feeling about this conversation.

She kisses me back, but she doesn't let it go on for long.

"Liam, what's going on?"

I take a deep breath, but I don't let go of her. I'm so nervous she'll run. Literally.

Spit it out, dude.

"I got… some news." I swallow against the driest throat I've ever had in my life. "My boss wants me to open a new office in Austin."

It's barely even a second after the words have left my mouth that she's tugging my wrists to get my hands off of her face and stepping backward.

I feel an immediate loss. I want to touch her. Tell her

everything will be okay. That I don't have to take the job. That I can stay here, and nothing has to change.

Her face has completely transformed. She's staring, but not at me. It's like she's looking *through* me. It's the same weird ghostly, zoned-out expression she used to wear all the time, except that I haven't seen it since before her birthday.

I hate it.

"Kate?"

She doesn't respond.

"Kate, please talk to me."

She blinks, but it doesn't do a thing to clear her vision. She's not seeing anything.

"It's not permanent. We do this… we go to new cities and open offices and train people and then we come back home."

Her head turns, but I swear she's not seeing anything new.

"It's probably about six months. The person who was supposed to do it had a family emergency and can't go."

The second-longest moment of my life passes in silence while she looks off into the distance. Finally, she makes eye contact with me. It feels both better and worse. I'm grateful she's looking at me, but I'm terrified of what she's going to say. For what I *know* she'll do.

I see something flicker across her eyes, but it's gone so quickly I can't tell what it was.

"That's great for you, Liam. I'm happy for you." She nods, like she's trying to convince herself that she's happy for me.

I shake my head. "Kate, I—"

"You deserve it," she cuts me off. "Really… I know you'll do a great job."

"No, Kate, let me—"

"I need to get out for my run before it's too late."

Her abrupt end to this conversation is like a kick to my chest. But I just look down and nod. I want her to get her run in and be home before dark. And I know she needs to work through whatever it is she's feeling.

She leaves me standing in the kitchen, staring at her retreating form and my stomach drops. None of this is a good sign.

I don't know how many miles she ends up running, but I know she's gone for so long that the sun starts to set, lighting the sky with brilliant color and reflecting off the lake. I made dinner and because she still wasn't back, I put the leftovers in the fridge when I was done. When she finally gets home, she makes a beeline for the stairs and disappears into her room. She doesn't come out for the rest of the night.

Not sure what else to do, I go through the motions of getting ready for bed and lie down, once again, staring at the ceiling.

Instead of being excited about this job opportunity—the chance to live in a new city for a while and experience new people and new food—I'm thinking about Kate and how this news is affecting her.

I picture that look on her face and my chest squeezes. I don't want to hurt her. I don't want to *leave* her. I'll happily stay here if she wants me to. But we can't work this out if she won't talk to me.

So I throw off the covers and walk across the landing to Kate's room. The door is cracked open as usual, so Beaker can come and go as he pleases. It's dark in the room, but the light of the moon shining through the window lets me see where Kate is on the bed. I walk over to the empty side of the bed and wait for just a moment before I hear the sheets rustle and then the duvet is thrown back.

It's a no-brainer to take the invitation, to slide into her bed, pull the duvet back up, and lie down to face her. I can barely see the whites of her eyes in the moonlight, but I can tell she's looking at me.

As my eyes adjust, I can see her more clearly. She looks… scared.

Reaching my hand up to her face, I brush my thumb over her cheekbone, partly because I want to touch her and partly because I wonder if she's crying. Her cheek is dry, but I swear I feel her chin quiver against the base of my hand.

"Kate, I don't have—"

I don't get to finish the sentence. She launches herself at me, silencing me with her soft, pliant mouth. Her arms pull me into her, so I wind mine around her body and press her completely into me.

Something feels different in her touch right now, but I don't want to overanalyze it at this current moment. I just need to feel close to her and I'm *almost* successful at it until I hear a tiny sniffle.

"Sweetheart…" I try to start again, but again, she stops me.

"Liam, please don't talk about it right now. Please… please just… I need this. Please just touch me. Hold me. Make me feel like everything will be okay."

Her voice breaks more than once, and it fucking kills me.

I kiss her and I taste salt. I bring my hand back to her cheek and gently sweep away the dampness from her soft skin. "Baby, please don't cry. There's no reason—"

"Liam, please…" Her hands curl into fists, taking bunches of my shirt with them. "Please…"

My chest squeezes painfully. I don't want her to hurt. I don't want her to cry. So I roll her onto her back and ease myself over her, letting my hips fall heavy on hers and cage her head in with my forearms.

There's still a question in her beautiful hazel eyes and I want to erase it from existence. I don't want her to have questions about me.

"I would do anything for you, Kate," I whisper.

23

YOU CAN'T UNRING THE BELL

Kate

"**Y**ou headed home soon?"

Elliot's voice breaks me out of my five-thirty haze. He's standing in the doorway to my office, hand braced on either side of the doorframe.

I should go home. I know that.

The thing is, I know that once I get home, Liam will be there, and he will be getting ready to leave for Austin and this whole thing just makes me *sad*. So fucking sad.

For a little while there, I was able to live in this fantasy world where my life wasn't in complete shambles. Liam and I were doing sexy things, having dinners at home together, watching the entire Jurassic Park catalog, and stumbling through this weird time alongside one another.

And ever since Liam came home on Monday, everything has been different.

The bubble has burst and there's no way to put it back together.

"Hello?"

I blink hard and look up at my best friend with the best smile I can muster.

"Yes, of course."

He nods, but he looks suspicious. Like he knows there's something up.

"Anything fun planned for tonight?"

"Nah." I shake my head. "I'll go for a run. Maybe read. Binge something on HGTV."

Elliot continues to study my face, but I'm trying really hard to keep my expressions in check. He knows me better than anyone. He'll know that something is wrong.

In the back of my mind, a pesky thought tries to remind me that July is quickly approaching. That Elliot was instrumental in getting me out of bed and integrated back into society.

That he has always, *always* had my best interests at heart.

I don't want to disappoint him.

He narrows his eyes at me for a split second and then seems to acquiesce. "We still on for tomorrow?"

Oh right, movie night. He and Leon are supposed to come over to watch a movie.

I'm not sure how the hell Liam and I are supposed to hide the awkwardness between us.

Does Elliot know about his job offer? Does Leon?

I clear my throat, suddenly feeling like a massive lump is making itself at home. "Yep. Still on."

"Good. I'll bring some munchies."

"That sounds great. I'll bring the wine."

"Perfect." He spins back toward the door but looks back over his shoulder, pinning me with a concerned frown. "You sure you're all right?"

I force a smile. "Of course."

"Okay," he folds. "I'll see you in the morning."

"Drive safe."

He leaves my doorway and I let my head hit the chair behind me with a thunk. I know I need to go home. I'm avoiding Liam. I'm sure he knows it, too.

With a groan, I force myself to stand up, gather my things, and leave my office. While I'm driving home, I decide that I will definitely go on that run and then attempt to get through dinner with Liam—if he's around, anyway. I need to try. I need to find a way to be normal around him.

So that's what I do. Liam is in the kitchen when I walk in. He's getting ingredients out for dinner, but he freezes when he sees me.

My stomach clenches with unease. I drag air into my lungs and squeak out the most pathetic "Hi" in the history of the world.

"Hey," he returns immediately. "How was your day?"

I shrug one shoulder and set my bags down on the bench below the coat hangers. "It was fine. You?"

He hesitates. I'm very aware that I'm asking him how his workday was and that's what has caused the tension this week.

"Stressful" is what he finally lands on.

I keep my face as impassive as possible when I respond. "I'm sure you have a lot to do before you leave."

His eyebrows furrow just a little bit and the muscle in his cheek jumps. Abruptly, he turns back toward the fridge and deposits the ingredients back onto the shelves, then shuts the door and turns to face me again.

"Kate, I wanted to talk to you about that."

Oh, I definitely do not.

"There's not much to talk about, Liam. You've earned an amazing opportunity and I'm really excited for you."

That muscle in his cheek jumps again and something flares in his eyes. Anger? Frustration? Probably both. I'm a fucking disaster of a human and he's been living with me for months. He's probably exasperated beyond belief.

"I haven't accepted the position," he tells me.

Oh.

Oh fuck.

Fucking hell.

"Oh? Why not?"

His eyebrows shoot up. "Why not?" He repeats my question back at me before palming the back of his neck and squeezing. "Because... because of *you*, Kate. Because of *us*. Because of whatever it is we're doing here."

My throat closes up tight. My mind is screaming at me, *There is no us!* But my heart knows it's a lie. I can't get the words out. I can't get *any* words out.

Liam takes a step closer to me, his palms up, beseeching. "Kate, please, talk to me."

Fuck fuck fuck.

I choke on a breath, my lungs starting to seize. I swallow compulsively. I open my mouth to attempt to say something —anything—but nothing comes out.

"Kate, I... I need to know."

I shake my head and try to speak again. This time, I'm able to get out a very breathy, "Know... what?"

"I need to know how you feel about this. About me."

My knees are suddenly weak. I grip the edge of the counter to keep myself upright. That's when he realizes I'm not okay. Not even close.

"Fuck." He rushes forward and cradles my face in his hands. "Kate... I need you to try to breathe."

I squeeze my eyes shut and hold on to his wrists as he tries to demonstrate deep breathing, as he's done so many times for me in the past. My eyes and my nose burn, but I can hear Liam murmuring to me through the fog, pulling me back.

"In... out... in... out..." he continues until I'm finally able to follow instructions.

"There you go... take it easy."

Once I'm able to get oxygen again, I pry my eyes open and he's right there. Blurry, but there. I still can't get any words out, not that he seems to mind.

He's so patient.

That thought brings me back to where we left off. I don't know what he sees on my face, but something in them flickers and then dies.

He drops his hands and steps back. I immediately want him back. I want his warmth and his steady breath. His strength.

I know we need to continue with this conversation, but not a single part of me wants to.

Liam clears his throat. "I, um... bought some time, but I need to tell my boss what I've decided."

I lick my dry lips and swallow hard. "Which is what?"

His head tilts to one side as he studies me. "Kate, I haven't decided. I wanted to talk to you."

"Why do I play a part in this decision for you?" I have a feeling I know the answer. I've been avoiding it. It's that pesky voice in the back of my mind that keeps trying to tell me I'm missing something.

I keep kicking it and telling it to shut up.

He sighs, looks out the back windows toward the lake and seems to come to some kind of conclusion. "I know that this isn't ideal timing. I know that you've had a horribly traumatic year. I know that you and I have been on different time lines."

All of those things are true. I still don't know how these topics relate to his decision.

"But I… I don't *have* to take this job. I could stay here. There will be other opportunities, and frankly, I didn't think this one would come up so quickly. When I took the job, I said I'd be open to opportunities like this, but I assumed it would be farther down the road. I don't have to take it."

Oh. Fucking hell.

I blink furiously. "Why… why would you do that?"

"Kate, you…" He pauses and I just know. I know what's coming and the tears have already started to blur my vision again.

Liam steps closer to me and takes my head in his hands again, wiping tears away with his thumbs.

"You *must* know…"

I shake my head. Not because I don't know but because I do, and I'm terrified to hear him say it.

"Kate," he whispers, tilting my head up toward his face. "I'm in love with you."

Something in my chest caves in and I try to shake my head again. This time, because this cannot be real. He cannot possibly. Now that he's said it out loud, my brain wants to deny something it knew with certainty just moments before.

He nods slowly. "I am, Kate. I love you. I couldn't stop it. I wouldn't want to stop it if I could, though. You're one of the strongest people I've ever met. You may not feel that, but I see it. You're strong and fiercely loyal and you love so deeply. Of course I fell in love with you. How could I not?"

"Liam, I'm…" I don't even know how to finish that sentence.

Liam, I'm a mess.

Liam, I'm not cut out for this.

Liam, I'm literally human wreckage.

"I mean it, Kate. I'll stay here if you want me."

With another swipe of his thumbs under my eyes, he leans in close and presses his lips to mine.

If I've learned anything about the effect Liam has on me, it's that I'm helpless when his mouth is on my body—any part of my body. And even though I've been crying, and he's been trying to calm me down and told me he's somehow in love with me and I'm definitely freaking out, I want to kiss him.

So I do.

With tongue and then roaming hands and finally, desperate *want*.

"I love you," he whispers again, his hands sinking into my hair.

The words feed my soul and somehow threaten to kill me slowly. I want a repeat of Saturday night. Or Sunday after the baseball game. Or even Monday after he told me about the job in the first place. Mostly, I want to go back in time.

But you can't unring the bell.

Liam's hands frame my hips as he maneuvers me backward, pressing me against the counter.

For a few moments, I consider it. For those precious moments, I live a lifetime with Liam. Steadfast, loving, handsome Liam. It's full of traveling and laughter and cool nights by a roaring fire, of dancing and quiet dinners at home and movie marathons. It's beautiful and tragic and I *want* it.

And that's when I realize what that pesky thought was on Saturday night that I kept trying to push away.

And I have my answer.

"Stop…" I pull my mouth from his. "Stop, please stop."

I slide out from between him and the counter, then pace a few feet away from him to get some space. I don't want to be able to reach out and touch him because if I do, I might kick that needling voice into the sun.

When I turn back to him, he's standing right where I left him, but he's facing me with wary eyes.

With a deep breath that wouldn't even be possible if it weren't for him, I finally face reality.

"Liam… you are… basically perfect. You took care of your ailing wife. You've been taking care of me for months now. You're kind and compassionate and *so* loving."

I have to stop for a second to catch my breath. My chest hurts. My stomach is revolting. I don't want to do this. I know I *have* to. I know it's the right thing. But I don't *want* to and it's making me feel sick.

"I can't give you what you want. What you deserve." My voice breaks entirely, and the tears are unstoppable. I just have to accept them as a fact. "I'm… I'm pretty broken, Liam."

"You're not broken," he says gently. "You're grieving."

I huff a laugh, shaking my head. "You are so incredibly kind."

"I'm only telling you the truth."

Closing my eyes, I drop my head into my hands.

"Hear me out, Kate." I hear him move, his footsteps getting closer on the tile, but he stops short of actually touching me. "We can take this as slow as you want to. We can step back. We can do whatever you need to feel comfortable."

I drop my hands and look at him. He's straddling the line between not listening to me and trying to prove me wrong, but he looks so sincere, I know he's not trying to manipulate me.

"Liam, I'm… I'm not like you. I can't accept that my husband died during what was supposed to be a relatively routine medical procedure on his best friend's watch." I swallow acid, just trying to say those words. It *still* hurts. "I'm not who I used to be. I don't know who this person is you think you've fallen in love with."

His eyes narrow. "Look, you can question your decisions and what you feel is best for you, but don't question my feelings for you." He taps his sternum with his fingertips. "I know myself. I know what I feel."

I grind my teeth together. "Then I'm confident you'll find someone else to feel this way about. I can't be it. I can't give you what you want."

That makes his eyes narrow even further. "And what is it that you *think* I want?"

The dam inside me breaks, the truth I haven't wanted to speak aloud finally flowing free.

"You have a fucking *legacy*, Liam. You are William Arthur Anderson, the *Fourth*. And I… I can't. I can't be pregnant again. I can't do all of that again. I won't survive it, I… You're asking too much of me."

"I'm not asking anything—"

"Yes, you are!" I can't help but raise my voice. "You're asking me to jump off a bridge with you when I can't even fucking swim. I can't *do* this, Liam. I'm not prepared. I'm a complete mess. You deserve someone who can give you all of these things—who will *want* to give you all of these things. You deserve someone who will give you William Arthur Anderson, the *Fifth*."

His expression hardens and I realize that this is the first time I've ever seen Liam angry with me.

"First off, William Arthur Anderson, the Fifth was never going to exist, Kate. Jill was never going to be able to have kids and I knew that. I wanted her and that was all that mattered to me. And second, I don't give a fuck about the *legacy*." He does the air quotes on *legacy* and everything. "It's *my* life, not my father's or his father's or any of the other Williams before us. I'm *Liam* and I fell in love with a woman who would die young and now I've fallen in love with *you*. I don't care if you want zero kids or five. I want *you*. Now… if you *don't* want *me*… then that's one thing. But if you don't want to be with me because of a legacy that *you* think I need to carry on… well, that's not an actual reason. That's you pushing me away because you're scared."

"Of course I'm fucking scared!" I shriek. "How are you *not* scared? My husband died. Your *wife* died. How are you not fucking terrified to fall in love with anyone ever again? How are you not running for the hills right now?"

He's quiet for a moment while my chest is heaving and I'm doing my damnedest to not fall prey to another panic attack. It seems like he's working something out in his brain, and he must find the answer because suddenly, his face softens and he leans against the counter.

"Because I want my life while I have it. You and I both know that life is short—sometimes devastatingly so. I don't know how much time I have here, but I want to spend it with people who bring joy to my life. I want to spend it doing things with those people that make my life better. That remind me why life is worth living. I want to live every possible moment with people I love because *that* is what I want to think about when I'm dying. I want to remember drinking bourbon on the patio with someone who's trying to keep me company when she knows damn well I'm not in a good headspace. I want to think about watching every *Jurassic Park* movie and throwing popcorn at each other. I want to remember baseball games and late-night conversations. When I die and my life is flashing before my eyes, I want those things. I don't want to *wish* I'd told the person I love that I love her. I don't want to regret not having the courage to say it. I'd rather say it and blow my whole life apart than keep quiet and *wonder*. Kate, I love you and I'm sorry if you're not ready for that. I'm sorry if this is too fast, too soon. Trust that I wasn't expecting any of this to happen, but now that it has… I don't want to let go of it."

My chest aches again. I could do good deeds for the rest of my goddamned life and still not deserve him. How awful for him to fall in love with a woman who cannot return the sentiment.

"We're not in the same place, Liam," I admit quietly. "I'm not going to insult you by claiming I don't have feelings for you. We both know I do. But you're right... I'm not ready for this. The truth is, I may never be ready. And you shouldn't have to wait around for me."

The wary look in his eyes returns. It's like he's silently begging me not to continue.

"I... I have a lot of shit to figure out right now and I think..." I swallow more acid. "I think I need to figure it out on my own."

The sigh he lets out comes from the bottom of his soul. He looks so defeated as he braces a hand on the counter where, just a moment ago, he pressed my body. His shoulders sag and the churning in my stomach intensifies.

I feel guilty. So fucking guilty for everything. For asking him to move in with me. For reaching my arm across his body all those months ago. For kissing him—that night and tonight and all those times in between.

For dragging him down with me, just as Jill had been afraid to do.

I broke him.

I broke the gentle man with the dead wife.

I am a horrible piece of shit for breaking this wonderful man's heart.

"I understand," he says quietly, lifting his head to meet my gaze. "I do."

"I'm sorry," I whisper, tears flowing from my eyes once again. "God, I'm so sorry."

"Me too."

We stand silently across from each other for a moment before he crosses the room and stops directly in front of me. Quietly, he speaks to me while he kisses my forehead, wipes tears from my cheeks, threads his fingers into my hair, and I let it all happen because… I may never have this opportunity again. This is very likely to be the last time Liam ever touches me like this.

"I hope you find everything you're looking for—no matter what that means."

My hands find his sides on their own and my arms tremble from fighting the urge to wrap around him.

"I just want you to be happy."

The reverence in his voice is far more than I deserve, and I already know that this moment will haunt me for the rest of my fucking life.

He lingers for only a half second longer before whispering, "Good luck, Kate." Then he steps away so quickly that I couldn't have changed my mind if I wanted to.

Liam leaves me standing in the kitchen, staring straight ahead at the back windows, blurry through my tears.

2 4

STARTING OVER... AGAIN

Kate

I wake up with a headache.

But not the kind that reminds you of the super fun night you had. More like the kind that reminds you your entire fucking life is in shambles, and you've actually managed to make it *worse* for yourself because you're absolutely terrible at making decisions.

Yeah. That kind.

I'd smack my own forehead, but it hurts like a motherfucker, so I'm not going to do that.

I drag my body to the bathroom and look at myself in the mirror.

Fucking fuck.

I didn't wash my face last night and I have mascara tracks down my cheeks. My eyes are puffy. My skin is pale as fuck. I look like I've been on a bender.

As I stare at myself, I'm struck by the realization that I

haven't looked like *this* in a while. It's been… weeks? Months, maybe? Since I looked in the mirror and found *this* woman staring back at me.

Nausea roils in my gut as I remember Liam's face last night.

Fuck, I hate myself today.

It's been a while since I've felt like that, too.

Whether I like it or not, today is a weekday and I'm taking over this business one day, so I try to shut off all my feelings and I get ready for work. I dab cooling gel on the poor, swollen flesh around my eyes in an attempt to hide the fact that I cried half the night. I keep the eye makeup light so I don't risk irritating my eyes even further.

Before I open my bedroom door, I take a deep, fortifying breath and prepare myself for the probability of seeing Liam. We're both adults. We'll figure this out.

Or I'll avoid him for the rest of my life.

Somewhere in the back of my mind, Gwen's voice reminds me that avoidance isn't a solution and I drop-kick the words into the fucking sun.

I open the door and am met with absolute silence.

I walk across the landing to find his door open, the bed made. Downstairs, there's coffee in the coffeepot, just like usual, but Liam isn't sitting at the breakfast nook with oatmeal and the newspaper. A peek into the garage confirms that he's already left for work. His car is gone.

A teeny, tiny part of me feels relieved that I get to avoid the awkward (and painful) encounter with him this morning. But mostly, I feel completely miserable. And guilty.

"Fuck," I mutter to absolutely no one but myself.

Beaker is suddenly chirping at my feet and headbutting my legs.

Cool, so I'm back to talking to the cat.

Note to self: don't tell Gwen.

I fill a travel mug with coffee, grab my overnight oats (something Liam showed me how to do, so it's super fun that I'll have *that* reminder every time I make them), and head out the door.

Work signals normalcy for me. Work is always there. I can bury myself in it easily. There's always something to do. An email to be returned. A property to be evaluated. A new listing to create.

I'm able to keep myself busy all day, not allowing for interactions long enough to signal that anything is amiss with me today. I don't want or need questions right now. I just want to keep my brain occupied so I don't have to think about what might be waiting for me at home.

The sunny dispositions of our employees complement the sun in the sky, but I'm certainly not part of the sunshine group.

"I'm gonna run home and get Leon. Then we'll head over to your place." Elliot's voice shocks the hell out of me for more than one reason. First, I was lost in my own world and second, I completely forgot about movie night.

I try really hard to hide the shock on my face. "Yeah… of course."

"Great! I'll see you in a little bit!" It's uncharacteristic of him, but he doesn't study my face or try to overanalyze what he sees. To my enormous relief, he dashes away.

"*Fuck*," I groan, dropping my head into my hands. I need to get home and talk to Liam. Maybe we should cancel. I could say I'm not feeling well all of a sudden. I'm sure we can find some sort of excuse, but I know I need to get home quickly in order to do it.

I slam my laptop shut, grab my purse, and practically sprint out the door.

I get home in record time and am surprised that Liam's car isn't in the garage when the door opens. He's usually home before me, but I suppose I'm not usually home this early.

As I'm gathering my things in the car, I try to find ways to talk to Liam about this. He's probably forgotten as well.

Beaker scampers across the floor to greet me when I open the door. My sweet little disaster.

"Hey, buddy." I squat down to pet him and rub the bridge of his nose. "Did you have a good day? I certainly hope so."

Shocker: he doesn't respond.

When I stand up, I see a folded piece of paper on the kitchen island. Frowning, I pick it up and hear something clatter on the granite.

My house key.

My stomach bottoms out.

Here's my house key. I couldn't fit all of my winter clothes in my suitcase and I probably won't need them in Austin, so I left them here for now. I'll come back and get them when I get back, or I'll send someone for them after I'm gone.

Thanks for offering me a place to stay.
Liam

My heart speeds up with every word I read, panic lancing through me like ice.

He just... left? Without telling me beforehand?

Clutching the note in one hand, I make a beeline for the stairs, my heels doing nothing but slow me down. I mutter obscenities as I bend to yank them off my feet.

I run up the stairs and whip around the corner, stopping short in the doorway of his bedroom, my heart in my throat. Everything looks the same... but then I remember that the furniture was already here when he moved in. Liam had barely brought a thing.

Frantically, I scan the space for anything that belongs to him—the photo of Jill on his dresser, his cologne on the bathroom counter, his phone charger draped over his night-stand. There's nothing.

I bound over to a dresser and yank open a drawer, but I already know what I'll find. Or rather, what I won't.

It's empty.

I yank open another and it's empty, too.

The third drawer holds thick sweaters.

Even though I know it's pointless, I cross the room to the closet and slide open the door. Aside from a couple of heavy jackets, it's empty. His suitcase isn't sitting on the floor any longer.

Slowly, I turn to face the room again and tears spring to my eyes. I'm still holding the note in my hand.

How could he leave without even saying goodbye?

I get to find out he left in a fucking note, scribbled and left on the counter with the key I gave him.

What did you expect, Kate?

With sadness weighing me down, I lie down on Liam's side of the bed. I'm not sure whether it's guilt, sadness, or gluttony that has me breathing in the scent of his cologne on the pillow. It's crisp and clean.

I fish my phone out of my back pocket. No missed texts or voice mails, but I already know he wouldn't have reached out. If he resorted to leaving a note on the counter, he's certainly not going to get hold of me directly.

Still lying on the bed, I replay last night's conversation in my head for the millionth time.

Kate... you must *know...*

I'm in love with you.

You're strong and fiercely loyal and you love so deeply. Of course I fell in love with you. How could I not?

I'm still flabbergasted that he claims to love me. I'm *such* a mess.

A better woman would have cried tears of joy and professed her undying love in return.

But I'm not that woman.

I may never be that woman.

And he *deserves* that kind of woman.

I don't know how long I lie in Liam's bed—which, unfortunately will probably *always* be Liam's bed in my mind—but at some point, Beaker jumps onto the bed. He meows and nudges my hand, reminding me that I didn't feed him when I got home.

"Oh, I'm sorry, Beaker. Let's get you some dinner, yeah?"

I haul myself up and off Liam's bed, trudge down the stairs, and plop some turkey feast into a bowl, topped with the customary treats, and place it on the floor. I pet his back a couple of times, then refill his water dish and grab myself a glass of wine.

Sinking into the couch, I turn on the TV. If anything, it's just for the noise. I don't know if I'll be able to pay attention to it. The house is just too goddamn quiet.

And that's where I'm sitting when I hear the door to the kitchen open.

"Kate?" Elliot calls out. "I'm here. I brought a movie. I know you guys have that one from Netflix you wanted to watch, but this one should be pretty funny."

His messenger bag lands on the counter with a thunk.

"Leon isn't coming. He got held up at the office and now he's exhausted and just wants to go home."

He comes around the fireplace wall and sees me on the couch, then glances around.

"What's wrong? You look gloomy. And where's Liam? I didn't see his car."

I can only meet his gaze for a fraction of a second before looking down into my wineglass. "He left."

"What do you mean 'he left'? Like, he's picking up dinner?"

I shake my head. "He moved out."

Elliot freezes in place. "Where did he go?"

I shrug. "I honestly don't know. He's taking that job in Austin, but he doesn't have to be there until July first, so…" I wave my free hand toward the garage. "My guess is his brother's place. His parents' maybe? I don't know."

Elliot slowly walks over to the couch and sits down next to me. "What happened?" His voice is so fucking gentle, I could cry.

"We had a… disagreement."

My response is met with silence before Elliot's hand begins waving in a circle, beckoning me to give more information. "About…?" he prompts.

"Well, technically, it was about him moving to Austin."

A peek at El's face shows me that he's frowning. "Okay, so then he just… moved out?"

"Apparently. I didn't exactly realize he was going to leave today." I hand him the note that I haven't been able to let go of since the moment I found it.

After a moment, he sighs and says quietly, "I'm sorry, Kate."

I shake my head. "I don't know how I got here. This time last year, I was…" Well, I wasn't happy, but I wasn't muddling my way through a deep depression, but Elliot doesn't know about my miscarriage, so I swallow the words. "I was happily married. Of course, I didn't know that my husband would die in a few weeks. And here I am now, upset because my roommate moved out." I huff a laugh and take a sip of wine. "It's all just so absurd."

I hear Elliot take a tentative breath. "Kinda seems like he was more than just a roommate."

My gaze snaps to his. I take a moment to study his expression—it's open, but with just enough *try-and-lie-to-my-face* energy that I don't bother.

"Yeah… I suppose so," I concede. "I've kind of been in denial about that."

"For what it's worth, I think he genuinely cares about you."

"Why? Did he say something to you?"

"What is this? Middle school?" Elliot chastises. "No, he didn't say anything to me. I've known the man for over a decade. I can tell when he cares about someone and when he's just being polite."

I roll my eyes. "I was just asking."

"If you have questions about how Liam feels about you, you need to ask *him*."

I stare into my wineglass. "I, um… I don't really have to ask."

Elliot's gaze sears into the side of my face.

"He told me how he feels."

"And…?" Elliot prompts.

I look over at him, pleading. I don't want to talk about this in detail. It hurts enough.

He raises his eyebrows expectantly.

"Oh, come on. Don't make me say it," I beg.

"Wow." He blinks with wide eyes.

I nod because I can't bring myself to confirm it aloud.

"And you… don't feel the same way?" he asks.

"Elliot, I…" I rub my forehead with my free hand. "I don't know how I feel. I care about him, of course. Maybe I even have *loving* feelings toward him, but I just… I can't right now. I'm not there yet. I don't know if I'll *ever* be there."

Memories from last night flash through my mind and tears spring to my eyes again.

Fucking traitors. Get your shit together, tear ducts.

"It's not really fair to him," I finish, swallowing against the burning sensation in my throat.

"Oh, honey—"

"It's my fault," I interrupt Elliot. "I told him to take the job in Austin."

Elliot lets out a big sigh. "Yeah, but I'm not totally clear as to why. You two obviously care about each other. I've known that for a while now. Why not just... see where it goes? No pressure. You could just hang out."

"I think it's too late for that. He already lo—" My voice cuts out. I can't even say the word. I close my eyes and take a deep breath before continuing. "Elliot, I'm a mess. I'm just... a disaster of a human. I can't be in a relationship right now. I'm not ready. I have no business dragging him down with me. He should go... live..." I take a fortifying sip of wine to cover up the total failure of my vocal cords.

My sweet, kind, wonderful friend takes my hand and holds it in his much larger one.

"I don't want to put you guys in the middle of this," I continue. "You're friends with him too, but it's not your problem. It's our problem. It's *my* problem."

"Don't say that," he says gently. "You've had an exceptionally tough year. I'm sure he understands."

My forced laugh is devoid of humor. "I'm not so sure about that."

Elliot leans forward to get my attention. He's frowning. "Honey, clearly he does. You told him what you needed and he's giving it to you."

I think about that for a moment and realize that Elliot is right, which still doesn't make me feel better. I close my eyes and rest my cool wineglass against my forehead.

"I'm sorry, sweetie."

"No, I'm sorry," I say, looking up at him. "I'm the one that got us both into this mess. I should have just kept my mouth shut. He could have gotten an apartment on his own and moved on with his life."

Great job, Kate! Solid life decisions!

"I hope I'm not making things weird between you guys and him."

"We'll be all right, don't worry."

Elliot settles back on the couch next to me and I take the opportunity to lay my head on his slender shoulder. He kisses my hair.

"For what it's worth, I think you did the right thing."

"Yeah?"

"Yeah... I do."

"Well, there's that, I guess."

We sit in silence for a few moments, the TV playing whatever the fuck it is playing. I wasn't paying attention to it.

"You still up for a movie? Or would you rather be alone tonight?" Elliot asks.

I lift my head from his shoulder and look up at him. My first instinct is to be alone, but really... how healthy is that? Gwen's voice reminds me that I need a support system.

Fine, Gwen. You win tonight.

"Yeah... why not? Maybe no rom-coms."

"How about *The Kingsmen*? Hot dudes killing other hot dudes?"

"Perfect," I agree.

"I'll get more wine."

Elliot pats my thigh and gets up from the couch.

I'm starting over.

Today is day one.

25

CAN YOU JUST INJECT ME WITH THE MEDS?

Kate

Life without Liam is… boring.

For the second time in one year, I'm figuring out how to live without a man who'd become important to me—and yes, maybe that makes me incredibly pathetic, but here we are. The circumstances surrounding the two situations might be completely different, but the end result is still the same.

I'm alone.

And I have to figure out how to live my life all over again.

This time though, I'm not paralyzed by depression and grief.

Don't get me wrong… I'm sad. I'm heartbroken. But I'm certain I did the right thing, and that provides me comfort sometimes. Particularly at night when the house is quiet and I'm watching movies with Beaker.

Liam and I haven't spoken since that Thursday. It's July

already, so I imagine he's already in Austin. I like to imagine he's living his best life and barely sparing me a thought. Some might find that depressing, but I find it liberating. If Liam doesn't want me, I can't hop on a plane to Austin and beg for forgiveness.

If he's happy, I did the right thing.

If he's thriving, I did the right thing.

And of course, if I'm thriving, I know I did the right thing.

Today is my first therapy appointment since Liam moved out. Between conflicting schedules and Gwen's vacation, we hadn't been able to get anything on the books, but I still checked in with her office manager every week to fulfill my legal obligations.

I'd call, tell Rosalie that I'm calling to check in and I'd relay the three things I'm grateful for, which was my assignment from Gwen in lieu of our regular check-ins for the two and a half weeks we couldn't find time together. Additionally, I told her my plan for the week. After that, I hung up and I assume Rosalie reported back to Gwen.

So for the past two weeks or so, I've been putting my money where my mouth is.

I've been allowing myself to process Liam's departure, evaluating my grief level post-Nick, and making some decisions about how I want to proceed with my life.

As usual, Gwen sits down in the armchair across from me, flips open her folder, and begins to recap our last session. "It's been a while since we last saw each other, but I have been receiving your updates through Rosalie. The last time we talked—"

"Liam moved out," I cut her off. It doesn't really matter what we talked about last time.

Gwen's eyes snap up to mine. "Oh?"

I swallow and nod sharply. "Yes."

"Did something happen?"

Gwen is using her gentle voice—the one she uses when she doesn't want to scare me but believes the subject at hand is very important for us to discuss.

I give her a brief recap, hitting the highlights and making sure to include Liam's declaration of love for me.

I still can't believe that happened.

I tell her my reasons for telling Liam to take the job offer in Austin. I tell her how the entire thing made me feel. I tell her that I need to figure all of this out on my own.

Alone.

When I finally finish, Gwen nods solemnly. "That must have been a very difficult conversation for both of you."

"Yes," I admit, my chest constricting with the memory.

"I have to say though… I'm very proud of you."

I frown. And blink. And shake my head.

"What? Why?"

"Because you stood up for yourself." Gwen's head tilts slightly to the right, her dangling earring falling away from her neck while the left earring falls to her neck. "You recognized that what Liam was proposing was not aligned with what you wanted, and you made that fact known."

Oh.

Oh, that actually… makes sense.

I find myself staring into the abyss while I think about that, and I feel a teeny, tiny flicker of pride in myself before the shame and heartache win out again.

"I hurt him. I could see it in his eyes." My chest constricts again, so I press my fingers to my sternum to try to alleviate it. "He's such a wonderful person and I hurt him. I feel horrible about it."

Gwen looks down to her notebook and nods ever so slightly. "I can see why you feel that way. But… I think you both know that it's most important for you to focus on your-self right now."

I don't know how to respond to that, so I stare out the window.

After a lengthy silence, Gwen's gentle voice drifts across the space between us.

"Do you think you love him?"

My eyes snap to hers and I start blinking compulsively.

Like... what? How am I supposed to know the answer to that?

So I answer truthfully.

"I don't know."

Gwen nods again and jots something down in her notebook.

I have a love-hate relationship with her jotting down notes in her notebook. Is she writing something good or bad? Is she making a note about diagnosis or planning what her Kate voodoo doll will look like?

"Regardless, I think you made a good decision. A *healthy* decision. I'm proud of you."

This quiet pride emanating from my court-appointed therapist solidifies a decision I'd made before coming here today. I clear my throat, trying to calm my nerves.

"I... I'm also ready to try medication."

Gwen's eyebrows shoot up her forehead. "Really?"

I nod.

"What changed your mind?"

I suck in a deep breath. "Clarity, I suppose." Scratching at my temple, I dig deep for the courage to keep talking about my goddamn feelings. "I suppose I've made progress in the past year... you know, since I'm not in jail right now. But I think I'm finally at a point where I need to figure out how to... build a new life." I stare down at my fingernails, run my thumb over the smooth, painted surfaces. "Find a new normal, I guess."

Gwen is quiet for a moment before she asks a question. "Does Liam moving out have anything to do with this?"

I really should have known that question was coming, but somehow, I'm still surprised by it.

"I mean… I'd be lying if I said it didn't. But it's not that he's *gone* specifically, it's that…"

God, this is going to sound absolutely pathetic.

I blow out a breath and force myself to keep going. "In his absence, I've realized that there is just *nothing* in my life besides my job. I've needed work. I've needed to focus on something tangible that I could do easily. The distraction has been important, but I can't…" I trail off when I realize that the word doesn't quite fit the way I feel. "I don't *want* to live like that for the rest of my life."

The words hung in the air between us for a moment before Gwen told me *again*, "I'm proud of you for making that decision."

When did my therapist, being proud of me, become a thing that mattered in my life? What the fuck is happening right now?

My throat is suddenly thick and my nose is burning.

Fucking feelings.

I grind my teeth together and get my shit together. "I want to get better. I do."

"That's a very big step, Kate." Gwen's voice is so fucking gentle I want to jump in it and wrap it around my body. "I'm glad to hear it."

And then lie on the couch and watch bloodthirsty dinosaurs.

With Liam.

Goddamnit!

I sniff and blink back my tears.

Can she just inject me with the meds now?

"I'll do whatever you tell me to. I just don't want to feel like this anymore."

Gwen's eyes soften and her mouth forms a gentle, barely there smile.

"I'm not going to tell you to do much of anything, Kate. I'm here to help you figure out what you want and then help you build the tools you need to achieve those goals." She pauses and tilts her head in thought. "I'll give you some homework now and then."

Skepticism activated.

"Like what?"

"Well, first of all, I want you to do one selfish thing every day. One thing that is for you and only you. Something that makes you happy."

I stare at her blankly. *What the fuck does that mean?*

And then I realize I didn't ask that question out loud, so I do.

"I want you to focus on yourself. You said that you want to find out how to move forward with your life… to find out who you are now. So… do things that make you happy."

I sigh and look out the window again, racking my brain for any goddamned thing that makes me happy.

"I like running. It makes me…" I mean, not *happy*, but… "It calms me down."

"Running is great. I know it helps you manage your emotions and relax a bit—as contradictory as that sounds," she adds with a sly smile.

Gwen's cheekiness makes me huff a laugh.

"What else?" she prompts.

Look, I'm fully aware that it doesn't say much about me that I literally can't think of anything that makes me happy. Nothing brings me joy except for Beaker and Elliot at this point. So that's what I tell Gwen: Beaker and Elliot.

"Spending time with your cat and your friend." Gwen nods. "That's nice. What else?"

I don't even try to hide my eye roll. "Gwen, what are you

hoping I'll say? Nothing makes me happy. Is that what you want to hear?"

"That is definitely *not* what I want to hear."

"Then what?"

Gwen sighs. "Okay, how about I give you some examples of things that make me happy?"

"Please do."

"Well, it's July, so it's hot all the time. That makes me rather miserable sometimes—"

"Off to a good start," I interrupt.

But it gets a laugh out of Gwen. "Hush you," she chides. "So I like to go to the beach. I put my chair right next to the water so I can put my feet in, and then I read a book under an umbrella. It's one of my favorite things."

In the back of my mind, I wonder if she's anywhere near my part of the beach, but I don't ask. It feels like an invasion.

"Sometimes, I get a massage because I carry tension in my lower back and every couple of months, it gets difficult to manage."

The thought of a near stranger touching me makes me outwardly cringe. "I can't believe you let strangers touch you."

That gets a laugh out of Gwen.

"You don't have to do things that make *me* happy, Kate. I want you to figure out what makes *you* happy, and then I want you to do those things."

I can't hide my grimace. "You make it sound so simple."

"It might be hard at first, but you'll get better at it with practice."

She sounds so confident, whereas I'm feeling anything but.

"Why don't we come up with something now? I can help you brainstorm."

I sag on the couch, my spine curling, body deflating.

"Gwen, I literally don't know. I like running. I like hanging out with Beaker and Elliot."

"I'm sure we'll find something." Gwen smiles.

Again, with the confidence.

"What do you enjoy doing with Elliot?"

"We watch movies together. Sometimes we go out to dinner. Elliot is my best friend."

"That's lovely. Maybe every couple of weeks, you ask Elliot to have a movie night with you? Or go out to lunch or dinner?"

I think about it, then nod. "Yeah, I can do that."

"What about the animal shelter? You're nearing the end of your court-mandated service there. Are you considering continuing with it?"

I nod again. "Yeah… I like it. I go every Sunday morning. I get to cuddle with cats and dogs for a while."

"Excellent." Gwen's smile is blinding this time. "That won't be every day, of course, so on days you're not hanging out with Elliot or spending the time at the shelter, try to find something else. No matter how big or small. Try things out. See if you can find a new hobby. Keep a note on your phone of what you're doing each day that makes you happy."

I grumble my agreement. It's not like I have much choice. Gwen is the person keeping me out of jail.

"I'm proud of you, Kate. You're making healthy decisions."

"Yeah, yeah, yeah," I grouse.

"I also want you to do one more thing."

"What's that?"

"I want you to write letters to Nick."

I blink. Once. Twice. Three times rapidly. "You want me to *what?*"

Gwen's lips twitch like she's holding back a smile and she glances down to her notebook while she composes herself.

Clearing her throat, she looks back up at me. "I'd like you to write letters to Nick."

I stare at Gwen, waiting for a crack in her therapy facade to see if she's joking. There's no crack, not even so much as a splinter. There's no laughter in her eyes. Just the same patient kindness as always.

"You want *me* to… write letters… to my *dead husband*?"

"Yes." Gwen nods once.

"Letters he'll never read?"

"Yes." She nods again.

"Why? What's the point?"

"The letters aren't for *him*. They're for *you*. To help *you* process your feelings. To help *you* work through your grief now that you're ready to do so."

Again, I'm staring at Gwen, a frown marring my face. Nothing about this idea sounds fun.

"You don't have to do it every day," Gwen clarifies. "Just whenever you're feeling up for it. Maybe when you're sad, or angry, or thinking of him. Whenever you feel drawn to do it… you should."

"And do what with them?"

"Whatever you want. Keep them in a box. Bury them in your garden. Burn them. Whatever makes you—"

"Happy, right." I roll my eyes.

"To be honest, I doubt writing letters to Nick will make you happy very often. Maybe sometimes. Not at first. Like I said, this exercise is about you… not Nick. You have a hard time talking about him, which is completely understandable. But you didn't have a hard time talking *to* him. So maybe if you talk *to* him, you can process what's happened."

I have to admit that Gwen is making a valid point. With a resigned sigh, I let my head fall into my hands.

"What's going through your mind?" she asks me.

I groan and rub my temples. "I'm thinking that you're probably right and I'm very annoyed about it."

Gwen makes a noise that I imagine is her trying to hide laughter. "And why are you annoyed about it?"

"Because—while this idea sounds like it could be helpful—it also sounds like it will be *horrible*."

Gwen is silent for a long moment before she nods.

"Sometimes, the most helpful things are also the most horrible."

26

I'M SUPPOSED TO DO WHAT?

Kate

The anniversary of Nick's death arrives with a heavy sense of dread from me. I've talked to Gwen a lot about it. She helped me develop a plan for the day, so I wouldn't just drink myself into a stupor and cry all day.

Not that that was a possibility.

Of course not.

Cough.

July fifteenth is a Friday. I wake up feeling fucking wretched. Gwen reminded me that it was perfectly normal to feel a lot of feelings—especially on the first anniversary of his death.

Remembering that comment made me want to punch something, so I let myself curl into a ball in my bed and cry for a while.

Because work always helps me find a sense of normalcy, I

dab cooling gel on my eyes, take a shower, and head into the office.

My dad and Elliot drop by multiple times during the day. Elliot brings me a salad to eat for lunch, knowing damn well I don't want to eat anything.

He's my best friend.

I love him so much.

At three o'clock, I'm doing research for a new client when I hear a knock on my door.

"Yeah?" I ask, not even bothering to look up. I assume it's my dad or Elliot.

"Hey, I was wondering if you could find me a studio space?"

I know that voice.

With a big gasp, my head snaps up, eyes wide toward my open door.

My brother is standing there with a massive smile on his face. He's wearing jeans and a T-shirt with a hoodie and his backpack thrown over one shoulder.

All the stupid feelings in my heart and my brain start warring immediately. I want to cry and also scream with delight and hug him.

I choose joy.

I jump up from my chair, shoot around my desk, and run toward him. He wraps me up in a big hug, his arms around my head and neck like he can't decide if he wants to put me in a headlock or protect me from everything awful in this world. I cling to his torso and beg my tears to keep it in check.

"What are you doing here?" I shriek as I pull away from him, holding on to his shoulders.

"I wanted to hang with my sister for the weekend. Is that okay?" he challenges.

"Of course it is!" I pull him back into a hug and make a

mental note to thank my dad and Elliot, who undoubtedly helped orchestrate this visit. "Where are you staying?"

He shrugs. "With you, maybe?"

"Yes!" I confirm. "Of course!"

The mere sight of his face is doing wonders for my mood, and I suspect everyone knew it would help.

"Come in here and sit down!" I pull him toward the club chairs in front of my desk. "Did you bring your laptop?"

"Of course."

I clap my hands together like I'm completely unaware of what day it is. I swear Benji is like a shot of serotonin straight to my brain, and I vaguely wonder if the antidepressants Gwen started me on are making a difference.

"Get it out! I want to see what you've been working on!"

He chuckles and unzips his backpack.

"I've been contracted recently for some magazine spreads," he says as he pulls out his MacBook.

"Ooooh, fancy."

"Yeah, I'm a little out of my element."

"You are not. You're a talented photographer and they know it."

He grumbles something under his breath. I have no idea what he said, but it doesn't sound complimentary to himself, so I smack him in the back of the head.

"Ouch, dammit, Kate." He rubs the back of his head. "What was that for?"

"I just assume you were saying something mean about yourself. Think of it as a Pavlov experiment."

He looks me dead in the eye and says, "There's something wrong with you."

I can't help the loud, cackling laugh that comes out of my face.

I mean, duh.

I'm not sure Benji knows that I'm in court-appointed

therapy or that I lost my absolute shit on this day one year ago, but he's definitely right that there's something wrong with me.

"Benji, I'm very aware that there's something wrong with me," I say, dabbing at my eyes before my tears can ruin my makeup. "I'm sorry if you're just now figuring that out."

He swats at my leg with the back of his hand. "Shut up, Katherine. Look at my shit."

I manage to calm down enough to sit up straight and pay attention to what's on his laptop screen.

He's photographed an A-list singer in a variety of colorful outfits, sprawled across a vintage couch, sitting in a window seat, holding an antique phone to her ear, face pointed toward the sun with her eyes closed and her dress blowing in the breeze. Her dark skin is playing well with all of the brilliant colors they've chosen for her, and he's done a brilliant job of capturing the contrast.

"Benji…" I breathe.

"You like them?"

"Of course, I do. They're brilliant."

"I've been doing some cityscapes, too."

Every young photographer does whatever they can. They need the work so they can get the money, but also the experience. Even accounting for my (severe) bias, Benji's work is excellent no matter what. But his landscapes—or cityscapes, in this case—are my favorites. It's where he really shines. He's not hindered by anyone else's artistic vision or input. He gets to just do whatever he wants.

"I did this one a couple of weeks ago," he says. "I'd been up super late w—" He stops so abruptly it makes me frown and look over at him. "I wanted to get the Brooklyn Bridge at sunrise. It's also one of the only times you can get the bridge with fewer people on it."

I want to ask him more questions. Specifically, I want to

ask him if that *w* was the beginning of the word *with* and if *Cassandra* was the next word, but I don't. I know him. He doesn't want to talk about it any more than I want to talk about the reason he's been summoned home.

He brings up his photos of my favorite bridge in his city and starts flipping through them. When he gets to one where the pinks and oranges of the sunrise are at their peak, there're some fog patches around the buildings that do their best to dampen the colors, but they're not successful.

"Wait, wait, go back," I say when he flips to the next one. "I want this one."

"Yeah?"

"Yes! For my stairwell. Can you do that for me?"

His eyes meet mine. "I'd be happy to."

We spend another hour looking through his photos and catching up on nonsense when Elliot shows up in my office doorway and announces it's time to leave.

"Where are we going?"

Elliot smirks. Benji chuckles.

"You'll see," Elliot says with a wink.

* * *

"Is your visor tight enough? We don't want to risk messing up your pretty hazel eyes," Elliot says.

"I think so."

Elliot tugs on the strap of my visor, just to be sure.

"All right. You have time. Don't worry about how much. Just go ahead and let it all out."

I look behind me at the random items placed all over the room—lamps, old tube televisions, empty bottles, furniture, dead computers.

"Here you go." Benji hands me a baseball bat.

"Am I... I'm really supposed to just break some of this shit?" I ask.

"Or a few things. All of it. Whatever you want," Benji confirms.

They both secure visors over their own faces to protect them from flying shards and settle back against the wall farthest from the objects.

I look back at them. "I don't know about this, guys."

"Why not?" Elliot asks.

"I mean... you're both just standing there waiting for me to get angry enough to break some shit. It feels weird."

"You want us to leave?" Benji asks.

If I'm being totally honest, I know this will be cathartic. I'm kind of into the idea of smashing some shit. But I don't know if I want Benji to watch it happen.

And also, it seems counterproductive to make myself ragey after such a lovely afternoon.

"Maybe?"

"No problem," he says, nudging Elliot. "We'll be outside. Take your time."

They both file out of the room and shut the door behind them.

I'm left alone with a bunch of shit no one cares about that I'm allowed to just smash to pieces.

This seems both healthy and unhealthy.

I blow out a breath and let myself think about the past year.

I remember this date and how it altered the course of my life.

I remember Nick's calming reassurance that everything would be okay.

I remember seeing him for the last time as Doug helped wheel his hospital bed out of his ICU room.

And then Doug coming back to deliver the news.

The part where I lose my shit is so painful to think about, but I make myself do it. I make myself remember every moment possible—even Doug on the floor in front of me, begging.

I picture the morgue.

I think about the moment we found out I miscarried, as painful as it is to ever think about.

I remember Nick telling me that we would be okay—that we still had each other and we'd get through it together.

It all comes to a head. My eyes and throat burn. And because I'm in a safe space, I allow myself to feel the anger I felt last year. I let myself tap into that part of me that is always simmering below the surface. The part that I repress on a daily basis.

And then I let go.

The first swing of the bat feels unpracticed. I hit my target—a lamp—but I hear Liam's voice in my mind telling me how I could improve my form. And that only serves to fuel my rage because if I wasn't so fucked up, I might be able to find happiness with Liam.

The second swing is better. I absolutely destroy another lamp.

And it feels *far* too good.

So I summon that same energy and I take a swing at an old computer monitor. It takes a few tries, but it finally gives way, falling onto the floor. But apparently, I'm not done. I swing at it time and time again as it rests on the floor.

I destroy a lot of things in that room. I swing the bat at some things, and I throw others. I'm sure I scream. I definitely cry.

Eventually, I lose all my rage fuel and I collapse to the ground, sobbing. I rip the visor off my head and bury my face in my hands.

I don't know how long I sit there, but at some point, I recognize Elliot's cologne. He puts his arm around me and squeezes me into his side.

"You're okay, sweetie," he murmurs.

"It's… not… *fair*…" I wail in between hiccups.

"I know," he responds, his hand moving up and down my arm. "I know, it's not."

Elliot lets me sit there, crying into his shirt for who knows how long. When my tears finally slow and I'm able to maintain a regular breathing pattern, Benji sits on the other side of me, sandwiching me between the two of them.

He plants a kiss on the side of my head and tells me that he loves me, which only makes me start crying in earnest again.

They manage to get me out of the building and back into the car, and then they drive me home. Elliot stays the night, sleeping in my bed. Benji stays in Liam's room.

Liam's room.

In the morning, I have a headache from crying. Beaker is cuddled up beside me, purring.

Elliot goes home to Leon after making waffles for us.

Instead of going for a run by myself, Benji goes on a long walk down the boardwalk with me.

He tells me about what's coming up for him, what he has planned, what he wants to accomplish for the rest of the year.

He specifically asks me about what I want to do and fuck, I wish I knew what to tell him, but I just don't.

"What if you start small?" he presses.

I scoff. "You sound like my fucking therapist." I do my absolute best Gwen impression that truly sounds nothing like her. "*What makes you happy? Keep a log of what you're doing every day that helps you feel happy.*"

Benji shakes his head, but I can see him smiling out of the corner of my eye.

"It's not terrible advice."

"It had better not be, I see her all the fucking time and she costs a fortune."

This time, he doesn't hide his snicker very well.

"Well, have you been keeping a list?"

With a dramatic eye roll, I admit the truth. "I'm working on it."

"Okay, so today is Saturday. What's the thing you're doing that makes you feel happy?"

I don't even have to think about it. "Spending time with you."

"And tomorrow?"

"I'll see you tomorrow, too."

"What about Monday?"

"Did you *talk* to my therapist or something?"

He finally laughs outwardly, not trying to hide it anymore.

"No, Kate. I just… I want to make sure you're okay."

I have to clench my jaw and look away from him to get my shit together.

It kills me that he feels like he needs to take care of me. I'm the older sibling. I've always taken care of him. He shouldn't need to feel this way. I feel guilty for not having my life together because it's led to him feeling like he needs to look after me.

Look at me naming my feelings again, Gwen! You can still eat shit!

"I don't… I don't want you to worry about me, Benji," I huff. "I'll be fine. I'm figuring it out."

"Katherine—" he starts but stops abruptly.

"Are you seriously full-naming me for the second time in two days?"

"Yes. Yes, I am." He stops walking and looks directly in my eyes. "And frankly, you deserve it."

I rear back. "*Excuse me?*"

"You don't have to do this alone. You don't have to 'figure it out' alone. I can be there for you, and I truly wish you'd let me."

I'm at a complete loss for words. I try to shake my head, maybe not to defy or deny his words but because I can't believe he's saying them.

He scratches at his scruff and looks around. Finding a bench, he grabs my forearm and pulls me over to sit.

"Kate, I *want* to be there for you. I *want* to support you."

"Benji, I'm fine. You don't need to—"

"Fuck, why can't you listen?" He threads his fingers into his hair and tugs at the strands.

I just can't help but needle him. "Don't pull too hard. You're too young to start balding."

My comment at least gets a laugh out of him and breaks some tension.

"Kate, I know I don't *need* to do anything, but I *want* to. I don't know why you're so adamant in your refusal of my support. It…" He swallows and takes a deep breath. "It hurts my feelings that you don't want my help."

I thought I'd cried myself out yesterday, but as I sit here, my tear ducts fucking betray me, making my eyes sting. I close my eyes and face the direction of the wind to make myself stop.

"I fully respect that you're a strong, independent woman," he continues. "I'm not asking you to be something you're not, Kate. I'm just asking you to let me help you. Because I want to be there for you the way you've *always* been there for me."

Well that does nothing to stop my dickhead tear ducts.

You fucking traitors! I would surgically remove you if I could.

I'm pretty sure a whimper escapes my lips as I reach over and grasp his hand.

"I'm going to text you and ask you what you're doing to make yourself happy."

Fucking fuck, why is he such a sweet kid?

In the deep recesses of my mind, I'm incredibly proud to have helped raise him.

I nod, swallowing a giant lump in my throat.

"You're my favorite sister," he says.

I laugh. I'm his only sister, obviously.

"I'll let you get back to me about your Monday assignment. You can think about it."

"How kind of you," I shoot back.

"I'm a nice guy."

We sit on the bench while I get myself together. I wipe my tears with my hands and dry them on my leggings.

It's still really bright out—the sun sets late in July. But we're due at our dad's house for dinner soon.

"I've been watching a lot of HGTV," I say, taking him seriously about wanting to help. "I've been thinking about painting for a while now. I just haven't had the motivation to do it."

"Oh yeah?"

"Yeah." I nod again. "Seems like a fresh start, you know?"

"That sounds like a great plan," he says quietly.

"Yeah, maybe."

Perhaps sensing the heaviness still in the air between us, Benji changes the subject. "Do you think dad will make us Manhattans tonight?"

"Hmm. That's a good thought. Maybe we should Uber."

"Yeah, I think so."

He gets up abruptly. "Race you back to the house?"

"Oh please, like you could beat me in any kind of foot

race." I jump up, knowing he'll take off before me to get a head start.

"I'm taller than you."

"But you're not in shape."

"I guess we'll see…" he says as he pushes off.

We're only about a quarter of a mile from the house. This won't even be a contest.

* * *

BENJI LEAVES ON SUNDAY. Oh, in case you were wondering… yes. I smoked his ass on our race home. He's horribly out of shape.

On Monday, I decide that I'm going to paint the living room that is seldom used. I'm not an experienced painter, so I figure it's a good testing space. I end up going down a rabbit hole on Pinterest ending in multiple boards that correspond to various rooms in my house.

On Tuesday, I research paint types and finishes, brands and theories on what painting techniques work best. I read about cutting edges and corners to ensure clean lines. I watch video after video of painters giving their best tips.

On Wednesday, I stop at the hardware store on the way home to pick up two gallons of paint—Soothing Green in an eggshell finish. Emboldened by my honorary degree in painting courtesy of YouTube University, I pick out brushes, rollers, trays, and drop cloths.

On Thursday, I manage to get a ladder off the garage wall by myself through sheer willpower and brute force. I move the furniture into the middle of the room and set down drop cloths. Because I'm not super confident in my edging skills, I tape off the baseboards.

On Friday, I rush home and open the windows for ventilation. I start with one wall—the one that would get the least amount of attention. I do the trim and then roll on a coat of paint. I do another coat immediately and then make myself a peanut butter and jelly sandwich to eat while I inspect my work. I think it needs a third coat.

So I get to work on it, but with each swipe of my paint roller, I can feel something in me shifting. I've been feeling it this whole time, but it's getting stronger and more difficult to ignore.

I'm physically changing the appearance of the house Nick bought for me. It's a strange mix of feelings to be glad to be doing something that makes me 'happy' while feeling guilty about changing things.

When I finish the wall, I stand back with a glass of wine and admire it. I *do* like it. I feel more prepared to finish the rest of the room tomorrow.

And then the feeling returns.

Am I erasing him?

I try to recall the times we used this room. We didn't use it often. It was usually a space people went to because they were looking for quiet during large gatherings. I try to remember what holidays or events are associated with those memories, but I have trouble with it. And *that* realization sends me down an entirely different spiral.

I can feel my memories growing hazy at the corners. They're *there* but I just… can't *quite* get my arms completely around them. It's like they're floating away on little wisps of clouds—impossible to grab, and even if I tried to swipe them out of the air, they'd disintegrate.

Panic lances through my heart. Will there be a day when I can't remember the things I've taken for granted for so long? Will there be a day I can't remember the scent of his cologne? Will there be a day I can't recall his voice?

With trembling fingers, I open the remaining voice mails

I have from him and email them to myself. I check my cloud storage backup to make sure the videos of him are saved and then I watch every single one of them, tears slipping down my cheeks.

I try to remember every single one of his facial expressions, even the ones I didn't like seeing... like when he was angry or frustrated or sad.

With my eyes closed, I picture his smile. I imagine the crinkles in the corners of his eyes—those eye smiles, as he called them. I listen to the videos over and over and over, trying to weave the sound of his silky voice into my mind, heart, soul, so it can never truly disappear.

It's this torturous trip down memory lane that makes me write my first letter to Nick.

Nick,

I have no idea what I'm doing.

I'm in therapy. I'm sure that's shocking to you, but don't you worry... it was court mandated. At this point though, I guess I'm doing it for me. The required time period is almost over.

And yet here I am, doing what she told me to... I'm writing you a fucking letter.

That you'll never read.

Because you're dead.

Fuck, that hurts even when I write it.

If I'm being totally honest, I'm still so angry with you. I'm so mad at you for dying. You weren't supposed to die. You were supposed to outlive me. You were supposed to take care of me and protect me and keep me safe and love me forever.

Instead, I'm sitting in this massive house you bought— without even asking first, might I add, because no, I will not let you off the hook for that, even in death—all by myself writing you a fucking letter.

Gwen would say that I'm latching on to anger because it's easiest to deal with. I've been watching videos of you for hours now. Going through pictures. Making sure it's all backed up properly because... well, I basically freaked out tonight.

You've been gone for one year. I still remember everything. I remember the good and the bad and the perfect and the shit I wish I didn't remember. But some things are starting to feel far away.

I don't want to forget anything. Not a single thing, Nick.

I don't want to forget that you used to put your coffee mug into the dishwasher with an over-the-top flourish because one time I was in a crappy mood and made a big deal about your cup in the sink.

I don't want to forget about the mundane nights watching TV any more than I want to forget our honeymoon.

I don't want to forget the little beauty mark on the lower right side of your chin.

I don't want to forget how soft your eyes got when you told me you loved me.

I don't want to forget the voice you used to jokingly mock me with when I was irritable.

Or your face the day I finished my MBA.

Or the tears in your eyes when we got married.

Or how you used to play with Beaker (who misses you terribly, by the way).

It all sucks, Nick. Everything about this sucks. And you aren't even suffering wherever you are. It's just me, alone, sticking this life out for reasons I'm not always entirely certain of.

I guess my point is that I miss you so much it's painful. Every single day, it hurts.

And for a while, I had something that made me forget about the pain... just for a little bit, when I was in the moment. And now thinking about that is painful, too. Because it's over. I'm not really ready to talk to you about that yet.

I love you, but I also hate you.

And you won't even read this.

God, this is stupid.

27

EVERYTHING IS TEMPORARY

Liam

"How's Austin treating you?" Marcus asks.

I've been here for about a month. For the most part, everything is going according to schedule and I'm hoping to be back home within the six-month time frame. I'd love to go home for Christmas and just stay home. We're really close to getting the occupancy permits and then we can get in the building. In the meantime, I've been working with the transferred staff and sorting through résumés in a temporary space nearby.

"It's fucking hot," I answer. "But you were right about the barbecue."

That shit is good and I've made it my mission to try as much of it as possible.

"And your lady? How's that going?"

My breath stalls in my chest.

During my flight to Austin, I was in physical pain. My

chest ached at the memory of my final conversation with Kate. That night, I'd lain in bed, emotionally exhausted and more depressed than I'd been in over a year. After a few restless hours, I gave up the charade of sleep and headed into work early.

I'd literally run away from her the way she'd run away from me all those months ago. Unlike her, I won't be running back. Not right now anyway.

As soon as Jake, my boss and the chief operating officer, entered the building, I made a beeline for his office and accepted the position in Austin.

Jake was thrilled, wanting to know what tipped the scales.

I mumbled something about never getting to Austin with Jill—how it was on our list. It's not *untrue*, but it's certainly not the whole truth. Not even close to it.

The truth, of course, is that I can't be within a thousand miles of Kate Rafferty.

And those two kernels of truth drove guilt straight through my chest, slicing through my body and leaving nothing but the remnants of a twice-broken heart.

I had to get out of there.

My parents had been sad about my rather abrupt departure after finally being home, but they were happy about the opportunity ahead of me.

Joe saw through me though. He knew there was more to the situation than I was letting on and he dragged it out of me with whiskey in the wee hours of the morning a few nights before I left.

Confessing all of my feelings did nothing to alleviate the tight feeling in my chest. If anything, it made it worse.

Maybe in some ways, talking to someone about my feelings for Kate felt like a relief. Finally, it was out in the open and thankfully, Joe just sat there quietly and let me talk.

In other ways, telling my brother about all of this made this entire situation very real, very quickly.

I wasn't happy to leave, but I'd be lying if I said I wasn't a little bit relieved to get away.

"Not well," I say. "I haven't talked to her."

"In how long?"

"Six weeks."

"Jesus, Liam. Why haven't you called her?"

"I can't. It's complicated. She needs time and I need to let her have it."

Marcus sighs into the phone. "Well… you might as well have fun while you're in Austin."

I snort. "Nah, I'm good."

"Is this what happens when you get old? You stop having fun? What are you going to do down there all on your own?"

"I got a list, man. I'm gonna see the sights. Eat all the barbecue. Do some of the shit Jill and I never got to do."

That seems to silence his comebacks.

"All right, fine," he concedes. "You need anything? Work related or not."

Isn't that a loaded question.

"Nah, I'm good. Thanks though. The transferred staff is really great."

Marcus sighs again.

"Whatever you say, man."

"I'll let you know if something changes."

"Sounds good. Listen, I gotta jump. Leena and I have reservations."

"Cool. Try not to be a douchebag," I joke.

"This fucking guy…" he mutters before hanging up.

I'm going to walk down to the next barbecue place on my list for dinner, so I hoist myself off the couch to grab my shoes. As I'm tying them, my phone dings.

Maybe it's my stupid, hopeful heart, or maybe it's that I

was just talking about Kate, but I find myself lunging toward it, wondering if it's her.

> Broseph: The boys are requesting FaceTime with Uncle Liam before bed.

I knew it wouldn't be her, but I'm still disappointed to face the reality.

Still a lost puppy.

She won't text. I know it in my bones.

She told me she needed time and I'm going to give it to her. I am. She deserves to choose how she navigates her grief.

But that doesn't mean I have to like it.

I miss her.

I feel like I'm starting on a new grief journey of my own. I've mourned my wife and now I'm mourning another woman in a different way. She's still living, still walking the earth, which makes it better and worse.

Better because she's safe and sound.

Worse, because Kate made the conscious decision to *not* be with me.

And because I love her, I want nothing but her happiness. So I'll let her go. I'll go to work and try to move on with my life. If one day, our paths cross again… well, I guess we'll just have to see where the two of us are individually.

For now, I'll just keep moving, just like I did after Jill died. One foot in front of the other. One step at a time.

I tap Joe's contact information and then the little video icon.

When the call connects, I see both of my nephews' faces vying for position in front of the camera and my smile is immediate.

"Uncle Liam, can you see me?"

"Can you see me, Uncle Liam?"

"Hey, brother!" Joe calls over the noise.

"Hey, everybody! Yes, boys, I can see both of you. You could back up a little and then I'd be able to see all of you."

"Fat chance of that happening," my sister-in-law scoffs from behind them. "Hi, Liam!" she calls.

"Hi, Tracy." I try to peer around the boys, but it's impossible. "All right, who wants to tell me what happened at school this week?"

Both boys erupt into chaos. They talk over each other and eventually, they decide to go get their artwork from the week and they sprint away, leaving Joe and Tracy on the couch behind them.

"When we ask what happened at school, they tell us they don't remember, but when *Uncle Liam* asks…" Joe complains, but he's laughing.

"Seriously, it's like they're different kids with you," Tracy confirms.

"I'm not their parent." I shrug.

"How's it going?" Joe asks.

I force a smile. "It's fine."

He gives me a meaningful look and the look of sympathy on Tracy's face tells me that Joe shared our conversation with her.

I scrub my palm down my face. "Guys, I'm all right. Wipe those looks off your faces."

They both seem to snap out of it and then the volume increases as the boys come back with their artwork, shoving it in front of the camera.

I can barely see any of it through the movement, but I tell them it's brilliant and that they're talented and I can't wait to see more. We talk about school (they had fun) and what they're doing the next day (organizing their toys).

I end up reading them a bedtime story that I pull up on my laptop and then they hang up.

The smile drops from my face slowly.

Returning home at the end of this is happening regardless of what's going on with Kate. I miss home so much.

But in the meantime, I'll check out every barbecue place in a one-hundred-mile radius and read bedtime stories over FaceTime to my nephews.

Everything is temporary.

STRAIGHT DOWN THE SPIRAL

Kate

When Nick was around, he hired landscapers to deal with our property. I never canceled them because I was entirely uninterested in dealing with all that nonsense. They showed up in the spring, as scheduled, to start on the gardens and they came to mow the lawn every couple of weeks all summer. They're ramping down now, but I went out to ask them some questions about the gardens.

The most patient landscaper in the world explained their strategy to me.

Landscapers have a fucking strategy?!

Apparently Nick had asked that flowers bloom continuously throughout the spring, summer, and fall, which is why they were there that particular day. They were planting tulip bulbs that would bloom in May.

The daffodils would bloom around the same time, she explained, but they were perennials, which—apparently—

meant they would come back every year, and supposedly get bigger each spring. Tulips were trickier, so they didn't count on them returning.

The irises and hydrangeas would bloom in June.

The lilies in July.

The magnolia tree and the sunflowers in August.

The daisies would keep blooming into September.

And in October, they'll bring in mums.

I listened intently, shocked at all of this information, to be honest. And then we talked about the following year. She mentioned some ideas they'd had and things they wanted to try out. Interested in any kind of pop of color I could get, I agreed to let her use my house as a testing ground.

Why the fuck not?

I'm still working on finding a thing every day that makes me happy. True to his word, Benji has texted me almost daily to ask what my thing that day is, which truly does motivate me. I don't want to let Benji down.

I'm still going to the animal shelter every Sunday.

I'm still going to therapy—now biweekly instead of weekly, thank you very much.

Elliot and I have lunch outside the office once per week. We take turns choosing the place.

And yes, I'm writing letters to my deadbeat husband.

Don't look at me like that. I'm allowed to make jokes. He's *my* dead(beat)husband.

The point is: I'm trying. I'm trying really hard.

Slowly—so slowly—I guess I'm building a life that is my own. It's not dependent upon anyone else but me. I'm painting rooms. I'm making travel plans. I'm apparently talking to the landscapers about what I want the house to look like next year.

See?

Look at me not wishing for death.

Let's throw a parade!

It doesn't feel like erasing Nick anymore. It feels more like taking back control of my life, which is the whole point, isn't it?

And honestly, changing the aesthetic of the house stopped feeling like erasing Nick and more like reconnecting with Nick. He bought this house for me. For us. Changing the way it looks doesn't make it less *him*. Just more... me. That's something I don't think he'd be angry about.

How could he be? He's dead. Remember?

Anyway, that's how I've ended up standing in front of his stupid headstone, holding a bouquet of daisies that I cut from the garden, tied with a satin ribbon. (The landscaper taught me how to cut them most effectively so I don't fuck up the plant. You know I would have killed the plant otherwise.)

I feel so awkward in cemeteries. Is it disrespectful to walk on dead bodies? Where should I stand when I get to his gravesite?

I haven't been here to visit this place in much longer than I *should*. I don't like it here. I don't feel him here. Truthfully, I don't feel him anywhere, but standing in front of his headstone with that fucking dash framed by two years feels so final. I absolutely hate it.

I stand a few feet from his headstone, feeling ridiculous. We were married, for fuck's sake. So I force myself to walk forward and kneel down to his flat headstone to brush the leaves and debris off the surface before I lay the daisies down next to his name. There's an empty space for my name next to it.

How lovely.

Finally, I make myself sit down on the ground and hug my knees into my chest.

I wondered earlier today if I might cry when I finally got here, but no tears come. Instead, I feel numb.

I stare at Nick's name, not entirely seeing it, thinking of the logistics of cemeteries and burials instead of the actual lonely truth of why I'm here. My brain prefers rational, logical thought one hundred percent of the time. In moments like these, I appreciate it.

Somewhere in the deep recesses of my mind, I remember my mother taking me to my grandfather's headstone after he died. I'd been expecting a tall, imposing headstone that drew attention and was quite underwhelmed when I saw a flat one sitting behind a mound of dirt.

I remember saying something to my mother about it and she said that groundskeepers preferred flat stones because it made lawn maintenance easier. The implication made my stomach churn all over again.

"Do they just… drive over you?" I ask Nick aloud. "You probably don't care."

I sit there another moment in silence, trying to remember every wrinkle on Nick's face. Trying to recall the exact timbre of his voice, the low rumble that shot straight through my chest sometimes, and the soft tones he used when I needed comfort.

"Are you here?" I whisper.

Nothing.

No gust of wind.

No sudden movement of nearby flowers or trees.

No supernatural signs.

I cannot possibly suppress my eye roll.

"I figured not. I just came by to bring you flowers. I'd tell you I grew them myself, but you know damn well the land-scapers did it. I did cut them though. And frankly, if you're not happy I brought them… I don't fucking care. You left me. If you cared what flowers I'd bring to your grave, you should have left better instructions. Or better yet, you should have stuck around."

I vaguely register the sound of a car in the distance, but I don't bother to turn and see the source. I just keep staring at the headstone.

"I've been painting your giant house. The landscapers and I are chatting about next year. I've been neglecting them."

Could I mow the lawn on my own?

Oh, fuck that. I'm not doing that.

"You bought us that house and now I'm left trying to figure out how to take care of it. With no one to fill it. No kids. No husband. Thanks for that, by the way."

I roll my eyes again and brush a stick I missed off his headstone.

"I'd apologize for painting that living room a different color, but you're dead, so I doubt you give a shit."

Silence.

Of course.

The silence just makes me angrier.

"I'm going to redo the master bathroom, too. Get rid of the fucking beige."

Still nothing.

"Jesus, Nick, you could at least figure out a way to acknowledge me. It's the afterlife. Aren't there endless possibilities there? Shouldn't you be able to conjure a gust of wind or something?"

Aaaaaaaand nothing.

"Not even a bee to sting me?"

Silence.

"A bird to shit on my head? Nothing?"

Absolute deafening silence.

"Oh, for fuck's sake," I mutter, getting up and dusting off my butt. "You fucking die on me and you can't even give me a sign from the great beyond that you still give a shit. What kind of eternal love horseshit is that?"

Grabbing my purse, I scowl at the headstone.

"Fuck this. You're not even here."

I turn to stomp back to the car and am startled to see an old woman staring at me, clear disapproval and judgment on her face.

"Oh, please," I spit. "Like you've never cussed at your husband before."

* * *

"We've never talked about your miscarriage."

I choke on my own spit.

Jesus Christ, Gwen. Going for the jugular today.

Once I'm done coughing like a pack-a-day smoker, I manage to squeak out a "So?"

Gwen raises her eyebrows expectantly.

I take a sip of my water even as my eyes continue to sting. "Do I have to talk about it?"

"Not if you don't want to."

"Okay, then. I don't want to talk about it."

She does that curious head tilt. "Why not?"

My eye roll is one for the record books. It's shocking my eyes don't get stuck in the back of my head. "I *just* said I didn't want to talk about it."

"And I asked why not."

I take a deep breath and try to formulate an answer that will satisfy Gwen. I know she won't leave this alone. I know it's a big deal that I didn't tell her until much later than I should have. I know that it's a thing I have to deal with in order to heal.

Eventually.

"Because it's painful, okay?" I clasp my hands in front of

me and glare at Gwen. "Because it was the beginning of the worst year of my entire life. That's why."

"That's understandable."

"So, can we drop it then?" The attitude in my voice is not kind. It doesn't seem to faze Gwen. She's used to it by now.

"If that's what you want."

I glare a little harder. "Are you saying you want me to talk about it?"

"If you want to talk about it, I'm happy to listen."

"But you think I should talk about it?"

"I think you should do whatever will help you process it."

The aggravation in my chest finally bubbles over. "Spare me the psychobabble bullshit, Gwen. Tell me what you actually think."

She's quiet for a moment, watching me intently. I refuse to look away. I try not to blink. Finally, she draws in a breath and says what's on her mind.

"In my professional opinion, talking through trauma is a very effective method of processing and making peace with it. In my personal opinion, you are no exception, and I believe discussing it would help you accept it and move on."

I stare back at Gwen in silence, but eventually my vision grows hazy as my thoughts spiral. I don't want to talk about it. I don't want to go down this road. I don't think it will help, but I have to acknowledge that Gwen has helped me immensely over the past year and a part of me feels like I owe it to Gwen to just… trust her.

"Fine," I concede.

"Fine?"

"Yes. Fine. We can discuss it. But when I say stop, we stop."

Gwen nods. "Of course."

And then we stare at each other.

Maybe she expects me to begin, but I don't know where

to start. So I wait for some kind of prompt. If she wants me to talk about it, she can get specific.

"Can you tell me what happened?" Gwen asks.

Cool, cool, we're starting with a question that has no answer.

"Does anyone ever know what happens? It just does."

"That's not what I meant. I apologize… I was unclear. I meant to ask how you found out. Were you having strange symptoms?"

I heave a resigned sigh and scratch my temple. "Yeah, I had some cramps. I called my OB. She told me to call back if I had any other symptoms. To rest as much as possible in the meantime."

My brain tries to shut off automatically, trying to avoid this conversation. My throat and my nose begin to sting. I close my eyes to block it out. To try to stop the surge of emotion that wants me to curl in a ball on the couch and go to sleep so all of this just *goes away.*

Gwen's voice drifts across the space between us so softly. "Take your time."

And then I can't stop the tears. They just come.

Fucking Gwen and her sympathy voice.

"And then I started bleeding." I don't open my eyes. I can't. I don't want to see her face when I talk about this. It's hard enough to see the look of pity on people's faces when they hear about Nick. This would be *so* much worse. "I knew. I just knew. Nick was trying to be hopeful, but I could see the fear in his eyes. The OB told us to come in. She confirmed it. Prescribed me some pills."

I reach blindly to the side toward the customary box of tissues on the end table and pull a few out, covering my face with them.

"And how did the two of you handle that?"

"Not horribly, I suppose." I finally open my eyes, but I still don't look at Gwen. I look at the coffee table between us.

"Nick was devastated, even though he was trying to play it cool. I was… I felt like it was my fault."

My voice cracks, so I clear it and wipe at my face.

"I should have stopped running. Nick asked about exercise, but my OB said that anything I was doing before I could continue to do. Maybe I had a drink before I knew I was pregnant and I hurt it somehow."

"It doesn't sound like you intentionally tried to end your pregnancy though."

"No. I didn't. I was excited. And Nick was just… over the moon. He always wanted kids. He was so excited to start a family."

"I hope you can understand—now that some time has passed—that it wasn't your fault. Like you said, it just happens sometimes."

"I know. I know that, rationally, it wasn't anything I did. But… still."

That fucking guilt suffocates me sometimes. Still. Even after all this time.

"Women often feel this way, so if anything, I hope you know you're not alone in that feeling. But it's important to keep repeating to yourself that it *wasn't* your fault. You didn't do anything wrong."

"Sure." I nod.

"You don't believe me?"

I crumple a tissue in my hand while I try to find a nice way to say that I don't believe her. "It's not that I don't believe you." A half-truth. "But how do you not blame yourself at least a little? You know?"

Gwen is quiet for a moment. A moment long enough that makes me look up at her. She seems to be waiting for that because she starts talking.

"Because if you allow yourself to believe you had something to do with your embryo's death, you'll always think there was something you could have done differently that would have changed the outcome… and that's simply not true in this case."

She pauses and I can't tell if it's because there are tears running down my cheeks again or if she expects me to respond.

"Miscarriages happen all the time," she continues. "Some women miscarry without ever realizing they were pregnant. Some women lose pregnancies much later. Some women have to make really difficult decisions halfway through a pregnancy because the fetus isn't viable. Pregnancy is not a neutral health state. It's very difficult on the body and it *always* comes with risks." She leans forward on her folders and I swear, her eyes stare into my soul. "Consider the actual freaking *miracle* that occurred in order for you to get pregnant. Sperm had to meet the egg at the *exact* right place at the *exact* right time, otherwise the egg wouldn't have been fertilized, or you could have had an ectopic pregnancy—which would have been no more your fault than the miscarriage you suffered. There are *millions* of things that can go wrong without human intervention, Kate. You didn't do *anything* wrong."

I dab at my face with more tissues, even though it's a fruitless activity. The tears won't stop.

"It's very sad. Devastating, even, especially given the loss of your husband shortly thereafter. But the miscarriage itself is not uncommon."

I suck a deep breath into my lungs and release it slowly. "How am I supposed to get past it?"

"Just like anything else. You talk about it. You process it. You accept it."

"Well, I don't want to talk about it."

"I know." Gwen gives me a tiny, sympathetic smile. "But if you never allow yourself to think about it or talk about it, it will be harder to get past it. You don't have to discuss it with anyone you don't want to. You can discuss it only with me if you'd like. Or write about it in a journal. But I *do* encourage you to allow yourself to process it."

I swallow hard and nod, turning my eyes toward the crumpled tissues in my hands.

"I'm done talking about it for now," I whisper.

"Okay."

Nick,

My annoying therapist got me to talk about... the thing I never want to talk about. I can't say she forced me into it, but she's the one that brought it up, so I'm blaming her. I never bring it up. I never talk about it. I just can't.

How can I talk about it when I can't even think about it without seeing the tears in your eyes when that stick produced a positive sign? When I think about the look on your face when the doctor confirmed I'd lost it. I'd lost your baby, Nick. It was my responsibility to care for it and I couldn't even do that right. I lost it before I even had much of an opportunity to screw it up.

Gwen (the annoying therapist) told me that it was not my fault. She was adamant about it.

Logically, I know she's right. But emotionally? Fuck, that's a totally different story. And knowing that I'll never have another opportunity...

Nick, I wanted your baby. I wanted to see you hold him. I wanted to see you play with him. To teach him everything and anything. To bond with him. And then I lost it, and then you were stolen from me, and now I have absolutely nothing of you. Every single part of you was taken from me.

So again... how am I supposed to talk about this?

How am I supposed to talk about losing the person who

*meant the absolute most to me right after losing the tiny thing
we'd made together?*

How, Nick?

*Because you're not feeling any of this wherever the fuck
you are.*

And I'm still mad at you.

*I'm still angry that I'm alone here and you're doing what-
ever the fuck you're doing wherever you are.*

*I'm so fucking furious that I'm writing you letters you'll
never read.*

When I die, I'm going to yell at you.

2 9

TRIP FOR TWO FOR ONE

Kate

"Are you sure you're all right going alone?" my dad asks for the hundredth time as I'm getting ready to leave the office on Thursday night.

"Yes, Dad. I'm sure."

The thing is, I'm single now. I have no one to go with. And I *won't* have anyone to go with.

My husband is dead and I released Liam from the shackles holding him down.

It's just me over here. Taking one step at a time.

"It's a long drive—"

"It's only four hours *with* traffic," I interrupt him.

He sighs.

"Dad, everything is fine. I'm only going to be gone for a weekend. I'll be back at work on Monday."

At that, he rolls his eyes. "I don't care when you come back to work, Katie. That has nothing to do with this."

I look up at him in question. I don't say anything. I just watch him. He's fidgety. He doesn't want to look me in the eye.

"Dad, do you have something you want to say?" I ask.

"I'm worried about you, okay?" he blurts out. "I'm always worried about you. Worrying about your kid doesn't just stop when they're done being kids. I don't expect you to understand, but dammit, Katie, I worry about you."

My eyes and nose begin to sting immediately, so I avert my eyes to the carpet.

He doesn't know. It was a completely innocent comment.

It feels like a sucker punch, nonetheless.

"I want you to be okay and you've been through a lot this year and now you're going away for a weekend alone."

The undertones are there.

He's worried about my safety.

And not that I might get into a car *accident* or *trip* and fall off one of those boats that go into the falls.

My dad—the greatest man I've ever known in my life and very possibly the most significant influence in my whole life —is maybe, possibly, worried that I don't want to be alive anymore.

I clench my hands into tight fists and let my nails dig into my skin in hopes that the pain will keep me from going into a shame spiral.

There're a lot of really hard truths in here, and no, I'm not ready to admit them to my father. Definitely not today, maybe not ever.

Perhaps in the confines of Gwen's office, I'd be able to admit aloud that I have wondered over the past year if being alive is worth it.

Maybe if I didn't have a Benji and an Elliot and—court-mandated or not—a Gwen, he and I wouldn't even be having this conversation.

I breathe in—*one, two, three, four*—hold it—*one, two, three, four*—and let it out—*one, two, three, four*. I unclench my fists and force my shoulders to fall back down so they aren't creeping up to my ears.

"Dad, you don't need to worry," I admit quietly before lifting my head to look him in the eye. "I'm getting better. I promise."

He swallows hard, watching me in silence.

"I'm just taking a trip. Nick always wanted to go to Niagara Falls." I shrug. "I know it's not a super fun vacation destination, but he wanted to go because his parents honeymooned there. I can't explain it, but I just feel like I *need* to go."

His brow furrows and he averts his eyes.

Are his eyes shiny?

Seeing tears *maybe* welling in his eyes stops me short. I've only seen my dad cry three times in my life.

The first time was at his mom's funeral when my parents were still married. We were sitting in church pews and we were supposed to be singing, but I didn't know the song, so I was just holding the songbook. I remember looking up at him and realizing that his cheeks were wet.

I took his hand and he seemed to startle out of whatever trance he was in, then looked down at me. Through his tears, he mustered a weak smile for me.

The second time was the day I left for college. He and Benji had driven me down to the university a couple of hours away. It wasn't a million miles away or anything like that, but it was the farthest I'd ever been from them for any meaningful period of time.

Benji gave me a hug and headed down to the car so dad and I could have a moment in private. He told me he was proud of me. He told me that he loved me and he had total faith in me. He promised that he was always just a phone call away if I needed anything. That I was still his baby, even if I was an adult now.

His eyes were already glistening, and then he hugged me. Even at the time, I suspected it was to hide his tears. But I still heard him sniffing.

Of course, sensing that he needed to break the tension, I asked if he had packed my condoms.

He choked on his own spit, but at least he was laughing.

The third time I saw my dad cry was sometime after Nick died. That time is such a blur to me, so I couldn't tell you exactly when it was, but I know that it happened because I was so surprised.

I remember we were at my house. I remember I hadn't showered in days. I remember the skin on my face feeling raw from tears. I remember we were alone.

The TV was on and I was watching *Law & Order*.

I remember him sniffing. And that's when I turned my head and saw tears on his aging cheeks.

Today might make number four, but I can see he's doing his absolute damnedest to stop them.

Choosing to give him a break, I close my laptop, slip it into its sleeve, and put it into my bag. I pack all of my things and then stand from my chair.

I wait silently, watching him until he faces me again.

"Dad, tomorrow I'm going to drive to Niagara Falls. I have a reservation at the Hilton on the Canadian side. I'm going to do touristy things. I'll stay there Friday and Saturday nights. I'll drive home on Sunday. I'll be back at work on Monday. Beaker will be fine alone for the weekend, but Elliot is still going to check on him Saturday." I nod firmly. "I'm fine. I'm just taking a weekend away."

He studies my face for a solid minute before finally speaking. "Okay."

"Okay." I nod again. "I'll text you when I get there."

"Okay."

* * *

APPROXIMATELY FORTY-FIVE MINUTES into my solo drive to Niagara Falls, I'm reminded that I hate road trips. Nick usually drove. He just liked doing it. I think he felt like he *should* as the man in the relationship, which—if I'm being completely honest—is one aspect of the patriarchy I'm all right with.

I have plenty of music I can listen to on my phone, but I'm bored with music within the first hour. I also have podcasts loaded up, so I decide to give one of those a shot. Nothing can make me less antsy and annoyed about the fact that I'm driving, so I decide to call people and see if they can keep me awake and alert for the drive.

I try Benji first because I know Elliot is at work. Benji's schedule is less predictable, but it also means he's available at random times of the day.

With a quick tap of his contact record, the sound of a call connecting is blaring out of the speakers. I quickly turn it down—damn podcasts—but in my haste, I very nearly miss a voice I don't entirely recognize coming through my brother's phone.

It's muffled and it's only a second before Benji says my name.

"Hey… what's goin' on?" I try to be as chill as possible, like I didn't just hear a woman's voice coming from wherever he is. I swear something's going on between him and his friend Cassandra. They kept sneaking glances at each other when I was in New York for my birthday. I know they've been friends for years, but… come on.

"Nothing, really. Just getting ready to head out to a photo shoot in—"

The sound is quickly muffled, like he's covering the receiver. But not before I hear the woman's voice again—it sounds like Cassandra, but I've only met her once, so I can't be totally sure.

Why in the world would he be hiding Cassandra from me?

I suppose it's technically the morning… but what do I care if they're sleeping together? Not that I want to spend too much time thinking about this, but… *go, Benji.* Cassandra's gorgeous.

"Benji, is this a bad time? It's fine if it is. We can talk another time."

"No, Katie, it's fine."

"Ben." I hear the woman's stern voice on the other end of the line.

What the hell is going on over there?

"I just called because I'm driving up to Niagara for the weekend. Text me later, Benji."

I hear him sigh. "All right. Be careful driving, please."

"Will do. Love you, Benji."

"Love you, Katie."

His phone cuts off in under a second.

Elliot. Must call Elliot.

He answers in two rings.

"Hey, sweetie. How's the drive going?"

"It's fine. I'm bored as fuck and I don't want to bother you too much at work, but I have to ask you a question."

"Kate, your father owns the company I work for. One day, *you* will own the company. I think if I'm talking to you on the phone without neglecting my duties, everything will be okay."

Fair point.

"Okay, when Ben was in town this summer, did he say anything to you about seeing someone?"

"Ummm…" He trails off while he presumably thinks. I'm not there. I can't see him. "Not to me, I don't think. I did pick him up at the airport, but we talked about you and work and weekend plans."

I search my brain for anything and everything he said that weekend. I can't remember him mentioning Cassandra at all. Except… one time, he stopped speaking really abruptly when he was talking about doing something *with* someone else and I wondered what that was about, but I hadn't pressed it.

"I wonder if he talked to my dad."

"Do you want me to transfer you?" Elliot chuckles through the question.

I'm torn on that idea. I don't want to worry my dad. But it would be good to check in with him. You know, reassure him I'm not dead.

"I suppose I should check in with him. He was worried about me going on a trip alone." I roll my eyes and I'm certain Elliot knows it because he snorts. "But I'm not going to talk to him about this, so don't bring it up with him."

"Yes, dear. Do you need anything else? Are you excited about your trip?"

Excited? I don't know how to answer that. Maybe a little.

Mostly, I'm nervous.

Not because I'm traveling alone—I've done this multiple times before—but because I feel so compelled to go there and I don't know why.

"I'm looking forward to a weekend away, yes."

"Are you going to hit up the spa?"

I grimace. "But then strangers will have to touch me."

Elliot sighs. "Katherine, you—more than anyone else I know—deserve a little pampering."

"Ugh…" I hate this idea, but my shoulders *have* been really tense and I wonder if someone could help me out with that. "I'll think about it."

"Good."

I hear his desk phone ring in the background.

"Okay, sweetie, I've got a call, so I'm going to transfer you to Jack."

"Okay, thanks, El."

"Text when you get there."

"Yes, dear."

Elliot transfers me to my dad, but he doesn't pick up. I leave him a voice mail to let him know I'm all right and about halfway to Niagara.

The diversion in my brain allows me to reset and when I stop at a Sheetz for more coffee and a restroom break, I find a serial-style true crime podcast that I can settle into for the rest of the drive.

The Peace Bridge in Buffalo is busy but efficient. It takes about forty-five minutes and then I'm headed into Canadian territory. Thirty minutes later, I'm parking my car in the garage at the Hilton and wheeling my suitcase toward the door.

And when I check in at the front desk, the kind woman working there tells me that I already have a massage booked for later that evening.

A little card says. *Treat Yo' Self. Love, L.L. Bean*

* * *

THE FOLLOWING MORNING, I wake to a spectacular view. From what I can tell, all the rooms facing the falls have floor-to-ceiling windows. My room has a king-size bed and a bathroom with a Jacuzzi tub, but instead of a wall blocking off the bathroom from the rest of the room, there's a window. If I sit on one side of the tub, I can still see Horse-shoe Falls.

And yes, that's what I did last night. I went to my massage, where the massage therapist had been prepped that I "desperately needed a massage" (via Elliot) but that I don't love strangers touching me. So Jennie talked with me for a few minutes to try and make me more comfortable before she left so I could get undressed.

She also asked me if I wanted quiet, at which point I real-ized that an hour of a stranger touching me while being alone with my thoughts was basically my idea of a night-mare. So I asked her to tell me about herself.

For the record, Jennie is a single mom to two boys who are, apparently, very rambunctious, and her ex-husband is a shithead.

She tells me the best places to eat and shop and gives me tips for not getting soaked on the Hornblower, which is the Maid of the Mist equivalent on the Cana-dian side.

She also got rid of a painful knot I'd had in my shoulder blade for weeks.

I've decided I like Jennie. I made sure to tip her well.

So today, I'm getting breakfast in the hotel, doing some sightseeing, getting lunch nearby at a place Jennie recom-mended, and then going on the Hornblower.

It's a gorgeous day. It's cool but not cold, and the sun is out. It's a perfect sightseeing day, in my opinion. You can wear long sleeves, but you're not sweating. You can wear jeans and flats and won't get all muddy. It's wonderful and I can't help but wish Nick were here with me. He would have loved it.

Eating alone is a thing I've gotten used to. I always have a book with me, so I just whip out a paperback and sit by myself. I briefly wonder if people think I look pathetic, and then I realize that I'll never see any of these people again and I don't give a shit.

And then it's time for Hornblower.

I put on my poncho and arrange myself the way Jennie recommended: purse slung across my body under the poncho, phone in my back jeans pocket, should I decide to take pictures. She told me where I could stand, but on that account, I don't listen. I go straight to the bow of the vessel and watch as we navigate down the Niagara River toward the giant waterfall ahead.

The sun reflects off everything, but I still lift my sunglasses onto the top of my head to keep my hair out of my face and prevent water droplets from blocking my view.

It's breathtaking.

As we get closer, mist sprays my face, and I feel an odd calm wash over me. The loud whooshing sound of the water fades into the distance and seems to quiet. People around me are pulling up the hoods on their ponchos and squinting into the onslaught of fine water droplets, but I stand perfectly still, staring up at the majestic arc of the falls.

I can't explain how it happens, but everything disappears for me in that moment. It's just me on that boat, thinking about Nick's parents all those years ago, coming here at the very beginning of their marriage—before drama, pregnancies and kids, before money struggles and fights. The beginning is so hopeful.

I imagine Nick being there with me, thinking about his parents. I think about our own wedding, our own honeymoon, and all the hope I felt back then. How I was *certain* that my life was absolutely perfect.

The fact that I'm taking this trip alone is more painful than I've let on for anyone. I'm here for Nick more than I'm here for myself.

With every tiny water droplet that lands on my exposed

skin, I can almost feel a piece of Nick weaving himself back into my soul. Mist soaks my hair and face and I vaguely recognize that I should be feeling cold, but I don't. Instead, I feel a warmth spread from my chest outward... like arms wrapping around me.

I close my eyes and imagine Nick standing behind me. That if I could just let my head fall backward, it would hit the solid wall of his chest. That his head would dip down and he would kiss the spot where my neck met my shoulder like he'd done countless times during the course of our relationship.

My chest feels odd—almost like it's stitching itself back together, love filling the empty spaces that Nick used to occupy so effortlessly.

It's peaceful and calming and all-encompassing.

Until it's not.

Until the moment reality crashes into my brain, reminding me that Nick is gone forever and that's the only thing I can fixate on.

Very suddenly, the warm feeling in my chest becomes overwhelming. I open my eyes, cold dread and panic swirling in my gut. It stretches up my torso, crawling up my throat, threatening to strangle me. It rips a new hole in my chest.

My eyes and nose start stinging—telltale signs that I'm going to cry, but I wouldn't know if I did. My face is already soaked.

My chest constricts painfully and my knees buckle. I grip the handrail tighter and suck in the most difficult breath I've ever taken.

I keep my eyes on the horseshoe. It's like I can't pry them away.

In this moment, I feel closer to Nick than I have since he died. Maybe it's because I'm in the place he wanted to visit but never did. Maybe it's a cruel joke from a deity I no longer believe in.

The horseshoe continues to pull at me. I squint against the mist, wondering if Nick would appear if I squint hard enough. As if he'd pop out of the water and climb up onto the boat and tell me the past year was a horrible dream.

My brain rattles with words I long to say to his face.

I miss you.

How could you die so soon?

I can't forgive you for leaving me.

I hate you.

I love you.

My vision completely blurs and I realize that I'm actually crying. The mist is no longer a scapegoat for all of my emotions. I clench my jaw, trying not to draw attention to myself with silly nonsense like hysterical sobbing.

Just as I'm starting to sink into misery, a violent gust of wind kicks up around me.

People brace themselves, their ponchos flapping around in the air. They grab railings and children and hunch down, turning their faces downward and away from the mist.

I can see fear on people's faces.

But for some reason, I'm not scared.

The calm settles back into my chest and the warm feeling of arms wrapping around me returns. I take a deep breath and fix my eyes back on the horseshoe.

I could almost, *almost* hear his voice. *Almost* smell his cologne.

"Nick..." My voice is a whisper that I'm sure no one can hear above the crash of water and wind whipping around us.

The wind stops as quickly as it started, leaving only a gentle breeze that seems to linger on my face, chilling my skin and relaxing me.

I clutch at my chest, pressing Nick's wedding band

against my skin beneath my clothing and the poncho. I trace the outline with my index finger and poke it through the center, like I'm trying to slip it onto the digit.

I stand at the railing, eyes on the horseshoe, even as the boat turns and heads back toward the dock. I'm sure I'm still crying—I can feel my nose running—but the hysteria has melted away.

I feel calm.

I feel the familiar pain in my chest.

But I also feel Nick.

30

JUST MIND YOUR OWN BUSINESS

Liam

"I'm impressed this project is running on time, given all the delays with the office itself," my boss, Jake, says during our biweekly Zoom check-in.

He's not wrong by any stretch. The office itself has suffered setbacks with the crew setting it up. Furniture was damaged in shipping and we had to reorder. They started installing the wrong carpet, which Isla, the new Austin office manager, thankfully caught toward the beginning of that disaster. We had to wait to put the furniture in until the new carpet could be delivered and installed.

Jake's comment sounds like it could be a compliment to me, but I don't look at it like that. I'm here to train the team, not get the physical office ready. "The team here is really great. Everyone has been very flexible and is dedicated to opening on time."

That part is true. It's absolutely true.

Jake's eyes narrow just a little bit.

"We've been able to do our training at the temporary space. Isla has been diligently watching over the installation crews—checking in every day. This office will do well, I'm sure of it."

His head tilts, and then he looks down and sighs.

"Liam, we're grateful for your dedication and tenacity. It's beneficial for everyone to have this location open on time so things can get moving."

I can read between the lines.

It will save us a metric ton of money if this office opens on time.

But then his tone of voice shifts. He no longer sounds like the chief operations officer he is. He sounds like a regular human. "But I also want you to know that it's very common for these projects to run long. Things happen. The wrong carpet gets installed. Furniture gets broken. People who agreed to relocate change their minds when they realize how hard it will be on their families and we need to replace them."

I nod slowly. I don't speak because something tells me he's not done.

"You work long hours," he points out. "I see you in Asana tasks late at night."

He's not wrong there either. I work a lot. Far more than nine hours each weekday.

It's very possible I've become a workaholic.

"Well, I'm here alone, you know?" I shrug. "I have a lot of time on my hands."

The thing is, work is a really great distraction. It keeps my mind off Kate, who is never far from my immediate thoughts.

She's always there.

So I'm always working.

If anything, to keep my hands busy so I don't pick up the

phone to text or call her. She asked for space and I'm giving it to her.

Maybe if I say it enough times, it will stop hurting.

Jake studies me for a long moment and then takes a deep breath and says things I don't want to hear. Things that human resources might frown upon.

"Liam, I know you've been through it the past couple of years. I fully respect your grief and your need to process it on your own time." He pauses like he's trying to decide how much trouble he could get into by continuing his thought.

I grind my molars together because I know what's coming. It's the same thing that people always say when they find out I'm a widower.

"I hope you know that it's okay to go out and explore the city," he says with a squint. "You're young. You've got plenty of life ahead of you. You should go live it. See the sights. Meet some new people. Enjoy your evenings and weekends in what is arguably the best city in Texas."

Human resources could absolutely give him shit for this conversation. But I know enough about Jake at this point to know he's being genuine. I can see he's legitimately concerned about the number of hours I'm logging. As much as Jake toes the line when he needs to, he's one of the most human corporate executives I've ever met.

I met his wife at the holiday party last year and I'm very certain she's the one that keeps him down to earth.

That thought hurts.

I hurt because Jill was that person for me.

And I hurt because something tells me I could have been that person for Kate.

I look away from my laptop screen and out the window of my very corporate apartment. It's a pretty cool city, I'll give it that.

Even better now that the heat has died down a little. I'll

happily take the October cloud cover over the oppressive heat of summer.

"I hear you, Jake. For what it's worth, I have a list of barbecue places I've been working through, and it's been *delicious.*"

My boss's face grows positively green with envy.

"Dammit, that's a good point. I might have to show up for the office opening. I don't necessarily do it with every location but… barbecue."

That gets me to smirk.

"Some of the transfers have gone with me. It's been a good time."

Jake nods. "I'm glad some of the team has joined you." His computer suddenly dings at him and he frowns, then sighs. "Sorry to bail on you, Liam, but I'm being summoned into my next meeting."

"No problem, Jake. Talk soon."

"Sure thing."

I end the call and close my laptop. I don't want to look at it right now. I just need a fucking minute.

I go to the kitchen and make tea. Yet another way Kate is never far from my mind. I have so many different kinds of tea. It doesn't make any sense when you live alone in a place with sweltering heat.

She had this lemon ginger that I really liked. It was one of the first things I picked up at the grocery store here.

Still a lost puppy.

As I'm standing in the window overlooking the city, my phone dings.

I've lost hope that it will one day be Kate. I know it won't be now.

I tap the screen to wake it up.

Broseph: FaceTime tonight?

I check the time. It's four thirty for me, which means it's five thirty for him. That means I have about ninety minutes.

Me: Sure thing. Call when you're ready.

So I figure I might as well get some things done.

I sit back down at my temporary desk. The apartment came furnished, so I'm just using whatever is here and I'll leave it all behind when I go back home.

I work until my phone starts ringing.

The moment the call connects, chaos ensues. Both boys are talking over each other at full volume. Joe's iPad is usually propped up against the TV so they can all be in the camera shot, so at least the camera is staying steady and I'm not getting motion sick. I can see Joe and Tracy randomly through the gaps between the boys' flailing limbs every couple of seconds.

"All right, all right, all right..." I borderline yell. "Let's back up. One at a time, boys! I can't understand you when you both talk at the same time."

My attempt doesn't work. They both pause while I talk, but then they both start back up.

It's honestly funny. But it's only funny because they're not my kids.

"Okay, let's take turns. Boys!" I bellow over them. I don't even know that they can hear me over their own voices.

A sharp whistle cuts through the chaos and both boys clap their hands over their ears. They turn around and I can see Joe in the same position, cowering away from Tracy, who rolls her eyes at my brother.

"All right. Boys, one at a time. Jackson, you started last time, so let's let Josh go first tonight."

Jackson crosses his arms over his chest and pouts, but he doesn't protest. Josh turns toward the camera again and immediately begins telling me about what he did in school that day.

When it's Jackson's turn, he does much of the same.

I can't believe how big they're getting. It all goes so quickly.

Joe and Tracy occasionally chime in with additional details or clarifications.

I read them the customary bedtime story and then Tracy ushers them off to their rooms. Joe picks up the iPad and settles back in on the couch so we can talk without all the yelling.

"They were extra special tonight," I say.

"They're so exhausting," he responds, letting his head fall back onto the back of the couch.

I can't help but smile. "You're a lucky man."

"I know it." He lifts his head and looks toward the direction his wife and boys went. "I do."

We catch up on our days and when I get to my conversation with Jake, his face changes.

"What?"

Joe palms the back of his neck and looks away. "I just... I don't know. Maybe he's got a point, Liam."

I let out a big sigh and rub my temples.

Why can't everyone just mind their own fucking business?

But Joe doesn't stop talking.

"You're young, man. Maybe you should download a dating app. See what's out there. You never know."

"Fuck, Joe..." The thought of downloading a dating app makes my stomach churn. I have absolutely no desire to do that. Or even date anyone. I scrub my hand down my face and clench my jaw at the sudden sting in my chest. "I don't want to know. I don't care."

I don't have to say anything else. He knows why I don't care what's out there.

We're both quiet for a moment while I try to compose myself and he lets me take my time.

"Liam, you're my brother. I've got your back no matter what. I just want you to be happy."

The words echo in my mind.

I just want you to be happy.

I said those same words to Kate the night before I moved out.

"You do whatever you need to. I'm not gonna try to bully you into anything. I'm just saying…" He shrugs one shoulder and shakes his head. "It might be worth considering."

31

THE TRUTH WILL OUT

Kate

"Talk to me about the letters to Nick. How are they going?"

Gwen's question doesn't irritate me like it once did. I've been writing them for about four months now, so I'm more accustomed to writing to Nick when I feel compelled to do so. Sometimes, it's because I've had a legitimately good day. Sometimes, it's because I feel horrible and miss him terribly. Other times, I write because I want to share news with him and I can't do it in person. He was always the person I shared news with.

Until Liam.

I find myself wanting to share news with Liam. I miss him. I miss him in a way I didn't realize was possible for me right now.

I try to shake off thoughts of Liam and bring myself back to the present, to Gwen, who asked me a question.

"They're… going. They're becoming more helpful, I suppose. More helpful, less hurtful."

Gwen nods, scribbling a note in her folder.

Definitely a Kate voodoo doll.

"I've been writing to him more often, I guess. More often than I did at first. He was…" I pause as that Nick-sized hole in my chest begins to ache. "He was my best friend. It's strange to know that I'll never get to just… rattle off a story about my day to him while he cooks dinner. Every once in a while, I still find myself picking up the phone to text him and realizing… I can't."

I take a deep breath and slowly release it. My breath shakes a little bit, but I'm not as embarrassed about that as I used to be. Regardless, I still close my eyes and enjoy the moment of blackness my eyelids offer.

"I miss him. Every day. Even on good days. But I…" My voice stalls out and my eyelids fly open, then away from Gwen. This thought feels strange, even in my head. Speaking it out loud might land me a grippy-sock vacation.

Gwen's head tilts to one side. The right. She favors the right side for head tilts.

"You what?" she prompts.

I lick my lips and swallow against my suddenly dry throat, searching for all of my courage to speak this aloud.

"Well… I was going to say that… I feel like…" I clear my throat.

Just say it, Kate. Spit it out.

"I've been thinking a lot about grief and legacy and memory. How we keep the memory of someone alive. And the more I think about it, the more I think that… maybe our loved ones live inside our heads."

Feeling self-conscious, I risk a glance up to Gwen. Ever reliable, her face is open, silently encouraging me to continue.

"Don't get me wrong... I fully recognize reality. Nick is dead. He's not coming back. But... he still lives in my head, you know?"

Gwen offers me a soft smile and I can't tell if she's about to call the psych ward or allow me to continue, so I bulldoze forward.

"The letters have kind of become this way for me to write down my memories of him, or my feelings for him so that they're a *record* of him. Because the more time that passes—Jesus, this will be my *second* holiday season without him—it feels like the world is just going on without him and I don't *want* it to. It's a weird mixture of wanting to heal and move forward but still wanting his life to *matter*. His brief, far too short, but *brilliant* life should *matter*. It should mean something important because he meant *everything* to me. He was everything to his family. There was no one better than Nick. He was kind and loving and so freaking wonderful. There will never be anyone like him, but I want people to know that they could *try* to be like him. If they wanted to."

I look back at Gwen, who still has her soft smile in place, her eyes thoughtful.

"I know this probably sounds insane, but... he died. I know that. But I don't want him to *stay* dead."

I watch Gwen carefully, wondering if she'll reach for her cell phone to call an inpatient facility.

Shit, who will take care of Beaker?

But Gwen just shakes her head. "Nah. It doesn't sound insane. It sounds like you're talking about legacy. About finding a way for his spirit to live on." She stops and looks up to the ceiling before bouncing her head back and forth, her brown hair swaying as she does so. "I don't mean that in a religious way, necessarily. I mean it like a metaphorical spirit. Like, the essence of what made Nick, *Nick*."

"Yes." I nod, eyes wide, grateful that Gwen understands what I mean.

"Have you thought about how you want to do that?"

I have thought about it. I've thought about it a lot. What I haven't landed on is *how* or *what* exactly.

"I haven't decided, but I've thought about some kind of scholarship or a sponsorship at the animal shelter."

Gwen nods slowly. "Well, if you want to do something to honor Nick's spirit, try to think about something that really impacted him. Something that would speak to his character. And then do *that*."

* * *

THE FOLLOWING SATURDAY, I work on the master bathroom—my newest home remodeling project—and then run some errands and pick up some flowers to take to Nick's gravesite. It's too late for anything in my garden, so I get something from a local florist.

I navigate the little roads and then walk between the rows until I reach his headstone. I brush the remaining leaves from the stone and lay the flowers down next to his name.

And because I'm me and I can't do anything with reverence, I whisper, "Nick... can you hear me? I'm standing on you."

I snicker to myself and then plop down to the side so I can talk without sitting right on top of him.

"I had to buy you flowers. All of ours are dead," I inform him. "Can you see it? Can you see the house? I'm working on the bathroom now. Just some tile changes and aesthetic stuff. Nothing drastic. I want it to look like a spa."

A gentle breeze rustles the last few leaves remaining on the trees. I smile, thinking that maybe it's Nick giving me a response I don't understand.

"I've been thinking about you… I mean…" I roll my eyes at myself. "I think about you all the time. Gwen and I are trying to work through everything that happened. Trying to get me to move through all the stages of grief so I can… I don't know… live my life again?"

I frown and swallow against the emotion clogging my throat. I'm just not in the mood to cry, so I shove it down. I'll cry later if I have the energy.

"I want to do something that will honor who you were deep down… loving, kind, thoughtful, helpful. And I always end up back at Beaker. I still volunteer at the shelter and I think that I might create an annual donation for them. Something that might help them fund their daily operations and take care of the animals. Provide medical care and whatnot. What do you think?"

A very slight breeze blows the leaves around me, making hair tickle my face and I choose to think of it as a sign.

"You like that, huh? I thought you might."

I hear the sound of a car driving along one of the cemetery roads and I think back to that woman I snapped at all those months ago. Embarrassment isn't a word I would use, but I'm not exactly proud of my behavior. I wasn't in a good place that day.

But also, that woman can take her judgment and shove it where the sun doesn't shine.

I roll my eyes and refrain from cussing at that woman under my breath.

"The holidays are coming up," I tell him as I lean back on my hands. "The thought of decorating doesn't make me want to vomit this year, so I guess that's exciting. Last year, Maggie helped me decorate." I stop and try to remember the last time I talked to her. It's been far too long. I suddenly feel guilt weighing me down. "Maybe she'd be up for helping me again."

The sound of leaves crunching near me has me whipping my head up, half expecting it to be Judgmental Old Lady.

But it's not.

I suck in a breath and start scrambling to my feet.

"Mrs. Rafferty…" I stammer as I brush my butt off. I can't quite meet her eyes.

"Mrs. Rafferty," she returns.

The formal name startles me into looking up at her, which is when I see her kind eyes—just like Nick's—staring back at me with a soft smile.

It's a punch in the gut. My eyes sting immediately, so I squeeze them closed to fight against the tears.

"I hear you've been coming here more often as of late," she says, her voice closer than it was a moment ago.

I open my eyes again to find her only a few steps away.

"How do you know that?"

Her smile widens. "An old teacher friend of mine got bored in retirement and helps out around here to maintain the grounds." She juts her chin in the direction of Nick's headstone. "He told me he's been seeing flowers here, so he kept an eye out to see who was visiting."

I nod, embarrassed for some reason. I have nothing to be embarrassed about. Nick was *my* husband. I can visit his gravesite as often as I want with whatever flowers I want.

Maybe I'm embarrassed that my not-anymore mother-in-law knows I've been visiting but haven't reached out to her family at all.

I don't know. I guess I'll talk to Gwen about it.

Fucking hell, I'll talk to Gwen about it. Who am I anymore?

"Yeah, I have," I acknowledge.

"Do you find it helps?"

I think about it for a moment, and then I think about lying. But then I decide I don't want to lie to her.

"Not really, no. Maybe sometimes."

Helen chuckles softly. "Then why do you keep doing it?"

"I guess… I just…" I look around the grounds and shake my head, letting out a big sigh. "I miss him. I guess I'm… looking for ways to feel him again."

My nose burns and I mentally slap myself on the forehead.

Why are you talking about your feelings? Shut up, Katherine!

"I understand." She nods. "It doesn't make me feel better either. In fact, it makes me feel like crap. It's just something to do, I suppose. Pull a couple of weeds. Leave some flowers." She lifts the small bundle in her hands that I hadn't noticed— also flowers from a local shop. "Spent a few minutes reminiscing."

I watch my not-anymore mother-in-law closely as she looks at Nick's headstone with a level of awkwardness I haven't felt since last Thanksgiving when I was at her house. I haven't spoken to her since, but not because I don't want to.

In fact, I *do* want to talk to her. Rather badly.

I've wanted to reach out to her many times because I *miss her.* I thought about it… I really did. But I never knew what I'd say when she picked up the phone and then everything with Liam happened and it felt like a betrayal I couldn't admit to Helen, and I was afraid she'd see right through me.

For years, this woman was more motherly to me than my own mother. I talked to her and saw her far more frequently than I talked to or saw my mom.

Helen Rafferty has a regal air about her I've always admired. She's classy but stern, like a member of the British royal family. She might seem cold if you don't know her, but I know better. She's quite warm under her brusque exterior. I always theorized that the toughness came from years of teaching, in addition to being a mom to all seven of her children.

We talked about so many things. She told me about her experiences raising so many children with differing personalities. Even her marriage advice was shockingly progressive, given the traditional, conservative way in which her children were raised.

She was open and honest and loving. And I adored her.

Whereas now, I feel like I might suffocate.

"You know, I saw Nick the day after your first date."

Her voice cuts through my guilty thoughts. "What?"

"Nick came over to the house the day after your first date." She looks up at me and smiles warmly. "He came over to help me make pies for Christmas. Initially, he said he'd just bring the apple pie on Christmas Day, but then he called and said he wanted to come over and bake it at the house. So he showed up with apples and baked with me all day."

A content, warm feeling spreads through my chest.

Sounds like Nick.

"He told me all about you. Told me about how he took you ice skating and then to dinner." She pauses, then chuckles. "He said the owner knew both of you and how he had no idea he'd accidentally taken you to your favorite restaurant. It was such a sweet story. I could just tell he was so smitten with you. He talked about you for quite a while."

Without my consent, my eyes are brimming with tears and when I blink, a couple of those asshole traitors escape and roll down my cheeks. "I didn't know that," I manage to squeak out.

Helen only smiles wider. "He said he enjoyed his evening with you, that he was looking forward to seeing you again. But it was the holidays, and you were about to head out of town to see your mom." She chuckles again. "He also said you made it a point to tell him that you were very busy and didn't have time for a relationship."

Fucking fuck, why does she have to remember that?

The thing is, I met Nick during my first semester of grad school. I was working full-time at my father's business already and going to school at night. I was busy *all the time* and I wasn't just saying that because I was looking for an excuse. I really *didn't* have time for a relationship, which is what I blurt out to Helen.

"I was just trying to be fair to him," I grumble.

She laughs harder. "I know, dear. I know. I'm not criticizing you. I'm just saying I'm glad you decided to make time for him. And so was he," she adds with a gentle smile down at her son's flat headstone that the grounds crew *definitely* drives over.

But it's that comment that sticks the final knife of guilt in.

You make time for the people you care about, so of course I made time for Nick. I wanted to spend time with him. Thinking back, I remember feeling surprised by how easy it was to find time for him. And truly, Nick had been accommodating to me.

He brought dinner to my office before I had to leave for class so we could eat dinner together. He went grocery shopping for me so I'd actually have food in my apartment—and then he'd stay to make me dinner so I'd have meals prepared to reheat.

He came by to help me practice presentations and proofread my papers between clients at work. He joked that he could record himself reading my textbooks so I could listen to them while I slept after I read an article about how we could retain information we heard during sleep.

Making time in my life for Nick wasn't difficult. At all.

So why was it incomprehensible that I should make time for the people he loved?

"Do you… maybe want to get some coffee?" I check my watch and raise my eyebrows. "Or a drink?"

Helen Rafferty swings her gaze to me in all its regal glory and I have to fight not to cower. But she doesn't make me wait for an answer.

"I would like that very much."

My smile is effortless. "That's great... I'll um... I'll just give you a minute."

I look at Nick's gravestone one more time and then turn to walk toward the little road so Helen can have a moment.

I'm excited. And nervous.

I've missed her so much.

* * *

HELEN and I go to a restaurant nearby that has a bar area. We sit down in a booth and catch up on what's been going on.

I tell her about house renovation things. She tells me about all the kids and grandkids.

I tell her about the idea for creating a legacy gift in Nick's name. She tells me she loves the idea and would love to be a part of it.

It's less awkward than I thought it would be. It's shockingly comfortable.

And then she asks a question that nearly makes me spit out my drink.

"Are you seeing anyone?"

I literally have to cover my mouth to keep my Manhattan from spilling out. With my eyes bugging out of my head, I stare at her while I force my throat to swallow the liquid.

"No. Of course not." I dab at my mouth with my bar napkin as I feel the flush spreading through my cheeks.

"Why do you say it like that?" she asks, appearing to be genuinely curious. She doesn't look like she's trying to bait me or hope I say something she can ridicule and even as I have the thought, I'm ashamed of myself. She would never.

It's my own guilt.

"I, uh…" I try to shake it off, willing the heat to leave my cheeks. "I don't want to see anyone."

Helen's eyebrows pinch together, just a touch, but she doesn't say anything.

"It hasn't been that long since Nick died. I'm not ready."

After another silent moment, she speaks in a voice so gentle it actually kind of hurts.

"Dear, I can understand if you're not ready. It's a traumatic thing to lose your husband—especially so early. I'm not telling you that you *have* to date…" Her mouth forms a tiny, sad smile and she sighs. "But I know my son, and under no circumstances would he want you to spend the rest of your life alone. At least, not if you would like to be with someone else."

My throat constricts as thoughts of Liam flood me.

His handsome face.

His quiet patience.

His warm embrace.

"If being alone is what you want, Kate," Helen continues, "then that's fine. I'm happy to support you in that decision. But if it's not… if you want to look for love again… then you should. Nick loved you so much. He'd hate to see you pining away for him for the rest of your life." She pauses, looking down at her old-fashioned and spinning the glass in a slow circle. "You're still young… you still have time to have children, if you want."

The breath stalls in my lungs, but I force myself to take a slow, measured breath, just like Gwen trained me to do when I'm feeling overwhelmed. I feel it the moment Helen looks up at me. I can feel the weight of her eyes on my face.

"Kate… I knew about the baby."

I freeze. Every single cell in my body stops moving except

for the ones in my stupid, broken heart, which begins pounding harder. So hard I can hear it.

When I can think coherent thoughts, I force my head to shake. "I'm… I, um… I'm not sure what you're… referring to."

Helen doesn't say anything as I continue to stare at my drink, trying to keep myself together.

Even now, after all this time, I still can't bring myself to admit this massive secret to the woman who birthed seven healthy babies.

Deny, deny, deny.

With a trembling hand, I pick up my drink and take a *very* healthy gulp. Somehow, when I'm setting my glass back down, her eyes snag mine and won't let go.

"On Memorial Day, I noticed that Nick was making you virgin Mules. I didn't say anything to him at the time—I didn't want to arouse suspicion when everyone else was around. But when I saw him a few days later, I asked." She shrugs with another sad smile. "He never could lie to me."

I can see it in her eyes.

She knew.

I'm caught.

I suck in a shaky breath and release it slowly, still looking into her beautiful green eyes.

All this time.

All this fucking time.

She knew, and she never forced me to talk about it. She never interrogated me. She never blamed me for losing the last piece of her son.

All of the horrible, terrible things I've said to myself since it happened, the ways I've blamed myself and sobbed until I was sick at the incalculable losses I've experienced in the past eighteen months… she knew this whole time.

I remember in that moment that Nick told me she'd miscarried at least one time. As much as I've always loved and respected Helen, a sense of kinship I haven't felt for her before blooms in my chest.

I swallow hard before I ask the question at the forefront of my mind. "Did you tell—?" I don't even finish my question before she answers it.

"No." She shakes her head quickly. "No. I didn't tell a soul. I swear. Not even my own husband."

The relief I feel is immediate. My chest releases tension that I didn't realize was keeping my back ramrod straight, my body sagging.

"He called me after your appointment confirming the miscarriage. He was devastated, of course. Having suffered more than one miscarriage myself, I understood at least a little bit of what the two of you were going through."

I frown. *More than one?*

"It's never easy," she continues. "Of course, for you... things were a little more complicated."

A tear escapes my eye, causing me to mentally cuss at my tear ducts. I dab at it with another corner of my bar napkin and try to take a deep breath.

"Kate, I'm so sorry."

I sniff and nod. "Yeah. Me too."

She takes a shaky breath herself, using her own napkin to dab at her own eyes.

"We have both lost children," she says.

I shake my head. "It's not the same. I lost a fetus. You lost a fully grown child that you knew and loved for nearly four decades. It's not the same."

Helen doesn't answer, but does seem to consider my words. Before she can try to convince me that my loss is comparable to hers (and let's face it, there are no winners here), I push forward with something I know I need to say to her.

"I um... owe you an apology though, I think."

That earns me a frown. "For what, dear?"

"For not keeping in touch." Tears sting my eyes again, but I push forward. "I was just... I was so devastated and wrapped up in my own grief that I didn't even think about how you'd lost a child. Or how his siblings had lost a brother."

I scratch at my temple in an attempt to buy myself time while I get myself together.

"You guys were so nice to me, and so sweet to try and include me in family events, still. When I came for Thanksgiving, it was so overwhelmingly painful to be around all of you. It was like... if I could take all the different parts of you and smash them together, I could see him again. I had little glimpses of him, but not *him*. I just couldn't bear the thought of seeing all of you again. So... I'm sorry I didn't reach out more. But I wanted to explain why."

Helen reaches across the table and squeezes my forearm. "You're forgiven, dear."

Another wave of tension leaves my body.

I had no idea how badly I needed to hear her say those words.

"You really should call Maggie, though," she says, withdrawing her hand and picking up her drink to take a sip.

I nod. I know she's right. "Yeah. Yeah, I need to do that."

"And listen, it's up to you, but I think everyone would really love it if you'd start coming to family dinners again."

My head snaps up. "What?"

"Remember family dinner? First Sunday of every month? We still do that, and we'd love for you to join us... whenever you're available and if you're comfortable."

My stupid, traitorous tear ducts well up again.

I try to think of something to say. Anything. Any word. But I come up with nothing. Everything that flits its way into my brain flies out immediately. I think I stammer a couple of words, but nothing is coherent.

After all this time, after refusing every single invitation to see his family in the past year, here is Nick's mother welcoming me back with open arms.

"Like I said, it's up to you. I understand why you may not want to come, but I wanted you to know you're welcome." She makes sure to meet my eyes when she finishes. "Always."

3 2

SURPRISE...?

Liam

"Ladies and gentlemen, this is your captain speaking. On behalf of the flight crew, I'd like to welcome you aboard flight..."

The pilot is talking, but I'm not really listening.

I'm going home, at least for a while.

We came to a mutual decision that it would be best to open the office after the new year, thanks to all of the delays we encountered with the supply chain and shipping delays and a million other tiny things that happened to slow our progress.

I'm flying home for the holidays and then I'll go back on the second of January to help them get up and running. I'll stay for a few days and then I'll be back home for good.

Or at least until I'm assigned a new office to open.

As the flight crew runs through their safety demonstration, I think about what I need to do when I get home.

I have a few days before Christmas, so I'll finish up shopping—I already had packages shipped directly to Joe's house so I could just wrap them at his house—and start looking for a place to live. Buying or renting, I don't know. But I'll figure it out. I can stay at Joe's in the meantime.

It's never a hardship to spend time with my nephews.

Once the flight takes off, I settle in and decide to get some rest. Those hellions are tiring and I admittedly haven't been sleeping well for the past few... months.

When I wake up, the flight crew is walking the aisle, collecting trash and the pilot is telling us we're beginning our descent.

"Local time is 8:39 p.m. and the local temperature is twenty-eight degrees."

Fuck, that's cold.

I grimace when I think about how warm it was in Austin when we left.

And then my eyes shoot wide when I realize that all of my really warm winter clothes are at Kate's house. I even left my really good coat. Because why would I need it in fucking *Texas* when I was in such a rush to leave?

"Great job, dumbass," I mutter to myself as I rub my forehead.

"What?"

The question comes from the guy sitting next to me. I look up at him and he's frowning.

"What?" I ask.

"Did you just call me a dumbass?"

"No," I assure him, shaking my head. "I was talking to myself. I'm a dumbass."

He looks skeptical.

"I just realized a decision I made six months ago was stupid and now I have to figure out how to correct it," I clarify.

He's still frowning, but he looks less offended.

"Sorry…" I say. "I'll stop muttering to myself out loud."

My seatmate goes back to whatever he was reading, and I go back to wondering how the fuck I'm going to get my stuff back from Kate's.

Joe picks me up at baggage claim, hugging me tight before grabbing my rolling suitcase and leading me to his car, updating me on the kids along the way.

Given the time, the boys are already in bed. Joe and Tracy made the very strategic (and very smart) decision to tell the boys that I wasn't coming home for a couple more days so they'd actually go to sleep tonight. Therefore, when we get to the house, everything is quiet.

Joe, Tracy, and I have a drink together, but it's getting late and we're all tired.

Tracy has already prepped the futon, making up the little mattress with a clean fitted sheet, top sheet, and two blankets. Two pillows are sitting on the end.

I settle myself in, fully prepared to wake up to two boys jumping on me. My spine remembers the feeling of digging into that bar in the middle of the futon very well.

Like I have most nights for the past six months, I lie there in silence, thinking of Kate. I even get out my phone to look at pictures of her that are still on my phone. I didn't take many, but I have a few. If they were printed, they'd be crinkled and worn from me taking them out so many times.

I try to steel my nerves to contact her. I know I need to. The moment I stepped out of the airport, my bones froze a little. I need that coat and the sweaters I left in the dresser.

It's late, so I'm not going to text her tonight. But I tell myself I need to do it the following day. It's already December 22 and I don't want to intrude on any of her holiday plans. I can stop by while she's at work.

If I'm being honest, I *need* to stop by while she's at work.

I'm not sure I'm ready to see her. I'm not sure I'm ready to be in the same city as her, let alone the same room.

So that settles it. I'll text her in the morning.

* * *

I WAKE up when a fifty-pound body lands on my chest.

Funny how the inability to breathe will do that to you.

"Jackson! I told you not to jump on your Uncle Liam! That's incredibly rude!"

Since my eyes flew open in immediate alarm when the wind was knocked from my lungs, I look up to find my sister-in-law's eyes wide as saucers.

"Liam, I'm so sorry. They're very surprised, obviously."

Josh is next to me, basically yelling about things he learned in school that week. I can't really understand any of it because all of my brain cells are devoted to remembering how to take air into my lungs.

"Boys." Joe's stern dad-voice cuts through their chatter and he mercifully lifts Jackson off my body. "I need you both to take a few deep breaths and let Uncle Liam wake up. He flew back from Austin last night and he had a long day. Just let him get acclimated, please."

I throw him a grateful look as I start to catch my breath. They keep chattering and I eventually sit up so no one can jump on my chest.

Tracy brings me coffee and the two of them start making breakfast while I sit on my temporary bed, chatting with my nephews and showing them photos of Austin. I tell them about all the barbecue places I went to, I show them the cool festivals my team eventually dragged me to, and assure them that I'll be here on Christmas morning.

Being with them feeds my soul in a way I had sort of

forgotten was missing. As much as I got used to living in Chicago, I figured being in Austin would be easier. But in the end, it wasn't. Having those few months at home just made me more homesick.

I realize I might have to leave again… it's part of my job. But I know now that I'll always return. I want these moments with them. I want to soak up their childhood.

We eat bacon and eggs for breakfast and then I head into the bathroom to shower. I use the time to mentally prepare myself for communication with Kate. It shouldn't be a big deal. It's just a text. It's a few words on a screen.

It just feels like a lot more.

I wrap a towel around my waist and pick up my phone. Before I can talk myself out of it, I type out the words.

> Me: Hey, Kate. I'm back in town for a bit. I was wondering if it's okay for me to pick up my winter clothes.

I read it back four times and then I tap the arrow to send the message.

Josh and Jackson and I play games for a while. Joe makes us lunch. Right after I'm done eating, my phone pings.

My stupid, hopeful heart leaps at the thought that it might be Kate, but I force myself to temper my reaction.

It's never her. You're a lost puppy.

Pulling my phone from my pocket, my stupid, hopeful heart is proven right.

> Kate: Hi! It's so good to hear from you. Yes, of course it's okay. I'll be home a little early today… around 4, maybe, but you can come over whenever. You know the garage code.

I know immediately that I can't go there once she's home.

I just can't. I need to go beforehand. I glance at the time… it's one o'clock. If I leave soon, I can get over there and back long before she's home.

Me: Thanks.

I can't bring myself to type anymore, though I want to keep the conversation going.

The weight of Joe's eyes is digging a hole into the side of my head, so I look over at him.

"What's going on?" He tips his chin in the direction of my phone.

Steeling my emotions, I tell him I need to go over to Kate's to get my winter stuff. He raises his eyebrows.

"I'll be out of there before she's home from work."

Joe's eyes narrow. "Are you sure you don't want to talk to her?"

"No, man. I'm not really sure of anything," I say, scrubbing a hand down my face. "But I do know I need my winter coat."

"I could go with you… if you want," he offers.

"Nah, I'll be fine. Thanks, though."

It will probably be fine.

"I'm gonna head over there. I'll be back soon."

My baby brother watches me too closely for a minute, then nods one time.

I trade out my sweats for jeans and borrow a hoodie, a coat, and a duffel bag from Joe, then brave the cold so I can drive to Kate's house.

My car stayed here while I was gone, and Joe drove it at least once a week so it didn't rust out and die. The gas tank is full and the oil was changed last month. Another rush of gratitude floods me. I really do have the best brother.

The drive takes about twenty minutes and during every

single one of those minutes, my palms sweat. I hope Kate gets home early while also hoping she comes home late. I hope she's living her life the way she needs to while also hoping she still cares about me.

I pull into the driveway and park by the garage door so I can make a quick getaway. Punching in the garage code, I notice that the garage door is a different color. It was stark white before, but now it's more like a muted gray. It's a subtle difference. I like it.

Finding the garage empty feels as much like a relief as much as it does a letdown. I don't let myself analyze that. I just make a beeline for the door that leads to the kitchen and run up the steps.

When I close the door behind me and face the kitchen, I'm assaulted by memories, despite my attempt at repressing them. I wade through them, push them away, and go toward the stairs, trying my damnedest not to look around.

Even so, I notice the decorations. The tree is set up in the same place it was last year. The mantel is decorated with lights and garland. Little Christmas knickknacks are on shelves and tables. I wonder if she did all of it herself.

When I start up the staircase, I notice something else is different.

The photos.

When I lived here, there were photos of Kate and Nick hanging in the stairwell—the two of them on their wedding day, looking like models in a fragrance ad. Them in front of the house, beaming proudly. Them on vacation somewhere in the Caribbean, sun-kissed and relaxed. Them in the colorful fall leaves, Nick kissing Kate's cheek.

Now though… they're all gone.

She's replaced them with landscapes and architecture—undoubtedly taken by her brother. They're beautifully matted and framed, climbing the wall gracefully.

The Brooklyn Bridge at sunrise. The Manhattan skyline on a cloudy day. A striking photo of her house in the fall with brilliant yellow and orange leaves surrounding it. A breathtaking view from atop the Empire State Building. The skating rink in town, full of people bundled up with rosy cheeks.

At the very top is a black-and-white photo of Kate's family. It's a candid from a family gathering on the back patio. Sophie is putting food on the table. Jack is talking, gesturing with his hands. Kate is laughing at something he's saying, head thrown back, hand on her stomach, eyes squeezed shut.

It's the version of Kate I love the most. It's also one I didn't see very often. The last time I saw her like that was at Leon's birthday party. Two days later, everything changed.

If this version is making an appearance more often, I'm grateful. I'm glad. I'm proud of her. I know how difficult this journey is… for her, in particular.

I force my feet forward and into my old room, intentionally not looking across the landing to her bedroom door.

When I look up, I almost wonder if I went into the wrong room.

The bed and furniture are the same, but the walls are a different color. Instead of the beige they were before, they're now a calming, warm green. There's a new chair in the corner of the room and a cascading shelf along one wall with photos in frames scattered on the shelves with books and various small items—shells from the beach, a tiny container of sand, souvenirs from other cities.

I grind my teeth together and open the closet, pulling everything off hangers and shoving them in the duffel bag. I rip open drawers, carelessly throwing their contents into the bag as well.

It's when I get to the bottom one that I freeze.

The jeans I was expecting. I knew I'd left them there.

What I *wasn't* expecting was a box with my name on it. I throw the jeans into the bag and sit on the bed with the box.

Inside, there's a stack of envelopes held together with a rubber band, Kate's handwriting scrawled across the top one in slanted cursive.

Forgetting everything about wanting to get out of the house quickly, I take off the rubber band and open the envelope on top. It's a letter, addressed to me from Kate and dated July twentieth.

Liam,

You're probably in Austin right now. You were supposed to start your new project on the first of the month. I assume you have.

I'm not totally sure why I'm writing this letter to you. I think because I miss you. I miss talking to you. I miss you talking to me. No matter what else went on between us, I counted you as a friend. And now you're gone.

I feel terrible about how we parted ways. I wish it could have been on better terms. Sometimes, I wish I could have seen you one more time before you left, but I think that might have made it more difficult to say goodbye.

As horrible as it was to discover you'd left without telling me, I might be glad you did it that way. I don't know if I would have had the courage to let you go otherwise.

Anyway, I hope you're doing well in Austin.

But I do miss you.

Kate

I read it again, just as confused as I was the first time. Why did she write me a letter she never sent?

I pick up the next envelope. It's marked August second.

Liam,

I'm painting the house. I started in that second living room no one ever uses. I figured if I sucked at this, that was a good place to figure it out. It didn't turn out too bad though. I'll do my room eventually, but I haven't decided how I'll do it yet, so I'm starting on the empty guest bedrooms.

Part of me wants to renovate your room. So badly.

Ha. Your room. Like you still live there. Like you'll ever be back, living in there. Look how delusional.

I want to paint it because I was never a fan of the beige in there. It's drab. I want to make it more welcoming. Warm.

But I also want to rip it apart so I can forget about the pain I feel when I think about you. I want to erase you from my mind while simultaneously imprinting you on my skin. I don't know how to handle that. I don't know what to do with those conflicting feelings.

My therapist would probably tell me it's normal or spout some psychiatrist bullshit.

For now, I'm going to leave your room alone. I don't want to touch it while I'm unsure of these feelings.

I hope you're doing well in Austin.

I miss you.

Kate

P.s. Beaker misses you, too.

I drop down onto the bed, my hand holding the letter hitting my thigh.

She missed me.

The hopeful parts remaining in my heart try to cling to that sentiment while my brain reminds me that she wrote these words in August and now it's December.

But would she give you the letters if she didn't still feel that way?

It's like there's a devil and an angel on my shoulders, trying to convince me that a crisis is a good move right now. In my old bedroom. In Kate's house.

The third envelope is marked September fifth.

Liam, I yelled at Nick's gravestone today.

I went there to put daisies from the garden on his headstone and I ended up yelling at him.

Were you ever mad at Jill for dying? I realize her illness wasn't her fault. I know the circumstances were different. But were you ever angry?

What am I thinking... of course you weren't. You're a hell of a lot healthier than I am. I'm sure you never yelled at her headstone. Only unstable people do that.

Honestly, if I were alone, it wouldn't have been a big deal. But this old biddy showed up—probably to see her own goddamn husband—and was giving me very judgmental eyes, so I snapped at her, too.

Things are going well, obviously.

Hot Mess Kate

This one makes me sad, but it also makes me laugh. Kate isn't unstable. She's grieving. Trying to make sense of the world around her that looks and feels totally foreign from what she expected.

And I would have loved to see her yell at that old lady. That would have been hysterical.

A feline sound chirps from the doorway, and then Beaker is bounding into the room, up onto the bed, rubbing his face all over me.

"Hey, buddy!" I set the letter aside and stroke his back from head to tail. He preens and purrs and headbutts my free hand. "I missed you. How's Kate doing, huh?"

Beaker doesn't answer. Instead, he rolls over on the bed a few times and then snuggles up against my leg. While he's happy next to me, I open the next letter, dated September fifteenth.

Liam,

I'm in Niagara Falls. The Canadian side.

Nick's parents came here decades ago for their honeymoon and Nick always wanted to go, but we never got here. So now I'm here alone.

I wanted to come here to feel closer to Nick, I think. I'm sure that sounds absurd... driving hours away into a different country so you can seek out your dead husband. Oddly enough, something happened today... and I sort of... god, I don't even know how to say this without sounding like I need to be admitted into a psych ward.

I swear I felt him today.

I don't know how to describe it, but I swear he was there.

For the first time in so, so long, I felt... peaceful.

I'm not sure what it says about this experience today that I wanted to talk to you about it. You and only you.

When we were living together, you became one of my closest friends. And then... something else as well. But still my friend. So when this momentous breakthrough happens in my brain, I want to talk to you about it.

But because I'm a mess, you're in Austin and it makes me hate myself. It didn't have to be this way. You could be here. Or maybe not "here" as in Niagara, but "here" as in, with me.

I don't know what you're up to. I've thought about reaching out so many times, but you haven't, and that makes

*me think I hurt you so badly that our friendship is
irreparable.*

*Of course, knowing you, you're just giving me space
because I asked for it.*

*Fucking hell, I should really just go to sleep. This is enough
thinking for one day.*

I still miss you, though.

Kate

I read letter after letter, Beaker purring alongside me. She talks about what she's doing to the house. She talks about conversations she's having with the landscapers. She tells me how she's opening some sort of fund for the animal shelter in Nick's memory.

She recounts events that happened before we lived together that help me understand more about her mindset when we moved in together—how her brother basically got her out of bed after one month.

In a letter dated November, Kate discusses those early days after Nick passed.

*I was not well. I was not okay. I truly didn't believe I would
ever be okay again. I wanted to die, but didn't often think
about actually killing myself. I just wished I was dead. I can't
say if I would have jumped in front of a bus if given the opportunity, but I'm not sure I would have resisted it very hard.*

*I couldn't think beyond the next hour in any day. The rest
of my life was supposed to be spent with Nick. That was the
promise. Until death do us part. Well... death parted us. And
far earlier than we'd anticipated. My future was completely
uncertain and devastating. Not focusing on the future was the
only way I could survive.*

People told me to make plans—to find things that made me

happy. Even little things. They tried to get me to make appointments for pedicures and buy concert tickets and plan dinners. But having something to look forward to seemed completely impossible. I wasn't looking forward. I was looking back.

So when I saw you at Elliot and Leon's, and you said you were looking for a place to live, it was my gut reaction to ask you to live with me. I had three empty bedrooms and a massive house I didn't think I could afford. It made sense in my head at the time. I didn't stop to think about how weird it might be until after I'd asked, and I wasn't going to pull the offer. Doing so felt rude and horrible.

I didn't think in a million years that we would develop feelings for each other. It didn't even seem fathomable. The thought literally never crossed my mind.

That night, I saw a grieving man who could use some company... even if that company was a grieving woman who probably wasn't going to be of any actual help. Perhaps not living alone would make you feel better, and it would help me pay some bills until I figured out what the hell I was going to do.

And then the unfathomable happened. Over time, we got more comfortable with each other, and I saw what a kind, gentle, generous person you are. I saw things in you I never expected to see through my mourning haze—you weren't simply my roommate anymore. You had become a legitimate friend, and then... something more.

I think in some ways, you saved my life. I don't mean that in a "love will prevail" kind of fairy-tale way... it's more subtle than that. The fact that you developed feelings for me had little to do with it. It was the fact that you developed feelings for anyone at all. It was the fact that you'd found a way to build yourself a new life. You showed me that it was possible to work through your grief and keep going. Little by little, day by day. And that night when you told me how you felt about me, I real-

ized that if I let you stay, I'd halt your progress. I'd destroy your life all over again because I couldn't give you what you needed.

I wish I could say I was trying to save you when I told you to go to Austin. Even though I knew I was bad for you, I can't claim to be selfless in that decision. I wasn't ready for a relationship, and it was time I said it out loud to you. Past time. I knew deep down I wasn't ready... that I wasn't emotionally prepared for what was happening with you. But I... I just couldn't say it. I couldn't stop it.

I'm sorry.

Kate

I set the letter down next to me and fall backward on the bed.

Every detail of that Thursday night replays in my mind. Everything I said. Everything she said. Even the feeling of her body against mine in the precious seconds when I believed that maybe... just maybe, it would all be okay.

And then she let me down as easily as she could, but even now, I feel the same pit in my stomach that I did that night. The same heartbreak. The same sting in my eyes.

I scrub both hands down my face and check my watch. It's coming up on three o'clock and I feel a sudden urgency to get out of the house.

I stuff all the letters back into the box, give Beaker a few more pets, then grab my duffel bag and practically run back through the house, shutting the garage door behind me as I leave.

Before I tear down the driveway, I make sure the door is all the way shut and then I head toward my favorite park in town. I don't get out of the car—it's cold as fuck, you might recall—but I do sit in that parking lot and read the rest of

Kate's letters. I want privacy for this and if I go back to Joe's, everyone will be all over me trying to figure out what I'm reading.

The letters pick up in frequency at this point. Where there might have been two or three per month, there are now sometimes two per week. It almost feels like she was writing to me when she wished she could talk to me. Like it was a substitute because I wasn't there.

She tells me how she reconnected with her mother-in-law. How her sister-in-law came over to help her decorate again this year—*this time, without the horrible awkwardness and general wishing for death*, she says.

She talks to me about getting ready for her second holiday without Nick… how that feels for her. How it's both better and worse.

> *Last year, I had you to share in my grief. I knew it was also your first holiday season without Jill and I felt a lot of comfort in that. I felt like we were both trying to navigate these waters… not together, per se, but alongside one another and it felt less lonely that way.*
>
> *But this year, you're in Austin—a city I've yet to visit but somehow hate only because you're there—and I'm trying to figure out how to do this all over again.*
>
> *It's better this year, but it's also worse.*
>
> *Liam, I miss you. And I know I have no right to. But I do. Like… a painful amount. And that makes me feel absolutely horrible all over again for the way things ended between us, which makes me sad and lonely and the cycle starts all over again.*
>
> *It sort of feels like I mourned Nick last Christmas, but this year… this year, I'm mourning a relationship I desperately wanted but was not ready for. What could my holiday be like this year if I weren't such a fucking train wreck?*

*None of this is fair to say to you, which is ultimately why I
probably won't ever give these to you. But fuck, I wish I had the
courage to.*

I'm frowning something fierce. She obviously found the courage to give me these letters. Why wouldn't she have wanted to initially?

What changed?

Did she really believe that my feelings for her would just disappear over the course of six months?

If she actually believes that, I didn't do a good enough job of showing her how I felt. Of course, there were complicated circumstances that made me hold back from showing the full depth of my feelings for her… so maybe there's a valid point here.

Right here, right now, I swear to myself that if I ever get the opportunity to show her, I'll do it and I won't hold back a single thing. I told my brother earlier that I don't know much of anything these days—with the exception of needing my winter coat in this frozen tundra.

But one thing I know with absolute fucking certainty is that I will never get over Kate Rafferty. I could live another sixty years, never speak to her again, watch her marry another man and have a family, and I would still love her just as much as I do in this moment. I will love Kate Rafferty for as long as I live, and long after I'm dead.

The next letter is from December thirteenth.

*Not long after you moved in, you came… "home" I guess,
and found me crying under the Christmas tree. Do you
remember that? You were so fucking kind. I was in full panic
mode and couldn't find my way out and you were patient and
wonderful and loving—things I later learned were just… you.
That's just who you are.*

You stayed with me and helped me breathe until I calmed down and then I was so embarrassed and overwhelmed that I fled to my room to hide from you.

I want you to know how much it meant to me that you took the time to sit with me that night. But I also realize I never told you what was going on. I'm sure you assumed it was just a widow grieving over her first Christmas without her husband—and I'm sure some of it was that—but that wasn't the major issue of the day.

That day was the day my baby—Nick's baby—was due. That day was the day I was supposed to be giving birth to a child. Or desperately wishing he would come so I could stop being swollen and large and angry.

Because I hadn't told anyone, I didn't have anyone that day. The only person who knew was dead. I don't think I'd ever felt more alone than I did that night, lying under that tree. That night was probably one of the lowest lows. I felt so empty.

You calmed me down under the tree, but I woke up from a dream about Nick and it threw me right back into a panic attack. I cried in my bathroom, hoping you wouldn't hear. It's the only time in my life I've cried so hard I threw up.

The following morning, I came downstairs with a wretched headache and a death wish. You'd made coffee and pancakes, and you were reading the paper in the kitchen. It was honestly jarring. It took me a while to get used to the idea that a different man was living in my house, eating breakfast in my kitchen. Sometimes, I'd hear you in there when I came down the stairs in the morning before work and I legitimately expected to find Nick in there. I thought about walking in and seeing that brilliant smile light up his face. But of course, it wasn't him in there bustling around.

Sometimes, having you around actually made me miss him more—which isn't your fault, obviously. And you couldn't

possibly have known. But having another man around some-
times just... hurt.

Flash forward one year and that man is in Austin (I still
hate that city). I'm alone (which I've accepted, and is probably
for the best). No one is making breakfast in the kitchen (you
know I hate cooking). No one is watching baseball in the guest
room (I tried watching after you left, but it just wasn't the
same).

It's a different life, but it's not a bad life. I'm doing all right.
I still miss you, though.

Kate

I stare at the letter in my hands for a while… I don't know how long.

I'm not ashamed to admit I have tears in my eyes. It's like I can physically feel her pain. My chest is tight and my stomach is in knots.

I knew she was having a hard time that day, and yes, I assumed it was because it was her first Christmas without Nick. But even after I found out about her miscarriage, I didn't put together the dates. I try to scan my mind for that ultrasound photo, but the only thing I remember is the kidney-shaped blob and the number of weeks she was. I don't remember a date on the printout.

I feel terrible that she continued to struggle after I went to bed. I wish I'd heard her crying so I could go sit with her. Not that wishing for something to be different that happened a year ago would do anything to change the circumstances, but I still wish it. She shouldn't have had to be alone in that moment.

Pressing my fingers into my aching sternum, I look down at the pile and find that I'm still not done—a fact that makes me both relieved and sad.

There's a short, lighthearted letter where she's telling me about something funny that happened at work.

There's a long letter where she tells me about her company's holiday party and how that's the night she knew things were changing with Nick. I'd never known this, but she met him because the company he worked for was a client of hers.

She tells me about how they talked all night and she finally agreed to go out with him. She tells me about their first date and the joke that he just wanted to take her on a decent first date because so many of hers had been so terrible. The details bring a smile to my face because I can feel the nostalgia in her words. I can tell in the words she chooses how different she feels now versus the way she felt on the anniversary of Jill's death when she admitted she wasn't sure if she'd do it all again.

In fact, she admits in this letter that she *would* do it all again. Just to have the chance.

The final letter is talking about her Christmas plans. Her brother will be staying with her starting December twenty-third—today, apparently—and I wonder if that's why she's coming home early today. Her dad and stepmom will join them at her house for brunch. She jokes that the only thing she's providing is the mimosas, but that her brother will make waffles and her stepmom and dad will bring food, too.

And then she starts talking *to* me *about* me again.

I don't know when you're coming back... if you're coming back. You still have winter clothes in your room, which is kind of funny in a way. It reminds me of that really terrible advice toxic women sometimes give to each other about intentionally leaving something behind at a man's house, but act like it's an accident so they have to see the dude again to get it back.

I'm fully aware that's not what's happening here, but it still makes me laugh.

At some point, you'll come get your stuff, or send someone for it and I'm dreading it. I'm dreading that moment because that's the last piece I have of you and once it's gone... you'll be gone.

Liam, I don't want you to be gone. I don't want to be rid of you. I miss you so much it hurts.

I've told you before that I don't know why I'm writing these letters to you and I'm not sure if I'll ever give them to you... it started as a cathartic exercise, but I'm not sure I can endure you actually reading them.

But I suppose... why am I writing them if I don't want you to read them?

So if you are reading this, please know that I am sorry for any pain or suffering I've caused you. I promise it was never intentional. I was clearly struggling and didn't cope well. But I'm eternally grateful for your patience when you lived here... and when we were together. And for letting me have space when I needed it.

I'm a better person today than I was when we met, at least in part because of you.

I hope Austin is good to you.

Kate

P.s. Fuck Austin.

The end of the letter makes me laugh. It's funny to me how she holds a grudge against Austin for reasons that are completely ridiculous. It's funnier to me that she *knows* it's ridiculous and hates it anyway.

I still don't know why she gave me these letters or why they were being stored next to the clothes I'd left in her house.

But I'm glad she wrote them and that they were in that drawer.

Even with the rough subject matter of some of these letters, I feel like a part of my chest has stitched its way back together.

I missed her so much while I was gone.

I still miss her.

But at least I have these letters.

And a tiny smidgen of hope.

33

I HAVE TO GET OUT OF HERE

Kate

"What time are you getting here?" Elliot's voice cuts into my thoughts of last-minute things to do before I leave the office for the final time this year.

Like a sane person, he didn't work today. He and Leon are throwing a New Year's party tonight, so he's prepping for that, but I came into the office to do some final wrap-up and prep for next year.

Three cheers for workaholism!

Don't judge me. This is going to be my company one day.

Also, it's only two o'clock in the afternoon. I have plenty of time to get home and get ready for the party. Besides, Elliot and Leon live five minutes from my house. *If* you hit all the lights.

"What time do doors open?" I ask, trying not to laugh at my own joke about how this is basically being compared to the biggest event of the year among our friend circles.

383

He mutters something I can't understand but am completely certain is directed at me.

"Any time after eight, you little shit."

I stifle my laugh, pulling the receiver of my phone away from my mouth.

"Sounds good. I'll be there, but without bells on because they don't really match my aesthetic."

He sighs and I swear I can hear him roll his eyes.

"Listen, I just want to make sure you know…" he trails off, but I already know what he's going to say.

"Spit it out, El."

Another sigh.

"Liam will be here tonight."

"Okay."

"Is it?"

"Of course it is."

There's a moment of silence before he continues. "I just… I want to make sure you're prepared."

I take a deep breath and let my head fall back against my office chair.

Am I prepared to see Liam?

I honestly don't know. I'm not sure anything could prepare me for seeing Liam again. But the thought of it makes my stomach flutter and my eyes sting.

I still miss him so much. And what does that say? Do I miss his friendship? Do I miss what we were? Do I want to see what we could be?

I'm not sure if I know the answers to any of those questions if I'm being totally honest.

But I do know that Gwen has been encouraging me to follow my heart while also examining my feelings and the thoughts behind them.

She and I talked at length about the letters I wrote to

Liam. See, she didn't assign *that* homework to me. I just did it. And when I told her, she was pleasantly surprised.

My sticking point was that I didn't know if I should give them to him. Frankly, I didn't want to make that decision and Gwen certainly couldn't make it *for* me.

So I kept them in a drawer of his dresser and told myself that if he came by to pick things up and found them… then so be it. It was up to fate at that point, right?

The day he texted to ask if he could pick up his clothes, I was already at work and unable to get home to take the box out of the dresser before my meetings were over that afternoon.

Therefore, fate decided he should have the letters.

The thing is… he hasn't contacted me since, so I don't know if he read them or threw them away. He might have burned them for all I know.

Regardless, he took them out of that drawer and I did not die.

"I'll be fine, El. But I appreciate your concern."

He doesn't respond for a moment, but he finally concedes and drops the subject. "I'm glad you're coming. Wear something cute. Oh, but there're icy patches, so be careful about your shoes."

"Yes, dear."

Someone calls his name in the background and I hear muffled conversation for a second before he comes back. "I have to go."

"I know, I'll see you later."

"Love you, bye," he says before hanging up before I can return the sentiment.

I heave a sigh and decide everything else on my list can wait until next year. It's not that important.

And I decide that—in and of itself—is growth worthy of celebration.

So I snap my laptop shut, pack up my things, and head out the door.

I have a party to attend.

And if at all possible… a Liam to win back. Even if it's just his friendship.

* * *

I'M RUNNING LATE.

That's actually out of the ordinary for me. I enjoy being punctual. But in this case, I couldn't decide what to wear because every single outfit I put on my body felt like it wasn't giving a great first impression of seeing Liam again.

Of course, this isn't at all his first impression of me. Not even the second or the third or one hundredth. We used to live together. We shared an active (and satisfying) sex life. What I'm wearing won't matter… not really. It's just that I want to show him I'm doing better.

And it's not a crime to want to look nice for a guy you have… feelings for.

What kind of feelings? My brain tries to ask me.

I don't know, they're just feelings. Leave me alone.

I wound up wearing a cute gray knit sweater with a pair of dark skinny jeans and warm ankle boots. I blew my hair dry with a diffuser, so the waves are still intact but tamed with product. I did my makeup in the most elegantly under-stated way I could manage—a subtle, lighter, smoky eye finished with lip gloss.

As I inspect my final appearance, I realize that I haven't tried this hard to look nice for someone since I started seeing Nick.

I close my eyes for a moment to endure the sting of pain in my chest, but I breathe through it and end up smiling at the thought of him. How lucky I was to get to know him for as long as I did.

When I open my eyes, they're glassy, but I dab at the corners so I don't fuck up the makeup I just applied.

I might not know exactly what my feelings are for Liam, but they're *there* and I want to explore them if he's willing to try with me.

After all, why would I miss him so fiercely—still, after six entire months—if these feelings weren't something... big?

So I pet Beaker's adorable head, make sure he has food and water, and head out the door.

The drive over is uneventful, as expected. It's five minutes.

I park in the designated parking area. Fortunately, it hasn't snowed much yet and the ground is hard enough already that people parking on the grass won't destroy anything. Otherwise, I could never imagine parking on their *lawn*. Elliot would die.

I check my makeup one last time in my visor mirror, then grab my clutch and the bottle of wine I bought for them and head up the driveway to the house.

My knuckles don't even make contact with the door before it flies open, Elliot standing right in front of me with a massive smile on his face.

It's a little alarming, if I'm being honest.

"Hi, honey," I say, trying to figure out if he's attempting to send me a message via his exaggerated expression.

"Hello! It's so good to see you! Come on in!" He reaches forward and grabs my hand, pulling me inside the house and shutting the door behind me.

"Are you sure it's good to see me? You seem weird."

"Yes, of course! Everything is fine. I'm very glad you're here."

I narrow my eyes at him.

"Elliot, what's going on?"

He blinks a few times. "Nothing, dear! Hosting stress. Everything is fine. Let's get you a glass of wine, shall we?"

This does nothing to tamp down my suspicion, but I let it go because I'm already dealing with enough, what with my nervousness over seeing Liam again.

Elliot leads me into the kitchen to get wine, where I find that everything is already hustling and bustling. There's a buffet set up on the island, set up by caterers, and the dining room table has an assortment of cookies and desserts. I can't be bothered to check out the selection though, because I'm already looking for Liam.

A glass of red wine is shoved into my hand and my coat is stripped from my body.

"I'll put your clutch in its place," Elliot says. Whenever there's a party, he puts my clutch in the same drawer in a console table so I know where to find it, but am not worried about leaving it somewhere.

"Thanks…" I turn to look at him, but he's already walking away from me.

"Kate, you made it!" Leon moves into my field of vision and wraps me into a hug.

"I wouldn't miss it," I promise. "What's wrong with Elliot? He's being weird."

"Is he?" He lets go of me and frowns. "Who knows. Hosting stress maybe? I don't know. I'll look for him though and see what's going on."

"All right. Let me know."

"I will, sweetie. Get some food," he says, gesturing toward the island. "I need to go check on the firepit."

"Sure." I try to give him a reassuring smile, but I'm not sure it works. When he's disappeared out the patio doors, I search for Liam again. I still don't see him, but I'm surprised to see a few random people outside. I think they're smoking, which is probably why the firepit is set up—so they can be warm out there.

A former classmate of mine and Elliot's finds me and starts chatting to me about the real estate market, but I'm only half paying attention. I still haven't seen Liam.

When she says she needs food, I follow her to the island and put finger foods on my plate—vegetables, little pockets of dough that are probably filled with something delicious, meatballs, and some fruit.

I eat it while she talks and I'm present enough to know it tastes good, but again… I'm not paying much attention.

It's not until someone else we know from school joins us that I feel someone's eyes on me. The hair on the back of my neck stands up and a shiver goes up my spine. I look around as discreetly as I can without being even more rude to the people I'm already being rude to by not listening to them.

And then I see him.

My breath catches before I'm able to deliberately take air into my lungs and blow it back out. My heart is speeding up, loud enough to pound in my ears and that's the only sound I can hear anymore. The people around me have dulled to a low murmur.

He's *right there*. All six feet of him, wearing dark jeans and a black Henley. His green eyes are soft and his blond hair is perfectly styled—whatever hair product he uses still allows for fingers to run through it, so I know that it's pliable and soft. My fingers twitch on their own volition.

He's standing about thirty feet from me in a group of people who are talking around him. But he seems to be in a similar situation… he's not really listening to the people in his group. No, he's just staring at me.

His eyes bore into mine and something inside me shifts. Very suddenly, I feel a clarity I haven't experienced in nearly two years.

I love him.

I've always loved him.

All those feelings I felt before he left… the ones I couldn't name and couldn't let myself think about that made my chest feel like it was going to explode. The goose bumps he gave me from simple touches. The way I wanted to talk to him about any little thing that happened. The way I wanted to just be around him, even if we weren't doing anything. The way my stomach flip-flopped when his husky voice murmured my name in bed. Even the guilt I felt for wanting to do any of those things…

All of those feelings were love.

How did I not see it? How was I so fucking blind?

Rationally, I know the answer—I was grieving and unable to see past it.

But things aren't the same now.

I'm not the same person I was when he and I were together before. I've worked hard to process all my trauma, and while I know I'm nowhere near whole and healed, I see things so differently now.

Back then, Liam was a Band-Aid. He was able to temporarily stop the bleeding, but he would never have been able to actually heal the wound.

That part was entirely up to me.

And I did it. I'm *still* doing it.

I've done everything I was supposed to. I did the work in therapy, I took the meds, I did my homework, and I did one thing every single day that made me happy. I've done the hard work. I'm sure it's not over. I'm sure the grief will continue to come and go in waves, but I'm *leagues* ahead of where I was when Liam lived with me.

Everything is different. Especially me.

I'm standing here in Elliot's house, staring straight into

Liam's soul and I understand more about myself in this moment than I have ever before in my life.

Liam may have been a Band-Aid before, but I don't want him to be a Band-Aid now. I want him to be a new fiber. I want him…

I just want *him.*

The force of this realization knocks the wind out of me and my eyes start to water. I swallow against the lump in my throat and I swear his weight shifts, like he's going to come over to me.

But then someone grabs his arm and pulls him toward a different conversation and this woman I barely remember from college is touching my shoulder and asking me if I'm okay and I want to kill her a little bit.

Liam blinks and looks away, but I swear my heart is trying to beat out of my chest and leap into his arms.

I keep looking back in his direction, only to find him doing the same thing… glancing back over to me. And because it happens this way, of course someone calls his name and beckons him across the room. With one last look at me, he follows whoever is ruining my goddamn life and he disappears from sight.

My body deflates so dramatically that I can actually feel myself sag.

"You done with this, sweetie?" Elliot asks me, already taking my plate from me.

I think I say some variation of *yeah,* but I can't really be sure.

He spins away and tosses the plate into a trash can, then spins back and takes my hand. "If you'll excuse me, I just need to borrow her for a minute," he says to our former classmates and then pulls me toward the wine bottle he'd poured me a drink from earlier.

"Why do you look like you're about to throw up?" he asks as he refills my glass.

"I just saw Liam," I breathe.

His eyes cut to mine. "And? What did he say?"

I sigh, rubbing my temple with my fingers. "I didn't get to talk to him. We saw each other across the room."

"Ahh," he says, placing a stopper in the wine bottle and placing it back on the counter. "Are you planning to talk to him?"

Oh my god, I need to talk to him.

What am I going to say?

Fuck fuck fuck.

"Uhh…" I stammer out some nonsense words that can't possibly make sense while Elliot stares at me with wide eyes.

I try to speak again and fail. Again.

His eyebrows shoot up his forehead. "You good?"

"Fuck, what is wrong with me?"

Finally, a complete sentence, Katherine.

I fan my suddenly very hot face with my free hand and glance up at my best friend's handsome, kind face just long enough to catch him looking across the room with a weird gleam in his eye.

"You know what you need?" he asks.

"A lobotomy? That crackpot doctor from *Eternal Sunshine of the Spotless Mind*? Edibles?"

He rolls his eyes, but there's a smirk on his face.

"You need *fresh air*, darling. Don't move."

I turn around and lean against the counter space Elliot just abandoned, taking healthy gulps of red wine, which I know in the back of my mind won't help my overheating situation at all.

When Elliot returns, he's holding my coat. "Here. Put this on. Go outside and get some air. You'll feel better." And then he tops off my glass again and practically pushes me toward the patio door.

The door slides shut behind me and I lean back against the siding just like I did last year.

Remember how I said things have changed? I'm realizing now that as much as they've changed, everything is basically the same.

I tilt my head back toward the sky and mutter some profanities under my breath. I stand there in the cold darkness, the firepit too far away to do much good, if anything.

Just as I take a step toward it, I hear a throat clear to my left.

An embarrassing shriek escapes my mouth as my head snaps toward the source of the sound.

And of course… it's him.

He's sitting on the same bench he was sitting on last November when we had our first real conversation and I offered him a place to stay for a while.

My free hand clutches my chest and my eyes immediately burn. He's *right there.*

I want to walk toward him, but my fucking feet are frozen to the spot.

I swallow so hard it's audible.

Fortunately, he can still move because, apparently, I cannot. He keeps walking toward me—slowly, like he doesn't want to scare me—until he's about three feet in front of me.

He's also wearing a coat. It's the one he left in my closet. It's unzipped, so I can still see that Henley stretching perfectly across his broad chest. I'm only a little bit ashamed to say that my mouth waters.

But the more pressing issue is my eyes. They're also starting to water.

You might call them tears. I'm just going to say it's because the smoke from the firepit is bothering me.

"Kate…" he finally says, speaking in that low, husky tone that I usually had the pleasure of hearing when we were doing… things.

His voice is better than I remember. My stomach does the flip-flop fluttery thing and I have to fight every single urge to cling to him like a koala. I have to remind myself that he may not feel the same way anymore. He may have gotten over me while he was in Austin.

"It's good to see you," he says.

If I had a baseball bat handy, I'd hit my beating heart pretty hard.

Chill out, dude! We don't know how he feels!

I take a deep breath before I respond.

"It's good to see you, too."

Five points for originality!

I scratch at my temple. I'm so fucking nervous.

We stare at each other for a minute or twenty before he tips his head toward the firepit. "Come on over here. You've got to be freezing."

He extends his arm like the perfect fucking gentleman he is and gestures for me to sit in one of the chairs in front of the fire.

I follow instructions and he settles into the chair next to mine.

"How are you?" he asks.

It's such a simple question, but it feels loaded.

Did he read my letters?

Did he throw them out?

"I'm good. You?"

"I'm okay."

Just okay? Why are you only okay, Liam?!

I have no right to ask, but I desperately want to know.

"It's… *really* good to see you."

I shouldn't be so proud that I formed a complete sentence, but that's where I am in my life, apparently.

"It's *really* good to see you," he echoes.

"How was Austin?" I force my face to withhold the grimace it wants to display when I say the name of my least favorite city.

He studies my face for a moment before he answers, his eyes roaming over all of my features, down to my jeans and boots, and back up again.

"It was all right." His voice is hoarse, so he clears his throat before continuing. "I'll have to go back… we had some delays. But then I'm coming back home."

"Oh…"

"Thank you for letting me swing by to pick up my stuff."

"Of course."

He and I are still watching each other like we're waiting for the other to flinch or call a bluff. It's awkward.

I take a deep breath, trying to figure out where to steer this conversation, because although I don't know what to say, I know for a fact that I don't want it to end. I missed him. I want to talk to him.

But he beats me to it.

"I read your letters."

I freeze. I don't even blink. My vision goes blurry as I stare at the stones that make up the patio, trying to remember everything I wrote in my letters to Liam. I don't know how embarrassed I should be right now.

"Thank you."

I frown and look up to meet his gaze, which I learn is still fastened to my face. "For what?"

"For writing them," he says gently. "For letting me read them."

Letting fate decide whether or not Liam would *get* the

letters was one thing. Thinking about whether or not he'd actually *read* them was a different matter entirely and I realize in this moment that I never gave that part of it much thought.

Nevertheless… he read them. And he was glad I wrote them and glad he read them, apparently.

"Did you really read them all?"

"Of course I did. You wrote them to me."

Of course he did. He wouldn't be Liam if he hadn't.

My voice is barely above a whisper when I say, "Thank you."

"For what?"

"For actually reading them. You didn't have to."

"I wanted to," he says immediately. "I um… I thought about calling or texting you so many times while I was gone, but… I wanted to give you the space you asked for. I wanted to respect your decision."

I don't know why, but this comment makes me feel a little bit better. Maybe because he has a good reason for not speaking a single word to me in the past six months.

"But I missed you. Very much," he continues. His eyes are so sincere, it's painful.

"I missed you too," I whisper. "I'm glad you're back."

"Me, too."

I want to ask where he's staying, but it feels awkward. If I bring it up, I'm basically reminding him that the last time he was here, he was staying with me—not that he'd need a reminder… but it might be hurtful to bring it up. I keep my mouth shut instead.

He looks behind us to the bench we sat on all those months ago.

"Do you remember that night… last year when you offered me a place to stay?"

I blink. "Of course I do. It's not something I've ever offered anyone else."

That night changed my life.

I'm too chickenshit to say it aloud.

He nods. "You talked about it in your letters. It's an evening I've thought about so many times since. It started off so similarly to everyone else who heard about Jill's passing… you told me you were sorry to hear about it…" His voice trails off while he stares into the fire for a moment. "But that's where the similarities end."

Liam looks away from the fire, eyes locked on mine.

"You were the first person in years—literally years—who didn't have that *look* on your face when you talked to me. That look of pity… like they were just so grateful they weren't in my position. People got that look the moment they found out she was sick… way before she died. Everyone…"

His eyes narrow and then rake down my face, lingering on my lips before coming back up to my eyes.

"… except you," he finishes quietly.

I don't know what to say to that, so I stay silent. I know my eyes are brimming with tears because Liam is getting blurry.

"You already knew."

I nod.

"It was really helpful for me to be around someone who wasn't constantly looking at me with pity. I tried to keep it from people at the office—my boss knew, but I hadn't told any of my team members. Inevitably, people found out, and I could tell immediately by just… the way they looked at me. All that pity."

The heavy emotion is evident in his voice. Liam is mostly very even-keeled, levelheaded. But right now, I can hear the pain he carries valiantly on a daily basis.

"But living with you… every night, I came home to a woman who didn't pity me. She poured bourbon for me and listened to stories about my wife and let me talk the way I needed to. It was refreshing."

I huff out a quiet laugh.

"Who doesn't want to hang out with a woman who has a lot of booze and a morbid sense of humor?"

He smirks. "It was exactly what I needed, Kate. I owe you a massive debt of gratitude."

I shake my head immediately. "No, you don't. You don't owe me anything. If anything, I owe you… many things. Endless apologies, my gratitude for your support, more meals than I could ever possibly tally up. Helping me keep my house."

Liam inhales, like he's about to say something, but thinks better of it and closes his mouth.

"What?" I ask.

He looks at me, questioning.

"You can ask whatever you want." I feel brave saying it, even if my voice doesn't sound confident.

He breathes in again, lets it out. "Do you… do you feel like you're doing better?"

I look off to the side, thinking, but my head is already nodding. "Yeah… yeah, I do. I mean, I'm not going to lie and say I'm totally fine. I may never be." If anyone would understand that, I feel like Liam would. I clear the lump in my throat before continuing. "But… I'm doing better than I was, yes. A lot better, probably."

I'm staring into my wineglass because I don't know where else to look. His gaze is so penetrating… like he can see through me.

"What changed?" he asks.

It's my turn to take a calming breath before I speak. "Everything, I suppose. Eventually, Gwen convinced me that I had to talk about Nick's death and… everything else… in order to process it." I didn't want to say it, but I knew he'd know what I meant.

There's one massive thing I never put in my letters and that I never told Liam. But something inside me is compelling me to talk to him about it now, so I'm going to go with it. If I love him… *holy shit, I love him…* then I should trust him with my trauma.

I take a large sip of wine, trying to gather some liquid courage to tell Liam my deepest, darkest, most shameful secret. "When Nick died… I just… lost it. I mean, completely lost it. Something in me broke."

I can't look at him while I say all of this, so I stare at the fire in front of me.

"One moment, Doug was telling me what happened while Nick was in surgery… how he didn't make it… and the next, I was storming down the hall in the direction they'd taken Nick… just *screaming* at Doug. Ugh… I—" Losing my courage for a moment, I cover my eyes with my hand and sigh.

Spit it out, Kate. He said he loved you. He said he knew his feelings and himself. This won't scare him away.

"I threw a vase full of fake flowers at him."

Liam doesn't say anything, but I don't really expect him to. Either way, I can't bring myself to look at him. But I do lower my hand from my eyes and continue talking.

"That's about the time the security guard tackled me. And then everything went black." I shake my head to try to get the memory out of my brain. "I found out later they'd sedated me. I woke up in Nick's hospital bed in his ICU room."

Not wanting to continue that particular story, I skipped ahead in the time line.

"After that, I was just *terrified*. I'd never behaved like that in my life. I'd never snapped like that. I couldn't think too hard about Nick. I couldn't really speak much. I was just so scared that I'd lose it like that again. And it was so incredibly painful to think about that I didn't want to anyway."

I want to look at him. I want to see his facial expression. To know what he's thinking. But I'm too ashamed, too embarrassed, too scared. So I just keep staring into the fire and trying to avoid anything in my peripheral vision.

But then, I feel a hand on mine. When I look down, I see Liam's strong hand gently taking one of mine off my wineglass. He interlaces his fingers with mine. Surprised, I look up at him.

He's watching me calmly, patiently. Just like always. Just like Liam.

He doesn't say a word. He just holds my hand, our fingers entwined, his thumb feathering across my knuckles in a soothing manner, as if he just wants to reassure me that he's here. I don't get the impression that he's judging me, and that's enough to encourage me to continue.

"I probably don't need to tell you that very few people know about this. Elliot and Leon do. My dad and Sophie. Benji. The people who were there. And of course…" I close my eyes and let my head fall back onto the chair. "… the judge who allowed me to do community service instead of actual jail time."

"For throwing a vase?" His voice sounds mildly amused, which reminds me that he's probably felt similar anger during his life, knowing that his wife would die far too young.

"I disrupted the entire cardiac ICU and endangered the lives of the staff and patients, so… yeah. Between Doug and Sophie, they convinced the hospital admins to drop it down. I did court-ordered community service and, of course… court-mandated therapy."

His eyebrows draw together, forming a line between them. "The animal shelter," he says slowly.

I roll my head to the side, still resting on the chair, and meet his eye. "Yeah… it's where Nick got Beaker."

He nods. "And therapy is good."

I consider that statement—because it *is* a statement. I know he's not asking. "I wouldn't have always agreed with you on that front, but I do now."

He smiles. "Do you like your therapist?"

"Yeah, I do. Gwen. She's really great. Again," I add with a smirk. "I would *not* have always thought that."

Liam chuckles.

He's still holding my hand, so I'm afraid to make any sudden movements that might draw his attention to it.

"I admit I wasn't very cooperative at first, but I came around eventually," I add.

"I'm glad you found her."

Laughter bubbles up in my throat. "You mean 'court-ordered to see' her."

A broad smile stretches across his face, and he gives my hand a quick squeeze. "I don't care how you found her. I'm just glad. You seem… I don't know… different. I don't mean that in a bad way…" He rushes forward when I frown a little. "I just mean you're…" He trails off.

My insides turn to jelly. I want to know what he wanted to say.

What?! What's different?!

But I take a cue from him and keep my mouth shut. Instead, I just wait.

"You seem like you've made some peace… I guess."

I study his eyes. They're a breathtaking shade of green—both calming and mesmerizing. They're earnest and kind and the way he looks at me makes me believe I'm the only woman in the whole world.

"I suppose that's true," I manage to squeak out. "I didn't have much choice, did I?"

"Right," he says quietly.

He's still holding my hand. I'm not about to take it away and he doesn't seem inclined to either. His thumb occasionally traces a crescent on my skin, causing my stomach to flip like it did when I was sixteen and the boy I liked held my hand. So I just stay still and hope it continues.

"What do you think was the most helpful?"

Wait, what?

"Hmm?"

"What do you think was the most helpful?" he asks again. "Therapy? Talking? Time?"

I take a moment to think about that, staring at my wineglass again. "Gwen told me to do things that made me happy. And as soon as she said it, I realized I didn't have a clue what made me happy. I wasn't sure I could ever *truly* be happy again."

Silence stretches between us and I don't have the courage to look at him, but Liam's thumb continues its random crescent pattern, which gives me the strength I need to keep going.

"So I just... started doing things that seemed like they would keep my brain occupied in a positive way. I traveled. Did minor renovations on the house. I ran. Learned more about gardening and landscaping." I shrug. "It eventually worked."

"It helps to stay busy, sometimes," his quiet voice encourages me.

"Yeah..." I agree, tentatively. "I don't know. I guess I've just come to the conclusion that we should do things we love. Because that's what makes us happy. Let's just... do things we love. But also, it's kind of a choice, isn't it?" I look over at him, and he meets my eye with a touch of confusion in his. "To be happy, I mean."

"Oh... I suppose, yeah."

"Not entirely, obviously… you can't control everything. Or anything, I guess. But you can choose to make the best out of the situation you're in. I didn't have any control over what happened to my family, but I can control how I choose to live the rest of my life."

Liam nods. "You certainly can."

"So I've learned to say no to things that don't sound like they'll move me closer to the goal of being happy. Within reason, of course. I still have to do annoying things, but the big stuff… how I choose to spend my time and who I spend it with… I'm picky about that."

We sit there in front of the fire for a few silent moments. Still holding hands. Liam's thumb still tracing that crescent along my skin. The only sounds are the crackle of the fire and the muted conversation from the rest of the partygoers inside.

It's an easy silence. I don't feel the need to fill it with meaningless chatter. I let myself sit, enjoying the gentle pressure of his hand around mine, the soothing sounds of the firepit, and the warmth in my chest.

"Kate?" Liam's voice breaks through the silence.

"Yes?" My voice sounds awkward, even to my own ears.

Liam licks his lips and opens his mouth, but then the patio door cracks open and someone calls his name.

"Come on, man. It's time," he says with a wink.

"All right. I'm coming," he says to whoever the fuck is now at the top of my shit list.

Liam sighs, then squeezes my hand one more time before letting it go and standing.

"You ready to go back in?"

"Almost," I say. "You go ahead. I'll just be another minute."

He nods slowly and then heads back into the house.

After the door closes, I take a deep breath and sag in my

chair. If I had a pillow, I'd scream into it. Instead, I take a gulp of wine and stare up at the sky.

What the fuck is it time for? Is it midnight already?

I glance at my watch and find that it's only ten thirty.

What is it time for?!

I groan and sink even further into the chair.

"Do you hate me? Is that what it is?" I ask a god I don't believe in, as if he or she or they are watching me from up above. Rolling my eyes at the expected nonanswer, I force my body out of the chair and make my way inside the house.

I have no idea where Liam went, but I need to pee and I need cold water.

And maybe also a cold shower because my brain managed to help me forget how hot Liam is in real life.

I wonder if rage rooms are open on New Year's Day.

I go to the bathroom and then help myself to some water. I'm meandering around the house, telling myself I'm *not* looking for Liam, when I finally catch a glimpse of him.

He's standing near the fireplace and he's smiling, intently listening to something someone is saying, but I can't tell who he's talking to.

His coat is gone—he must have hung it back up. He came in maybe fifteen or twenty minutes ago. I still don't have any clues as to what it was time for.

I haven't moved any closer. I'm staring at him like a creeper. But then someone else moves out of the way and I finally see who's capturing his attention.

It's a woman. Blonde. Thin. Moderately attractive.

I've never seen her before.

And they're standing just a *little* too close together for them to be casual acquaintances.

Every hair on the back of my neck stands up for the second time that night, but this time, it's not because I can feel his eyes on me.

No… this time, it's because he's enthralled by someone else.

And then she reaches forward and squeezes his forearm, head tipping back with laughter.

Everything around me seems to slow down. I try to blink away the vision, but I can't. It comes back every time I open my eyes again. A sharp pain spears my chest. Meanwhile, my knees go weak and I have to grab on to the nearest piece of furniture for balance.

I can't move, no matter how much I try to make my feet go somewhere. *Anywhere.* I just stand there watching Liam talk to some blonde woman who I've grown to hate over the course of the last sixty seconds for no legitimate reason. People maneuver around me, momentarily blocking me, granting a brief reprieve for my eyeballs.

Liam leans casually against the mantel, one arm resting on top of it and the other gesturing while he speaks. The blonde is hanging on every word he says as if he's the most incredible thing she's ever spoken to.

I can't blame her, as much as I hate her very existence. Liam is very easy to talk to and a wonderful listener. He has this uncanny way of making you feel like there's no one else around. Of course she's standing there with her mouth open, drool practically dripping from her mouth.

I was literally in the same position within the last thirty minutes.

Tears prick my eyes, threatening to seep out. When her hand lands on his chest, I can't take it anymore. I spin on my heel and hightail it in the other direction as fast as I can.

With a quick stop by the coat racks, I grab my purse out of its hiding place, swipe a bottle of water from Elliot's fridge, and speed walk toward the front door.

Someone opens it just as I'm about to open it and I jump back.

It's Leon.

"Kate!" His surprise morphs into confusion in the same second. "What's going on? You're leaving before midnight?"

I blink quickly, knowing there are tears trying to escape my stupid eyes.

"Honey, what's wrong?" he asks more quietly, leaning toward me.

"Nothing," I lie. "I just need to get going. I'm sorry, sweetie."

One foot in front of the other, I force myself forward and make my way toward my car, but Leon is hot on my heels.

"Kate, what's going on? Did something happen?"

Oh no, no, just my heart shattering into a million fucking pieces. Seriously, everything is fine.

"No, of course not," I lie again, pulling my keys from my clutch.

"Honey, no offense, but I don't really believe you. You're practically sprinting to your car."

I get close enough to the car to make the fob work and I immediately hit remote start.

"Everything is fine, Leon. I just need to go. Please tell Elliot I said goodbye."

He balks. "You didn't tell Elliot you were leaving?"

Fuck.

I hadn't really meant to admit that to him.

With what I'm sure is a guilty look on my face, I look back up to him.

"Kate... what happened?" he asks again. His voice is gentle and it touches a nerve somewhere in me. My eyes tear up again.

"Look, it's really nothing, okay? Nothing happened. No one did anything wrong. I just... I can't stay. I'm sorry."

I take a step forward and hug him, tightly but fast, and then hop into the driver's seat.

Leon stands back as I reverse out of the faux space on the lawn and make my way down the driveway, my tail tucked firmly between my legs.

Part of me is mad at myself for being such a fucking coward in July. Part of me is mad at myself tonight for *just now* figuring out that I'm in love with Liam. The remaining parts of me are just sad.

If I was mourning the loss of a relationship I never got to see come to fruition before, I'm devastated by the loss now. The blonde woman—who I'm having a very difficult time not calling names in my head—hammered the last nail in that coffin and it will take the rest of my life to get the image of her touching Liam's chest out of my head.

Whether I like it or not, it's time to accept the facts.

Liam has moved on.

Liam is ready to date other people.

I missed my chance.

And if I love him—truly love him—I have to let him go so he can be happy.

BUT WHAT DOES IT MEAN?

Kate

Beaker wants cuddles.

I'm sure he can tell something's bothering me. He's intuitive like that.

I'm trying *not* to think about Liam or that blonde woman or the way she touched him. It's best I not think about it.

It's best that I think of Liam being happy.

Of Liam finding happiness after the death of his wife and a failed… rendezvous? Affair? Whatever… with a woman who was an absolute shit show.

For the second time tonight, I complain to the god I don't believe in.

Why couldn't I have met him later?

Why did I have to meet him when I was a complete train wreck?

But Beaker wants cuddles, so I'm trying so hard to focus

on that. I scratch the bridge of his nose the way he loves and let him headbutt me over and over and over again.

Therefore, I'm on the couch, still in the clothes I wore to the party, petting and cuddling the biggest scaredy cat in history when the doorbell rings and scares the hell out of me.

Very, very tentatively, I stand from the couch and move toward the wall so I can peer around the corner.

When my head is far enough around the corner, I see a familiar winter coat on a familiar body topped with familiar blond hair. It may be broken into pieces thanks to the window design, but I'd know Liam anywhere.

There's a flash of movement toward the side and the doorbell rings again. Twice, quickly in succession.

What is he doing here?

I take a deep breath and walk around the corner. I don't bother hiding myself. He knows I'm home. I know it's him.

I think I'm prepared to see him when I pull the door open, but I'm not.

His hands are braced on either side of the doorframe and he's breathing harder than usual.

I frown at him, immediately concerned.

"Liam? Are you okay?"

He ignores my question.

"You left."

I blink and do my best to wipe the image of him with that fucking blonde woman from my mind. It's not working, so I squeeze my eyes shut and scratch at my temple.

"Why?"

My eyes fly back open at his question. "Why what?"

"Why did you leave?"

I have no idea what to say. I search my brain for any helpful thing to say, but I draw a blank.

There's a look on his face that I realize is vaguely familiar, but I can't properly place it. It's maybe determined and also frustrated?

"Can I come in?" he asks when I don't manage to form a sentence.

"Yeah, of course." I step to the side to make more room for him. He walks into the house and stops well within my personal space. My whole body heats up with memories of what it feels like when he touches me.

My eyes land on his chest, right in front of my face, but I can't resist the pull of his gaze. I can feel it on me, moving over my features.

His gorgeous green eyes are waiting for me when I look up and I *wish* I could say it has the calming effect it normally does.

This time, it hurts.

This time, I want to look away.

But I don't… because I don't want him to know there's something wrong.

Something flashes in his eyes. Some kind of knowledge being confirmed, and then he leans over, gently takes my hand off the doorknob, closes it, locks it, and turns toward the interior of the house.

"Come on," he says.

I frown after him as he moves into the living room and disappears around the corner.

I find him in the kitchen, where he's already filling up my teakettle with water.

"Wh-what are you doing?"

"You're tense. I'm making you tea," he says simply.

Setting the kettle on the stove, he turns on a burner and then goes to the pantry to get out my tea box. He doesn't even set it on the counter before plucking out a bag of chamomile and selecting a mug from the cabinet. He puts both on the island before meeting my eyes.

My very confused eyes.

"Liam, what are you doing here?"

Shit, that sounded rude.

"Not that you're not welcome here." I rush out. "You absolutely are, but I'm... confused as to why you're here *right now.*"

"Why did you leave?"

His voice is gentle, but I still clam up.

I don't want to talk about this. I don't want to talk about the blonde bit—

Dammit, don't call her names, Kate.

I swallow hard and try to keep the emotion off my face, but I look away because I don't want to look him in the eye when I lie to him. "I just... I was tired."

"Bullshit."

My eyes snap to his.

"What?" I blink compulsively.

He shakes his head slowly. "That's not why. Why did you leave, Kate?"

"Ugh..." I press on my temple. "It's nothing, Liam."

"It's not nothing, or you'd tell me."

God-fucking-dammit.

With a sigh, I admit a partial truth.

"Look, I just... I saw you with some woman and it... caught me off guard. I just hadn't seen you with another woman yet. But now I have and it's fine. It was just... surprising. It was bound to happen sooner or later. I was unprepared. But I'm fine."

Did any of that make sense?

I don't know. I'm not sure I care.

He doesn't even frown. He just keeps looking at me with a weird look in his eye when he asks his next question. "Why did that catch you off guard?"

I fight the urge to roll my eyes. I clench my jaw instead. "Because of our history, okay?"

In that moment, the kettle screeches. He spins around, turns off the burner, and pours boiling water into the mug on the counter. He rips open the tea packet and plops the bag in the water.

And then he looks up at me again.

"Did it bother you to see me talking to that woman?"

He's not even denying it!

I swat at the thought. He didn't do anything wrong. It's not his fault I'm an idiot.

I scratch at my temple to buy time.

He tracks the movement and his eyes narrow.

"It did," he answers for me.

I lose my battle with the eye roll.

"It's none of my business, Liam…"

"Why did it bother you?"

"It doesn't matter be—"

"I think it does."

"It doesn't th—"

"Kate, tell me why it bothered you."

"It's none of my business."

"*Kate.*"

It must be the pleading tone of his voice that causes me to lose my fucking mind.

"Because I'm in love with you!" I shout.

And then gasp.

And then clamp a hand over my mouth.

There's an inscrutable look on Liam's face. He's not mad. He's not happy. He just *is*. And it freaks me out even more.

"I'm sorry! I'm so sorry. Oh my god…" I squeeze my eyes shut so my brain will stop trying to scrutinize every muscle on his face forming an expression I cannot understand.

I turn away from him and open my eyes so I can start pacing furiously around the kitchen, fidgeting relentlessly.

"Fuck, I'm sorry. I realize I have absolutely no right to tell you that I'm in love with you. I'm the one who put a stop to us. I'm the one who destroyed everything. I mean… I did it for a good reason, I swear, and I really did need that time. Despite being an absolute mess in this moment, I truly am better off than I was in July."

FUCK, HE READ YOUR LETTERS!

Why did my brain take this moment to remind me?!

"But the fact remains that I have no right to tell you I love you *so long* after you were brave enough to tell me." I pause as a semi-hysterical laugh escapes my mouth. "Goddammit, I can't stop saying it. I'm so sorry."

I want to look at him, but I can't.

And for reasons I don't understand even a little bit, I can't stop talking either.

"I… I started writing you letters because I missed you so much. And I didn't understand why. Obviously, there was something between us, but I could never let myself examine it too closely, so when you offered to stay, I just… fuck, I *completely* flipped out. I couldn't fathom you making a decision like that with me in mind. And then you told me you loved me…" My voice breaks and tears fill my eyes. I quickly swallow the lump in my throat because the word vomit won't stop.

"And I wasn't ready for that. *No part of me* was ready for that. It was too much. Too fast. Too soon. I couldn't let you stay. But then once you were gone, I was so sad. Even though I *knew* I'd done the right thing. I missed you every single day. I wanted to talk to you. I wanted you to come back. But I *knew* that it wouldn't work out even if you did because I wasn't in a good place for something like that. So I… I worked hard. I worked *so* hard on myself, the house and the general shit show that was my life. I *wanted* to get better. For myself… not for anyone else. And I did, Liam, I really did."

I can see him in my peripheral vision, standing ramrod straight, watching me. I can't look at his face. I'm too scared.

"Elliot told me you'd be there tonight, so I thought I was prepared, but holy shit, I was *not*. I was so excited to see you again. The biggest part of you I missed was your friendship. The way you just… understood me. You were the first person I really opened up to and you made it easy because you knew what I was talking about. I didn't have to explain why I felt the way I felt about anything. Even things that were probably *horrible*. And then when I actually *saw* you tonight, I just…"

I squeeze my eyes shut again and swallow yet another lump in my throat. I can see him across Elliot's house, watching me. Just like I know he's watching me now.

"I knew immediately. The moment your eyes met mine, I knew that all that confusion and all those feelings I'd felt for so long that I didn't know what to do with… didn't know how to process… they were love. That whole fucking time and I was too scared or stupid or buried in grief to see it."

My eyes fly open because that train of thought leads me back to guilt.

"And honestly, that made me feel *even worse* because it made me feel so guilty for how I treated you. I feel so terrible… like I took advantage of you. You were grieving and I should have just left you alone to mourn in peace. Ugh, but… I really did need you. I wasn't ready for you, but I absolutely needed you. I think…" I pause, not sure if I want to admit this out loud.

I stare at the tile for a moment before my mouth starts moving again without me even thinking about it.

"I think you saved my life."

It comes out quietly, which I suppose makes sense. It's a delicate thing.

"I was… in such a dark place. I couldn't have found my way out if you'd given me a light-up path pointing in the right direction. But you… you pulled me out. As grateful as I am, I feel just as guilty for dragging you into… everything, I guess. For butting in. For not just letting you grieve alone. For… low-key initiating a… relationship or whatever with you. You deserved—still deserve—better than what I could give you, and if I would have left you alone, you could have found it by now."

Which brings me back to that blonde b—

Seriously, Katherine. Get it together.

"But maybe you did… with that woman. And that's… great." I have to choke out the last word because thinking about that possibility makes me feel like I'm going to die.

Silence descends around us, and I feel more foolish by the second. I'm still afraid to look at him.

After another moment, I see him move. His feet enter my field of vision and then the mug of tea is in front of my face.

I look up at him, finally.

He looks calm. Relaxed.

"Here," he says. "Take a sip."

I take the mug from him and do as I'm told. It's my favorite chamomile. Of course he remembered.

"I just met that woman tonight. My friend wanted to set me up with her."

Salt. Wound.

I open my mouth to tell him I don't need to know the details when he continues.

"I'm mildly ashamed to admit this, but I don't even remember her name. I was… distracted."

"Well, she was *very* focused on you," I mumble, still staring into my tea.

I swear I hear him snicker, but I'm still too scared to look at him.

"Kate, I'm not going out with her."

"Why not?" I grumble.

He captures my chin between his thumb and index finger, forcing my head up, so I kind of don't have a choice but to look at his face.

His eyes are sparkling. His features are relaxed.

"Because I don't want to."

"Why not?" I whisper.

My breath catches when his gaze dips down to my mouth for just a second.

Except that he lets go of my chin and nods to the tea in my hand again.

I dutifully take another sip.

"You said in your letters that you felt awful about the way things ended with us. I also felt terrible… about the way I left you, specifically. I got up early that morning and left for work before you'd be out of your room and then left work early to pack up my stuff because I just couldn't bear the thought of being in this house with you… seeing your face every day without being able to kiss you… sleep across the hall from you, but not able to touch you…" he trails off as his head shakes slowly.

"I ran away… it was my turn, I suppose," he added with a self-deprecating laugh. "I ran away and it was incredibly difficult. But I needed to get away from you. Not because I didn't care about you or I was mad at you—neither was, nor is, true—but because I cared so deeply for you that I couldn't be around you if you didn't want to be around me."

He takes a breath and eyes my hands, which are gripping the tea mug with a white-knuckled death grip.

"Drink," he says gently.

So I do.

"I didn't know what to expect… coming back here. I—" He looks to the floor between us, his cheeks flushing an endearing shade of pink. "I purposefully came to pick up my stuff when I knew you'd still be at work. I just didn't know if I was ready to see you. Or if you even wanted to see me. I was… shocked to find your letters, but I read them all the day I found them. And—if I'm being honest—many times since then."

A shy smirk tips his mouth up on one side and I have a very strong urge to kiss that corner. But I sense he's not done, so I stay put. I even take a sip of tea to appease him.

"I didn't know what your letters meant though. For you, or us, or anything. So I didn't want to push you."

He pauses and I feel like I'm on the edge of a fucking cliff.

I take a big gulp of tea, which has begun to feel like the gateway to keep him talking.

"I had *years* to get used to the idea that my wife was going to die. *Years* to plan her funeral and make sure everyone knew what they needed to do. Everything was meticulously planned and she had a say in all of it. So when she passed, I had the *comfort* of knowing she was done suffering and that she died with as much dignity as we could give her. That she was dancing again… wherever she was. I had a lot of warning, and then closure when she died. But you didn't have any of that. You were completely blindsided. I can't even begin to comprehend the life changes you experienced all in one day." And then, in a softer voice, he added, "And so soon after you'd miscarried."

I take a shaky breath into my lungs and then release it, not breaking eye contact at all. I don't like talking about it, but I don't feel the compulsion to hide from him when the subject comes up.

"I felt like I took advantage of *you*. That I was pushing *you* while I was living here. To… move on. Or face things you weren't ready for. And I probably wasn't ready either, but I guess I kind of leaned into it because… whether I liked it or not… I was falling in love with you."

My chest floods with warmth just from him saying the words. He's not even saying them *to* me.

Loser.

"So, *I'm* sorry, Kate." He flattens his right hand against his chest, as if he's trying to show me he's literally speaking from his heart. "*I'm* sorry I tried to push you into something you weren't ready for. I don't know what you want. Or what you're ready for. But… I pushed you once, and I lost you, and Kate, I… I wouldn't risk that ever again."

My heart speeds up.

What does that mean?

WHAT DOES IT MEAN?

His voice is lower both in tone and volume when he speaks his next sentence.

"I'm not seeing that woman because I don't want to see any woman but you. *I'm* in love with *you*. I never *stopped* being in love with you."

My lungs are suddenly burning and I don't know why until my body expels the air I'd been holding in them. There isn't a single hope of holding back my tears at this point. They fall freely down my cheeks.

Liam gently takes the mug from my hands and sets it on the counter. Then he takes my face in his hands and wipes away my tears with his thumbs. I grip his wrists immediately, needing some kind of anchor in the tumultuous storm of my emotions.

I find it in his tender touch, the clean scent of his cologne, and the steady rhythm of his breath.

Slowly, so slowly, he tilts my face up toward his, resting his forehead against mine, sliding his fingers into my hair. But he doesn't kiss me. Somehow, I know in my bones that he's waiting for me. Letting me decide where to go and how fast I want to get there.

I can't stop more tears from gathering in my eyes, but his thumbs brush them away quickly.

Is this real life?

This remarkable man who fell in love with me when I was at my absolute worst is standing right in front of me, holding my head in his hands, putting all of his faith in me.

The beauty of it astounds me. In that moment, every single broken piece of my soul gathers and weaves back together. It's not what it was before… it's different. Probably messy and patched. But it's there. In one piece.

Unable and unwilling to wait another second, I wrap my arms around him and press my lips to his, throwing myself into my future instead of clinging to my past.

The weight of this decision doesn't seem as heavy as it once did. Shockingly, it feels… right. Natural. Like this is where I'm supposed to be.

Liam responds immediately, like he'd been silently begging me to kiss him. His lips part and take my bottom one between his, sucking gently before parting them wider and seeking my tongue with his.

Sparks shoot down my spine.

I take the opportunity to let my hands wander, reacquainting themselves with the texture of his hair, the broadness of his shoulders, the steady heart beating in his chest.

I will never run from this again. I'm *in* it.

I want Liam for the rest of my life.

"God, I've missed you," I whisper in between kisses.

"I've missed you, too," he says without missing a single beat. His hands roam just like mine, touching my ass, sliding under my sweater to sear the naked skin of my back, moving back into my hair to tug my head in whatever direction he wants it. His touch is fervent, but gentle, like he's been waiting for this moment since July and he wants to savor every sensation.

Liam eases me backward, pressing my low back against the island, causing zips of desire to travel up and down my spine.

Will the countertop be too cold?

I'm not sure if I care, to be honest. But then his hands slide back down, over my ass, and firmly grip the backs of my thighs.

"Come here."

His voice is low, commanding.

It's hot as fuck.

I tighten my arms around his neck, letting him lift me and guiding my legs around his trim waist. It takes longer than it should for me to realize he's not setting me on the island, but actually carrying me out of the kitchen. We don't make it to the stairs though.

I'm kissing his neck, getting drunk off the scent of his skin, when I realize we've stopped by the mantel. I look up, frowning.

"What are—" I start, but the words die on my tongue when I see him open a small ceramic Tiffany box that's been on my mantel for years. And when he pulls out a condom, my jaw drops. "*What?*"

He chuckles, burying his face in my neck and I assume we're going upstairs.

Instead, he drops a knee to the couch and gently lays me down before settling his big body on top of me. I want to ask him about how and when those condoms got in there, but his mouth is on mine again and the hidden condoms are forgotten. I hold him close, touching every part of him my hands can reach, not letting his mouth get too far from mine at any point. He rocks against me, runs his hand down my side, over my hip and down to my thigh.

Part of me wants to savor this moment. Part of me wants to slow things down and drag this out as long as I possibly can. But the part of me that denied my feelings for him for so long… the part that is overjoyed to the point of being overwhelmed… it needs an outlet. And it needs it *now*.

My heart feels like it's ready to explode. I need to feel his whole body. I need every inch of his warm skin pressed against mine. I slide my hands up his shoulders and into his coat—

How is he even still wearing this?

—and try to yank it down, but I'm blocked by his position. He sits up, kneeling before me on the couch with a twinkle in his eye and a small, warm smile on his swollen lips. He peels the garment off and lets it drop to the floor.

Before he can stretch back out over me, I sit up and push his shirt up his hard torso, leaving wet kisses along his stomach. He takes the hem of his shirt from my hands and pulls it over his head. I hear it hit the floor.

But then he slides a finger under my chin, tilting my face up, beckoning my eyes to meet his.

And everything manic in me calms down.

That feeling… that's the one I usually have around him.

I watch his eyes soften and his smile gets wider. He brushes the backs of his fingers against my cheekbone, making me sigh. My eyes drift shut as he slowly, slowly trails his hand down my neck, over my shoulder, down my side, and to the hem of my sweater. I feel his warm breath against my neck, and then his soft lips brushing against my skin.

His fingertips are light against my sides as he lifts the sweater up and over my breasts. His mouth leaves my neck to make room for my arms to go up and the sweater to go over my head. When I open my eyes, I greedily take in his expression as he gazes down at me. It's happiness, arousal, and awe.

His voice is soft as he looks into my eyes. "God, you're beautiful…" He drops a kiss to my lips before making a trail down my neck to my collarbone, easing me back onto the couch once more. "It's been torture not being able to see you all these months… not being able to touch you."

Holy fuuuuuck.

Fortunately, what comes out of my mouth is a lot more eloquent than that.

"You can touch me as much as you want. However you want. Whenever you want."

"I'm going to take you up on that."

He kisses the soft skin of my breasts above my bra, dipping a finger into the cup and brushing over my nipple. Tingles shoot across my chest and through my abdomen. My breath hitches in my throat and my fingers slide into his hair to keep him close.

"Do you have any idea how soft your skin is?"

He slips one bra strap off my shoulder, pulling it down far enough to expose my nipple and suck it into his mouth. My mouth falls open, but I don't answer his question. I think it was rhetorical. I do, however, toss up a silent thank you to the basket of moisturizers in my bathroom.

"I've missed it," he murmurs as he pulls the second strap down and moves his mouth to my other nipple. For reasons I don't entirely understand, that one feels more sensitive right now. Maybe it's the culmination of everything that's happening… his words, the emotion evident in his voice, his tongue —that *expert* tongue—on my body.

I feel him slide a hand under my back, so I arch to make room for him. With a pinch of his fingers, he unclasps my bra. Without that hand ever leaving my body, he trails his fingers around my ribs, then down between my breasts, slowly pulling the garment away, his fingertips leaving a trail of goose bumps in their wake.

"I've missed the hitch in your breath."

He drops slow, gentle kisses along my stomach as he inches farther down the couch.

"I've missed the way you shiver when you're really turned on."

When he reaches my jeans, he pushes the button through the hole and drags down the zipper, pausing to leave a kiss on the sensitive skin just above my underwear.

A sound somewhere between a gasp and a pant escapes my mouth, and as if he'd done it on purpose—and maybe he did—a shiver moves up my spine.

"I've missed how responsive your body is."

He pulls my jeans and panties down over my butt, leaving another kiss on my hip bone before sitting back on his heels and pulling the clothes off my legs. He tosses them in the general direction he'd tossed the rest of our clothing and then kisses the inside of one ankle.

No one has ever done that to me before, but holy shit, it's hot. I'm not sure if it's Liam or the action itself, but I'm not going to question it. I don't plan to try it out with anyone else.

"I knew how I felt about you, and I wondered all the time how you felt about me. But when we were in bed together… I didn't have to question it. I could see it in your eyes. I could feel it when you came. And I've missed that, too."

Liam releases a sigh that seems to contain every last bit of air in his lungs.

"I can't wait to see it again. To *feel* it again."

Holy shit.

I swallow so hard it's audible.

Is my skin on fire?

I'd look down to see if my skin is literally burning, but I can't tear my eyes away from his face.

One hand is still on my ankle, the other trails down the

inside of my leg, and apparently, he's intent on scrambling my brain because he keeps talking.

"Talking to you at Leon's took so much self-control. You were a foot away from me and I still couldn't pull you into my lap. I had to settle for holding your hand. I couldn't *not* touch you…"

He squeezes my ankle before setting it down and sliding his arms under my bent knees.

"I have missed everything about you, Kate. Your good heart. Your intensity. Your mind. Your body."

His arms wrap around my thighs as he stretches out before me, his head sinking lower. But before his tongue touches my body again, he looks up, his heated gaze searing me while he reiterates his point.

"Every. Single. Thing."

And with that, his tongue reacquaints itself with the most sensitive parts of my body.

With purpose.

My poor brain can't handle the sensory overload, so my eyes drift shut, my head falls back onto the couch. I reach for his hands, still holding me in the position he wants me in, our fingers intertwining against my thighs.

Part of me thought I'd been inflating how good he was at *all the things*, but now I see it was just my mind playing tricks on me. Liam is just as in tune with my body now as he was six months ago. He knows when to adjust, when to ease back, when to push harder. And he keeps going until I'm arching, panting, chanting his name, every nerve ending exploding as I hold on to one of his hands for dear life. His other hand is buried between my legs, stroking, coaxing, filling me.

As the tremors continue to ripple through my body, I can feel him slowly traversing the length of my torso, leaving loving kisses on my belly, chest, and jaw. I wrap my arms around him, holding him close again, our bodies pressed together, our foreheads and noses touching.

"Liam…" I breathe.

"Kate… my love."

His lips meet mine again, impossibly soft, his tongue slipping past the open seam of my mouth and gently, gently stroking my tongue.

I shouldn't be surprised at all that Liam managed to expel the frantic feelings in my body. While I'm still filled with need, I'm better prepared now to slow things down and savor every second of this reunion.

"I love you," I whisper.

Saying the words again feels freeing. I'm not blurting them out accidentally. I'm not trying to hold them back. I'm *choosing* to say them. *Choosing* to share my feelings with Liam.

He takes a deep breath in and out. He seems relieved. Happy. Content.

I kiss him again, moving my hands down his chest to his jeans. He lifts his hips to give me better access. I slide the button through the hole and pull the zipper down.

He lets me blindly explore while continuing to kiss me, but when I slip my hand into his boxer briefs, he tears his mouth away on a gasp. I greedily watch his face as I stroke him. His eyes are shut, and his jaw is clenched. He's tense. So tense. A groan rattles deep in his chest just before he drops hungry kisses on my collarbone and neck.

His movements become more forceful and urgent. I don't need him to speak to let me know what he wants, but I'm still glad he does. And when he speaks, his voice is like gravel, adding fuel to the already-burning fire in my body.

"*Fuck…*" His lips are still on my neck, his breath heavy on the thin skin. "Kate, I need you."

Liam lifts his head to look in my eyes, pleading. Even

behind his quiet confidence, there's something else there. Hesitance, maybe? Concern that I'll fall into old habits and run away right after?

Regardless, I'm not running, and I need him to know that.

I release his length so I can push his jeans down with his boxer briefs.

"You can have me," I whisper.

His blink is slow, like he's trying to process the words.

A heavy breath sweeps across my skin before he balances on one forearm and threads his free hand into my hair, guiding my mouth back to his. With his fingers in my hair, his thumb tipping my jaw up, and the delicious weight of his body pressing me into the couch, I feel cherished. And very… *very* aroused.

We work together to get his pants off without sacrificing too much space between us and then he's sliding a condom on.

From a hidden condom stash!

Now is not the time, Kate! Focus!

Liam settles his strong body over mine again, eyes devouring my naked body.

"Liam?"

His eyes meet mine. "Yes, love?"

"You can have me for as long as you want. I'm not going anywhere."

He watches me for a moment, staring into my eyes intensely. Finally, he swallows and says, "I want everything, Kate. I want the good days and the bad days. I want lazy Sundays on the couch and *you* when I get home from work during the week. I just want *you*. Forever. Every day. For the rest of my life and beyond. I want you to be mine, and I want to be yours."

I feel a tear escape my eye, rolling down my head and into the shell of my ear. "I want you to be mine, Liam…" I guide his lips to mine, kissing him softly before whispering, "But I'm already yours."

"Kate…" he sighs, brushing stray hairs off my forehead with a soft touch of his fingertip. "I've *been* yours…" He drops a kiss to my lips, then my jaw. "I've been yours for a long time now."

My chest swells with urgency. Sliding my hands down his back, I wrap my legs tighter around his hips and whisper desperately, "Liam, I need you. Please."

His attention returns to my eyes, watching me as he eases into me, clenching his jaw as he sinks deeper, a groan vibrating in his throat.

It's not like I didn't know what to expect. I've been with Liam many times. I know how big he is. I know his body as well as I'd ever allowed myself to get to know it. I know what turns him on. But this time—the way I feel with him now… the way he looks at me—it isn't what I expected.

This is different.

This is deeper.

Stronger.

More intense.

I feel burning in my eyes, tears threatening to ruin my life, so I slam them shut and kiss him, trying to ignore the sensation. I don't want to be a woman who cries during sex and I've already shed one tear too many while lying naked beneath him. I refuse to cry while he's inside of me, filling me, moving with me, making me feel like I'm fully alive for the first time in years.

But I do need to get my mind off the emotion trying to choke me. So I focus on his strokes, slow and steady. On his lips, soft and perfect. On his chest, grazing mine with each movement, sending little zings across my skin. Everything feels incredible.

Liam feels incredible.

Every single thing about him.

"God*damn*, Kate…" His lips move to my collarbone, my neck. I move my head so he has more room. "You feel better than I remember… I didn't even think that was possible."

A single, breathy laugh escapes my lips. "I'm glad I'm not the only one who feels that way."

His lips curve into a smile against my skin. "God, no." And then he slides a hand under my butt and pushes up.

Oh shit.

Apparently, he's not forgotten a thing. The effect is immediate. My back arches, head thrown back, and he takes the opportunity to lick the hollow between my collarbones and leave open-mouthed kisses on my throat.

I can't do much except hold on, my nails scratching his back, shoulders, scalp… whatever I can reach and try to grasp.

When I'm close, he pulls his hand out from beneath me and grabs my right knee. Hooking his elbow around my leg, he pulls it up so he can hit *that* spot and reaches between our bodies so he can touch a deft thumb to that *other* spot.

I gasp. Choke on air. Cry out. Shiver from head to toe. I manage to say his name only once before my whole body contracts and explodes.

Liam makes a strangled sound before he stops breathing entirely, his movements becoming jerky, his body pressing against mine in earnest. I cling to him.

He releases my leg, but I simply intertwine it with his.

Seconds, maybe minutes, pass while we both try to catch our breath.

He kisses me tenderly, strokes my hair, my cheeks, trails his fingers down my neck.

Even though I grumble about it, he has to pull out. *Stupid condoms.* As much as I want to eradicate barriers between us, I'm glad he was prepared because I sure as hell wasn't.

Reaching over to the coffee table, he grabs a couple of tissues and discards the condom in the tiny trash can under the side table. I'm glad he doesn't leave me on the couch.

Then, he lies back down with me and pulls me into his arms. My skin cools, and I shiver against his warm body. Because he's always paying attention, he reaches out for the blanket on the back of the couch and pulls it over us both.

I snuggle closer to his body, resting a contented hand on his chest and registering the gentle tapping of his heart against his ribs. I'm lying there with my eyes shut, enjoying the easy, intimate nature of the moment with Liam when the condoms return to the forefront of my brain.

"Liam?"

"Hmm?" he murmurs, his hand moving up and down my arm in a soothing motion.

"Why are there condoms in my ceramic Tiffany box?"

Liam's body goes completely still for a moment, which makes me adjust my position so I can see him better. He's staring at the box on the mantel, brow furrowed. His hand seems to squeeze my arm absentmindedly.

"Hey…" I murmur, using my index finger to tilt his face toward me. "What is it?"

His face is still serious, eyes boring holes into my soul before he finally opens his mouth to answer. "I put them in that box the morning after the baseball game…" He trails off.

I search my brain and quickly remember the afternoon at the ballpark, followed by hot sex on the couch. The following day, everything blew up.

"Oh, Liam…" I turn my face into his chest. "I'm so sorry."

"Hey…" He shifts on the couch, sliding out from underneath my arm and scooting me beneath him. He lies on top of me, pinning me in place. "Please stop apologizing. Was I heartbroken? Yes."

Ouch.

"But you were right to do what you needed to do. If those months were what it took for you to start to heal… if those months were necessary for you to decide you wanted to give it a shot with me…" He shakes his head before dropping soft kisses on each of my cheekbones, then my collarbones, before continuing. "… then I'd be willing to live those months alone all over again."

Forehead resting against mine, he secures the last remaining sutures in my heart.

"There's not a doubt in my mind how I feel about you. I'm in love with you and I want to be with you for the rest of my life. But I wanted *you* to be sure about *me*." His thumbs brush against my cheekbones as he gazes into my eyes with a sincerity that kills me a little.

My eyes burn again.

"Liam… I'm sure. I'm *so* sure. I want you forever. I don't want to let you go. Ever again."

"Thank god…" His voice is ragged as he wraps one hand around my neck, thumb under my jaw to tilt my head up as he pulls me in for a searing kiss.

"I love you…" I whisper in between kisses.

"I love you…" he returns immediately.

We make out on the couch for a bit and eventually end up in round two, which requires Liam to raid his Tiffany box condom stash, but this time, it's funny as all hell.

After we've come down from our respective highs, we're lying on our sides, limbs intertwined and heavy. I have no idea how long we've been occupied on this couch or what time it is, which reminds me of what day it is.

"I think we missed midnight."

He chuckles. "I think we used the time wisely."

"No arguments there." I smile. This was the best way to usher in the new year.

Last year felt like the end of something—the last year

Nick would see, the end of our marriage, the life I thought I'd live.

But this year feels like a new beginning. A new life. New choices. A new path.

Neither is perfect. Both have shown me how fortunate I am to have people in my life who love me.

I finally feel free. Relaxed. Happy. My eyes are closed and I can feel sleep pulling me when Liam's voice brings me back.

"Kate?"

"Hmm?"

"Can I take you out on a date sometime? Preferably soon."

I open my eyes and look into the depths of his green eyes, at the lock of blond hair flopping over his forehead. "Um… yes? I'm not really sure you have to ask."

"I think I do."

"Why? We've kind of skipped a bunch of that stuff, haven't we?"

Liam traces the features of my face with his index finger, ending on my lips. The featherlight touch sends shivers down my spine.

When he meets my eyes again, I suddenly know why he's asking. I know why he's making a big deal about it.

I remember writing about my first date with Nick and why he was so insistent on taking me out on a great first date… because so many of mine had been so terrible.

I was… shocked to find your letters, but I read them all the day I found them. And—if I'm being honest—many times since then.

He must see the realization in my eyes because he nods once and then kisses the back of my hand.

"Okay," I whisper.

His responding smile is small, but it lights up his eyes and in that moment, I can see my whole future ahead of me.

It's full of laughter, love, light… and Liam.

Thank you so much for reading! In the immortal words of Ted Lasso: I appreciate you.

If you enjoyed *Meet Me at Home*, please consider leaving a review. As a brand new baby author, reviews can go a long way in helping people find my book.

Looking for more of Kate and Liam? Using your smartphone's camera, scan the QR code below to download the epilogue and see what they're up to a few years down the line.

ACKNOWLEDGMENTS

Is it weird to dedicate a romance novel to your grandfather? Some might think so, but I did it anyway. It's my book, after all.

The thing is, my grandfather has been a major influence in my life. He's always supported me—no matter what. While I would have probably perished at the mere *thought* of him reading this book, I know he would have told every single person he came across that his granddaughter published a book. He would have told everyone how proud he was. He would have done anything he could to help me.

I am who I am today because of who he was. He was the best man I've ever known and he deserves my first book dedication. Unfortunately for him, I write romance.

I've had the idea for this book in my head for an embarrassingly long time. Years. It wasn't until a couple of years ago that I decided I was going to publish it, come hell or high water.

Thank you to Amy Pennza and my bestie Matt for reading early editions of this book and providing valuable feedback.

Special thanks to S.L. Prater, my podcast cohost Rae, and my friend Ashley for beta reading for me. You're all wonderful unicorns and I appreciate you more than you'll ever know.

S.L., I truly don't know if I could have published this without you. Your advice and support has meant so much to me. I'll try not to make you cry next time.

Shoutout to Becka Mack, who fielded frantic Instagram messages and emails and encouraged me to keep going. And of course, thank you for pointing me toward my cover designer.

Aliyah, you whipped up this gorgeous cover and gave me ideas for additional series covers. You are talented and I can't wait to see how you grow.

Ellie and Rosa at My Brother's Editor, I appreciate all the hard work you put into this book—your comments made me giddy and brought tears to my eyes. I'm so grateful you took me on.

To my partner in crime, Rae, you are one of the most important people in my life. I'm so glad you randomly asked me if I wanted to start a podcast in 2020. This has been an immense joy and I wouldn't have wanted to do it with anyone else.

Extra special thanks to my husband for never taking it personally when I ignored you most nights of the week so I could write. I fell in love with you all over again when I saw you lying in bed in the dark with a headlamp on so you could read a printed copy of my unedited manuscript.

Thank you also to the numerous people who supported me through this experience, including my coworkers, Rachel Weingarten (THE INDEPENDENT!), Alice, Jess, Kendra, Melissa, Liz (the Christina to my Meredith), Leigh, Annette, Meg, and of course, my mom, who I guarantee is better than your mom.

And an extra-special thank you to you, dear reader. Thank you for reading my words and spending time with Kate and Liam. It means the world to me.

ABOUT THE AUTHOR

Veronica Wynne is a writer managing her anxiety one romance novel at a time.

She enjoys writing about strong heroines because she believes with her whole chest that women are capable of absolutely anything and that any hero worth his salt will love them for being strong.

When she's not writing, she's reading, knitting, thinking about writing, forgetting to water her plants, and talking about kissing books with her bestie on The Chick Lit Book Club Podcast. She lives in northern Ohio with her husband, highly energetic child, and rescue dog who is probably digging flower bulbs out of the garden at this very moment.

Find more at www.veronicawynne.com.

ALSO BY VERONICA WYNNE

Meet Me at Home

Meet Me Book 2 (Coming Late 2023)

Meet Me Book 3 (Coming 2024)